China Affair

China Affair

Evert Warren

VANTAGE PRESS
New York

Wars generate many intriguing stories. The most bizarre of these are often kept locked in the minds of the participants who fought and suffered—and sometimes loved. Only now, many years after the end of World War II, is the story told. It has been said fact is stranger than fiction. This story is based on fact. Any similarity, however, between the characters appearing herein and any real persons, living or dead, is purely coincidental.

Cover design by Polly Quillen

FIRST EDITION

Copyright © 2004 by Evert Warren

Published by Vantage Press, Inc.
419 Park Ave. South, New York, NY 10016

Manufactured in the United States of America
ISBN: 0-533-14941-X

Library of Congress Catalog Card No.: 2004093187

0 9 8 7 6 5 4 3 2 1

To the MIC

*Her patience, support, and love
made this possible.*

China Affair

Prologue

It is no accident that Tientsin, China (now known as Tianjin) is an international city. As the gateway to the Yellow Sea and linked to Peking (now known as Beijing) by the Grand Canal, Tientsin received the attention of many foreign powers interested in the Chinese trade which flourished.

The Boxer Rebellion (1899–1900) changed Tientsin in a peculiar way. As part of the reparations China was compelled to make, sections of the city were given over to the nations involved. These nations were allowed complete control of their respective areas, known as "concessions." The infusion of people world-wide was truly unique, because each nation tried to make her concession as much like the mother country as possible. Street names and businesses reflected the nationality. Chinese was the basic language, and English was common throughout the city. However, each concession fostered its own language, and Tientsin developed a distinctly European character. These concessions were eventually returned to Chinese control, but the Sino-Japanese War had already altered lives in China.

Japan invaded Manchuria in 1931 and continued her aggression. By 1937 Japan controlled not only Manchuria, but northern China, the Chinese coast, and much of southeast Asia. Tientsin, like many other cities, was in the firm grip of the Japanese, whose strict and often cruel rule was final for anyone who dared to oppose them. Then, on December 7, 1941, the Japanese attack on Pearl Harbor started the full-blown state of war with America.

Knowing they were in a vulnerable area of World War II, residents of Tientsin trembled, and many foreigners were caught in this net of circumstances. Americans and British were moved to restricted areas by Japanese soldiers, and property of the two countries was confiscated. Despite the war concerns, the concession-created lifestyles lived on, and the influence of foreigners persisted. The population resigned itself to the rigid Japanese rule and conditions which were often disagreeable.

Mixed amid all the anxiety was China—China at its best, and its worst. The wealthy and beggars could be found on the same street. In luxurious restaurants, sable-draped ladies with suited escorts picked at the best food, while in the streets outside, half-clothed urchins and haggard adults stretched out hands to beg for food. Street scenes were radically different, and in many locations barely a city block separated dirty, squalid China from a clean, busy city not unlike one in any progressive country.

Such was this city of over two million people in 1945. A city seething with wealth and poverty, love and hate, cleanliness and filth, beauty and ugliness, refinement and vulgarity. This metropolis bubbled with excitement, romance, and intrigue. It is no wonder this story should have its beginning in Tientsin, China.

1

It was early January, 1945 and cold in Tientsin. She pulled the small white envelope from the door handle of the wholesale house where she worked as a bookkeeper. One of her additional duties was to open up the offices in the morning to get the chill off before the owner arrived, so she rushed to turn on the heater. When she returned to her desk, the white envelope was there where she had dropped it. The name written on it was hers, Sonya Petrovna.

Sonya had never received a letter at her workplace. It surprised her, and her hands shook with anticipation as she read the short note written in Russian.

Sonya,

Please do not be offended by my writing you like this. I have seen you many times and think you are an outstandingly beautiful woman. You are important to me, and I regret this method is necessary to ask you for a date.

It is impossible for me to meet you otherwise, so I will be waiting for you this Friday at 8:00 P.M. on the corner of Bureau and Foochow. Look for a man wearing a light blue suit and red tie. Please grant me this. I tell you now, I will not give up.

An Admirer

Sonya sat thinking about the strange note. Who could it be? Her work at the wholesale house was conducted primarily in English, occasionally in Chinese, rarely in Russian. Was he Russian? Her use of the Russian language was practically limited to her home and friends of her parents. Only vaguely could she remember Russia and their home there.

It had been such a big, grand home, and she liked it so well. Then it was gone in her mind, and she often thought the gorgeous mansion was only a child's dream. Sonya was much too young at that time to realize her father and mother were

3

forced to leave Russia.

Ivan and Katilka Petrovna had rushed to China with their only child and were lucky to reach Tientsin with their lives, let alone any of the large estate which had always been theirs. They were a stately family when they arrived in Tientsin, and everyone spoke respectfully of the Russian gentleman and his beautiful wife. However, life proceeded badly for the Petrovna family when Ivan was forced to make a living, because he had never been trained in trades or in the business world. The years broke his pride, and only the strong will of his kind, soft-spoken wife prevented him from deteriorating completely. Now his working days were spasmodic, and his earnings were barely enough for food.

Sonya read the note again. The word "beautiful," written by some man, excited her. Now barely twenty, she possessed a self-confident way with males, and men fancied her. Beautiful did not say enough. Her long, golden hair fell in natural waves. Big brown eyes and a dark creamy complexion seemed to create a sultry atmosphere which hovered wherever her long shapely legs carried her. The curves of her tall slender body were enticingly perfect. Sonya Petrovna was truly more than just beautiful. She was a seductive woman.

Sonya got up and stretched to clear away her rambling thoughts, carefully putting the note back into the envelope and into her handbag. She could hardly wait to show it to Netti, her longtime friend and confidant. She wondered what Netti would say. But that would have to wait until she finished work and could go by the dress shop where Netti worked.

Though younger than Sonya, Netti Rurik always seemed more mature and calculating. She stood by and often advised Sonya at difficult times. Like the time some years before when Sonya said she was pregnant. Netti listened and believed the information. Sonya thought she was in love with the Italian man and lost control at that ever so crucial moment. She said he loved her! And she never saw him again after she told him she was pregnant. Netti came to her rescue, was the friend who kept the secret, and helped her with the abortion that followed.

Netti had been born in a small village in Manchuria and was

4

a small child when her mother, Catherine, brought her to Tientsin. Soon after, Catherine met and married her second husband, Mischa Rurik. He was an importer of sorts and died of a disease contracted while buying furs in the exterior of China. Catherine was left with barely enough to start a tiny dress shop in the British concession, where she made or altered most of the items for sale. By working hard, with long hours, the business soon flourished and evolved into an attractive boutique which catered to the occidentals in Tientsin. Catherine was devoted to her daughter and made sure Netti was able to attend a British school and receive private tutoring in the arts and languages.

Now in her late teens, Netti was an intelligent, well-developed young lady. She could not be considered beautiful, but her sincerity and good nature made her attractive. Her long auburn hair touched off the smooth fairness of her cheeks and expressive blue eyes. Despite a short stature, she had a strikingly proportional figure which drew second looks from men even twice her age. Pointed attention from a male, however, made Netti uncomfortable, and she wished she could be more like her friend Sonya when addressed in a suggestive way. She envied Sonya's nonchalant handling of the male sex. Rarely dating, she did so only at Sonya's urging.

Despite her shyness, it did not show when Netti was working in the boutique, because her ability to read, write, and speak four different languages made her an excellent salesperson in the multinational Tientsin. But all was not well in Tientsin, nor with the clientele the boutique serviced.

The Japanese/American conflict of World War II had been raging for over three years. Japanese control of Northern China and Manchuria was very evident, and often cruel. The aura at the boutique, amplified over many years, was obviously British/American. Because of this impression, Catherine and Netti were careful to conceal any such partiality, but they tried to keep up on how the war was progressing. It was nearly impossible to learn anything except what was advertised by the Japanese: Japan was winning! They remembered the time the Japanese came to the dress shop. The soldiers ransacked the place, destroyed the English-written style magazines, and carried away anything typically British or American. Later, they learned from friends that this ruthless search was made throughout the city by the Japanese gendarme under the precise direction of a tall, quick-tempered officer.

2

Sonya opened the door of the dress shop and beckoned with her usual greeting to Netti behind the counter. "Come on. It's quitting time." The wholesale house where Sonya worked was a short distance from the shop, and they often met for a walk on the way to their homes.

"Be with you soon as I lock up."

"Come on. I need to get home and dressed for a date with Joe tonight, and you too. He wants me to have you go with Ross. Will you?"

Netti was locking the door. "I'll see. I don't particularly like Ross Petra or Joe Roncini either, for that matter. Those Italian fellows are pretty old for us, and Mother wouldn't like it."

"You don't have to tell your mother everything. I tell my parents only what they want to hear, and I'm old enough to do my own thing."

"Yes, you are. But your father would give you a bad time if you gave him a reason."

"Don't change the subject. Will you go?"

Netti was evasive. "I'll think about it."

As they started along Victoria Road, the girls walked briskly in the chill air of the evening. Snow covered the ground and roofs, and a cutting wind swirled little eddies of it along the street where the feet of rickshaw boys had beaten the fluffy cotton of nature into a dirty sheen of ice. Their Russian-style boots clicked merrily, but they did not reflect the mood of these two young ladies. It was impossible to be merry when the thermometer refused to rise above freezing and coal could rarely be obtained because the Japanese controlled it. In fact, the Japanese controlled everything—even the lives of these two girls. Emphasizing this fact, a passing Japanese policeman looked back and deliberately stared at the retreating girls.

Sonya leaned toward Netti and whispered, "I just hate the

Japanese. Seems like they have been shoving us around all our lives. Wouldn't it be wonderful if the Americans came to Tientsin? Mr. Hecht told me today he heard the Americans are making advances in the war, and it is sure to end soon." Mr. Hecht was Sonya's employer at the wholesale house, and despite the Japanese censorship on war information, he was usually well-informed.

"I hope he's right. And I pray it ends all at once. I don't want fighting here," Netti replied quietly.

They were passing the sweet shop, and it prompted Netti's next remark. "Remember we used to get candy and chocolates there until Japan went to war. Now we can't even get decent material for dresses, let alone chocolates."

Suddenly Sonya stopped short in the middle of the sidewalk. "The most peculiar thing happened today, and I could hardly wait to tell you." As she spoke, she fumbled in her handbag and drew out the white envelope. She handed it to Netti, explaining in a matter-of-fact tone, "I found this sticking on the door handle when I opened up the wholesale house this morning. You know I usually open up." After a slight pause she added, "I think it's ridiculous. What do you make of it?"

Netti stopped in the glow of one of the dime streetlights to read the note. As she read, her eyebrows drew together and her head cocked to one side, showing a perplexed expression. "It sure is strange. Are you going to meet him as he asks? He doesn't even give his name, and you have lots of admirers."

Sonya was quick to respond. "Of course not. If that was written by someone I don't know, he's probably some nut. It is probably a joke one of the boys dreamed up."

Netti still wore a puzzled frown. "No. My intuition tells me something will come of this."

"You and your intuition. You're always using it overtime." Then, as an afterthought, Sonya added, "But somehow your intuition does seem to be right most of the time. Well, anyway, I'm definitely not going. He can meet me properly if there is such a man."

"I guess you're right," Netti agreed. "It wouldn't be exactly proper. And besides, that is a bad part of the city. There aren't even streetlights in that section."

8

"You're telling me," Sonya commented dryly. "I'd be scared stiff to go there in the dark, let alone to meet some man I don't even know."

The two girls had reached Netti's home and were standing at the iron gate opening into the little yard. Netti and her mother occupied a small apartment in one of a long row of two-story apartment houses just off Victoria Road. Of red brick, the buildings were exactly the same, and a common wall ran along the road in front of them. Within this wall, dividing walls separated each apartment house, thus forming a series of small identical yards. These walls were necessary in Tientsin to restrain mobs and add security, as well as privacy.

Netti pushed open the gate and turned to say goodnight when she saw the rickshaw. Excitedly grabbing Sonya's arm, she exclaimed, "Look!"

Sonya spun around to see the rickshaw vanishing in the darkness, with the rickshaw boy pulling faster with each bound. Peering back at her over the high seat was the face of a man, and he wore the cap of a Japanese officer.

"I feel so funny," Netti blurted, "and that face. Did you see it?" She was trying to control her emotions, which showed.

"Yes, I did. So what? Looked just like another military with money," flipped Sonya. "What I want to know, are you going with me tonight?"

"No, I don't think so. I don't feel well. Tell Ross thanks anyway—see you tomorrow."

"Goodnight, Netti. Maybe I won't go either," mused Sonya. Her mind was not on dates. She was thinking about the strange note, what Netti had said, and that rickshaw with its staring passenger.

Absorbed in her thoughts, Sonya had not been conscious of walking far and was surprised to find herself before her own home. The dilapidated building where she lived in the Russian concession presented an ugly picture to her in that minute, because she had been living in a world far away, a sort of romantic world the events of the day had fashioned for her. She begrudged every step up the creaky stairs, always spotlessly clean from her mother's scrubbings. It seemed to her she had lived in the dingy second-floor apartment forever, but long ago she had made up her mind it would not be forever. A small step was taken toward her goal when she went to work. She furnished her tiny room to her tastes and carefully saved her meager wage to buy the clothes she had always wanted.

Her room was off the hallway, so in effect she lived alone, rarely seeing her father and seldom seeing her mother. Her mother sometimes came to Sonya's room to talk, but it was not often. Sonya enjoyed those talks and wished there were more such times, but her days were too full of work and her nights too full of play to spend much time at home.

As she settled herself in her little room, she began to change clothes, moving leisurely and stopping now and then to admire her figure and exotic face in the small mirror over her dressing table. Sonya was proud of her beauty, and she was vain. But why was she putting on her new dress? She had decided to stay home, and a call out the window brought the Chinese boy who was soon running to give Joe the note from Sonya saying she was not feeling well and they could get together another time.

Sonya had dated Joe Roncini a number of times, and the last one gave her cause to be concerned. He was becoming ardent and jealous. The ardent part she liked, the jealous part she loathed. He loved her, of that she was sure, and he had practically proposed to her that night. Somehow she wanted that proposal, but the mere thought of marrying him was absurd. Of course, he was great fun, but fun was not all Sonya wanted. Going with Joe was only a game—a game she well knew was often a bit dangerous. Recently, his passionate embraces had been more than a little demanding.

3

On Monday morning, Sonya was surprised to find the door to the wholesale house unlocked. She was relieved when Mr. Hecht's voice greeted her.

"Good morning, Sonya. I opened up this morning. Had some things to take care of before office hours. There is a letter on your desk. I found it in the door handle and discovered it was addressed to you. Rather an odd place to leave mail."

"Why, er, yes, it is, isn't it?" stammered Sonya. The news of the letter confused her, and she forgot to say good morning to Mr. Hecht.

There lay the letter with her name on the plain white envelope. Exactly the same as before. Why did her hands tremble as she held the harmless little piece of paper? Was it simply that she knew what would be found on the inside? Or was it premonition of some impending disaster? She ripped open the envelope, unfolded the single sheet, and read the Russian written there.

Sonya,
> *Maybe you did not understand my last letter asking you for a date. I prefer to think so and shall forgive you this time for not meeting me. Please, do not disappoint me again. I am determined.*
> *It bothers me to know you date that Joe Roncini. He is not good for you. Give him up and turn your attentions to me. I think I love you, and I don't know why. I will not give up.*
>> *Your Admirer*

Sonya could not believe what she read. She read the letter again. Shocked, she sat down to ponder the meaning of the weird note, which still hung loosely from her now calm hand. Was he professing love or threatening her? Then, without hesitation, she picked up the telephone and asked for Netti's number.

"Netti? I was afraid you wouldn't be in the shop this early. No, nothing wrong. Just want to see you as soon as possible. I have something to tell you. No, not now. I'll stop by at noon and we'll have lunch. I'll tell you everything then."

Sonya dropped the receiver and turned reluctantly to her work. It was difficult to concentrate on figures when there were more important matters on her mind. Mostly, she wanted to tell Netti about the letter and ask her advice. The morning passed slowly, as if the hands of the clock refused to move. Sonya tried in vain to concentrate on the books spread on her desk but realized she was accomplishing nothing.

"Miss Petrovna, are you so industrious you don't care for lunch?" Mr. Hecht's voice startled her. She looked up to see him standing in the doorway while slipping on his coat.

Sonya smiled, instinctively glanced at her wristwatch, and stood up. "Guess I got involved with the balances and didn't realize it was that late," she lied.

It took Sonya less than fifteen minutes to meet Netti and lead her to a secluded corner of the Victoria Café. Being the largest restaurant in the city, the Victoria Café was no place for privacy, but Sonya always preferred it. It was the most American café in Tientsin, and she liked the modern chrome and leather furniture, the winding staircase to the mezzanine floor, and the swank tea lounge. Also, the stringed orchestra which played soft chamber music during the dinner hours appealed to her champagne tastes.

Well aware there was a matter of importance weighing on Sonya's mind, Netti waited impatiently for her to begin. She curbed her impatience and allowed Sonya to set her own time for an explanation. When they had ordered, Sonya handed Netti the letter and said simply, "Here it is. Mr. Hecht found this in the door handle when he opened up this morning."

Netti read the letter and regarded her friend calmly. In a sober tone she said, "I told you there was something to that other letter. This is only the beginning, and I'm wondering about the end."

"But what can I do? You know I don't like it."

"Not much right now. All you *can* do is wait and see," Netti answered absently as she gazed out the window in deep meditation.

Sonya did not have long to wait for further word from the

self-appointed "admirer." Only three days had elapsed when to her utter amazement she found herself talking to him on the phone. The phone had rung on her desk, and she had answered with her customary, "Good morning, Hecht's Wholesale."

"Sonya. This is your admirer," a voice said in Russian. It was low and softly rounded, with an accent she could not place.

Swift realization froze her hand to the receiver. Her first impulse was to hang up, but her hand would not move. She tried to think, to answer that voice, but her lips moved without speaking.

There was a brief moment of sickening silence, then he spoke again, slowly, as though groping for the right words. "You needn't be afraid. I expected you would be confused."

It dawned on her the voice was gently soothing. She fought furiously with her befuddled mind to think of an answer, to say anything.

"Are you all right?" she heard him ask.

Words came to her in a rush, but with a mighty effort, she kept them from tumbling out. Instead, she answered as calmly as she could, "Of course. I just hardly know what to say."

"You needn't say anything. I prefer you listen." He went on placidly, confident of every word. "I adore you and must meet you. If only you'll be sensible and cooperate, we can have many pleasant times together." He paused, and then, as if to entice her, went on, "I can give you what you have always wanted. Meet me as I ask. I'll be waiting for you tonight at eight-thirty in the doorway of the old bottling works on Ewo Street, and I'll be wearing the same outfit as before. Remember?"

"Yes, I remember. But I can't meet you. I won't meet you. I don't even know who you are, and it isn't my habit to go out with a man before a proper introduction. Besides, you ask me to meet you in the worst places in town."

"That can't be helped. Listen to Netti's advice. This is the beginning. I will not give up."

A sharp click told her he had hung up. It was useless to scream out all the questions tumbling through her mind. She sat there, unable to move, still holding the receiver. He had referred to Netti. How much did he know about Netti, or herself? She had not recognized the voice. It was unlike any she had ever heard,

13

and it had practically hypnotized her into listening. The confident tone was as if he had her entire future arranged.

Sonya decided to keep this incident to herself, because she knew Netti would give her advice she didn't care to take quite yet. Nevertheless, she spent an uneasy evening with Joe Roncini and wished more than once she had told Netti everything. She and Joe had gone to The Forum because he was aware Sonya liked this rendezvous of the elite, international set. However, this particular night she wished she had stayed at home because Joe became impossible.

"Let's go, Joe. I've had a couple of drinks too many, and I'm tired," she suggested.

"What's wrong with you? You haven't been yourself the past couple of weeks. We've been going together for a long time, and you've never been so distant. I love you, can't you realize that?"

"I simply said I was tired. Is there anything strange about that?" quipped Sonya.

He fondled her hand across the table. She withdrew it abruptly and started to rise. "Let's go. I don't care for another scene tonight, especially here."

Joe followed her, sullenly silent, and refused to speak until they arrived at her door. She did not care. Her mind was not on Joe Roncini.

"Aren't you going to kiss me goodnight?"

"Yes, of course." She kissed him mechanically and pried herself away from his eager embrace. "Don't, Joe. I'm not in the mood." She left him standing there, brutally quiet.

The next morning, the note was in the door handle at the wholesale house. It startled Sonya more to realize she actually expected to find it there than the fact she had not been disappointed. *A routine affair*, she thought absently as she opened the letter. Secure in the knowledge of what the letter contained, Sonya felt no unusual emotion and deliberately paused at the door to read it. However, her unperturbed attitude changed as she read, and when she looked up, her face was ashen with fear. She turned swiftly to look up and down the street, but no one was there. Without thinking, she found herself half-walking, half-running in the direction of Netti's shop. It was closed, so she turned toward Netti's home. She stopped when she saw Netti less than a block away.

"Why aren't you working?" Netti asked.

"I don't know, I mean, I don't care, I—I don't know," Sonya stammered breathlessly. "Netti, I'm in danger. I must talk to you. I'm…"

"All right, all right," Netti interrupted. "Calm down and quit waving that paper. People are watching you. We can talk in the shop." Quickly she took Sonya's arm and propelled her in the direction of the dress shop.

When she had seated Sonya in the back room, Netti demanded disgustedly, "Now tell me what is wrong with you. I don't believe I've ever seen you lose your self-control as you did out there on the street. I suppose it's some more about this 'admirer' of yours, right?"

"Yes, that's it. Here's another letter. I just found it in the door handle, as usual," Sonya replied. "But this is serious. He's threatening me."

Netti took the letter and read:

My Darling Sonya,
    You do not take me seriously. That is your greatest fault, because I have told you I want you. Again you refused me and went dancing with Joe Roncini. I am a patient man, but my patience ebbs. Do as I ask or I shall be driven to extreme measures you will not like. I will not give up.

                                                            Your Admirer

Netti was visibly affected by what she read and did not try to conceal her feelings. "This is something, isn't it. Is there anything about this you haven't told me? Be honest." She looked Sonya squarely in the face.

Sonya explained the phone call of the preceding day and asked, "What are you thinking?"

"I'm wondering, just wondering."

"Wondering what?" snapped Sonya.

"I'm wondering who this man can be, and I'm trying to think of some connection somewhere," Netti explained thoughtfully. "If only we had some idea of who he is we could turn it over to the Japanese gendarme. They'd take care of it in a hurry. But we can't take it to them without some facts. They would laugh at us

15

if we said some man calling himself 'admirer' was the problem. No, that's no good. I don't trust them anyway."

"Maybe we should tell our parents," Sonya suggested.

"That would never do," countered Netti, adding emphatically, "your father would say you are lying, and if my mother knew, she'd worry herself sick. No, that's out of the question. We have to work this out by ourselves."

"But what can we do? What can I do? I'm scared," Sonya admitted. "This man knows everything you and I do."

"For one thing, I think you had better stay at home for awhile. There's no point in asking for it. If only we had some idea to work on," Netti mused. Then suddenly she looked up. "I *have* it! Do you remember the time about two months ago when that Japanese fellow stopped you in the bank? Remember, you told me about it? Have you ever seen him since?"

"Yes, I remember. No, I've never seen him again. I'm sure of it." Sonya was nervously twisting her watch back and forth on her wrist when suddenly it dawned on her she was supposed to be at work. She jumped up. "Oh my gosh! I'm over an hour late to work! Mr. Hecht will be mad. See you tonight. I must run."

"Okay. Oh yes, and don't forget the Russian Club meeting at Zota's tonight," Netti called as Sonya raced into the street.

Walking hurriedly toward the wholesale house, Sonya thought about the incident which Netti's words had brought to mind. It had been at least six weeks ago when the Japanese man annoyed her. Each afternoon, Sonya customarily took the company's daily receipts to the bank, and since it was only a short distance, she usually walked rather than take a rickshaw. That particular day, she had just reached the bank when a large automobile pulled up to the curb and a voice hailed her in broken English, "Oh Miss, please, you care go for a ride?" She had turned to see the small narrow face of a Japanese civilian staring from the back seat of the car. Yes, he would be Japanese, because only they possessed automobiles.

She had curtly answered, "Don't be absurd!" and continued into the bank, showing him an impatient shrug of her shoulders amid a flying mass of golden hair which fell in waves down her back. But that had not been all.

He followed her into the bank, and, to her amazement, had

accosted her in perfect Russian. "Why do you refuse me, Miss? I merely asked in a gentlemanly way if you cared to ride with me. I will indeed be honored by an affirmative answer."

Sonya's temper had run uncurbed about that time, and the little man had hurried to take leave from her stream of violent words. Sonya now remembered the incident and wondered.

Applying the last dab of makeup, Sonya worked feverishly in order to keep her appointed date for the Russian Club meeting. She had a habit of being late, but tonight she was determined to prevent Netti's reproving remarks, and in a few minutes she was walking rapidly in the directly of Netti's home. The dirty narrow street, with its row of dingy Chinese shops, seemed unusually quiet as she hurried along. Maybe it was because the shops were closed and without streetlights. It was so dark she could not see if the street was deserted or not.

She heard the sound of feet behind her and turned to see who was there, but she turned too late. Cold strong arms encircled her waist and jerked her toward a dark doorway. Numb with fear, she could not scream, but she instinctively twisted in the vise-like grasp and clawed desperately at the dim outline of a man's face. He cursed under the cutting fingernails and grabbed at her flying hands. That was enough for Sonya's escape. When his arms left her waist, she broke and ran for her life. Thank god Netti's home was not far away.

Sonya's hysterical screams brought Netti racing to the gate. "Sonya, Sonya, what's wrong?" Netti shook her roughly in an effort to stop her unintelligible screaming. Sonya's screaming stopped abruptly, for she went limp in Netti's arms.

"Mother, Mother, come help me," Netti shouted frantically.

Appearing at the door, Catherine ran to Netti's aid when she saw her daughter struggling with Sonya's unconscious form. "What's happened to her?" she asked, as they more dragged than carried Sonya to the living room sofa.

"She's fainted—I don't know," Netti panted. "Get some water, a wet towel, something!"

Catherine was already on her way to the kitchen.

When Netti sprinkled the cold water on Sonya's pale face, her eyes opened, her lips moved slowly, and they heard her mutter, "What happened?"

Netti stroked Sonya's forehead and reassured her. "You're all right. Just relax. We can't tell you what happened. We want you to tell us."

Recognition dawned on Sonya's frightened face, and she clutched Netti's hand. "Oh, Netti! It was horrible, horrible! A man attacked me...dragged me toward a door..."

"What are you saying?" Netti interrupted. "Do you mean he, he..."

"No, he had me in his arms only a second. I scratched him in the face—got away—ran here."

Catherine interceded to reprimand both girls. "I have repeatedly told both of you never to go out alone after dark. Maybe this incident will prove my point." She rose and started for the kitchen. "I'll go see if I can find you something hot to drink. It will help calm your nerves. I'll also phone Zota and tell her you girls shall not be coming tonight. I think Sonya had better rest, and then we can take her home later."

When Catherine left he room, Sonya turned her big, brown eyes on Netti and whispered hopelessly, "It's him, I know it. We have to do something. I tell you, we *have* to do something, something, before he kills me."

"Yes, we *do* have to do something," Netti agreed. "But what?"

4

After the night Sonya appeared hysterical on her doorstep, Netti decided to try and solve the problem by learning about the "admirer." She believed it might be possible to solicit aid from someone, or at least obtain valuable advice. She decided not to include Sonya, because many women distrusted Sonya, probably due to her attractiveness to men. Also, it was logical to turn to a man for help and that would rule Sonya out. But Netti did not know a man with whom she could discuss this strange situation, so her probing had to start with women.

Since she thought it would be inadvisable to reveal many details, she had to be subtle in her approach. Such was her method when she talked with Zota Seivberg two days after the Russian Club meetings which she had not attended. Zota was a pretty girl but somewhat on the plump side, and had a jovial nature. Characteristically, such was her mood this particular day when she greeted Netti in the shop.

"Since when do you and Sonya have to have your mother make up stories to keep you from attending drab functions? We missed you at the meeting. You were needed."

Netti laughed. "Quite some story, too, wasn't it?"

"Yes, it certainly was. Wish some man would attack me. I wouldn't struggle a bit. Men are at such a premium these war days, and Sonya has them all chasing her anyway. Does she have to hold sorties with strange men to simply add excitement?" Zota joked.

"What do you mean, she has all the men chasing her? I didn't realize she was that much in demand. Have you heard someone talking about her?" Netti spoke casually and busied herself with a bolt of goods on the counter.

"Why sure. Everyone is talking. I've heard at least a hundred men say they wanted to go with Sonya," Zota continued in jest.

"I mean, anyone in particular?"

"No, of course not. How did we get started on Sonya's love life, anyway? I'm more interested in my own." Zota dropped the subject. "The reason I stopped in is to find out if you and your mother are going to Peitaiho Beach with us this summer. It's time we made arrangements for a beach house if we want it at the right time, and with all the red tape one has to go through to get traveling visas from the Japanese gendarme, we should get started on our plans."

"Yes, I'm sure we'll be going. Don't we always?" Netti answered. She noticed the calendar on the wall read February, 1945. "But it's months before we go."

"We know that," Zota acknowledged. "But just the same, we'll obtain the reservations for the house, okay?"

"All right," Netti agreed, as Zota started toward the door. "Where are you going?"

"Out to find myself a good-looking guy!" Zota smiled and disappeared into the street.

That ended Netti's attempt to extract information from Zota. She was confident Zota knew nothing, so why press the matter further. If only she could think of someone to talk to, someone older with whom she might discuss the problem. Mikela, of course, she was just the person!

Mikela was sort of a cousin who lived with Netti and Catherine. Netti did not know the exact relation, because her mother had always been a little vague on the subject. She knew Mikela was in her thirties and had been married at one time while she lived in Manchuria, but she had come to live with them about six years before, and without a husband. Since then, Mikela had been going for at least four years with an Italian man by the name of Felice Miletto. Mr. Miletto was a fine, gentlemanly person, and they would have married a long time before if he could have obtained a divorce from his estranged wife in Italy.

If one stopped to scrutinize it, the romance of Mikela and Felice was an odd one. Mikela did not speak Italian, and her English was little better than none. Felice, on the other hand, did not speak Russian, and his English was about on par with Mikela's. Hence, they had no common language, and through their years of close contact, they originated a language of their

20

own—a conglomeration of three or four national tongues, complete with accents and expression. It was truly a language of love, because others could not follow their strange chatter. And their love was another point which confused Netti. Mikela was out nearly every evening, returning almost every night, or more likely, early in the morning. Consequently, Netti assumed Felice and Mikela were living together but creating the appearance to those outside the circle that they were just steady romancers. Catherine ignored the situation, basing her views on the fact Mikela had been married and was old enough to care for herself. She never discussed it with Netti, and the matter rested there. Netti loved Mikela, held confidences with her, and respected her judgment. Therefore, the more she thought about it she realized Mikela was the ideal person with whom to discuss Sonya's problem.

Before Netti conferred with Mikela, more pieces were added to the puzzle. Netti was closing the shop when Sonya walked in and calmly told her what had happened. Her manner was evidence she had gained control of her emotions as she began to explain what had just happened.

"He phoned me this afternoon—just the same as before. Believe it or not, I wasn't scared. He was very gentlemanly, and his tone was kind. I chatted with him as I would to an old friend. He told me how much he loved me, adored me, and how beautiful and desirable I was. He gave me goosebumps just talking over the phone. He has the finest voice, sort of makes you listen whether you want to or not. He talked about you and how much he likes you. He seems to know everything we do, *everything*!"

Sonya paused for a comment from Netti. None was given, so she hurried on, eager to tell all. "He insisted again that I meet him, but when I refused without a proper introduction, in a proper place, he got mad. He changed completely. One minute he makes me want to meet him, and the next I'm afraid to. He stormed on and on, wouldn't let me talk. His last sentence was almost a command, and it scares me when he says he won't give up. He told me to come to the Kit Kat Club tonight and he'd be waiting."

"Did you say the Kit Kat Club?" Netti cut in, completely flabbergasted.

"Yes. The Kit Kat Club. That's what I said. Then he hung up before I could even answer." When Sonya noticed Netti's amazed look, she added, "I know the Kit Kat Club is a whorehouse. Don't look so horrified. I'm not going there."

"Of course you're not. But why on earth would he ask you to come to a place like that? The man must be insane."

"As far as I'm concerned, there's no doubt about it. But when he wants to be, he's just the opposite. He changes completely in an instant. And he is so sure of himself, always seems so confident, emphasizing he won't give up."

"Incidentally, did you find out anything about him? His name? Where he lives, what he does, anything?" Netti quizzed. "Did you ask him *anything*?"

"Don't be ridiculous," Sonya snapped. "Do you think he'd have told me, even if I had asked?"

"Well, at least you could have asked," Netti insisted. "It's time you tried getting some information from him."

"I'm certainly not going to do it until I meet him, *if* I ever meet him," Sonya countered with determination.

Netti had been letting an idea revolve in her fertile brain and spontaneously decided to tell Sonya what she was thinking. "We must talk this over with someone who might help us, and it can't be our parents. What do you think of telling Mikela? She is worldly, knows men, and may be able to help us. Also, we can trust her. What do you think?"

Sonya agreed, because she was ready to try anything if it removed the dreadful thoughts she harbored. They immediately started out to talk to Mikela.

Once on the street, Netti started the conversation. "Zota dropped in this afternoon. She is making plans for going to Peitaiho Beach this summer and wanted to know if Mom and I were going along. Seems awfully early to think about such things when there's still snow on the ground, but she insists it will take months to get a beach house and arrange for traveling visas. Maybe she's right."

"She's right about the visas. It takes Mr. Hecht two to three months to get one from the Japanese for his business trips. He insists they hold them up just to be mean."

Netti interrupted to exclaim, "I said there was snow on the

22

ground. Look! It's about gone. So absorbed with our worries these past couple of weeks, I didn't notice."

The two girls had failed to notice much of anything since the "admirer" started his antics, and life in Tientsin had surely not stopped because of it. The snow was gone from the roofs, and only periodic patches of ice on the streets reminded one that snow had been everywhere a couple of weeks before. Tientsin was due for an early spring if the signs were correct, but the warm spring breezes from the desert were still many days away. Even yet, the puddles of muddy water in the gutters were filmed with ice each morning. The most noticeable evidence that it had warmed up was the increased activity on the streets. Sidewalk vendors were more plentiful, and Chinese waifs swarmed the streets in the midday sun. As a whole, the city's population had taken on a happier expression, and even the beggars seemed cheered by the prospect of a miserable winter gone and a warm summer ahead.

The girls found Mikela at home alone, and the time was ideal to discuss their problem privately with her. Netti did the talking in Russian, because all conversation in Mikela's presence had to be in Russian for her to understand. She explained the escapades of the "admirer" in sufficient detail to give Mikela a full picture—to include the possibility of imminent harm to Sonya.

"That's the story. We don't know what to do and decided you may be able to help us. You, of course, understand why we don't tell our parents," Netti pointed out.

Mikela acknowledged she understood by a slow, deliberate nod of her head. She was thinking and not quite ready to give an opinion. After a period of calm meditation, she said, "This 'admirer' story is almost unbelievable. In fact, Netti, if it weren't you telling me, I wouldn't believe it." Mikela looked seriously at both girls who were watching anxiously, then continued. "I can't help you. After all, I'm a woman like yourselves. The solution is to find this man. That, Sonya, means *you are going to have to meet him!*"

Sonya gasped. "But Mikela, he might do anything."

"I know," Mikela cut in. "But you *do* have to meet him. Tell me how else you shall ever know who he is?" Before Sonya could

23

answer, she added, "What we have to do is arrange to protect you at that meeting."

"We must protect her!" exclaimed Netti, obviously surprised at such a suggestion.

Mikela explained. "Felice is capable, and he has a number of strong friends. We could ask him to help—if you are willing?"

Netti and Sonya were eager to affirm her request, and each nodded agreement without waiting for the other.

"It's settled then," Mikela decided. "I will talk it over with Felice tonight and let you know his answer tomorrow."

The girls were enthusiastic but a bit uneasy, and when Sonya started to leave, Netti asked if she wanted her company. Sonya agreed, and Netti began gathering up the few things she needed to spend the night with Sonya. When they had put on their coats and started toward the door, Netti turned to Mikela. "When Mom comes in, tell her where I've gone. I'll walk to work with Sonya and see her at the shop in the morning. Thanks, Mikela. Thanks for helping us."

The girls stepped into the night, walked through the courtyard, and pushed open the iron gate. They were soon in the street. "I don't think my parents are home tonight. Maybe we should stop by the café and get a sandwich," Sonya suggested in an apologetic manner. Seldom did Sonya spend an evening at home, and her hours were irregular. Therefore, Katilka Petrovna had long ago ceased to make provision for her daughter's meals. Consequently, Sonya's meals at home usually consisted of whatever she could find in the kitchen, and she hesitated to ask Netti home to eat for fear there would be nothing there.

"Suits me fine," agreed Netti. She caught Sonya in a serious gaze. "Tell me, why is it your parents are never home? It isn't right for you."

Sonya flushed. "Father is rarely at home, and I guess Mother goes to visit her friends simply to have company." Sonya walked on silently. Abruptly she turned to Netti, and Netti could see the tears in her eyes. "I expect I'm as much to blame as anyone, but I can't stand to be around them. It's so miserable, and I continually see how unhappy mother is. All the pride she used to have is gone. I feel like crying when I see down on her knees, scrubbing the floors. That's why I want money, not only for

24

myself, but for mother. I want to give her the things she used to have, servants, a nice home."

Netti adopted her motherly tone. "I wonder if you're doing the right thing. You can't run away from it by not going home. You could be a great comfort to your mother by being with her more often. Besides, you run around too much. As for obtaining money, you may as well be practical and realize your chances of ever having lots of it are pretty slim."

"Oh, I don't know," Sonya replied defiantly. *"I'm beautiful*, and I'll have money somehow. Wait and see."

"You scare me when you talk like that. I believe you'd do anything for money. Yes, *I do believe you would do anything!"* Netti repeated slowly, as though amazed at her own acknowledgment of a fact she had always realized but feared to admit.

Sonya did not answer, because she was pushing her way through the swinging doors of the Victoria Café. Once inside, the girls hurried to find a table in an effort to be as inconspicuous as possible. In the evenings the café was overrun by Japanese soldiers, and two unescorted women might very easily be placed in trying circumstances. Without looking, they could always tell when the crowd was predominantly Japanese because of the silent atmosphere they created. They always sat quietly and talked in low undertones. Their arrogant manner and threatening glances prompted others to act likewise.

Netti picked a vacant table near the wall and seated herself facing the room. Sonya sat down on the opposite side while Netti glanced around the room of brown uniforms. She felt uncomfortable in this crowd of Japanese and found it difficult to conceal her nervousness. Sonya felt much the same way, because she leaned toward Netti and whispered, "I wish I were sitting where you are. I have the feeling that one of these little devils is slipping up on me and I'm afraid to look around to see."

Netti did not answer, because her attention was focused momentarily on a group of Japanese officers making their way toward the door in their neat brown uniforms, highly polished boots, and long shiny sabers which swung impressively as they walked. Those sheaths held a blade of cold steel, razor sharp, each one the pride of its owner and probably his ancestors, for more than likely the saber had been handed down for centuries.

Netti knew full well those swords were not just ornaments, because many people of northern China had been decapitated by a quick stroke of their flashing blades. *Damn them*, she thought, *damn them*.

These officers evidently were high ranking, for other soldiers stepped smartly to the side as they sauntered past, and those seated talked in timorous undertones as they nodded in the direction of the passing officers. The group crossed in front of the table where the two Russian girls sat, and as they did so, the leading officer turned his head to look Netti squarely in the face. His glance was almost fleeting, for he did not break his stride, nor did he look a second time as he walked to the door. Nevertheless, that officer impressed Netti—not by his glance, but by the fact he did not look Japanese. He was taller than his associates, and his broad shoulders dwarfed the others. *Had his complexion been the faded yellow of the typical Japanese?* Had he shown her eyes which were characteristically slanted? Subconsciously musing these questions and trying to remember their answers, Netti was startled when Sonya spoke loudly.

"Netti, will you please answer me?"

"Why, er, yes, what were you saying?" Netti asked insensibly.

"I was saying," Sonya mimicked, "What are you going to eat? The boy wants your order."

"Oh, anything. Anything you're having. I'm not very hungry."

As the girls ate slowly, the conversation turned to the lighter things of life. They discussed the lack of American fashion information, and quite appropriately so, as the Russian ladies of Tientsin had always been zealous in their efforts to imitate American styles. Materials were still plentiful, at reasonable prices, when the Japanese allowed their sale. But ideas were lacking, and like many others, the girls hoped for the day when they might again thumb through the latest copies of style magazines and pick out a new dress. It was nearly impossible to buy the ready-made article for a white woman's wardrobe, but the Chinese tailors needed only a picture of the garment to reproduce it exactly.

The girls did not discuss silk stockings or lingerie, because

26

they were blessed with quantities of both. At least they thanked the Japanese for one thing: prices were kept low. If a merchant was found marketing goods at exorbitant prices or was involved in the black market, the officials were efficient in disposing of the merchant, and his goods. He simply "disappeared" was the only explanation people were given. Consequently, it was wise to play along with the Japanese, even though your ideals told you otherwise. Because of this many businessmen collaborated reluctantly. Also, there were some who did so enthusiastically because it paid them well to work with the right officials.

Sonya and Netti were comforted by each other's presence when they left the café. They spoke very little, resuming their conversation only when they reached the security of Sonya's little room. Netti began. "How nice it would be to have a decent radio so we could hear something besides that dribble put out by the Japanese. It's times like this when I like to hear good music."

The Japanese had confiscated most of the radios in Tientsin and allowed only small sets which restricted reception to one station—which was Japanese operated.

Sonya removed her dress and stood half concealed as she held her slip high above her head, squirming to rid herself of the clinging satin. Between curses she answered in a muffled tone, "I know what you mean. I don't even know who is winning the war. The Japs tell you one thing, and what you hear via the underground tells you another. Oh, damn this slip. It's too tight, or I'm too big in spots."

Sonya stood practically nude, in sheer panties and brassiere. The scene prompted Netti to pull the blind—something Sonya had neglected to do. As she did so, she asked reprovingly, "Don't you ever close the blind before you undress?"

"Oh, that window opens on the alley, and no one is ever in the alley. Even if there was, so what? I'm not that modest," Sonya answered impishly.

"Well, you should be," was Netti's only comment as she followed suit and began to undress.

Clang! The window pane rattled from the impact of something outside. Both girls stood transfixed, unable to speak, staring at each other.

Sonya found her tongue, and her voice quavered uncertainly. "Could it be? I was supposed to meet him tonight. We're the only ones home!"

The glass rattled once again from some thrown object, but with it came the reassuring voice of Mikela. "Sonya, Netti, are you up there?"

Netti's relief was so spontaneous she nearly tore the blind in her effort to open the window. "Coming right down," she called.

"Felice is with me. Make yourselves decent," Mikela warned.

Taking only enough time to throw on robes, Netti and Sonya raced downstairs to greet Mikela and her escort. When Sonya opened the door, she exclaimed, "Mikela, don't ever—don't ever do that again. My heart stopped when that window rattled!"

"It was the only way we had of getting your attention. We pushed and pushed the doorbell," Mikela explained defensively.

"It doesn't work," Sonya inserted. "Netti and I should teach you our secret whistle we always use to call one another. Come, let's go up to my room."

Once settled in the room, Mikela explained their reason for the late-hour visit. Felice sat silently, since he was left out of the conversation by not being able to speak Russian. However, Mikela occasionally stopped to discuss certain points with him.

Mikela had taken Sonya's problem to Felice, and the plan they worked out necessitated an understanding with Sonya before the "admirer" phoned again. Since the possibility existed that he might phone the next day, they had come immediately to arrange the details.

Though simple, their plan seemed effective. The next time the "admirer" phoned, Sonya was directed to arrange a meeting on his own terms, providing he simply wanted to meet her on a street of the city. Then, when the place and time had been designated, her instructions were to inform Felice. He said he had three friends who were dependable and would be available on short notice. The four would station themselves at strategic places around the appointed meeting place when Sonya appeared to keep her date. Felice pointed out they would not be armed, but he felt confident four strong men could easily handle the culprit no matter how fanatic he might be. When the "admirer" arrived to keep his appointment, Felice and his men were to capture him and end Sonya's worries.

One thing remained to be decided, and Mikela bluntly put it to Sonya. *"Are you willing to take this chance?"*

Sonya hesitated and answered reluctantly, "Yes, I guess it's the only way. I think I can handle it."

"It's settled then," Mikela said decisively, as she and Mr. Miletto were leaving the room. "Don't forget to let me know the minute you hear from him. We must give Felice as much time as possible."

Having closed the door on Mikela and Mr. Miletto, Sonya turned to Netti. "I guess this will end it—or will it?" Sonya did not sleep well that night.

5

The wholesale house phone rang. Sonya's hand trembled as she lifted the receiver. It was just another business call. She had answered the phone at least ten times during the morning, and they were always business calls. If the "admirer" did not phone soon, she would be a nervous wreck, for instead of working, she had spent the entire morning rehearsing in her mind just what to say and how to say it when he did call. He had to phone her. She knew he would. It was nearing noon when it finally happened.

He spoke in Russian, and as always was surly and gracious by turns. He snapped vehemently about her not meeting him as he asked, but became pleasant when she agreed to do so now. Yes, the corner of Dillon and Rue de Paris would be all right, and eight would be satisfactory. Sonya had trouble believing she had really agreed as she put on her coat preparatory to seeking Mikela. She made the excuse to Mr. Hecht that she felt suddenly ill and hurried off on her mission.

Sonya found Mikela at the Rurik home. Mikela's sole source of income was derived from knitting, and she often spent the entire day over her yarn and needles. Upon being informed of the phone call and the arrangements made, Mikela decided they should immediately contact Mr. Miletto. Apparently she knew where to find him, even though it was early afternoon.

It occurred to Sonya they should go by the dress shop to inform Netti, and she said as much to Mikela who responded, "No, we won't tell Netti. She can't help, and she would want to go with you tonight—which is out of the question."

They hailed rickshaws and were on their way. Sonya did not know where they were going, so she told the boy to follow Mikela before settling herself comfortably in the rickshaw. She listened absently to the steady patter of her rickshaw boy's feet as they rhythmically beat the hard pavement, and she contemplated the evening ahead. The thought of seeing him did not worry her. Quite the contrary, it relieved her—for she wanted the "admirer" brought out into the open and herself freed of his constant shadow.

They finally stopped before a low, brown stucco building. The structure appeared to be a cross between a residence and a business establishment, with large windows on one end displaying bottled goods, and windows on the other end closed by blinds. As Sonya pondered these facts, Mikela got out of her rickshaw and instructed her to wait. A moment later she disappeared down a narrow alley alongside the building.

Sonya had never been informed as to Felice Miletto's livelihood, and she wondered about it. This was a better section of the city, and Mikela seemed thoroughly acquainted with it. Surely Mr. Miletto must be a fine man to have squired Mikela for so many years. And yet, as she waited, she kept thinking. *Her unhappy affair with an Italian man had left her with a distrust of Italians. Was this where he lived? Was this where he worked? Was it possible he or some of his friends knew the man they were trying to catch?* She dismissed the latter as ridiculous when Mikela returned with Mr. Miletto.

Sonya started to talk, but Felice silenced her with a short gesture of his hand. He made it known, through Mikela as interpreter, that it would be better to discuss the matter in a private place. Mikela responded by saying Catherine and Netti would be at the shop working, so their home would be a good spot. Felice agreed and said he would find a city map somewhere and meet them there.

Mikela and Sonya waited for what seemed a long time for Felice to join them. In only a few seconds he had unfolded a map and asked, "Where are you supposed to meet him?"

Sonya had trouble understanding the weird language Mikela and Felice used but was able to make out the question. "The corner of Dillon and Rue de Paris, at eight tonight."

Nodding to Mikela to interpret for him, Felice began talking. "I know the place pretty well, and it will suit our purpose. I better draw a sketch of that area and explain where all of us will be."

He picked up a pencil and paper and motioned Sonya and

31

Mikela to the table. Then, with deft strokes, he drew a rough map showing the streets and buildings in the immediate vicinity of the proposed meeting place.

"The proposed spot is an industrial district, and most of the buildings are warehouses. The buildings will be dark at that time of night, and street lights there are little better than none. It makes it perfect for your man—but also perfect for us." Felice paused to look squarely at Sonya. He was trying to decide if she was capable of playing her part in this dangerous scheme. Her eyes were steady under his searching scrutiny. Satisfied with her reaction he continued, "One of us will be on each street, concealed in doorways—and each will have the meeting spot in sight. The man will be surrounded and can't possibly get away."

Felice looked straight at Sonya again. "I will follow you at a reasonable distance and keep an eye on you before taking up my position. That should give some assurance."

Mikela, who had been interpreting for Felice, questioned him further. "Do you want to see Sonya again before tonight?"

"It won't be necessary. We have just a few hours, and I must round up my friends. We'll be in position well before eight, and I'll start trailing Sonya about a block from the corner." He prepared to depart. "Come, Mikela, I have a lot to do."

Looking at Sonya, Mikela suddenly felt sorry for her, because there was no doubt she was scared to death. "Don't worry now, Sonya. Everything is going to be fine. All you have to do is be present on that corner at eight. And remember, not a word of this to anyone." She hesitated at the door to give Sonya some last minute advice. "I suggest you do something this afternoon to occupy your time. Read a book or something. Bye."

"Bye, Mikela. Bye, Mr. Miletto."

She felt terribly alone. She tried to read but found herself reading the same paragraph over and over. She paced the floor of her room until the walls seemed to crush her. She looked at her watch: 4:30. There was still a lot of time.

Finally, in desperation, she threw on her coat, descended the stairs, and stepped into the street. As she threaded her way through the afternoon throng of jabbering Chinese, the loitering masses composed her, and the biting breeze acted as a tonic. Her muddled brain cleared perceptibly, and she realized her feet

32

were wet from the icy slush along the streets. In her rush to abandon her repugnant room she had forgotten her galoshes.

Sonya walked over three blocks before becoming aware that a Chinese beggar followed her. Actually, she could not be sure such was the case, and she turned into an alley to watch his action. Halfway through the alley she stopped, bent over to lend the impression of tying her shoe, and looked back. The beggar lounged near the entrance of the alley, but he was not following her. Maybe she had been wrong, but she was suspicious of everything these days.

She stopped at her familiar small restaurant and sat alone near the window to watch the procession on the streets. It was China and typical Tientsin. Rickshaws and bicycles were everywhere, with an occasional car tooting loudly to clear its path. Skull caps, cloth shoes, and mandarin coats frequently pushed aside by American slacks or English costume complete with knickerbockers and knee socks, dirty-faced and half-clothed children begging, old men and women in ragged clothing squatting on the cold pavement, sidewalk peddlers selling everything from moldy bread to exquisite jewelry and arguing over the price with every customer. Yes, Tientsin was just the same. And Sonya was convinced it would be the same forever. *Was she doomed to live here all her life?* It was not so bad if one had money. The wealthy lived very well, and it did not take much to be wealthy in China. She watched the passing populace, and her thoughts were not on the dubious evening she faced.

Her eyes caught on a beggar loitering just outside the window, and recognizing him as the one she noticed earlier was a rude awakening from her musing. She thought he was following her, and his presence now confirmed her suspicions. He must be an employee of the "admirer," for who else would want her followed? The "admirer" seemed to know everything she did! She looked carefully and saw a typical Chinese beggar with scant white beard. Wearing no more than enough clothing for the chill weather, his long coat was repulsively dirty, torn, and patched with various colors. If he were not a beggar, he certainly played the part well, for even his face seemed lean from malnutrition.

She paid her bill and hurried outside, eager to see if the beggar would follow her again. Sure enough, he slouched along after

33

her. Having waited for such an action, Sonya turned abruptly, and her voice rang viciously in Chinese. "You beast, why do you follow me?"

The beggar crouched and held out a grimy hand. "Pardon Miss, I do not follow. I only beg so I do not starve."

Sonya's temper rose, and she clenched her fists in rage. "Go," she screamed. "Go, before I call the police and have you beaten."

Under the glare of her accusing eyes, the beggar bolted and ran down the street. That was enough. Sonya turned and started home, anger burning in her soul. Now she was determined to meet the "admirer." Nothing could keep her away from the scheduled meeting, because she wanted the privilege of scratching his eyes out.

She looked at her watch. It told her she had thirty-five minutes before meeting this person who made her life so miserable. Moving unhurriedly, Sonya gave herself the last fastidious touch of makeup, brushed her trim brown suit, and put on her raincoat preparatory to leaving the house. She decided on a raincoat, because the weather looked unpredictable with a cold mist settling. When she began her walk along Victoria Road to Dillon Street, she had complete control of her emotions and prayed silently that Mr. Miletto would be true to his word and plans.

The damp air, coupled with a near freezing temperature, chilled Sonya to the bone—so she pulled her collar high and clasped her hands tightly within her fur-lined muff. Regardless of how hard she tried to stop, her teeth chattered, and she shivered constantly. She wondered if it were only the nasty weather which chilled her, or was she being nervous after all. She kept telling herself she was not frightened and was well-prepared for this climactic date.

Three blocks to go! The dilapidated streetlights shined dimly in the murky night, and their yellow light fought against the depressing darkness. Shadowy forms moved along the street. A passing rickshaw appeared grotesque against a hazy background, and the steady patter of feet died in the wake of echoing silence. Sonya stood her ground, fighting a desire to turn and run.

"Go on, Sonya. Everything is ready," Mr. Miletto's voice whispered from an obscure doorway. She recognized his voice.

Only Felice murdered the Russian language so thoroughly. Finding confidence in his pressure, Sonya proceeded along the street. Watching straight ahead, she aimed herself toward the designated corner which was less than half a block away.

Just as she was beginning to wonder if the "admirer" would be on time, a strong hand covered her mouth, cruelly crushing her lips against her clenched teeth. A strong arm encircled her waist, pulling her close to a powerful male body. Sonya had not seen nor heard anything and was now struggling as blood pounded in her head with a deafening roar. She struck out aimlessly to free herself from the ruthless grasp. Over her shoulder, her hand felt something soft. Instinctively, she dug in long fingernails and hung on. She evidently clutched a vulnerable spot on her assailant, for the fingers left her mouth and she felt a stinging sensation on the back of her hand as she fainted.

When her mind cleared, Sonya found herself sitting in the middle of the sidewalk, looking dully at the blood on her left hand. The sound of running feet and Mr. Miletto's excited voice awakened her as though from a dream, and she looked up to see three or four men huddled over her.

"Take me home," she whispered. "Please, take me home."

*   *   *

Sonya opened her eyes to see natural surroundings. She was in her own bedroom. Mikela and Netti were there, watching her carefully. Then the events of the evening came back to her with a rush. She started to speak, but Mikela interrupted. "You aren't hurt, just a little scratch on the back of your hand. Relax, you've had quite a shock."

"What I want to know is—did they catch him?" Sonya's expression begged for an affirmative answer.

"No, they didn't," Mikela answered reluctantly. "Felice said it happened so fast they couldn't get to you, and he just vanished."

"What do we do now?" Sonya was having difficulty talking and muttered, "He is really going to hurt me, *maybe even kill me.*"

35

"Felice thinks you had better go to the Japanese police."

"You know we can't do that," Sonya said. "I'm more afraid of them than him."

Mikela prepared to leave and turned to Netti. "You should get some ointment and a bandage on her scratched hand. It probably will be all right in the morning."

Netti spoke pointedly to Mikela. "Certainly you know we can't go to the police. They are more against us than for us. They would laugh at us, or make a big issue out of it."

"You're probably right," Mikela agreed, "but there is little more Felice can do."

"Tell him thanks anyway," Sonya said.

Netti spoke up. "Well, none of us can do anything tonight, and I think Sonya should get some rest. Mikela, go on home and tell Mother I'm staying with Sonya tonight. She shouldn't be left alone." As an afterthought, she added, "And don't mention a word of this to Mother."

Mikela agreed with a shrug, slipped on her coat, and departed.

Netti proceeded to undress while Sonya started to apologize for not including her in the plan to capture the admirer. She had seemed a little miffed about being left out.

"You don't need to explain. Mikela told me all about it," Netti said as she settled herself in the bed beside Sonya and switched off the light. "He must have been scared, because he barely got away. Maybe he has learned a lesson and won't bother you any more."

"Maybe," whispered Sonya, "*maybe not.*"

6

The days slipped by, and Sonya heard nothing from her self-appointed "admirer," now referred to as Mr. X. It had been decided she should give him a name, and Mr. X seemed appropriate. At first, she worried about the absence of his attention, but as the days wore on without further contact, she pushed him from her mind.

She was relieved and happy in the life she had almost forgotten, and she turned again to Joe Roncini for the good times he presented. They were together almost every night. They danced and drank, sometimes too much, and she tantalized Joe until he burned with desire. His advances were regularly squelched by her laughter and attention to others in the crowd. But he loved her and wanted to marry her. When she rejected his earnest request to marry, he sometimes turned bitter and lost control of his emotions. He reasoned there was no cause for the marriage rejection. He truly loved her. He made good money in his small fur business. The war could not last forever, and soon he would have an export trade. Having failed to win her consent, his idea was to start a truly intimate affair which, over a period of time, would end in her desire for marriage.

The evening had been a hilarious one, dancing and drinking at The Forum, followed by sandwiches and more drinks at Joe's apartment. As usual, Sonya made herself the spark of the party and inspired everyone to gaiety by her vivid antics and clever jokes. Her imagination simmered as her drinks multiplied, and Joe shrewdly provided her with plenty of drinks. He also made sure the party terminated in good time by quietly herding the couples from his apartment.

He pushed the last person through the doorway and locked the door. Then he turned to Sonya who still waltzed around the room, singing gaily while she balanced a half-empty glass in her hand. She reeled into his arms, and they swayed together as Joe took the glass from her hand and placed it on the table. His arms tightened about her, and his lips gently brushed her ear. They rocked dizzily, locked in close embrace, and then Joe lowered her to the sofa. His lips hunted hers and crushed them cruelly with burning eagerness.

"I love you," he cried hoarsely. "Do you understand? I love you. I must have you." His hands were exploring her warm body, caressing her. Clumsily, he fumbled with the belt knot at her waist while his lips kissed her throat. Sonya's benumbed brain fought to overcome her mixed emotions and Joe's violent advances. But the excitement of the moment sobered her, and the realization came that she was about to give herself to a man she really didn't like. She struck him viciously, full on the face.

"Stop it, Joe," she spat. "*Stop it!* Did you think I'm a pushover for a couple of drinks?"

Joe's ardor raged uncurbed. Without answering, he continued to maul her. With superhuman strength willed to people for such emergencies, she managed to push him back and jump to her feet. Joe sat on the sofa, staring vacantly as Sonya gathered up her coat and bag. At the door she spun on him and said disgustedly, "You needn't take me home. You've made a stinking heel out of yourself, and if I never see you again it'll be too soon. *Believe me, Joe, I mean it.*"

She stormed out of the apartment, slamming the door behind her as Joe buried his face in his hands. Yes, he had made a heel of himself, and he had lost her. He knew it.

Sonya sat down at her desk, thinking about Joe Roncini. It had been a number of days since she slammed the door in his face. She had not agonized over it, but she was reminded of him by Zota at a lunch they had just finished. Joe had taken to unrestrained drinking, and his friends were worried about him. His work was in shambles and he spent most of the time cursing himself and talking about how much he loved the one he lost. But she was determined not to feel sorry for him. It was a closed book, and it must stay that way.

The ring of the phone on her desk broke the silence, and Sonya answered mechanically, "Good afternoon, Hecht's Wholesale."

"Hello, Sonya."

The room spun before her as she realized it was Mr. X. That voice brought back memories that were not too deeply buried. "You!" she exclaimed. I thought . . ."

He cut her off rudely. "You thought I had forgotten you. No, I can never forget you. You are constantly with me in every thought, and I'll continue to pursue you until you are mine. I won't give up."

His voice was pleasant and musical. When he paused, Sonya said nothing, for she did not know what to say. He continued, "I was away from the city for a few days, but now I'm back and more eager than ever to take you out. To prove my love and show you a magnificent time is all I ask. Please, I beg you again, meet me as I ask."

"Meet you," she retorted. "You profess love or something and then strangle me when I keep the date. No thanks."

He laughed softly and answered good naturedly. "I'm sorry about that, and you weren't hurt. Scared maybe, but not hurt. It's ridiculous to think you could trick me, and my actions that night were to impress you that no one should try it. Getting Felice Miletto and his henchmen involved was stupid." There was a long pause, then he spoke again. "How about it? When do we get together?"

"Don't be absurd," snapped Sonya. "You must be crazy. Leave me alone or I'm going to the Japanese gendarme."

His voice changed and he spat viciously, "I warn you. If you do, you will regret it."

Sonya shuddered with terror. Though she could not see the person whose voice made her quake, she visualized a fiend uttering those words. She groped for words but could not speak.

"*Remember*! I know everything you do, every place you go. I warn you, do not go to the police. And stop going out with other men. I won't give up."

Without thinking, Sonya slammed down the receiver and held it there with both hands. Maybe that way she could hold him out of her life. But the days that followed were a continuous nightmare. There were regular phone calls, interspersed by notes left at her door, and Mr. X was constantly on her mind. He was usually very romantic, but on occasion evidenced a quick temper which left her shaken and worried.

39

Sonya confided every event with Netti but was afraid to tell anyone else about her dilemma. Being a witness to the sad situation, Netti covered her own emotions by continually consoling her friend. She pleaded with Sonya to get hold of herself, warning that she was losing weight and her very appearance demanded an explanation to other friends. However, it was futile advice, for Sonya could not just will Mr. X out of her life when he was regularly phoning or sending messages, alternately threatening or professing his love.

Sonya dreaded another evening alone. She sat looking through the window of her tiny room, wondering if Netti was home. Earlier that day, Sonya informed her that she was determined to sleep, and true to her word she came home and prepared for bed. Thus, she was attired in a nightgown and hated to dress for the walk to Netti's home. Still, the warm spring evening beckoned her. It seemed foolish to waste these pleasant nights, and she had been doing just that because of Mr. X.

Spring had come early and seemed to be here to stay. The Hai Ho River, free of its icy shield, moved easily through the middle of the age-old city, its dirty water carrying more and more of the winter restricted traffic. Shop doors were propped open during the day to invite in the sun warmed breezes, and the cloudy haze on the windows could no longer be accredited to condensation but more honestly to the greasy grime collected there. All of Tientsin rocked to the rhythm of spring, evidenced by the strolling couples out to catch the scent of romance which rode on those first balmy breezes.

Caught up in the warm weather, Sonya gazed out over the interesting old city with its ageless oriental buildings, faint lights, and surging crowds. She missed the male companionship to which she had been accustomed before Mr. X interrupted her routine, and she missed the stimulating emotions akin to that companionship. If Mr. X had not cautioned her, she might have dated some of the many men who perpetually waited on her, but she knew and feared his ability to execute his threats.

A shrill, diminutive whistle pierced Sonya's mood, and it immediately lifted her low spirits, for the whistle was the secret one she shared with Netti. Hastening to put on her negligée, Sonya heard the whistle a second time. Already on her way,

Sonya hurried down the stairs, left the door open, and moved to the gate, fumbling for the latch in the dim light. "Just a minute, Netti."

Suddenly, the gate was flung open, knocking her down. There was a blinding flash of pain when her head hit the pavement. She layed there unconscious. When she came to, she became aware of a heavy pounding in her head and her body felt numb. Sluggishly, she opened her eyes to see the gate swinging like a monster over her. Realization of what happened came to her in a rush, and she struggled to get up but could not rise beyond a sitting position. How long she had been lying there she had no way of knowing. Her long white legs stretched out in front of her, and their contrast against the dark pavement drew her attention.

Complete horror enveloped her as she became aware that her gown and negligée were wadded in a crumpled mass about her breasts, leaving her completely naked from the waist down. She felt a warm burning sensation on her face and rubbed it. When she brought her hand away, it was covered in blood, blood from a cut there. And there was also blood on her face! As tears burst forth, she held her silence for fear of drawing attention, but she wanted to scream. "My God, my face—*my face is scarred!*"

The words raced through her mind over and over as she half-crawled, half-ran up the stairs to her room. Clutching the dressing table for support, she looked in the mirror. Blood was smeared over her left cheek. "My face is bleeding," she moaned as she collapsed to the floor.

Sonya thought she was dreaming, but she really was being lifted by Netti and Mikela. They were in her room talking softly and helping her. They had been out for a walk, enjoying the evening air, when a Chinaman stepped from a doorway into their path. He bowed respectfully, held out a white envelope, and said in Chinese, "Please, Miss Rurik, would you mind delivering this letter."

Without thinking, Netti took the letter. The Chinaman bowed again and disappeared around the corner, while Netti stood there with the letter in her hand. Then she looked to see it was addressed to Sonya Petrovna. That was a fortuitous happening, because it took them immediately to Sonya's residence

41

where they found the doors open and Sonya huddled on the floor of her room, covered with dirt and blood.

Netti choked on her words, "She's dead—she's dead."

At that moment, Mikela saw Sonya's eyes flutter. "She's not dead. She just moved. Here, help me get her to bed. Hurry, get some water. She's only passed out."

Netti and Mikela managed to remove Sonya's torn and dirty gown, bath her, and get her comfortably settled between clean sheets. She still did not open her eyes, but was showing signs of returning consciousness.

"My god, what do you think happened to her?" Mikela asked as she examined the cuts on Sonya's cheek. "Look, she's opening her eyes."

"Yes, she is. She must be coming to. Sonya, do you hear me?" Netti questioned eagerly.

Sonya stared blankly at Netti for a moment. She then spread her arms to receive Netti's embrace and began sobbing. The crying increased as she clung to Netti as if her life depended on her presence. Netti made no effort to detach herself but instead held her close and consoled her softly.

Finally Sonya began to speak. Little by little she managed to tell them what happened, her voice quivering and spaced by sobs. "It's him, intent on torturing me. And he says it's 'cause he loves me. *Is that love?*"

"It's a strange love, that's for sure," Netti agreed.

"And now he has done what he has threatened, he's scarred my face!" Tears burst forth again as she turned to the wall.

"No, those cuts on your face are like scratches. You could have done it yourself when you fell. They will be healed up in a day or so," Netti said with assurance.

"Are you sure?"

Mikela supported the conclusion. "Netti is right. Nothing more than scratches. Quit worrying about it."

"Thank god he spared me that. But people will notice. My mother will ask. What will I say?"

"You won't have a problem." Mikela spoke matter-of-factly. "Makeup will cover them. Wear a scarf around your hair. You often do, anyway. No one will notice. And more importantly, right now, Netti, where is that letter to Sonya the Chinaman gave you?"

"Oh, yes. Sonya, a Chinaman on the street handed me a letter for you." Netti reached over to her coat, pulled the enveloped out of the pocket, and handed it to Sonya. "Here it is. It's addressed to you. Another strange way for you to get a letter."

Sonya handed it back. "Read it for us. I'm not up to it. It's probably just another awful letter from Mr. X."

Netti opened the envelope and unfolded the single sheet of paper. "It's in Russian, and there is no date or address on it." She began to read:

Dear Miss Petrovna:

I hoped it would never be necessary to write you this letter. There have been many times when I felt you should be warned in some way.

By way of explanation, I am a friend of the man who professes to be an admirer of yours. Since the first day he saw you, he has seemed to have little else on his mind. I know that he loved you at first sight, and it has grown to where it consumes him. He is a good friend who I have known for some time, but it has come to the point where I do not understand him.

He is a strong-willed, intelligent person who has changed and is sometimes almost irrational. That worries me, and it is possible he could cause you great harm.

In the interest of your safety, I recommend you follow these suggestions. Never go out after dark unless accompanied by a friend, and preferably do not go out at all. When moving about the city during the day, keep to the main streets. Never ride in a rickshaw if you have never seen the boy before and are not reasonably sure he is all right. Do not ride in an automobile unless you know the driver.

I hope you will believe me and take these suggestions seriously.
Sincerely yours,
A friend of one who loves you.

Netti quietly returned the paper to the envelope while Sonya gazed listlessly at the ceiling.

"That letter comes sort of late," mused Mikela. Her words ushered in a cloak of gloom which settled over the three of them and hung heavily in the room.

7

World War II information whispered around Tientsin said the Allies were crushing Germany, and the Americans had been dropping bombs on Tokyo. The oriental and occidental communities secretly hoped America would win the war—and soon. Of immediate interest, Americans had just landed on another Japanese island. Netti looked at the calendar. It read April 1, 1945. She knew she would never forget that date, even though that island where the war raged was over thousands of miles away. Was Japan on the verge of defeat? Could the fighting extend to northern China—and Tientsin—where the Japanese had been in control for years? She knew the answer was yes!

Spring was evident in Tientsin. Sunny days were bringing summer, which Netti enjoyed. The scent of growing plants was already mingling with the common odor of China. Even the old trees along the street and in the unkempt park across from the Astor House were showing some life, and grass was beginning to break through the winter-trodden soil.

Netti preferred summer to winter, even though the brutal sun of mid-summer scorched north China and made life unbearable. Cold weather left her depressed, and she lived only for the relaxing days of the season ahead. They meant enjoyable hours of lying on the beach at Peitaiho, splashing in the invigorating ocean, playing on the sand, joking with friends, laughing and having fun. There would be refreshing evenings of dancing and perhaps even romance.

Romance! How naturally it came to mind! She rather liked flattering remarks and was determined to get over her uneasy feeling with men. Remembering the last summer and how men seemed to stare at her when she roamed the beach in a skintight bathing suit brought a flush to her face. Secretly she hoped for similar attention again, and there was little doubt she would receive it. The past year had improved her poise and helped her confidence.

A shiny black automobile drew up before the dress shop, stopping directly in front of the show window. Netti watched and hoped the occupants would not enter. She hated to serve Japanese. However, the man who stepped out of the car was not Japanese, and this fact drew her intense scrutiny. He was meticulously dressed in a brown, English-style suit and wore a brown felt hat to match. When he stopped to look over the items displayed in the shop window, Netti was surprised to see he was Chinese. His well-groomed appearance and confident manner stamped him as one of those rare Orientals of good breeding and education. The glasses he wore gave him a fatherly look. Netti guessed he was well over fifty.

Somehow, she suddenly realized the man standing there idly peering through the shop window was none other than Feng Hu, the influential Chinese solicitor of Tientsin. She had never seen Mr. Feng, but his reputation was common talk, and this man fit the description perfectly. No other Chinaman would dare display his wealth so brazenly in front of the Japanese.

During the years of Japanese occupation, Mr. Feng had become chief mediator between the subjected Chinese and their rulers, braving the wrath of the Japanese to force the hand of justice. Always he upheld the Chinese people and pled for them. Any thoughts the Japanese had toward executing him soon dissolved when they realized his strong influence over the people of China. The Chinese loved him, and the Japanese hated him, enduring him as one tolerates a blackmailer. It was easiest that way. Consequently, Mr. Feng's reputation grew, and although he could not always help, he was known to listen and willingly give advice to all who called on him.

Netti's mind caught on that thought! *Could he help Sonya? Would he help her?* It was worth a try, and she found herself hoping desperately he would enter her shop. If he came in, she would ask him—but how might she be sure this man was truly Feng Hu? She settled on a simple plan: she would call him by name, and if wrong, he would undoubtedly correct her.

The man still stood on the street, contemplating the display of materials which Netti had placed in the window that morning.

Evidently satisfied with what he saw, he moved to the door and stepped into the shop.

"Good afternoon, Miss," he said pleasantly in Russian. "I am looking for materials—a dress for my wife. Your display in the window is attractive, and I want to know if the blue material can be made up for her. I presume it's the best?"

"Yes, Mr. Feng, that is satin-silk, our very best, and our tailors can make a dress to suit whatever you want."

"You know my name," he responded good-naturedly. "I don't believe I've ever been given the pleasure of meeting you, but I am flattered by such an attractive lady."

"I recognized you from what I've heard," Netti admitted, blushing uneasily.

He chided, "I wasn't aware my reputation with young ladies was so prevalent."

"I assure you, Sir," said Netti, slightly confused, "it wasn't that."

"No, of course not," he laughed. "I am much too old—and with a family. But I did mean it when I said you flattered me."

Netti spoke impulsively. "Sir, could you help me? I mean, would you help a friend of mine?"

"I don't know what you have heard about me, but my ability to help people is somewhat restricted and usually along definite lines. I am a solicitor by trade, and compelled to be a politician. Other than that, my knowledge is limited."

"May I tell you about it, and then you can see," Netti began, and then added cautiously, "but you must promise to treat what I tell you with secrecy."

Mr. Feng looked at her a bit amused. "That does add interest. What is your problem? Or rather, your friend's problem? I will help only if it makes sense to do so and only if I can."

Netti needed no further urging. She offered Mr. Feng a chair, which he took graciously, and she began the story of Sonya's "admirer." She finished out of breath, having talked hurriedly to keep from delaying him and waited for his comments.

"A truly amazing chain of events. I believe I may be able to help your Sonya. In fact, this Mr. X you speak of also presents a problem to me, and I want to find him. I give you my services free."

"Free!" Netti gasped.

"Yes. I daresay it would necessarily be so anyway," chuckled Feng Hu.

"Yes, I expect so, "Netti admitted.

"Come now, where may we find your girlfriend? I have a little time to myself this afternoon, and there are some things I should tell her."

"I could phone her and have her come here. She'd be here in a few minutes."

"An excellent idea. In the meantime, I'll pick out my material."

Netti phoned Sonya at the wholesale house and insisted she come to the shop immediately. Sonya was reluctant but agreed when told it concerned Mr. X. Netti returned to Mr. Feng to find he had laid an assortment of materials out on the counter. Pointing to two of them, he gave specific instructions for making them into dresses. He wrote the necessary measurements by memory and selected the patterns from pictures she provided.

Mr. Feng's efficiency impressed Netti, and the more they talked the greater became her confidence in him. She believed he would end Sonya's strife as easily as ordering a dress.

Sonya flew through the door in her customary turbulent way. After being introduced to Mr. Feng, she listened tolerantly while Netti explained the circumstances that required her presence. Sonya was not angry because Netti had taken matters into her own hands. However, she believed, and quite naturally so, that no one was capable of helping her. She doubted this Chinaman could do so when others had failed.

Mr. Feng looked directly at Sonya and spoke in a confident manner. "This man you call Mr. X is obviously smart and has above average ability. Which all leads me to believe he would give some thought to his position if he knows I am helping you. Modestly speaking, my influence can be quite far-reaching, and it occurs to me that fact may drive your Mr. X into the open. In other words, we'll allow him the privilege of coming to us."

"You mean, if he knows you are going after him, he'll come to Sonya or tell her who he is?" quizzed Netti with amazement. Sonya continued to sit quietly, refusing to show any enthusiasm.

"That is somewhat the idea," confirmed Mr. Feng. "Maybe he

won't do just that, but I think he may do something to bring his escapade to a climax. Now, Miss Sonya, the next time he phones I want you to give him an ultimatum. Tell him he must give you his name or meet you in the presence of your friends, wherever you desire. If he refuses to do either of those, and I'm quite sure he will refuse, tell him you are turning the matter over to your solicitor, and tell him I am that person. I suspect his action will be passive, but if anything unusual transpires, come to me immediately."

"There, Sonya, that's simple enough," encouraged Netti.

"Yes, I suppose it is," Sonya conceded. "It sounds almost too simple."

"That, Miss Sonya, is why our plan will work," Mr. Feng asserted as he started toward the door. "I shall pick up the dresses next week, Miss Rurik. Good-bye, and good luck."

Without further explanation, Feng Hu bowed gracefully and made his exit. A moment later, the two women watched the black automobile disappear down the street.

"You weren't a bit courteous," reprimanded Netti. "Mr. Feng is a big man in Tientsin, and he offered to help you without charge. You acted as if you resented it."

"It's not that. It's just I don't have faith in anyone or anything anymore," Sonya retorted.

"I know how you feel, but I have a feeling this is it. Soon you're going to know your admirer by a name," Netti guessed with conviction.

"If that's your intuition again, I hope you're right. And further, if Feng Hu is the solution by your way of thinking, I hope Mr. X phones soon so it won't take more waiting."

Had Sonya only known at that time the events which were to follow, she would have considered herself a prophet. Be it Netti's intuition or Mr. Feng's efficiency, only a few days were to elapse before a calamitous incident occurred, and Sonya waited barely a day for the phone call she wanted.

The call came in the morning, as it customarily did, and Sonya lost no time in giving the ultimatum to Mr. X. His reaction, when she demanded his name, was a sardonic laugh. When she demanded he meet her in public, he gave her a vehement refusal. However, when she said the matter would then be placed in the hands of Feng Hu, she met silence. The click of the receiver told her it was a victory, because for once Mr. X revealed a lack of confidence. Sonya was now ready to acknowledge the potency of the name Feng Hu. At least the mention of it had surely disrupted Mr. X's trend of thought. She felt rather elated over this turn of events, although she could not imagine what the consequences were likely to be.

In the days which followed, Sonya's elation turned into more than mere hope. The phone calls ceased, the notes stopped, and she regained her peace of mind. She allowed herself the belief that her troubles were over and Mr. X had at last decided the situation too hot to handle. Nevertheless, the memories which were still quite vivid did not keep her from thinking about stepping back into the swing of the gay life she missed.

Netti continually emphasized the need for caution. "Now, more than ever," she kept saying. "Call it intuition if you like, but I have a feeling."

It was late afternoon when Sonya started for the bank to deposit the company's funds. She carried the stack of currency and checks in her hand as she strode serenely along Victoria Road toward the bank. Having left her coat in the office, she found it necessary to quicken her step, because the day had turned cooler. Also, a glance at her watch indicated the bank would soon be closing.

Less than a block from the bank, a hand reached around her and wrenched the stack of money from her grasp! Uttering a stupefied gasp, Sonya turned to see the Chinese thief running down the sidewalk, weaving in and out among the throng of people clustered there. Sonya was panic-stricken! On her small salary, it would take her a lifetime to pay back all that money!

She ran after the Chinaman, screaming at the top of her voice, *"Stop that man! Stop that man!* He's a thief! He's stolen my money. Stop him, please. Someone catch him."

Not a soul made any effort to apprehend the thief. They preferred to watch the comical spectacle produced by the hysterical woman running as fast as her high heels permitted. Impeded by people in her way, Sonya's progress was slow, but the thief did not gain, and she managed to keep him in sight. Her tight skirt and high heels crippled her stride, and she reluctantly gave up the chase, weeping and praying someone would stop the disappearing man.

"Jump in, Miss," the voice said in Russian. "I will help you catch him."

She looked up to see a car beside her, the door open for easy entry. Hope flared on Sonya's tear-stained faced, and she jumped toward the open door. With one foot on the running board, Sonya raised her head to see the man who sat in the back seat waiting for her to enter. As she did so, a ray of light from the back window shone on his face, and a spark of recognition seared her memory. *The warning! The warning letter!* Reflex action helped her withdraw from the gaping door. She had barely stepped clear of the car when it started with a roaring jerk and sped away, the door still swinging open. Instinctively, Sonya's mind photographed the rear of the fleeing auto, and she memorized the license number: *976, 976, 976* she kept saying, over and over and over. Above all, she desperately wanted to remember that number.

Her heart pounded as though it would leap from her heaving chest, and her whole body vibrated from spent emotion. She leaned against a lamppost to steady herself, while vaguely contemplating her next action. A commotion down the street drew her attention, and she looked up to see two Chinamen tussling with each other. They were about half a block away, and their noise and violence attracted her. The dress of one of the Chinamen looked like that of the man who had escaped with her money, but Sonya could not be sure. As the thought revolved in her mind, the fight ended abruptly, and one Chinaman ran in the opposite direction while the other came briskly toward her.

Though still some distance away, the Chinaman made it evident he meant to accost her. Then she saw the money! The man held it in his hand, and the intense joy which surged through Sonya upon seeing it could only be shown by the grateful tears which sprung from her big brown eyes.

Upon reaching Sonya, the man held out the stolen money, made a short bow, and said in Chinese, "Miss, I have the pleasure of returning your money. The thief got away, but I retrieved this for you."

"Oh, thank you, thank you," Sonya blubbered gratefully as she took the money from his hand. When she started to say more, he brushed past her and made his way hurriedly down the street.

Still confused from her terrifying adventure, Sonya stood quietly, trying to dry the tears which persisted. Then she remembered the bank and her primary purpose. She turned toward the bank, knowing she must hurry if she were to make it before closing time.

After depositing the funds, Sonya retraced her steps to the wholesale house, but her mind was not on her surroundings. The entire money-stealing incident was strange. The running thief could have outdistanced her with ease, but he had elected to keep only a short way ahead of her, as if intent on staying just out of reach. And the car arrived at the most opportune moment, tearing away when she refused to enter it. As the car drove away, a benefactor appeared on the scene, assailed the thief, and retrieved her money while the thief just happened to escape. Also, the tussle for the money seemed a trifle staged, now that she thought it over. *And that man in the car, where had she seen him before? Why did his presence effect such spontaneous action on her part?* His face rang a bell in her memory—a bell of fright! *Where had she seen him?* Sonya wrestled with her memory, but each time she pinned his countenance to familiar surroundings, some part of the picture watered and flowed out of her grasp. She was still pondering the matter when she stepped into the wholesale house.

"Were you held up at the bank?" questioned Mr. Hecht.

"No, I just met a friend in the bank and stopped to chat for a minute." She hated to lie to Mr. Hecht, but telling him the truth would only complicate matters, and he accepted her explanation of delay without a word. *Met someone in the bank.* The phrase clicked in her mind, and Sonya spun around on her heel with exaltation. Now the face in the car fell into its proper setting, and she remembered where she had seen that man before. It had been the time in the bank when he asked her to go riding with him. Netti had reminded her of that incident and promised he would show up again. It had happened!

Preparatory to closing, Sonya tore around the office. Experiencing difficulty in containing herself with the newfound knowledge, she raced to see Netti. Now she was positive the whole

51

money-stealing episode had been staged for the sole purpose of enticing her into the automobile. Undoubtedly, the plan must have been conceived by the cunning mind of Mr. X. *Was the man in the car Mr. X?* Sonya assumed he must be.

8

Netti sat in the shop, thinking of quitting time and contemplating the advisability of closing a little early. Her mother had departed for a buying tour of the city, and the responsibility of locking the shop rested with Netti. Six-thirty was closing, and her mother would be furious if she left before then, but there were no customers and had not been any all afternoon. Such was usually the case these days. Most of their customers were occidentals and Russians who now had limited purchasing power.

Though the Russians were not molested by the Japanese unless for good reason, their means of livelihood had been reduced by the restrictions imposed on them. Many were forced to work for a ridiculous wage, or not work at all. They preferred the latter, but the majority worked because the Japanese looked with disfavor on those who refused, and to stand in a good light with the Japanese was the best assurance of a longer life. Consequently, money was scarce and business slow, but the Japanese had a way of keeping prices down, so people were able to manage, even if not well.

When Sonya burst through the door and excitedly asked where to find Mr. Feng, Netti sensed the significance of the question. Methodically, she began closing the shop, giving not a second thought to the fact a few minutes earlier she had questioned doing so. All the time, she kept firing questions at Sonya, not giving her time to answer, ending with, "What's happened?"

"If you give me a chance I'll tell you on our way to see Mr. Feng. You do know where to find him, don't you?"

"Yes, I think I know where his office is," replied Netti. "Come on, I'm ready. It isn't far."

By the time they reached Mr. Feng's office, Sonya had told Netti the full story. Netti also believed the entire money-stealing incident had been staged. However, she laid stress on the reappearance of the Japanese man who had accosted Sonya in the bank.

As they rang the bell to Mr. Feng's office, she was saying, "I told you that man had something to do with all this. I knew he'd show up again, and he's probably the type who would fall in love with a girl by mere sight."

"Good afternoon, Miss Sonya, Miss Netti. I was just leaving the office," Feng Hu greeted pleasantly. "Please come in."

After seating themselves in his office, the girls were so anxious to tell the story they both started to speak at once. Mr. Feng held up his hand, grinned, and suggested maybe it would be best if only one proceeded. Netti curbed her impatience and allowed Sonya to outline her experiences of the day. She told Mr. Feng everything, beginning with the phone call during which Mr. X had hung up, the stealing of her money, the man in the car who wanted to help, her recognition of the man and where she had seen him before, the car speeding away when she refused to enter it, and the amazing return of her money.

Sonya paused momentarily to catch her breath before continuing. "And I remembered the license number of the car. Do you think it will help? I just know the man in that car fits in somewhere, and my money was stolen with the intention of getting me into that car."

"I am inclined to agree with you, Miss Sonya," Mr. Feng said thoughtfully. "But there are other matters to be considered. What is the license number of the car?"

"Nine, seven, six."

Mr. Feng wrote down the license number, hesitated over the paper, and looked seriously at Sonya. "I hope you are sure of this number. A lot may depend on it. Most of the licenses in Tientsin are small numbers. Three digits could be right, and there isn't a possibility of there being a foreign license plate in the city."

"I'm positive that was the number," avowed Sonya.

Mr. Feng was enthusiastic. "I'll take action to find out who owns the car." He stopped short and added, "However, I have some concern about it. Most automobiles in Tientsin today are operated by Japanese."

"We realized as much," Netti offered.

"Don't worry about it. I'll still find out," Mr. Feng said confidently. "Now, Miss Sonya, there are a few other facts I need to know. First, how long has it been since this Japanese man stopped you in the bank and wanted to take you riding? Had Mr. X made an appearance at that time?"

"It's hard to remember exactly, but I think it was about the same time. Yes, I believe this man stopped me in the bank quite some time before I received the first note from Mr. X."

"Can you identify him as the man who attacked you on any one of those occasions?" quizzed Mr. Feng.

"No. I have never seen the man who attacked me."

"Back to the car again. Can you describe the car for me? Do you know what kind it was?"

"I don't know the kind, but I can describe it. It was light brown and had four doors."

"Well, that is all I need to know," declared Mr. Feng. Slapping his knees as he rose to his feet. "This time tomorrow, the bloodhounds will be running close on the heels of your Mr. X."

"We do hope so," Netti said, leading the way to the door.

Feng Hu opened the door and stepped to one side. "I have no doubt of it. I will phone you tomorrow, Miss Sonya." The door closed behind them.

*   *   *

When the phone rang in her office the next afternoon, Sonya knew it would be Mr. Feng. He was quick to come to the point. "Miss Sonya, is it possible for you to come alone and be at my office at nine o'clock tomorrow morning?"

"Why, yes, I expect so."

"Good. We have a visit to make." He added in a deliberate tone, "The car belongs to the Japanese gendarme. We are calling on Colonel Yosuki in the morning."

His last sentence chilled Sonya and left her petrified with apprehension. She did not sleep well that night, but she arrived punctually at Mr. Feng's office the next morning at the time set. He greeted her with "Good morning," before ushering her into his car and being on their way, heading north on Taku Road.

Tensely silent, Sonya sat beside Feng Hu in the back seat of his automobile. He had given specific instructions to the chauffeur, and when the car turned left of Taku Road and then right again on Chaylord, he made no comment. Instead, he held his reserve and abstractly watched the passing parade of peddlers, beggars, and bounding rickshaw boys who seemed to engulf the car. Movement was further delayed by the streetcars, which jerked wildly, gaining speed only to stop abruptly to belch out a mass of clawing people before inhaling another.

Sonya maintained her composure as the car crawled hesitantly through the French concession, passing the intersection of Chaylord and Marshal Foch Streets. It was one of the busiest intersections of Tientsin because of the French bazaar which was located there and attracted the multitudes who jammed the streets. Sonya smiled as she allowed herself a short memory of the four-floor market with its myriad tiny independent shops where she often browsed with her near-empty purse. She thought of the many times she had been there with Netti to argue the price and buy small items.

The car finally turned on Fukushima and stopped before an open gate guarded by two Japanese sentries. One guard stepped to the rear window of the automobile, cocked his rifle, and challenged Mr. Feng in Japanese. In return, Mr. Feng spoke briefly and presented a card. At the sight of the card, the sentry stepped smartly to one side and bade him enter. Mr. Feng nodded, gestured to his chauffeur, and the car moved through the gate into the small courtyard, stopping before a large gray building. Located in the center of the Japanese concession, Sonya guessed this building was the headquarters for the Japanese gendarme. Her heart skipped a beat when she thought of what the place might hold in store for her.

Sonya followed Mr. Feng up the short flight of steps to the main door. In Japanese, Mr. Feng conversed with the uniformed sentry standing there. A few moments later, Sonya found herself walking behind the soldier and Mr. Feng as they were led along a broad corridor. She was plagued with the feeling she should never have gotten involved and they were walking into the wrong place.

9

Feng Hu and Sonya Petrovna waited in a comfortable room at the Japanese gendarme headquarters in Tientsin. The room was luxuriously furnished, with two overstuffed divans, a number of big lounge chairs, and a variety of end tables and coffee tables set around on the heavily carpeted floor. Sonya experienced the sensation of entering a family living room rather than the headquarters of the Japanese gendarme. This pleasant feeling vanished when she became aware of the Japanese officer seated behind a small desk at one end of the room. The officer was beckoning them to be seated and made no effort to rise or say anything.

Once having seated themselves, Mr. Feng leaned toward Sonya and whispered, "That door beside the desk leads to Colonel Yosuki's office. He will receive us shortly. We are a few minutes early." Then he noticed Sonya tugging nervously at the handkerchief in her hand and added, "Relax, Miss Sonya. You have nothing to fear. Colonel Yosuki is coldly efficient, and I understand brutally cruel, but he is one of the fairest men I have ever met. He'll listen to our story and see that justice is done. Of course, we must know what we are talking about, and I wouldn't have brought you here if I thought we didn't."

"But when everyone talks in Japanese I don't understand, and I get the impression something is amiss," Sonya pointed out.

"I didn't realize you don't speak Japanese," apologized Mr. Feng. "I shall ask the colonel to carry the conversation in Chinese for your benefit."

"Thank you."

The officer behind the desk interrupted their conversation to say something to Mr. Feng in Japanese. Mr. Feng nodded approval, stood up, and said to Sonya, "Colonel Yosuki wants to see me alone. I should be only a moment."

Suddenly alone, Sonya could not dispel the feeling she was

abandoned by her only savior. Actually, she knew better, but the sensation persisted, and she wished for Netti's comforting presence. She had wondered why Feng Hu directed that she come alone. She had not even told Netti about her appointment with Feng Hu and Colonel Yosuki. In fact, she had told no one! None of her friends knew were she was, and she worried she had made a mistake.

Mr. Feng called from the door of Colonel Yosuki's office, "Come, Miss Sonya. The colonel will see us now."

Rising, Sonya experienced the impression of leaving her body on the divan. Her head seemed fluffy as the room momentarily reeled before her eyes. She had to collect her senses and calm her emotions. Standing still for a moment, she steadied herself with one hand on the back of a chair. When her head cleared, she walked toward Mr. Feng.

Colonel Yosuki's office presented an amazing contrast to the luxuriously furnished lounge where they had waited. In the middle of the barren room stood a massive, glass-covered desk, supplemented only by a number of hard, straight-backed chairs placed against the walls. The mood thus created chilled Sonya, and when her eyes fastened on Colonel Yosuki, she knew the room was characteristic of the rotund little man who scrutinized her. Mr. Feng introduced her and the colonel nodded but did not rise. Fearfully watching him, Sonya could not tear her eyes away from his impassionate face. The face was round with fat, cold, expressionless, and piercing black eyes which were almost hypnotic. The whole of Colonel Yosuki's fifty-odd years of living was carried in those ruthless but intelligent eyes.

At a gesture from Colonel Yosuki, an orderly stepped forward with two chairs, placed them beside the desk, and made a hasty exit. The colonel asked them in Chinese to be seated.

With Sonya and Feng Hu facing him, the colonel announced curtly, "Miss Petrovna, Mr. Feng has made known certain facts in your case. I intend to close the issue immediately. If one of my men is responsible, he will be punished. We do not include women-play in our duties. If no evidence is produced to implicate my personnel, all accusations of guilt will be removed from this organization, and your complaints will not be welcome here." Emphasizing the full intent of his words, the colonel continued,

"We admit ownership of the automobile you describe, and I know who was in custody of it on the afternoon you refer to. However, it is necessary that you identify the man. Come this way, please."

Colonel Yosuki rose and led the way to a door. He moved easily, despite his flabby body, for his stride was brisk and his back straight from years of soldiering. When he opened the door, Sonya was dumfounded by the scene before her. The room was enormous and completely filled with even rows of desks. At each desk sat a Japanese man, some in uniform, some in civilian clothes. Some were working industriously at their desks while others were walking along the aisles with their hands full of papers, conversing or examining the documents on the desks.

"Our workshop," Colonel Yosuki stated simply. "Miss Petrovna, your man is in this room. Do you mind picking him out for me?"

"Not at all." Sonya mustered all of her will power to make her voice sound confident, but she held no hope. Every man in the room looked the same to her—Japanese had always looked the same to her.

"Feel free to move anywhere you please," the Colonel stated. There was an obvious sarcastic note in his voice.

Without further comment, Sonya began walking slowly along the row of desks, starting systematically on the row nearest the wall. She moved slowly, peering intently at each upturned face, as Colonel Yosuki and Mr. Feng followed. The occupants of the room exhibited signs of interest in the proceedings, but their interest was restricted to furtive glances and whispered words, for Colonel Yosuki's presence prohibited any demonstration. Some dared to turn and gaze after the gorgeous girl as she passed, and the action brought a withering glare of reprimand from the colonel.

Sonya stopped, looked closely at the man before her, started to point to him, and then moved on without comment. Time after time she thought she had found him, but each time something failed to match in her memory, and she could not be sure. Halfway through the room, she was convinced her chance of recognizing the man was small. After more futile looking, she was positive no chance existed. She turned to face Colonel Yosuki to acknowledge defeat, and then she saw him! The action of the man had drawn her attention, because when she looked in his direction, he quickly dropped his face.

"That's him!" she shrieked, pointing in his direction. His desk was some distance away, and Sonya almost ran toward it while she kept pointing at him with one hand and beckoning with the other for Mr. Feng and Colonel Yosuki to follow. Her own ability to identify the man had stimulated Sonya to the extent where her enthusiasm ran unbounded.

"This is the man. This is the man," she repeated breathlessly. "I'd know him anywhere. He's the one who stopped me in the bank, and he's the one who was in the car the other day."

"That will suffice, Miss Petrovna," spat Colonel Yosuki. In Japanese, he gave a rapid order to a subordinate standing nearby before striding down the aisle in the direction of his office. Mr. Feng and Sonya followed silently.

Once again in his office, Colonel Yosuki motioned Mr. Feng and Sonya into chairs. Sonya felt ill at ease. She wanted to ask the colonel what he planned to do, and if the man she selected actually had been the one in the car.

Colonel Yosuki occupied himself with the papers on his desk and ignored his visitors. Finally, he looked up and said, "Now we shall interview our defendant." He pushed a button on his desk and the door opened. Three men entered. Sonya recognized the center man as the one she accused, and the other two were strong-bodied Japanese soldiers. She guessed these two must be the colonel's right-hand men. The man in question, dressed in civilian clothes, stood at rigid attention before the colonel's desk. The other two stood at attention to one side, like executioners awaiting orders from the fat little man behind the desk. Orders to kill would be taken for granted by such men.

In Japanese, Colonel Yosuki rapidly questioned the accused man. He answered the colonel's questions in short phrases, emphasizing his answers with vigorous movements of his head. After first nodding affirmatively, his gestures then became negative.

Colonel Yosuki turned to Sonya and said in Chinese, "The man before me is named Nasioto. He works in my intelligence department. He is competent and efficient. He admits having the automobile on the day in question but denies all of your accusations. He further states he has never seen you before today."

"But he is the man. I'm positive. He's lying," Sonya exclaimed in Russian, with grim determination.

Colonel Yosuki again quizzed Nasioto, and at one point Nasioto turned to look at Sonya before shaking his head negatively. It was evident he was denying any recognition of her.

"Miss Petrovna," Colonel Yosuki said coldly, "I cannot uphold your accusations. The evidence is too meager for me to take action."

It was all too plain! Sonya's word against the word of a Japanese, and Colonel Yosuki naturally accepted Nasioto's story in preference. Blood pulsed hotly through her veins as her rage mounted with the realization of how futile it could be to contest a Japanese in his own backyard. She jumped to her feet, and her fury broke free in a vicious tirade of words.

She faced Nasioto squarely and screamed in Russian, "You know me all right. You lie, you lie! Do you hear me? You lie! You remember as well as I do the day you stopped me in the bank and said in Russian you wanted to take me riding. I told you where you could go, remember?"

Under the onslaught of her searing words, Nasioto stood with mouth agape. Mr. Feng was tugging at Sonya's sleeve, trying to quiet her, trying to seat her. Her wrath was uncontrollable, and she shrugged his hand off her. Then Colonel Yosuki halted the proceedings.

His words, for the first time spoken in Russian, pierced the room with deadly intent. "So, Nasioto, you do lie. The girl knew you speak Russian perfectly. How would she know that if you had never seen her? Admit your guilt. Admit your guilt I say!"

"I know nothing," Nasioto answered in Russian, visibly trembling with fear.

"Know nothing, eh?" spat the Colonel. "You should be aware of our methods of making people talk. You know they are not pleasant. You'll talk."

His hand flipped toward the guards in a short gesture. Quick as lightening, one of the guards jumped to obey, leaving the office at once. The other guard smiled menacingly at Nasioto, seemingly delighted at the prospect of torturing another victim. Nasioto was terrified, and he looked furtively from one occupant of the room to the other. His expression was that of a whipped dog, desperately trying to find a place to hide. The colonel's face showed no expression, and his eyes glittered with a certain grim pleasure as he watched Nasioto squirm under his glare.

Mr. Feng pulled Sonya into a chair as the guard returned with a gruesome looking whip and a length of rope. From then on it seemed to Sonya that she was dreaming the scene taking place before her. The helpless man was stripped to the waist and tied to a stool. The whip rose and fell, again and again. Numerous strands of sinewy rawhide bit pieces of flesh from Nasioto's bare back, leaving a bloody mess. All the time there were the sickening groans of the tortured man, blending with the cold voice of Colonel Yosuki.

"Talk, you fool. Talk, I tell you. Talk."

The door swung open, and the whip stopped in mid-air. The soldiers came to instant attention. Colonel Yosuki and Feng Hu stood up, showing respect for the towering figure standing in the doorway.

The newcomer spoke in Chinese, unhurriedly, and with a soft deliberate tone. "Release that man. He is not responsible."

Silence reigned. The two guards fell over one another in their race to untie the unconscious man and drag him from the room. Then the tall Japanese officer stepped into the office and strode directly toward Colonel Yosuki. As he passed Sonya, sitting limply in her chair, he whispered five words. Those words shocked Sonya like a bolt of lightening, leaving her rigid in her chair. In Russian he had said, "I will not give up."

Without thinking, Sonya jumped up and pointed excitedly at the officer now facing Colonel Yosuki. "He is the admirer," she shrieked. "Mr. X, the man who—"

Her emotions out of control, and not believing her own words, Sonya sank into her chair. She sat silent, scrutinizing the man who professed love, pursued her, and hurt her. She wanted to remember every feature exactly.

Mr. X calmly returned her gaze, and there was a quirk of a smile on his lips as he slowly nodded in the affirmative, nonchalantly acknowledging her accusation. His eyes were devouring her bit by bit, and she had the sensation she was standing naked. When he finally spoke, his voice was familiar. "Yes, I am the man you seek. It is regrettable, Sonya, we had to meet in this manner."

His simple confession ignited Colonel Yosuki's temper, and he shouted indignantly, "You, you of all people! Sir, you have made an idiot of yourself, a ridiculous fool! You have used our agency to spy on and track a woman for purely personal reasons! You should be court-martialed! I'll see to it myself."

"I think not, Colonel," Mr. X said with authority. "I have arranged for a transfer to another area." Confronting Sonya and Feng Hu, he bowed and said in a pleasing tone. "I believe that arrangement should be satisfactory to my accuser and her solicitor. My orders are forthcoming."

"Yes, of course, my client finds the arrangement satisfactory," Feng Hu agreed. "Thank you, Colonel Yosuki, for your cooperation. Good day."

Once again in Mr. Feng's car, Sonya expressed her overwhelming gratitude. "You've been so kind. You have removed the blackest shadow of my life, and I feel as if I've just been released from a prison. I'd have gone crazy had this gone on much longer."

"I know you have been under a terrible strain, and I'm pleased I could be of help."

Sonya said impulsively, "I want to pay you something. I feel I must pay you for ending my nightmare. It won't be much, but something."

"My dear girl," Mr. Feng stated in a fatherly tone, "you owe me nothing. Forget it. I told you I would help you without charge, and I am as good as my word. My retribution lies in the fact that such a lovely young lady has thanked me and shown her gratitude. I did hate to subject you to the scene you just witnessed. I knew it might be gruesome, but under the circumstances, there is little one could do. It simply is not good practice to question anything a Japanese does these days, particularly Colonel Yosuki."

"I understand," said Sonya. "I wonder who that man is, Mr. X, I mean. Do you know him?"

"I was wondering the same thing. I should know him, but I don't. I believe he is Colonel Yosuki's superior. I've heard of him. It is evident he is a powerful man. You are fortunate that he acknowledged his guilt and took the stand he did. Having him leave this territory is the best you could hope for."

"Yes, I know," Sonya observed. "But isn't it strange he acts as he does. He is a clean, good-looking man."

"Well said, Miss Sonya," agreed Mr. Feng. "I am left more in the dark every day Japan rules our city. But now, where would you like me to take you?"

"I'm off work for the rest of the day, so I think I'll go see Netti. Could you let me off at Mrs. Rurik's shop?"

A short time later, Sonya bade Feng Hu good day and thanked him again for being so kind. She hastened into Netti's shop, bubbling over with excitement and eager to tell her faithful friend the astounding story. Mrs. Rurik greeted Sonya and informed her Netti had gone home for the day—she had not been feeling well. At this news, Sonya wasted no time in starting for the Rurik residence. She found Netti lying on the couch in the front room. After inquiring about her illness, she hailed her with the sensational statement, "We've found him! We found Mr. X! I saw him with my own eyes!"

Netti jumped straight up on the couch. "Do you mean it?" she gasped, unbelieving.

"I do mean it," Sonya replied as she pushed Netti down on the pillow. "Just relax and listen. If you won't interrupt me with a lot of questions, I'll tell you the whole thing. By the way, what's the matter with you?"

"Oh, you know, I'm always sick the first day or so," Netti answered impatiently. "Get on with it. Tell me about Mr. X. Who is he? What's he like? Tell me."

"All right, just give me time and listen." With that, Sonya related the events of the morning.

"And you still don't know his name, or what he does?" Netti asked when Sonya had finished.

"Certainly not," snapped Sonya. "He isn't the kind of person you question about anything, and besides, I was eager to get out of there."

"What does he look like?" Netti queried eagerly.

For the first time, Sonya gave thought to his appearance, which she had carefully stashed away in her mind. "Well, let's see. The first thing you notice about him is his height. He is taller than most Japanese. He's straight and muscular, broad-shouldered like an athlete. He had black hair and dark eyes. Now I remember what was so peculiar about him. His complexion wasn't like a Japanese—it was brown like that of a well-tanned white person, not pale like most Japanese. And his eyes, they're sort of slanted and large. You could almost forget they are Japanese. His nose is sort of narrow, small and straight. In fact, his whole face is more long than round. He has beautiful teeth and thin lips. His chin matches the rest of him. There, I think that's a pretty good description, don't you?"

"Yes," admitted Netti, visibly impressed. "I think I've seen that officer a number of times. His uniform fits him perfectly. And he's actually rather handsome, in an oriental way, right?"

"I expect it's the same person. I've never seen another just like him," acknowledged Sonya. "And, now that you mention it, he is handsome. In fact, quite handsome."

"What's he like otherwise?"

"He is very sure of himself, like a man who is used to being obeyed," answered Sonya. "He seemed calm and deliberate. I'm sure he must be well-educated. Not at all like the man I thought he would be from his letters. He didn't appear to be a person who would chase a woman, at least in a mean fashion."

"You describe him as a rather intriguing character," grinned Netti, flinging her head to one side with a joking air. "And he does love you. Now I wonder?"

"Netti," quipped Sonya, "if you're thinking what you're insinuating, you're being ridiculous. Besides, I told you he is leaving Tientsin for good."

Netti smiled and said in a knowing tone, "Well, maybe."

10

More than ever before, rumors were prevalent concerning the war. Information lines into Tientsin brought daily news, and tongues wagged—very carefully. The Japanese did not like news from sources other than their own, because they wanted the people to hear only what they wanted them to know. Their radio and controlled newspapers told of the invasion of Okinawa, saying the United States' losses were tremendous. They spoke of victory and their forthcoming drive to complete supremacy. Their optimistic propaganda even carried the intimation of an actual invasion of the United States. However, they didn't bother to mention the battles which had been fought and lost—Guam, Saipan, Tinian, and Iwo Jima.

Despite their propaganda, the Japanese failed to convince the people of Tientsin, because the secret information lines told a different story. Tinian-based bombers were making regular sweeps over Japan, with little opposition. Japan's Navy was essentially gone, and Japan wobbled under the impact. The entire empire quivered on the brink of collapse.

Those were the rumors of Tientsin, and the observing citizens would verify them by the Japanese actions around them. The soldiers were more brutal than ever. Their drives against the enemy agents, whom Tientsin harbored, evidenced meticulous planning. Large movements of troops were more prevalent, and they often occurred at night.

Netti and Sonya were mildly attentive and secretly pleased with the word they heard concerning the progress of the war, but like most young women of their age they were more interested in their own private affairs. Sonya now felt free to go and come as she pleased, and she regained her optimistic hold on life. She included Netti and showed her that men would provide fun without being serious.

Actually, their dates were few and far between, and the parties or get-togethers were made up of girls. Zota Seivberg could always be depended upon for a hilarious time and was included in their group more often than before. The girls sometimes went boating on the river and bicycled the city in the summer sun. They shopped for trinkets and bought nothing. Mostly, they spent their free time at the Russian Club, talking about dresses they would have after he war and the real fun which might be forthcoming if and when the Americans came to Tientsin. It would be exciting to have American soldiers roaming the streets instead of Japanese. The trains might again run regularly, and they could travel without restrictions or fear of being killed.

Their life, however, was not all pleasure. Bare necessities for her family's existence absorbed all of Sonya's meager salary. Netti's mother worked hard to make a living from the dress shop, and even with Netti's untiring help, they found it necessary to do without many things. All items requisite to a pleasant subsistence were scarce and hard to obtain if they were available. The girls found their life somewhat trying and therefore enjoyed all the little stimulations and common recreations available.

The big event of the season, which all of the girls anticipated with enthusiasm, was their forthcoming vacation at Peitaiho Beach. With their respective mothers, the girls made plans for their stay there. They had saved and worked toward that end and were discussing it at the Russian Club. Zota asked, "What have you decided, Sonya?"

"One thing is definite. We can't go up there and stay for two or three months," Sonya answered. "When do you plan on going?"

"Well, Netti and I have talked of leaving about the middle of next month and staying as much as three months," Zota explained.

"I expect if Mother and I get to spend a month there, we'll be lucky," Sonya said, showing a sad reaction.

"Look," inserted Netti, eager to help, "why don't we work it this way. We'll go on up next month, and then you and your mother can come up and join us when you feel like it. Maybe you can arrange it so we could all come back together. All you'll have to do is let us know when you're coming, and we can make arrangements for your accommodations. If nothing else, we can crowd up in our beach house."

"Sure, that would work," emphasized Zota.

"I think it might be alright," agreed Sonya. "Let's leave it that way."

Zota rambled on. "I'll write and get the reservations. I can hardly wait. Lying on the beach, swimming, dancing. A number of boys are going to Peitaiho for the summer. What a time we'll have!"

"May I remind you we're not there yet," Netti interrupted. "We still have to get our visas to travel. Remember?"

Zota picked it up again. "I'd completely forgotten about them! Oh well, we shouldn't have any trouble."

"Maybe not," replied Netti, "but we'd better put in our applications right away. I'll feel better when we have them. The Japanese can be very difficult about visas."

Sonya had not been following the conversation too closely. A certain event that morning had perplexed her, and she was thinking about it. Feng Hu had stopped at the wholesale house to thank her for the beautiful silver mug she had sent him as a token of her appreciation for his help. He said the words on the card that came with it were very appropriate. She was taken unaware because she had not seen Mr. Feng since the unforgettable day in Colonel Yosuki's office—and she had not sent him anything. Bewilderment had caused her to stutter over words of explanation, and Mr. Feng, misinterpreting her confusion for emotion, had bowed out the door and departed before she could tell him the truth. She reasoned only Netti and the people at the meeting in the colonel's office could be aware of her association with Feng Hu. The expensive gift ruled out Netti, and also Sonya, had Feng Hu thought about it. So she had to come to the conclusion she did not want to believe. It had to be Mr. X—but why?

Sonya left Netti and Zota at the club and started for home, walking along Taku Road in the direction of the Victoria Café. She was in no hurry and took her time gazing at the merchandise displayed in the shop windows. When the car stopped in front of her, she paid no attention. But when a man stepped out of the automobile and walked toward her, she stopped short in utter amazement. The man coming toward her was none other than Mr. X. She recognized him despite the fact he did not wear a uniform. He was meticulously dressed in civilian clothes. The light gray suit, white panama hat, and white shoes were in keeping with the warm spring day. A plain blue tie and matching handkerchief, which fell loosely from his breast pocket, provided the necessary color for his conservative dress. He tipped his hat and, speaking in Russian, greeted Sonya in the mellow tone to which she had become familiar.

"Good afternoon, Sonya."

Sonya had trouble getting the words out, but said, "I thought you had left Tientsin."

"Obviously I haven't left yet," he smiled. "I will be leaving as promised. That is why I am begging a few minutes of your time. I want to talk with you alone before I leave."

Sonya looked at him and saw a perfect gentleman standing before her, smiling good-naturedly, and looking her squarely in the face. Confused and unbelieving, her feelings were mixed with involuntary acceptance of this man, yet she felt harassed by the memories of his repulsive connection with her life.

As though hearing the debate going on in her mind, he said warmly, "You needn't fear me. I'm here to try and make amends. I want to explain my actions. You must know the truth. Please go for a ride with me so I may do so?"

"No thank you," Sonya heard herself saying, as if someone else did the talking for her. Her heart beat swiftly amidst rising agitation. She kept losing track of the fact that this man was a hated Japanese officer.

"Please, you must hear my story," he begged. His steady eyes watched her honestly, pleading for acceptance.

"All right," she said impulsively. Sonya could not explain the reason for her answer.

"Thank you. You won't regret it."

Graciously he opened the car door, waited for her to enter, and then stepped in behind her. At his order to the Japanese chauffeur, the automobile moved away from the curb. Sonya revealed her aloofness by sliding to the far side of the seat and remaining there. Knowing she was ill at ease, Mr. X relaxed on his side of the seat, maintaining his patience.

When Sonya could not stand the silence any longer, she

69

demanded, "Well, what is it you wished to tell me?"

"Don't be impatient," he soothed. "I shall tell you everything in good time. I'm sure we can find a better spot for my explanation than in the back seat of a car. You don't have any urgent engagements."

Sonya reddened. "How do you know?"

Mr. X turned halfway around in the seat in order to face Sonya squarely. His eyes were unflinching and his manner charming. When he spoke, his voice was steady and sincere. "I have made it a point to keep track of you."

For the first time, Sonya realized their conversation was being conducted in Russian. His Russian was so genuine she had not noticed. "I'm glad to know that," Sonya said flippantly. "Tell me, where are we going?"

"I thought the Country Club might be nice. You can hear my story over a drink. Maybe you will be move receptive in a nice environment."

"I can't very well object now," Sonya said rudely, though secretly pleased at the prospect of going to the Country Club. Her interest in the Country Club could be classed as curiosity. She had never had the privilege of going there during the years the Club had been known as the elite spot of Tientsin. The Japanese had taken it over when they occupied Tientsin, and prior to that time, she was too young to be interested.

Located on Race Course Road at the edge of Tientsin, the Club was originally built as part of the racetrack nearby. Reserved for select members comprised of the wealthy and prominent personages of Tientsin, the Country Club had been built for the most expensive of tastes. Then the Japanese had taken it over for their officers, and few people knew whether it remained intact and as elegant as before.

Sonya felt somewhat dubious about going to the Country Club. She did not like the idea of being seen publicly with a Japanese in a Japanese place. However, she dismissed her uncertainty, thinking it would be well worth a gossiped word to see the Club and not offend the man sitting beside her. Anyway, there was little else she could do now.

Mr. X made no effort to talk, apparently satisfied to wait for a more appropriate setting. He offered her a cigarette, which she

70

coolly declined. Despite this, she was thawing out. She was strangely impressed with this man. His gentle manners and fascinating personality bespoke good-breeding and encouraged her respect. His easy confidence and fluent speech evidenced a good education. Also, his mannerisms were definitely not Japanese, and she found herself wondering about his heritage—his background, his age. She guessed he was in his mid-thirties.

The car stopped before the entrance to the Country Club, and Sonya found herself standing within the massive building. While Mr. X talked to a white-coated Chinese attendant, Sonya methodically turned around to get a complete picture of the hallway in which she stood. On the left of the main entrance, a broad stairway led up to a mezzanine floor, and high above she saw a colored glass skylight shaped like a dome, through which the sun threw brilliant hues of light. Huge pillars of highly polished wood reached up to support the mezzanine floor. Another stairway led down to a carpet-covered lounge, and on the right of the entrance another hallway led off to parts unknown.

"This way, Sonya. It will be nice today out on the veranda," suggested Mr. X.

Mr. X and the attendant stood at the stairway, waiting for her to join them. When she did so, the attendant led the way down the stairs to the lounge, and Mr. X took Sonya's arm. When his hand touched her bare arm it warmed her, and she felt a tingling sensation throughout her body. She liked it, but she drew her arm away automatically. Never would she admit the feeling she had just experienced by the mere touch of a man's hand!

They followed the attendant through the lounge, along a short hallway, and into the barroom. Here, Sonya paused momentarily to view her surroundings while Mr. X waited patiently. The attendant moved through the French doors to arrange a table on the veranda. The barroom was not extraordinary but rather fitting to its location in the Club. It was long and narrow, separated from the veranda by a series of French doors, and the numerous tables were skirted by comfortable-looking wicker chairs. The bar reached across one end of the poorly proportioned room.

Mr. X seated Sonya at a table on the veranda and, after dropping cigarettes and lighter onto the table, seated himself

71

opposite her. "And now, Sonya, what do you prefer in the way of a drink?"

"Lime and vodka."

Mr. X gave the order to the waiter, taking the same himself, and watched the waiter disappear through the French doors. Then he turned to Sonya as if to acknowledge their privacy.

"I'm surprised," remarked Sonya. "There's no one here, only the waiter and the bartender."

"Rarely does any one come here at this time of day. That is why I thought it would be a good place for our talk," Mr. X explained.

"Oh, I see. But it sure is strange."

"Yes, Sonya." He paused. "I hope you don't mind my continuing to call you Sonya. I feel I know you that well."

"That's just fine. So what do we call you? What is your name?"

His good nature seemed to cloud over as he said, "I only wish I could tell you my name right now. But there are good reasons why I cannot. Sometime, hopefully in the near future, I will be able to do so. Now I must ask you to be patient."

Sonya looked a bit disappointed when she heard his reply, but he seemed sincere, and she did not want to be insistent. "Guess we'll have to keep calling you Mr. X until that time."

"Thank you," he grinned. "Help yourself to the cigarettes when you care for one. They are not the best but all we have to offer these days."

Sonya rarely smoked but decided to try his brand. She plucked one from the package. "They are much better than what I'm used to," she commented.

The waiter brought their drinks and departed. Mr. X leaned cross the table, lit Sonya's cigarette, and said nothing. His expression indicated he was thinking of a way to begin telling her the information he had promised by asking her to come with him. Sonya slowly exhaled a puff of smoke and waited. Finally he started talking, and his demeanor told Sonya it was time to be quiet and just listen.

"I appreciate your not pushing me. I know I have been confusing. Also, I know you must have a hundred questions. What I want to tell you should answer most of them, and I hope above all else it will encourage you to regard me differently than you do now." He paused to sip his drink. When he returned it to the table, he turned the glass slowly between his hands and looked into it as if to find the words he wanted to say. "This may seem strange to you, and it may not answer all. I just hope you will understand. Feel free to stop me to ask questions whenever you like."

He raised his eyes from the glass. With his voice low and toned as if pleading guilty to some horrible charge which had at last consumed him, and keeping his words deliberate and evenly spaced, he continued. "First, I am not a full-blooded Japanese. I am half occidental. My mother was white, my father is Japanese. I am what is vulgarly called a half-caste, what is politely called eurasian."

The meaning of those words startled Sonya, piercing her coldness and letting down her bars of reserve. She sat, bewildered, wanting to say something but not knowing what to say. This simple admission of his unorthodox heritage filled her heart with sympathy. She flushed with embarrassment, trying to understand his feelings. She leaned forward to offer some word of consolation, but he turned his eyes back to the glass and went on in the same low tone.

"All the details are not necessary to what I want to say. My mother has been dead a number of years. My father is in Japan and regarded there as a very influential person. I tell you this about my father because it is important."

Seemingly over the difficult barrier of what he wanted to say, Mr. X regained his easy confidence. He took a long healthy drink from his glass and smiled at Sonya, who looked more radiant than ever. He suppressed an impulse to reach across the table and take her hand in his. Instead he lit a cigarette, exhaled the satisfying draught of smoke, and watched the thin column rise upward into nothingness. When he spoke again, his eyes were locked with Sonya's, and they shone with a light of complete sincerity.

"When I was ordered to northern China, my superiors, knowing of my white blood, took steps to remove me from all temptation. Specifically, they forbid me to fraternize in any way with white women. They recognized that due to my mixed blood, such contacts could influence me, particularly with the opposite sex. But they did not reckon that I would see you." His voice was tender and tinged with loneliness as he continued softly. "That first day I saw you—I shall never forget it. Something clicked within me, and I knew I must be near you. You and Netti Rurik were walking along Victoria Road, gay and carefree, laughing as you talked. Your long hair shone like gold against the white snow, and your olive complexion reminded me of warm desert sands, even though the day was freezing. The way you walked, the way you tossed your head—I liked everything about you. As I rode along behind you in a rickshaw, I made up my mind I must meet you. However, the rules laid down for me said I dared not do so. We could not be seen in public. That is why I asked for you to meet me secretly. Do you understand?"

His soft voice had carried Sonya away in a dream, and his abrupt question caught her in a fog. She could only nod.

"From then on I wanted to know more about you. In a way, I wanted to live in your world, even though I knew it was impossible. Because of this, I had some of my trusted and loyal associates report on you. They have been very efficient and have kept good track of you—your friends, and your family. In this way I got to know Netti and how close you two are. It was natural for me to want to know everything—your desires, your feelings."

"Natural!" exclaimed Sonya. "Natural to spy on me?"

When he answered, his voice was barely above a whisper. As she looked into his eyes, a light seemed to grow and held her spellbound. She watched him closely and leaned over to catch every word.

"Yes, natural, because I love you."

Sonya need not have listened, because his demeanor spoke for him. She jerked forward, caught herself, and remained rigid in her chair. The words "love you" needed no comment. In the sickening silence which followed, he made no effort to speak. He sat with his hands spread on the table, and completely at ease, he peered deep into her eyes. His gaze seemed to wrest the soul from her body and leave her vacant. She knew he expected an answer, but it was impossible for her to diagnose the racing sensation within her breast. Struggling for the right words, she was finally able to speak.

74

"How can you say that?" she demanded. "It's a strange love when you have to threaten me, hurt me—in the dark." Remembering the agony, she wanted to scream out at him, but something indefinable tempered her feelings and left her next words passive. "How can you expect me to believe you?"

"I'll will try to explain it." The light died from her eyes, and he tried once again to wear the cloak of gentlemanly aloofness. The sound of his voice calmed Sonya. She snuffed at the forgotten cigarette and leaned back in her chair.

Looking across the table, eye to eye with Sonya, he started talking in a sad, matter-of-fact way. "Apparently, white blood and Japanese blood do not always mix well. At least, all my life I've lived with an internal state of turmoil, and I blame it on my heritage. I have been filled with suppressed desires and uncontrollable emotions. I know it, and I've always had to work at controlling my impulses. Perhaps I have rationalized and blamed my eccentric changes of disposition on that heritage, but there it is—deep in my being."

It was evident he had been over those words many times in his mind, but Sonya did not comprehend the whole meaning of the words and said so. "Tell me what you really mean. Are you just making excuses?"

"I mean this. I have a violent temper, and I know it. I curb it, but on rare occasions something snaps within me and I can't control the brutal feelings and actions that sometimes follow. Maybe it *is* an excuse, but a deep feeling drives me on. Then I get hold of it and conquer that feeling, becoming what I really want to be— a full-blooded white, considerate gentle person."

Sonya was closely attentive. She felt sorry for him, but suppressed her sentiment, for there were many questions she wanted answered, and she was not going to let her emotions interfere. She waited a moment and said, "I'm beginning to understand. Also, I received a letter telling me to be aware of your dangerous moods."

"From who? I don't know anything about it," he snapped.

"I don't know. It said it was from a friend of yours."

"Some friend," he ground out through tight lips, and Sonya suddenly saw the vehemence she had felt in some of their telephone conversations. It lurked deep within him and seemed to jump to the surface without his consent. Realizing now why he had grabbed her, and hurt her, Sonya sat motionless and silent while he regained his composure.

Finally she spoke when a warm smile crossed his lips. "Sorry I mentioned it. It isn't important. But I do want to know why you wanted me to meet you at the Kit Kat Club—a house of prostitution. That was a ridiculous request."

Mr. X laughed outright at the way Sonya gulped over the word "prostitution."

"Well, yes, it was. But posing as a legitimate nightclub. I didn't realize well-bred young ladies knew its real function. I thought only soldiers and certain men-about-town were aware of that. Sorry for assuming that. But no matter. It has not been open for a long time. It is a nice building, and I purchased it. I use it as a private getaway office and stay there sometimes rather than going home. I thought you might like to see how I furnished it."

Sonya had difficulty hiding her embarrassment. She felt strangely uncomfortable. Her one desire was to be free of his scrutiny. He seemed to enjoy the moment, and she wanted to flee, to lock herself in her room where she could slowly digest the meaning of all he had told her.

"It's getting late. I must return home," she lied. "May we go now?"

"Of course," he answered congenially. "I'd forgotten the time. Is there anything else you would like to know? You also should know I sent Mr. Feng a little gift and signed your name."

"Yes, I know. He thanked me for it. I thought it had to be your work. Why?"

"He deserved it. He brought us together, even though I didn't like the circumstances of our meeting."

Sonya rose impatiently, and Mr. X hastened to do likewise, at the same time tapping the table bell to summon the waiter. When the waiter appeared, he pointed to the large bills lying on the table. A broad smile spread over the countenance of the aged servant, and words of gratitude tumbled out as he bowed over and over again. The old Chinaman was not accustomed to receiving tips from his Japanese employers.

At the automobile, the chauffeur opened the rear door for

them to enter, but Mr. X reached out, closed the door, and spoke to the chauffeur in Japanese. Acknowledging his orders by a smart salute, the chauffeur stepped back. Mr. X opened the front door of the car, bowed low with a smile, and waved her into the car with a sweeping gesture.

Sonya hesitated. "What are you going to do?"

"There are times when I like to drive myself. This is one of them. Please get in. I'm really a rather good driver."

A bit reluctantly, Sonya entered the car. She debated his reason for wanting to drive but was forced to trust him. As a matter of fact, she found herself trusting him, regardless of the situation.

Driving back toward the city, neither made an effort to speak. Sonya was content to think about the strange man beside her and to wonder about this sudden turn of events. *What did it all mean?* She needed to start some kind of conversation. "Were you there that night I was knocked down at the gate? Was it Netti who whistled?"

He took his eyes off the road long enough to laugh at her. "I had a terrible time learning your secret whistle."

Without warning, he suddenly turned onto a side road. There was no reason for not taking the closest route to her home, and Sonya demanded, "Why are you taking this road?"

"I want to drive along the canal," he answered casually.

"But it's quite a bit farther."

"It could be," he acknowledged. He was evasive, and Sonya detected the mischievous grin which slipped momentarily across his brown face. There could be no doubt he planned something— something she could not or would not think about. She dared not allow herself to believe what she imagined. Yet, the fact remained that he was in control and she sat in a fast moving car, powerless to prevent him from taking her wherever he pleased. Terror gripped her. She contemplated opening the door and jumping, but knew that hitting the pavement at this speed would kill her instantly. In desperation she settled on a plan to jump out the moment the car slowed down.

Despite Sonya's fidgeting, Mr. X appeared nonchalant and indifferent to her obvious fright. He drove without turning his head in her direction, yet he watched her reactions from the corner of his eye, thoroughly amused. He was aware of her thoughts, and it delighted him because his scheme would be an even more exhilarating surprise if she were just a little infuriated.

Nearing a bridge, he suddenly swung the car sharply onto the rough surface of Canal Street and stopped abruptly on the bank of the muddy stream. Knowing Sonya's hand rested on the door handle for a rapid exit, he did not move. Instead, he spoke rapidly and agreeably.

"Please don't jump. I've no intention of molesting you."

"Oh," Sonya sighed, not sure if she believed him. However, she did not turn the door handle, but left her hand there, still dubious.

Before she could make a comment, he reached into his pocket and drew forth a small blue velvet box, holding it out to her in the palm of his hand. Sonya relaxed—not because he offered her the box, but because of the happy, open expression on the strangely handsome face before her. She never wanted to forget the way he looked at her in that fleeting second. Still, she hesitated.

"Take it," he urged. "Open it. It's for you."

Spellbound, still a bit uncertain, she took the box from the palm of his hand and, grasping it in both of hers, snapped it open. "Oh my!" she gasped. Clipped in a dainty slot of blue satin was a sparkling diamond ring. The single diamond was so large it appeared too heavy for the intricate gold setting. It glittered like a thousand tiny fires, and as Sonya turned the box back and forth in the sunlight, the huge stone threw brilliant beams of scintillating light around the car, seeming to dwarf all else in sight. Sonya could not tear her eyes away from the gorgeous ring.

"It's—it's a diamond, isn't it?" she stammered.

"Yes. It's a diamond," he answered, holding back the warm laughter bubbling in his heart. "Put it on. See if it fits."

"But why? Why do you give me this—this lavish present?" Sonya felt strangely uneasy, as though there was something wrong in this wonderful setting. "I don't understand."

"Simply this. I am leaving in a few days—being transferred to Shanghai. I may never see you again. You have been kind to listen to my problems and you've suffered because of me. It's a token for all of that, and, too, I want you to remember me." His last words were strained with emotion.

Still, Sonya hesitated. As much as she wanted to own the ring she knew she dared not accept it. In no way could she ever explain her possession of such an expensive item. Even to have it hidden away would mean living in constant dread of its being discovered. Sonya fought for the right decision, even though she knew from the start that that decision was going to be. She was fighting for the courage to refuse this man who was so happy in presenting it to her.

"Try it on. Come, Sonya, I'm eager to see if it fits."

Sonya continued to hold the box in her hand. She had the feeling that once the ring was on her finger she would never be able to part with it. He interrupted her debate by taking the ring from its resting place and lifting her hand into his. Carefully, he had selected her right hand. A gentle push, and the ring glittered merrily on her third finger. It fit perfectly.

Sonya smiled and turned her hand back and forth, as if to imprint its glitter in her memory. Than she reluctantly slipped it from her finger and replaced it in the box. Closing it, she offered the box back to him in her outstretched hand. "Take it back," she said faintly. "I'm terribly sorry. I can't accept it. It was awfully kind of you to offer, though."

"What do you mean you can't accept it?" he questioned in a stiff voice. "There are no obligations attached. I told you that."

A feeling of guilt surged through her, and Sonya found it impossible to meet his gaze. She focused her attention on the object in her hand and spoke apologetically. "I could never wear it. I would even be afraid to have it in my possession. You see, I could never explain an expensive jewel like this."

"Don't be silly," he argued. "You must take the ring. I bought it for you, for *your* finger."

"Yes, I know. But I can't take it. Here," she said, thrusting the box toward him.

Without a word he took the box and jammed it into his pocket. She could see him fighting for self-control, and she could feel the tension surrounding him as he started the car, crushed the accelerator to the floor, and sent the vehicle speeding down the road. A short time later he slid the car to a stop on the corner a block from Sonya's home. He leaned across her to open the door and said unemotionally, "You better walk from here."

Even as Sonya fled to the seclusion and safety of her room, she knew she would see him again. Oddly enough, she wanted it that way and hoped it would be soon.

11

Sonya lay in bed. She had scarcely left her room in two days, and her mother was disturbed when she had called Mr. Hecht to let him know Sonya would not be able to come to work. She had accepted the explanation Sonya was simply tired and wanted to rest, but actually Sonya wanted time to herself to try and analyze what was happening in her strange association with Mr. X. She did not even know his name, and it did not seem important.

Since her person-to-person contact with him, she had thought of little else. It was odd how he affected her with his mixture of self-confidence, deep-rooted emotions, and boyish enthusiasm. Remembering his suave courteous manner, she smiled to herself and wondered why he was attractive, when she abhorred Japanese. Willfully she rejected him as Japanese but approved of him as a man. His strange personality made him even more intriguing and made her want to know him better. He presented an abundance of food for her appetite for excitement, and she found herself dreaming of the possibility of a daring romance.

Thoughts of her loving him she dismissed as impossible. But he evidently loved her more than was good for him, and it was a new and thrilling experience to have a man literally insanely in love with you. However, of concern was the obvious fact that he must hold an authoritative position in the Japanese hierarchy. This was detestable to Sonya and did not fit her warm feelings, so she dismissed it. But she could not ignore the man who had wanted to give her an expensive diamond ring. That, she would always remember with a warm feeling.

Her daydreaming was interrupted by Netti, who burst into the room, demanding, "Sonya, what in the world is wrong with you?"

"Hello, Netti," Sonya answered serenely. "What brings you rushing in here?"

"You. I met your mother on the street, and I came along

home with her. You have her worried sick. What's wrong with you?"

Sonya threw back the covers, slipped into her negligée, and laughed as she said, "I think I've just been lazy." Netti watched as Sonya walked to the window and threw it open. "What beautiful weather, and I've been missing it. What time is it?"

"It's almost noon," Netti said impatiently. "I see there *really isn't* anything wrong with you."

Sonya flitted around the room preparatory to dressing and ended up making faces in the mirror while she combed her hair. Netti followed her actions skeptically. There could be no doubt Sonya's pretty head harbored some secret, and Netti wanted to know what it was.

"All right, what are you thinking?" Netti demanded. "You're acting like a schoolgirl after her first date."

"Am I really?"

"Has someone been to bed with you?"

"You're kidding of course," Sonya snapped, turning to give Netti a nasty look. Having twisted around on the dressing stool till she faced Netti, Sonya continued to draw the comb slowly through her hair as thought planning what to say. "Aren't you going to sit down?"

Netti still stood in the center of the room. At Sonya's question, she settled herself in a chair and waited. "I had a date with Mr. X," Sonya said simply.

"Really?"

"Yes, really." Sonya smiled impishly. "Want to hear about it?"

"I'm listening," replied Netti, trying to conceal her eagerness.

Sonya took her time and told Netti in minute detail all that had taken place on her so-called date with Mr. X.

"It's amazing! What's his name? You didn't tell me, and I'm getting tired of referring to him as Mr. X."

"I don't know. He said he would tell me sometime later when the time was right."

"You didn't ask him," sighed Netti. "You spent all day with a man who has been chasing you for months, and you didn't get his name. I give up."

"I'll see him again. Maybe this time will be right for him to tell me," she replied in an off-hand manner.

"I thought you said he was leaving for Shanghai."

"He said he was, but I'll see him again. Wait and see."

"Ohh—I see," Netti purred. "Could it be I'll be using Chanel before long?"

As young girls, they had made an agreement that the first to marry was compelled to give the other a bottle of Chanel perfume. Sonya remembered and readily grasped the meaning of Netti's insinuation.

"Don't be ridiculous," snapped Sonya. Seeing Netti preparing to leave, she added, "Where are you going in such a hurry?"

"Mother doesn't know where I am, and I must get back to the shop. I just ran up here a minute to see what was wrong with you."

"Wait another second and I'll walk to town with you. I must go tell Mr. Hecht I'll be back to work tomorrow," said Sonya as she rushed around the room to put herself in final order to go with Netti.

When they were in the street, Sonya wondered why she had spent the past two days in her room when she could have been enjoying the delightful weather. At this season, it was comfortably warm in Tientsin, but soon it would be unbearably hot, and she had wasted some of the perfect days. Not only the weather, but all of Tientsin looked good to Sonya. Either the rest had given her a new outlook on her surroundings, or her attitude had changed. More likely, Sonya found herself looking forward to some exciting days which would break her dull routine. She never liked Tientsin and would have left had the war not bound her there. She had been living in anticipation of the end of the war. Now she lived in anticipation of something indefinable— maybe a romantic interlude which would offer the stimulant she needed and craved.

Sonya left Netti at the shop and mounted a rickshaw for the remaining distance to the wholesale house. She wanted to catch Mr. Hecht before he left for lunch. Relaxed in the comfortable rickshaw, Sonya watched the shop windows slip by. The scene was familiar, for Victoria Road was as though a part of her. She had been along this street untold times, but now the typical English setting seemed different. Previously, the old three and four-story buildings seemed shabby. But on this particular day, they appeared quaint and old-fashioned. The constant hum of the jabbering Chinese on the streets provided a melody to the rhythmic beat of the rickshaw boy's feet on the smooth pavement. Even the faint odor of cooking rice and scented tea, which usually bothered her, now smelled great.

Thoroughly enchanted by her stimulating ride, Sonya was more surprised than infuriated when the rickshaw boy turned off Victoria Road and away from her ordered destination. She screamed at him in Chinese, "You take me the wrong way, you fool. Turn back. I told you the wholesale house on Victoria Road."

The perspiring boy in front of her leaned into the shafts and responded with an added burst of speed, which threw her against the back of the seat. Again she reprimanded him in a cutting tongue. He answered by turning his head as he ran and gave her a big grin, which showed a mouthful of dirty, jagged teeth. Not frightened, but ill at ease, Sonya decided to wait and see where he was taking her. Then, abruptly, he turned into an alleyway and stopped. There in the alley, lounging against a stone pillar, stood Mr. X!

Glaring at him, Sonya remained in the rickshaw. He returned her cold scrutiny with a good-natured smile and said, "I'm sorry, Sonya, but I've been waiting a long time to see you. I had you brought here because it isn't wise for me to meet you on the street."

Sonya refused to answer. Mr. X turned to the rickshaw boy and complimented him on his efficient work. Having dropped the rickshaw shafts to the ground, the boy moved to one side and bowed. He was evidently quite pleased with himself and verified his feelings by grinning broadly. A further signal from Mr. X prompted the boy to walk obediently down the alley in order that he might wait out of hearing distance.

Sonya defiantly crossed her arms, emphasizing her refusal to dismount from the rickshaw. At this motion, Mr. X moved closer and said in a low tone, "Please, Sonya, don't be angry. I had to talk to you, to apologize for my conduct the other day and to ask you for a date. Could we go out tonight?"

His pleading attitude melted Sonya's reserve, but she held back, still undecided. She noticed once again that he was dressed immaculately in civilian clothes. Absently she wondered how he dared wear civilian dress and if it were not dangerous for him to do so.

"What's the matter? Refusing to talk today?" he joked.

"The situation is more serious than that," rebuked Sonya. "I was brought here against my will."

"Quite true. But I believe you like it."

"I suppose you're reading my mind now?"

"Not at all, but that's beside the point. Will you go out with me tonight? You won't regret it," he implored seriously.

"Yes, I believe I will. At least it should be interesting," she retorted. Sonya did not question the answer she gave, for she had known she would consent. "What time shall you pick me up?"

"I can't pick you up. You'll have to meet me. I thought you realized that."

"You don't ask for much. First you want a date, and then you can't come for me. What do you want me to do—pick you up?" she asked sarcastically.

"Hardly, but you'll have to meet me," he explained. "Say, the Avon Street Bridge over the canal at eight. I'll be waiting in my car. The rickshaw boy who brought you here will be waiting in front of your house to bring you to the bridge. It will be dark then, and we can move about easier without being seen."

"All right. Now may I go?"

"Certainly," he replied. A large, warm grin spread over his face, and he signaled for the rickshaw boy. Sonya was soon jostling along on her way to the wholesale house. She had not even bothered to say good-bye when she left Mr. X standing in the alleyway.

Sonya made her stop at the wholesale house and decided to go see Netti. She thought it best to tell her friend about the forthcoming date. Maybe she had acted impulsively, and maybe she should not keep the date. She wanted the comforting feeling of Netti's concurrence and knowing where she would be just in case it went badly.

"Back so soon? I didn't expect you," greeted Netti.

"It didn't take long, but a good deal has happened."

"Now what? I swear, I can't keep up with you."

"I met Mr. X. He asked me for a date tonight, and I said yes. We are to meet at the Avon Street Bridge at eight." To prevent interruption, Sonya gave all the facts in one swift expulsion of words and waited while Netti recovered from the shock.

Finally Netti said, "It sounds exciting. Now you can find out something about him. For instance, find out his name."

"I'm glad you think it's all right," Sonya said, relieved by Netti's reaction. "And I can learn his name." She pondered her next words. "Frankly though, I'm a little frightened. What can we do? Where can we go? He says he can't be seen with me."

Netti was thoughtful. "There's hardly a place you could go under those circumstances."

"Maybe I was wrong in accepting the date."

"Relax. We should almost be able to determine his plans. Look, what are some of the things he could do on a date under those circumstances?"

"Well, he might want to go boating," suggested Sonya. "Or some out of the way restaurant."

"Or go riding in his car," added Netti.

"Or—" Sonya stopped her words and blushed profusely.

"Or take you to his home," Netti supplied the rest of the uncompleted sentence. "Isn't that what you were going to say?"

"Yes, I expect so," confessed Sonya, the color still high in her cheeks.

"Well?" Netti taunted.

"I'm convinced he's a gentleman. He'll allow me to make the decision as to what we do."

"Yes, he naturally should—and if he does?" Netti was being a bit cruel.

"I'd refuse. Of course I'd refuse," Sonya repeated for emphasis.

"But should you?"

Netti's statement astounded Sonya. "You're joking, of course."

"No, I'm serious. I'm confident you're capable of taking care of yourself, and he probably would be a gentleman on at least the first date. Also, you still know nothing about him, not even his name. By going to his home, you could learn where he lives and pick up more information about him."

"True enough," agreed Sonya, "but you might remember that I'm the one going, not you."

"You'll be safe enough," Netti assured her. "I know it."

"We'll see. I'm still not convinced. I'll have to see." Sonya rose to go. "I'll let you know what happens."

"Bye." Netti did not try to say more. From here on, she felt the decisions rested with Sonya. After all, Sonya was right. She was the one who had the date.

The rickshaw boy was waiting at her gate, even though she was a little tardy, and it was ten minutes after eight when she walked onto the canal bridge. Through the dusk she saw a figure pacing impatiently back and forth beside a parked car. Mr. X evidently believed in punctuality, for he seemed upset by her tardiness, and Sonya knew well how he acted when provoked too much. Consequently, she hastened forward, having decided on the lesser of two evils—to run away and have him accost her later, or to face his wrath now.

"Hello," she said nervously.

He stopped his striding and spun on her. "I had almost given up." Strangely enough, he was not angry, but she did detect irritation in his tone. His next words erased that impression. "I'm delighted you came. I was doubtful about it from the minute you accepted."

"Well, here I am," she said simply.

They stood there, rather awkwardly looking at each other, as if neither knew quite what to do next. Finally he assumed his natural manner and said, "Here, please get in."

He helped her into the car, walked around it, and slipped behind the wheel. He did not start the car but instead turned halfway around in the seat and looked at Sonya. One hand rested on the back of the seat while the other gripped the steering wheel. He was convinced the girl beside him looked more lovely than ever before. The mellow moonlight drifting through the car windows was reflected on her long, velvety hair which fell carelessly over the shoulders of her light suit. Her smooth, olive complexion appeared soft under the dim glow, and her large eyes shone with a deep luster like twinkling patterns of light on a moonlit brook. Under his gaze she lowered her eyes, revealing long eyelashes. He loved her. He couldn't help it. If only she could be made aware of his deep yearning. He wanted to crush her soft-ly rounded body to his, to drink from the freshness of her warm yielding lips, to fondle those perfectly formed breasts that pushed against her blouse. He caught himself leaning toward her and somehow felt guilty because she had looked the other way.

"I'm sorry," he stumbled. He squirmed in the seat. "What do you want to do? Do you have anything definite in mind?"

"No, I don't," she answered, ignoring his apology.

"Would you like to suggest something?" he asked.

"I think it's up to you," she replied evasively.

"Well, let's see," he said, looking past her as if intent on something along the canal. "We could go riding, within the limits of the city, of course. We could have a lunch at some quiet little café." He paused. "Have you had dinner? I do hope you haven't."

"No, I haven't." She smiled, raising her face. Sonya was enjoying the game and wanted to watch his expressions. "I had a late lunch."

"Good. Then it's dinner somewhere. That much we've set-tled. Now, where should it be?"

"Again, I say it's up to you."

He wrestled with the words in his throat. He wanted to be sure of just the right approach. Finally, in desperation, he offered half-heartedly, "I don't supposed you'd consider dining at my home?"

"It's hardly the proper thing," returned Sonya, cocking her head to one side.

"Yes, that's true, but please accept. I've arranged a superb dinner, and my plans will be wasted if you don't accept."

Sonya laughed outright. "So, you *did* have plans—plans from the very start. All right. Let's go."

He laughed with her. Then he started the automobile and they were off with a jerk, which threw her back against the comfortable seat.

Thanks to Netti's suggestions, Sonya set her mind to remembering the route when they started for his home. She knew close observation would be necessary because, although she had lived in Tientsin practically all her life, she was not familiar with many parts of the city. This was attributable to the fact Tientsin was a conglomeration of different localities, many of which were never safe for men, let alone a white woman who would attract undue attention. Therefore, Sonya's acquaintance with many sections of the city had been restricted to occasional rides with friends who knew the area.

Now, as they drove through the night, Sonya watched closely and made a mental check of the landmarks, streets, and turns which Mr. X made. Fortunately, the conversation lagged, and she found plenty of time to apply her mental processes to her purpose.

Mr. X seemed completely absorbed in his driving, intently watching the road and honking to clear the streets of stumbling Chinese and rickshaws. He was trying to make good time, but it was almost impossible in most areas because the occasional automobile had to clear a path as it moved along the oftentimes narrow, littered streets. Sonya realized her escort was driving at an excessive speed, and she couldn't help but be disturbed.

She became even more ill at ease when his frequent turns began to confuse her. He had intentionally left the main avenues and taken to the backstreets and alleyways. He drove back and forth, up one street and down another, criss-crossing and even reversing directions. His actions made no sense to Sonya. She debated asking him about it. Then, swift realization of what he had done stunned her! She did not know where they were! Having no desire to divulge this fact, Sonya sought to maintain her silence.

After more changes in direction, she could no longer be silent. She steadied her voice and said, as placidly as possible, "Aren't you taking a number of unnecessary streets?"

"For a purpose," he replied, keeping his eyes glued to the road.

"And what might that purpose be?" she probed. She felt the blood pounding her temples.

"I dislike being followed," he responded dryly. "My object is to keep the location of this home anonymous, both to my friends and my enemies. It gives me a certain privacy which is necessary to what I do."

Sonya breathed a sigh of relief. She judged it quite natural for a high Japanese official to want the location of his private home kept secret. But being with him, alone and not sure of where she was in the city, continued to bother her. When Mr. X stopped the car in a dark roadway bounded by trees, she looked around expectantly. As far as she could discern through the blackness, there were no buildings near. Doubt plagued her. While she peered through the window, he opened his door and stepped from the car. A second later he opened the door on her side. "Come, we're changing cars here."

"But why?" Sonya refused to move.

"I just explained that," he said impatiently. He smiled as he added, "My cooks are temperamental, so best we hurry. They might throw out our dinner."

Dubiously, Sonya allowed him to take her arm and steer her through the trees for a short distance. There, screened from the road by the trees, another automobile waited in the dark. Once in the car, Mr. X drove slowly along the short road to the main street, and only when he had pulled onto the main street did he turn on the lights.

"What about the other car?" Sonya asked.

"It will be taken care of."

Her curiosity was reaching the breaking point when the car finally stopped before a walled archway closed by a huge wooden gate. She noted they were in a congested district where the buildings stood one to the other, divided only by the tall heavy walls. The walls were next to the sidewalk which bordered the paved street, and though the buildings were near the street, very little of them could be seen. Since the enormous wall where they stopped looked no different in the darkness than any of the others, it would be impossible for her to recognize it at a future date. She would not be able to tell Netti or anyone else where she was. Sonya was hopelessly lost.

12

Mr. X turned the car and stopped at the solid gate that filled the walled archway. When he flashed the car lights, a Chinaman in baggy trousers appeared from the shadows. He moved to the car window and flashed a tiny light in the face of Mr. X and around the interior of the car, taking in the back seat and then Sonya. He muttered something in Chinese and disappeared into the deep blackness along the wall.

A moment later the huge gate swung open and Mr. X drove into the courtyard. Sonya heard the heavy gate swing closed behind them and began to feel as if she was caught in a net. However, the sight before her demanded all of her attention. Before them, silhouetted against the moonlit sky, was a huge mansion. Two long wings, two stories high, stretched out evenly on either side of the main structure, which reached a third story to dominate its position in the center. From the wing on the left could be seen a series of archways which evidently provided a cover for the sidewalk, stretching from the main building to a small home lounging among the gardens of the compact estate. Around all, the impressive wall was obviously there to repel invaders and block prying eyes. Past the right wing of the mansion, and barely visible through the night, were probably the servants' quarters, and the dim lights from their windows lent an atmosphere of quiet seclusion. As they drove the short distance along the gravel road to the manor house, Sonya perceived the gardens to be beautiful. Even in the dark, she could see the elevated flower beds made of stone.

Mr. X opened the car door and ushered Sonya through two large doors which swung open from the middle and which opened onto the hallway of the home she was now eager to see. To her surprise, she was standing in a sort of outside hallway. The floor was an intricate design of colored marble, and the fountain along one side was constructed of the same material. A series of lion heads along the wall spit water among the ferns and water flowers in the fish pool below. Large colorful vases on carved stands stood everywhere, holding cascading masses of ferns and flowers. The row of arched windows above the fountain were covered with pictures painted in bright colors and spanned the distance from the fountain to the high ceiling which was supported by heavy wooden cross-beams. She reasoned the wicker furniture placed here and there was used when the front doors were pushed wide in the hot summer to make an outside garden of the hallway.

Noticing the amazed expression on Sonya's face, Mr. X said, "Do you like it?"

"Oh!" she gasped. "Very much." Sonya was moving around, inspecting everything, smelling the flowers, dangling her hand in the fountain spray, and watching the goldfish scoot around among the rocks and ferns.

"I've gone to great lengths to make this place outstanding in the years I've been here. I enjoy beauty." His mind wandered for a moment, and his next words came as though he meant to say them to himself. "Lately, I've wanted it beautiful for you."

Sonya gave him one of her little sidelong glances and swung about as though to disregard the subject. She started in the direction of the French doors leading into the main hall. Mr. X caught up with her as she reached the few short steps up to the level of the hall. When he opened the door and she moved into the main building, she felt like she was in a palace. She wondered if her aristocratic Russian relatives had known a place like this.

In contrast to the aged outside, the interior was ultimately modern. Large squares of marble made up a checkered floor for the enormous hall. A broad, carpeted stairway circled halfway around the room on its gentle rise to the second floor, and the chromium banister could have been a part of the latest international mansion. Even the huge chandelier gave a modernistic touch in an ornate way.

Mr. X enlightened her obvious perplexity. He explained rapidly that the living room, bar, sun porch, master bedroom suite, lavatories, and bathrooms were on the left, while on the right could be found the ballroom, dining room, kitchen, and servants' waiting rooms. Upstairs were another living room, a reading room, and various bedrooms and bathrooms. Finally, he assured her she would get to see it all, but right now he was hungry and thought they had better prepare for dinner.

He clapped his hands and, as though by magic, a young Japanese girl appeared and bowed before them. Typically dressed in a Japanese kimono of brilliantly colored silk, she looked like a painted doll. Rarely had Sonya seen such a pretty Japanese girl. She seemed quite young, but knowing appearances often lie as far as Japanese were concerned, Sonya guessed her to be older than she looked.

"This is Kimiko," said Mr. X by way of introduction. "She'll take you upstairs and help you prepare for dinner. She speaks only Japanese, so you two may have a little difficulty in making yourselves understood. She has her instructions, and I'm sure you'll find her cordial and efficient."

When he finished speaking briefly to her in Japanese, Kimiko started up the stairs and beckoned Sonya to follow. She did so slowly, still somewhat dubious as to why she should have to be "prepared" for dinner. Having progressed nearly to the top of the stairs, Sonya stopped when she heard Mr. X call. She turned to see him standing in the middle of the hall, looking up at her and smiling like a mischievous child.

"I forgot to mention. I think you might find Kimiko has a surprise for you." Then he spun on his heel and walked down the side hall.

Fully resigned to numerous surprises in the company of Mr. X, Sonya did not allow herself too much concern over his words. However, she found herself totally unprepared for the procedure which took place when Kimiko escorted her into a large elaborate bedroom with wide closets and an attractive dressing table.

Kimiko began making motions which Sonya rapidly interpreted to mean she was supposed to take off her suit. Automatically, she rebelled. Whatever his instructions had been, she was now sure she objected to them. In no uncertain terms, she made it clear to Kimiko that she intended to remain dressed.

The puzzled expression which spread across the delicate features of Kimiko's face was pathetic. She hesitated uncertainly, as though trying to decide whether to run for her master or insist further. Then an idea struck her, and with that idea appeared a broad knowing smile. She bowed low and moved with short rapid steps to the closet. Standing on tiptoes, she reached within the closet and withdrew a black evening dress. She stood holding it high above her head to keep the bottom from touching the floor.

Kimiko's gestures to the dress were superfluous. Sonya uttered a squeal of delight, scooped the dress into her arms, and stood admiringly stroking the fine black crepe. Next, she bounded to the full-length mirror and held this amazing creation up to her, turning back and forth like a schoolgirl appraising her first formal. Exquisitely made, the dress was plain with a high neckline in front, a narrow strap for circling the neck, and a low open back. It was fitted tightly through the waist and hips to a gentle flare at the bottom. *Like one of those dazzling gowns shown in the American* Vogue *magazine,* thought Sonya.

Completely oblivious of Kimiko's presence, Sonya began removing her clothes, remarking to herself, "The length seems all right, if it will only fit!"

Attentive to her adopted mistress, Kimiko hastened to help Sonya with the buttons of her blouse. Sonya paid little attention, for her mind spun dizzily, visualizing herself in the dress now spread there on the bed. She would not be able to wear her slip or brassiere. *Oh well,* she thought to herself, *they were not necessary in an evening dress.* Suddenly, she stopped short in her busied actions. *Shoes! What would she do for shoes?* The tan pumps she wore would never do.

She turned to Kimiko and shrugged her shoulders, pointing to her shoes. Whereupon Kimiko grinned, bowed again, and hastened to the closet. This time she produced a pair of high-heeled sandals made of black patent leather and, proudly gesturing, she presented them to Sonya. Sonya grasped them as if her entire world had been fulfilled by the entry of a pair of sandals. She tried one on, and it fit perfectly!

When Sonya removed her stockings and slip and stood barefooted before the dressing table she hesitated. The color began to rise in her cheeks. She had never been naked before the eyes of a Japanese woman, and the more she thought about it, the more she blushed. Standing close by to be of assistance, Kimiko watched innocently. Sonya looked at Kimiko and then with some degree of determination, removed her brassiere and panties.

Kimiko quietly took over her duties. She seated Sonya on the dressing stool and began brushing her hair in such an experienced fashion that Sonya placed herself completely in the hands of her newfound attendant. Kimiko accepted her responsibilities readily and with delight. She powdered and perfumed Sonya, worked on her makeup from a line of cosmetics on the dressing table, dressed her, and fixed her hair. Had time permitted and Sonya agreed, she would have bathed her, given her a manicure or pedicure, or whatever else Sonya may have wanted. When Kimiko slipped the gown over Sonya's head, she crossed her fingers and prayed. It just had to fit—and it did, as though made for her! In fact, it must have been made for her. It clung to every curve as if molded there, outlining her perfect figure in a seductive manner.

Next, Kimiko produced a gorgeous string of pearls and snapped them around Sonya's trim neck, thus indicating completion of the preparations. Moving back to appraise her work, Kimiko clasped her hands enthusiastically and motioned Sonya to the big mirror. There, in the mirror, Sonya beheld an alluring lady, so stunning in beauty that she pinched herself to be convinced it was not all a dream. Never in her life had Sonya been dressed so attractively, and so expensively! Then she made her way to the door and, followed by Kimiko, walked down the hall to the stairway.

Waiting for her at the bottom of the stairs was Mr. X, dressed in a tuxedo. At the sound of her footsteps, he turned and looked up expectantly. He was not disappointed. Standing there at the top of the stairway, Sonya reminded him of a queen. Excitingly enticing, she looked just as he knew she would in the dress he had so carefully selected. He could not tear his eyes away from her, and he followed every one of her graceful steps until she stood before him, beaming happily.

"Sonya, you are breathtaking," he greeted, peering deep into her eyes. "You are even more gorgeous than I had imagined a woman could be."

"I'm bursting with excitement," she flushed. "Where did you ever obtain these divine clothes? And they fit me so perfectly!"

"They were purchased in Shanghai for you," he explained simply.

Sonya started. "But how—?"

"I know," he interrupted. "How did I know your measurements." Then he smiled and added, "That's my little secret. After all, how is a man to buy clothes for a lady unless he has the measurements—or the lady?"

His words carried a meaning which was obvious. They were said in a low, soft manner, and Sonya detected the pent-up desire and longing contained in them. The way he faced her churned her soul, and she found it necessary to lower her eyes to prevent his seeing the feeling there. She was determined to retain the reserve she had built between them, even though cheating may be required to accomplish it.

He broke the spell by suggesting a drink before dinner. "How about it? Since we've waited this long to eat, we may as well have a drink before dining. How would you like your martini? With an olive or without?"

"Are you kidding! Do you actually have gin and olives? They have been unheard of since the war."

After walking with her a short distance down the hall, he stopped and disengaged her hand from his arm. Pushing open a door, he said, "This is the bar."

Soft lights greeted Sonya, and as Mr. X slipped behind the small semi-circular counter, she swung around the room, looking carefully. Along one wall were two low half-moon tables made of mahogany, and around them were a number of low-seated chairs covered with red leather. On the other side of the room was a large overstuffed set, comprised of a sofa and four large lounge chairs. These, too, were done in red leather. Everywhere, there were end tables and coffee tables. The mahogany bar was just large enough to take care of the four leather covered barstools. Having made the round, Sonya perched on one of the stools. While Mr. X vigorously shook a cocktail shaker, she studied the labels on the number of bottles lined neatly along the shelves of the mirrored back bar. Though they were mixed freely with labels from many countries, she was impressed by the number of bottles which bore American labels.

"You have many whiskeys from America," she observed,

mildly curious. The words no sooner escaped her mouth than she was sorry for having uttered them, for she remembered with regret that Mr. X, being a member of the Japanese gendarme, assuredly hated Americans.

His answer astounded her, however. Nonchalantly continuing to shake the cocktail, he said, "Yes, they're excellent liquors."

Sonya watched as her host selected two cocktail glasses and poured their drinks. She started to speak but stopped short and looked intently at Mr. X. "Do you realize I don't even know your name. I just started calling you Mr. X—the nickname Netti gave you."

"I'd wondered how you referred to me," he joked. He pushed Sonya's glass close to her hand.

"What *is* your name?" she asked firmly.

He curved his hand around the glass and looked thoughtfully into the milky liquid. Raising his eyes, he hedged, "Let's see. Suppose we think of a good name for me."

"I want your real name," she demanded.

He ignored her plea. "How about Paul. I've always liked that name."

She spoke hesitantly. "Isn't that an American name? Why do you pick such a name?"

Strains of low music drifted through the room, and Sonya turned to see where it originated from. He took the opportunity to change the subject.

"I suspect Kimiko is on duty. She loves to play the record player. It's in the ballroom and is piped in here. I can turn it off if you like."

"Oh no. I love music."

She turned to press her original question, but one glance at him instantly told her she had lost her opening. By his manner she knew the subject of his name should not be mentioned again at that time.

He lifted his glass. "May I? To you, Sonya."

Looking squarely at her admirer, Sonya likewise raised her glass. "To you, Paul." Significantly, she had used the name he chose. "I'm going to call you that until you tell me differently."

"Suits me," he grinned. "I'll answer by it."

They were sipping the last of their second drink when there

was a knock at the door. Paul answered, and a Chinese voice informed them dinner was served.

"How about it? I think we've put the dinner off long enough. I'm starved," he said, glancing at his wristwatch. "You should be hungry, too. It's past ten."

"Yes, I am," she acknowledged, slipping down from the barstool. "It is different for me eating this late."

"I'm used to irregular meals," Paul remarked as they started for the dining room. "I have a terrible habit of eating when I'm hungry."

Two Chinese servants, dressed in neat white coats, awaited them in the dining room. While these servants seated them at one end of a long table, Sonya took in her surroundings and again was duly impressed. She did not, however, like the dining room. It was too large and gave one the feeling of being lost in one end of it. It obviously had been expensively furnished and fit the rest of the mansion. The enormous and intricately designed chandeliers held her eye longer than anything else. She could not remember having seen anything quite so ornate.

The dinner proceeded faultlessly. There could be no doubt Paul had planned every detail with meticulous care. They had course after course, interspersed with a variety of excellent wines. Throughout the meal the two servants attended them courteously and efficiently. It was easy to note they had been carefully instructed.

The conversation during the meal both interested and disturbed Sonya. She had started by referring to Kimiko and saying she thought her to be nice and very helpful. Paul agreed and, after a degree of questioning by Sonya, told the story of Kimiko's presence in his home. At first, he seemed reluctant to say too much about her, but evidently decided to be honest and give her the facts.

While he was deliberately vague concerning dates, he said he made a trip to see his father in Japan. While there he met Kimiko. It had happened when he decided to spend a few days with his aunt, who lived a distance from Tokyo. Though actually an attendant to this aunt, Kimiko was more like her own daughter. He was instantly attracted to Kimiko, and she made it a point to be constantly underfoot, doing for him and waiting on

98

him in every way. He had rather liked her, too. She was pretty and exceedingly useful. In due time she had offered herself to Paul, gracefully and shamelessly. He accepted her in an abstract way but was forced to make a decision when he prepared to leave for China. She begged to go along, according to him, as his housekeeper. Sonya understood the real meaning behind his words and thought the term "mistress" would be more fitting. She wondered if Kimiko meant anything more to him. But he insisted Kimiko just managed the house and was good at it. Nothing more, and he would be lost without her. That closed the subject.

After their meal they retired to the living room, and Sonya found the room most pleasing. The thick oriental rugs, the sofas, and the overstuffed chairs were all of the same design, done in the deep red characteristic of China. The big fireplace with its brass screen and filmy curtains accentuated by heavy drapes gave the room a homey atmosphere. The furniture was arranged in a way to make the larger room seem small and intimate.

When Paul rose and slid back a panel in the wall, Sonya's curiosity was instantly aroused. It appeared that he had slipped away part of the wall. Wanting to see what it concealed, she moved to his side. He was busy manipulating some dials and when she brushed against him, he looked around and smiled. "Thought you might like to listen to some music from the other half of the world. This is my radio," he explained matter-of-factly.

"You mean you have a radio which brings in broadcasts from all over the world?" asked Sonya, astonished.

He continued to play with the maze of dials before him. "That's right."

"But the Japanese gendarme! Won't they—?"

"I am the gendarme," he interrupted mildly.

Soon she heard an announcer speaking in English, and the contrasting tongue reminded her that all her conversations with Paul were conducted in Russian. It seemed peculiar to hear English on a radio and even more peculiar to realize the announcer was telling them they were listening to the voice of San Francisco. Then she heard music, soft mellow music, and Paul stopped operating the dials.

"Satisfactory?" he asked.

Sonya nodded as she swayed back and forth to the tantalizing rhythm. How she adored American music! She returned to her chair, and after sliding the wall panel closed, he pulled his chair close and joined her. Offering her a cigarette, he took one himself and then relaxed comfortably. Neither spoke. Sonya felt dreamy, listening to the music, and Paul seemed satisfied just to watch her.

"You know, we like the same things," she mused.

"I knew we would."

"But some of those things are distinctly American," she pointed out cautiously.

He evaded her inference. "Yes, one can find something to like about every country. I try to be broad-minded." He puffed on his cigarette at length and then asked, "Are you enjoying yourself?"

"Very much," she answered emphatically. She meant it, and she wanted him to know just how much she meant it.

"Would you like to dance?"

"Of course."

Paul turned back one corner of the rug to expose a portion of the hardwood floor. He held out his hand, and Sonya glided into his arms. They had barely started to swing to the rhythm of the romantic strains when, much to their consternation, the music stopped and the announcer began giving them a long dissertation on fine tobacco.

"Let's go to the ballroom," Paul invited. "I have a collection of records, and we can play what we like."

Sonya nodded and linked her arm with his. In the ballroom they found Kimiko. While he turned down the lights, Paul conversed with her in Japanese. Soon, Kimiko had the record player issuing forth lazy romantic music.

Again in his arms, Sonya discovered him to be a superb dancer. As they glided past Kimiko, she clasped her hands together and bowed. Somehow, that act of submission bothered Sonya, but Kimiko was soon forgotten and Sonya danced in a dream. She found pleasure in the easy way he held her, and she liked the feel of his agile body next to hers.

Paul, too, was content. At first, Sonya seemed reserved and stiff, but the mood of the moment which enveloped them brought her close to him. She relaxed and snuggled in his arms, laying her head on his shoulder. He held her closer as they danced as one, each completely absorbed in the other. They forgot how many times they danced past Kimiko, and they forgot how many times she changed the records. Sometimes they forgot the music and danced while the records were being changed, picking up the swing of the new tune when it started. Sonya and Paul were truly in a little world of their own.

Too soon the dancing was over, and they found themselves back in the living room. He had not wanted to stop, but Sonya insisted. Truthfully, she wondered why, because she had not wanted to stop either. Deep within her there seemed to be a self-induced reserve when with this man. Yet, it was not natural for her, and she enjoyed his company, even though she did not want it that way. In his arms she had been stirred to complete acceptance of her happiness. This very fact provided the reason for insisting they stop dancing.

"Would you believe it, Sonya, that's the first time I've danced probably in years," Paul said, still holding her hand. "I was surprised we did so well. It seemed natural. With you I can do everything better."

"That's a nice compliment."

"It is more than a compliment. I mean it. You can help me always do better."

Sonya had no appropriate words for Paul's comment, and she felt a little uneasy. She looked at her wrist only to remember she had left her watch in the bedroom, not wanting to wear it with the evening dress. "It's very late. I must be getting home."

Her statement prompted Paul to lean back on the sofa and push a button in the wall. He then waited expectantly for the entry of his servant. He was not disappointed, because the servants were well trained, and one soon appeared at the door, waiting obediently for his master's orders.

"The box, Chang."

At these simple words, Chang nodded knowingly and disappeared. When he left, Sonya studied her escort. She had been watching him closely and knew he must be up to one of his tricks. He wore that same mischievous look which always appeared before one of his surprises.

She did not have to wait long before Chang returned carrying a cardboard box tied with a broad red silk ribbon. He started to hand the box to Paul, but Paul pointed to Sonya. Chang then placed the box in Sonya's lap. For a moment he looked at her, beaming delightfully, and then he left the room. Instead of opening the box, Sonya gazed reprovingly at Paul.

"Go ahead, open it," he urged. "It's for you."

"Oh, Paul. Why do you insist on giving me things?" she scolded.

She burned with desire to open the box, yet she dreaded its contents. She knew it would be something unusual and probably expensive. She also knew she would be unable to accept it. What then? Would he be hurt? Or angry? Somehow, she feared him in those times when he was displeased. With misgiving she proceeded to open the box, untying each knot with care.

When at last she lifted off the top and pushed away the flimsy tissue paper, she was totally unprepared for what she saw. There lay a gorgeous fur coat! For him to give her a fur coat at this time of the year only added to her confusion, but she could not restrain her impetuous burst of delight. She made no effort to remove the coat from the box but sat stroking the soft golden fur. She could not control her excitement. "A gorgeous mink coat," she blurted.

"Not really. It's not mink. It's kolinsky, sometimes referred to as a Siberian sable. That gold color is natural."

Paul stepped over to her and withdrew the coat from the box. "You can't see it properly half wrapped up." As he shook the coat and held it up, he added, "I had no intention of buying a fur coat in this season, but when I saw these kolinsky pelts, I knew they were for you. They are rare and hard to find, particularly good ones that are well-matched, and I couldn't resist them. Chinamen smuggle the pelts in from Siberia by sewing them together like a poncho and hiding them by wearing it under a coat."

Sonya was so caught up with the beauty of the coat she did not follow all his explanation about kolinsky pelts. Somewhere in the past she had heard the word kolinsky, but she did not remember ever seeing the fur. She was accustomed to crude fur coats commonly seen in Tientsin, and this one looked like the latest creation from Paris.

Seeming to read Sonya's thoughts, Paul said, "I was pleased

to see it finished and think it is really gorgeous."

In Sonya's view the word gorgeous could not begin to describe this coat. She took it and started to put in on when she saw her name, SONYA, embroidered on the beautiful silk brocade lining. As she stroked the soft fur, she gasped, "My name, and the design of this coat. Wherever did you have this done?"

"A friend of mine in Shanghai made it up. Come, let's try it on. It won't look right unless you're on the inside."

Slipping into the coat, Sonya already was thinking of some gracious way to refuse it. Once again, she found herself faced with the same problem, and this time she knew what the result might be. If only he would be content to give her inexpensive things which she dared keep. The situation was becoming more difficult by the minute, for he was expounding at length on how well it fit her, how beautiful she looked in it, and how it was made for her alone. He took her hand and turned her around before him, his eyes dancing merrily. How could she disappoint such a man?

Sonya decided to face the truth and his wrath. She spoke deliberately. "It is magnificent, Paul. And it's the most beautiful coat I've ever seen, but you know I can't take it."

Paul stopped short in amazement. She could not have shocked him more had she slapped his face. He battled with mingled emotions and then, as if finding her meaning, he burst out laughing. "Please don't joke with me. I almost thought you meant it."

"I did mean it," she retorted, honestly afraid of her own words. "Oh, Paul, can't you see I would give anything in the world to own a coat like this. I should say, be able to wear a coat like this. It's like a dream, but I wouldn't dare. Maybe some day. Can't you see what I'm trying to say? It's not for me—not now anyway."

Sonya saw the blood rushing to his face as he stood dully in front of her. Even as she watched, the mellow light died in his eyes and was replaced by a vacant stare. As he fought for self-control, she watched his hands opening and closing, as though they were flexing every muscle in his body. He quickly relaxed and a thin smile soon vanished. He grimaced as he bluntly said, "I should have known."

As Sonya started to remove the coat, Paul grabbed the collar, jerked it off her back, and flung it across the room. Dazed by the display of violence, Sonya dropped to a chair and looked stupidly at the coat barely visible under the sofa where it had been thrown. Kimiko's presence drew Sonya's attention. Standing beside her, Kimiko gently tugged on her arm, showing a sorrowful little smile. Her timing was perfect, and Sonya eagerly followed her to the bedroom.

By the time Kimiko had dressed Sonya in her own clothes and hung the evening gown in the closet, Sonya had regained her composure. She hoped Paul would not still be angry. She dreaded the drive home. While these thoughts plagued her, Sonya made her way down the stairs and to the living room. Paul was not there. Chang was busy straightening up the room and had not touched the coat, which still lay on the floor where it had landed. The sound of footsteps caused her to turn around.

There in the doorway was Paul, dressed again in a business suit. His face wore a congenial though troubled expression, and Sonya knew well what was on his mind. He did not advance but remained at the door, as though waiting for her to make the first move. Not sure of herself, Sonya remained silent and waited. Each looked awkwardly at the other. When the embarrassing silence started to become unbearable, Paul stepped forward almost timidly.

"Sonya, how—," he faltered, "how can I ever apologize? I make no excuses. Please forgive me. *From this minute forward, I pledge myself to hold that part of me in check. To you, Sonya Petrovna, I make that pledge.*"

Sonya found herself seeing him as a little boy, confessing and hoping his truthfulness would spare him a spanking. She visualized him kicking his toe in the ground and hanging his head, when actually he stood before her, straight and unfaltering. All this she read in his eyes, for they were pleading with her, asking forgiveness from the depths of his soul. She reached out and linked her arm with his. He put his hand on hers and held it tightly as they walked to the car. They had taken up where they left off dancing.

They did not change automobiles on the way home, but he took all the other precautions. Suddenly, Sonya found herself in the familiar surroundings of the Russian concession, but she could not have retraced their path had her life depended on it. She really did not care where she had been. All she knew was that she had enjoyed her evening, and would enjoy more like it.

Paul stopped the car just around the corner from Sonya's home, explaining it might not be wise to take her farther. This continual caution seemed unnecessary to Sonya, particularly so early in the morning when the streets were deserted. She said as much, but he only grinned and informed her all of Tientsin had eyes and ears twenty-four hours a day. Sonya waited quietly for Paul to get out and open the door for her, but he did not move. She reached for the door handle herself, but his hand beat hers to it as he leaned across in front of her and turned the handle.

"Pardon me for not getting out. People are easier recognized outside a car than in one."

"I understand."

His hand still rested on the door handle. His body pressed against her shoulder, and his face was close to hers, so close she could feel his breath on her cheek. Sonya spoke low, and her voice was warm with feeling as she said, "Thank you. Thank you for a glorious evening. I'm only afraid I'll wake up tomorrow and discover it's been a dream."

"It's going to be one long endless dream," he whispered, and his voice vibrated huskily.

As he spoke, his faced moved even closer, and Sonya found herself swimming in the murky depths of his dark eyes. She did not think but acted instinctively. She lifted her face and kissed him full on the mouth. Drawing away quickly, his lips followed and hunted hers, finding and devouring them in a tender embrace. Sonya's senses spun dizzily in the dark, and far away she could feel his arms crushing her body. Then her arms were around his neck, and she gave without reservation the passionate response his hungry soul craved.

Reluctantly, Sonya slipped out of his arms. Only when she had walked the block to her home did she become fully conscious of the event which had just transpired.

13

Sonya sat daydreaming on company time. Her work for the morning had been accomplished, although it was still half an hour until noon. Since Mr. Hecht did not believe in his employees leaving early, she remained in the office.

She held a note from Paul, which had been delivered a few minutes before by a Chinese boy. The note said he was out of town and missing her. Of course, it included a few endearing phrases which were expected. A number of days had passed since she went to Paul's home for the first time. During those days they dated regularly and she had heard from him almost every day. She initially refused his requests for dates but finally agreed when it could be arranged and done secretly. He took her on a canoe ride, paddling along the Hai Ho in the evening sun. One day they slipped away to a dumpy little Chinese café in a dark corner of the city. She had never heard of the place, but he knew it well. He knew they would be alone and inconspicuous there, and he knew they would receive superb service and an excellent meal. Sonya was led to believe this tiny spot, located in a dilapidated building with greasy windows, was operated for the sole use of Paul. For sure she had never eaten a better Chinese meal or enjoyed one more.

And there were times together at his home where they danced, drank, ate, and listened to his radio. She now knew where his home was located in the old elite part of the city. That was no longer important, because all that mattered was being with Paul. But when she was forced to remember his Japanese position, his race, and his changing personality, Sonya could not sort out how she really felt. In his arms it was all forgotten. She liked him immensely and wanted more than just passionate kisses. *Was she in love with him?* Again and again their embraces left her shaken, because she wanted him intimately, and she wondered why he did not take her to bed.

He should have let her know he was fighting to keep his promise and hold his emotions in check. Some day that had to change.

"Hello, Sonya."

Sonya jumped at the unexpected sound of Netti's voice. "Netti," she acknowledged. "What brings you to Hecht's Wholesale?"

"I talked to Zota this morning. She and her mother received their travel visas to Peitaiho over a week ago. Mother and I still haven't received ours."

"So?" questioned Sonya, fumbling for the significance of Netti's angry mood.

"So," mimicked Netti, "we are ready to leave for Peitaiho with Zota and her mother and can't go without visas."

"You act as if you're mad at me," Sonya snapped, perturbed by Netti's attitude. "What am I supposed to do about it?"

"I'm not blaming you, but I am blaming your Mr. X. I just know he's behind this."

"Oh, don't be ridiculous. Why would he want to hold up your visas? He thinks you're wonderful."

"Well, it's funny to me the Seivbergs received theirs when we applied at the same time. I checked at the gendarme office, and they just shake their heads like a bunch of fools. They know nothing. I'm positive he has something to do with it."

"I'm sure I wouldn't know," retorted Sonya, "but I doubt it."

"Anyway, will you ask him about our visas the next time you talk with him?" asked Netti. "At least he may be able to help us. We wanted to leave this week."

"Of course, I'll ask him when I can. He's out of town now, and I have no idea when he'll return. The note he sent today didn't even say where he went."

Sonya looked at the clock on the wall, and seeing it was quitting time, rose and prepared to leave. Aware of her intentions, Netti suggested they have lunch together. Sonya agreed, and the two girls left the wholesale house to select a restaurant. They decided on the café in the Talatai House Hotel, since it was close and fairly decent.

While they ate, they became aware of the numerous Japanese soldiers and civilians in the café, which was used mostly by the clientele of the hotel. That must mean many were transients staying there. The Japanese forces took rooms they wanted, by force if necessary, for their transient soldiers, and the girls concluded such was the case here.

Though they were served a fair meal, they did not enjoy it. The environment was not conducive to good appetites, and they were more eager to leave than to eat. They picked at their food and said little to each other, since even a whisper would have been overheard in the quiet room. As always, the characteristic silence prevailed in the Japanese filled room. As they stepped onto the street, both looked at each other as if acting from one mind, and drew deep breathes of fresh air to emphasize the distaste they had shared in the café. They picked up their normal conversation of dress styles, men, parties, and the forthcoming trips to the beach. Before either realized the time, Sonya remembered she was due back at work.

Once again in the office, Sonya turned to the task of accomplishing her duties in the shortest possible time. She had just started when the phone rang. Answering it, her pulse quickened on recognizing Paul's voice. Somehow, he always affected her that way.

"I am in Peking," he said, "and it appears I'll be stuck here for a number of days. Just wanted to phone and let you know. Darling, I'm certainly going to be disappointed about the date we planned for tomorrow night."

"Don't worry about it," Sonya answered softly. "There'll be more dates."

"I wonder if you know how much it means to me to hear you say that."

How easy it was for him to put her on the defensive by some innocent statement. Sonya groped for a suitable answer, and not finding one, came up with Netti's problem. "Paul, before I forget, there is something Netti wants me to ask you."

"Yes," he answered congenially.

"Well, she and her mother applied a number of weeks ago for travel visas to Peitaiho Beach, and they haven't received them. She thinks you may know something about them."

"I feel sort of foolish," he said. "I think I have them with me in my briefcase."

"But why?"

"Well, I wanted to help her," he hastened to explain. "When they came across my desk, I pulled them out—was going to expedite them. I completely forgot. When does she want to leave?"

"Sometime this week. She didn't say when."

"Tell you what I'll do. Since it's my fault, I'll send them down by messenger," he declared, eager to right himself with Sonya and Netti. "They'll be delivered to you sometime tomorrow. Maybe you'd better tell Netti so she can go ahead and make her plans."

"I'll tell her today," agreed Sonya.

"Now, since we have that settled, I want to look forward to being with you when I return, which should be in a couple of days, probably Saturday."

"That's rather indefinite." Sonya still tried to be evasive, or at least not overly eager.

"Saturday, definitely," he said decisively. "I'll be there."

"All right," Sonya conceded, as though giving in reluctantly when actually she looked forward to the date. "The bridge at the same time?"

For their recent dates, they had met at the Avon Street Bridge at eight, so their meeting place and time had become well-established.

"Bye, darling. See you Saturday."

"Bye, Paul."

Sonya carried Paul's message to Netti and received the expected, "I told you so." The next day she found the visas on her desk when she returned from lunch. There was no note or evidence as to how they got there. It was typical of Paul's methods. Sonya promptly delivered the visas to Netti, who was busy preparing to leave. When Netti informed her they were going to Peitaiho the next day, Sonya could not conceal her despair. She wanted to go also, and this, coupled with the loneliness she would feel by Netti's absence, added to her dejected frame of mind. Netti noticed her friend's attitude and consoled her by reminding her only a couple of months were to elapse and Sonya would be joining them. They made their farewells, and Netti continued with her packing.

As she proceeded with her last-minute preparations, Netti

did not let herself think about Sonya. She hated leaving Sonya, particularly now when Sonya was carrying on a dubious romance with Mr. X, or Paul, or whatever his name was. She experienced a twinge of reluctance when she thought how she would be unable to keep an eye on her vivacious friend, who would be lonely without her. Consequently, she pushed Sonya from her mind in order to keep those disturbing thoughts from developing into mountainous doubts. The next day she was on the train headed toward the beach.

Netti may have thought Sonya would be lonely without her, but such was not the case. Although she missed Netti, her mind was filled with Paul, and his unorthodox courtship stimulated her to the point where it was more and more difficult to control her desire for ultimate love. The fondness she had for this Japanese official she learned to call by an American name was becoming something deeper and grand. The romance she once contemplated abstractly was now a part of her daily diet. She decided he must have lots of money, because he seemed to be always buying something—many somethings—for her. It was not really important to Sonya, but she often wondered from where he derived his evident wealth. She recognized a man in his position had means of obtaining the material things at little cost, and yet, his gifts to her were obviously expensive. Also, the fact he had not been transferred as originally understood added to her concern about his business affairs. She did not think it wise to inquire, and really did not care, as long as she could be with him.

Paul's uncontrollable temper never again sprung loose after the last outburst over the fur coat, and Sonya found herself trusting his judgment and actions. His uncanny instincts sensed her every desire. When he kissed her, she wanted to be kissed, and when he held her close, she wanted to be loved. But he had not overstepped the trust she bestowed on him. Their dates were exhilarating, and Sonya looked forward to the hours she spent with him, invariably in his home. Those hours were always pleasant, because he altered the routine. The dinner boasted a new dish, or there were different records, or a new gift. She had learned to accept the gifts graciously, because she knew he derived pleasure by giving to her. Although some of the gifts

110

were jewelry, he particularly liked giving her clothes, and she soon possessed an extensive wardrobe in the closet of the bedroom set aside for her use. Both Sonya and Paul recognized use of these items were limited to their dates and had to be tucked away in his home. Despite the restriction, Sonya enjoyed her newfound worldly goods and the times with Paul when she could use them. But all was not right in her world!

Sonya was worried about the mounting tension in her home. Her parents were asking questions about her activities and wanting to know about her friends and acquaintances. She did not lie but worded the truth carefully, and she was tired of the scrutiny. She had been old enough for a long time to leave home and be on her own, but she stayed largely to help a little with the finances. Her father was now working regularly and would be able to provide the basic needs for her parents, so Sonya was determined to find a place where she could come and go as she pleased.

She needed help to find an inexpensive apartment and ruled out Paul, because she knew he would want her to move into his home. Also, it was going to be necessary to increase her salary, which brought her to the conclusion Mr. Hecht might be the answer to her problem. She had been a faithful employee, so she decided to ask for his help and a raise at the same time, explaining her desire to be on her own as a responsible adult. Further, in a couple of months she was supposed to go to Peitaiho Beach, and he would have to arrange for her absence. Actually, Sonya was not looking forward to the beach and would like to forget it, but she had promised her mother, and Katilka really needed the vacation.

Sonya was eating the lunch brought to work when Mr. Hecht came to her desk and pulled up a chair. He always tried to keep her apprised of the war developments, and he had learned some more from sources he would not divulge. The American advances were still going on. Back in February, the Russians had cancelled their nonaggression pact with Japan, and now Mr. Hecht thought they might declare war on Japan. He worried it would effect the Russian population in Japanese held Manchuria and here in Tientsin. American planes were regularly bombing Japan and returning to their island bases, unlike the bombing of

Tokyo in early 1942, when the planes crashed in China. Japan was on the brink of collapse. Mr. Hecht rambled on, eager to tell someone what he had heard.

All this was important to people in the Japanese controlled areas, so Sonya knew she must show interest. However, her greatest interest at the moment was how to ask Mr. Hecht for help and a raise in salary. Now was as good a time as any. Without thinking it through, the words tumbled out. "I want to move out, away from my parents. I need some freedom, and I'm too old to be staying there—I need a place of my own, just a little flat. I'll need more money, though. Could you help me find something and increase my salary so I can do it?"

She was surprised at Mr. Hecht's simple response. "You've earned it. Of course I will help you. About the salary, first we better find the rental and know what it takes. We'll talk about it."

Sonya was ecstatic, and she wanted to give her boss a hug, but she restrained that emotion. Almost in tears, she said, "Oh, thank you, thank you. I was afraid. Can we do it soon?"

Mr. Hecht spoke in his mature, thoughtful way. "I know some people knowledgeable about rentals in this part of the city. I'll find out as much as I can as soon as I can. Just be patient."

The phone started ringing and broke the awkward silence. Mr. Hecht got up to leave. "You had better answer it. Maybe someone finally wants to buy something here," he joked as he walked away.

Sonya heard Paul's voice on the phone and was mildly surprised he would be calling twice in the same day. "Look, Sonya, could you meet at four on Saturday?"

"Why, yes, I suppose so," she stammered, somewhat alarmed he wanted to see her at such an hour in the afternoon. "Is something wrong?"

His voice came back laughing at her apprehension. "No, just think we should do something different. I would like to see you in the daylight."

Sonya was amused at his humor and retorted, "I'll ignore that last statement. You can see all you want of me any time."

His response was quick and pointed as he mimicked her. "Guess I should ignore your last statement, but I won't."

Getting away from the word game, Sonya expressed her concern. "What about your being seen with me? Isn't that dangerous for both of us?"

"Don't worry, I'll take care of it. See you Saturday. Bye for now." The click meant he had hung up.

Sonya busied herself at the office, determined not to think about Paul. It would take forever for Saturday to come! The next day, Mr. Hecht gave her something to think about that helped pass the time. He had talked to a friend who said there was an efficiency apartment for rent in the neighborhood. Apparently, the owner had died or left the city, and it had been vacant for some time. The rent was reasonable, with no down payment required.

Mr. Hecht had obtained the key and the address and thought they should go see it immediately. They found it on the second floor of a decent-looking building, set back from the street and protected by the usual iron gate. He had been told there were four apartments in the building, this being the small one, and the others were occupied by elderly married couples. It seemed too good to be true, and they were surprised to find a clean room with a window, a little kitchen, and a bath. *But what about the price, and furniture?* Again, Mr. Hecht took over.

"Sonya, I will raise your salary enough to let you live here, but you will have to manage your funds very carefully if you also want to eat and pay the utilities. I can find you some used furniture free, which should be comfortable."

This time Sonya gave him a big hug, saying, "How will I ever make it up to you?" That hug was all the payment he needed.

Sonya could not stop her gush of enthusiasm. "When can we do it? Can we start right away? What should I do?"

"The first thing you have to do is think of a nice way to tell your parents. No real hurry, because it will take awhile to draw up the papers and move in furniture. I'll take care of it and let you know when it's ready."

Yes, Sonya knew the first thing that had to be done was telling her parents, and she dreaded it.

14

Saturday came, as it always does, and it was four o'clock. As always, Paul's rickshaw boy had waited at Sonya's home, picked her up, deposited her in the same meeting spot, and left. She was puzzled. The car was not there as usual. It was noisy with rickshaws and people going by. She reasoned Paul had forgotten the time and wished she had not let the rickshaw boy go.

"Sonya, we have a couple of blocks to walk. Follow me." It was Paul's voice. She turned to see him, barely recognizable in common street clothes, a cap, and large, very dark glasses. Without a word she followed as he walked away. She was thinking he was always doing something strange with his ability as a master of disguises.

He soon turned into an alleyway, walked to the next street, and stopped in front of a large door in a building that looked like a closed warehouse, except for windows above the door. He opened the door and stepped in. Sonya followed, somewhat surprised to see how bright the windows made it inside. The room was vacant, except for a scooter parked there. It had two seats, and it was immediately obvious to Sonya that Paul was going to take her riding on it.

"Wherever did you get that?" she asked. "Do you think you are going to get me on it with a skirt? I don't like those things anyway."

Paul was picking a bundle out of the little rack on the front of the scooter. "It's old, but it runs pretty well on very little petrol. Saw it for sale some time ago and bought it. I used it to run errands. Here, put this on." He handed her a pair of slacks she knew would fit, because everything he ever gave her fit. She paused. Seeing her hesitation, he added, "Don't worry. I'll look the other way."

Sonya stepped out of her skirt to reveal see-through lace panties and a garter belt holding up filmy cotton stockings. She smiled. "Look if you want to. I don't mind." And he did. She knew what he must be thinking, and she wanted it that way. He did not have to guess at the reason for her pointed invitation.

A cap and dark glasses completed her outfit. Paul placed her skirt in the scooter rack, pushed the scooter out the door, got on it, and said, "Get on the back and hold on to me, tight, and don't let go. We won't be going very fast, but a spill can hurt."

They were on their way to somewhere. She wondered where. He need not have told her to hang on tight, and she was glad she had not worn high heel shoes because the little pads for feet were difficult. As he maneuvered the little machine slowly past people on the street, Sonya was really enjoying the ride. When they reached the outskirts of the city, he pushed up the speed. Sonya leaned forward around his side, enjoying the warm air brushing over her face. It was the month of May, and the weather was perfect.

Half shouting, she spoke in his ear. "It's really good to be out on such a pleasant day. Being with you in the daytime is a nice change."

Driving carefully, he turned slightly and answered, "Exactly. That's why I thought of it. Glad you are enjoying the ride. We'll stop after a bit."

Sonya was enjoying the ride, hanging on and watching the countryside slip by. They were riding along a shallow canal, and other than an occasional shack, the area was devoid of habitation. Around each hovel, unkempt children romped and played in the litter. Rarely were they dressed, because these Chinese families found clothes for children under five unnecessary. As they passed, the noise of the scooter drew attention, and the little waifs stopped their antics to stare in true Chinese fashion. Sometimes they even tried to run along with the scooter while the mother watched nonchalantly. And here was a broad barge moving slowly in the muddy water of the canal, propelled by coolies standing upright and pushing with long poles.

Paul guided the scooter across a bridge and followed a now-unused dirt road toward some red brick structures. It was an area of brick factories that had been closed by the Japanese, and he was undoubtedly aware of that. He finally stopped near a kiln surrounded by soft swamp grass nurtured by underground moisture from the swamps nearby.

"How about a rest here before we start back. We've come quite a ways," he suggested while helping Sonya off the scooter.

"Gladly. I'm stiff all over. I can hardly walk."

Stiff indeed, Sonya's first steps resulted in her stumbling and falling into Paul's outstretched arms. Trying to steady herself, she allowed him the satisfaction of holding her close, and she enjoyed the feel of his muscular arms around her waist. Further, she liked the way he bent to kiss her and the way his lips burned desire into hers. Looking into his eyes to find them animated with emotion, Sonya leaned back in his arms and tenderly took his face in her hands. Her own eyes glowed like smoldering embers. Her arms slipped around his neck, pulling his face down to her moist lips. His hands were tangled in her silky hair as they dropped to the ground on the bed of grass.

After a long time, Sonya's mind cleared the gap back to earthly things. She found herself lying in his arms with her head on his shoulder. "Darling, it's so pleasant here, just being together. Like Tientsin is a million miles away." Her voice was mellow, and she evidenced her contentment by relaxing in his arms.

He, too, felt the mood as they watched the setting sun moving down to perch on the horizon. When he spoke, his voice sounded far away. "Yes, a million miles away—the whole world with its war and grief and unhappiness—a million miles away. I've found something here, by a brick factory, that I've never had before. I guess you would call it contentment. Heaven must be like this."

The word "heaven" dropped naturally from his lips but grated on Sonya's reasoning. *Why?* He was Japanese, and the way he said it did not match his religion. She raised her head to look into his face, and she wore a questioning frown. "Paul, you spoke of heaven. I didn't think you believed—"

"Yes, I think of heaven quite often," he interrupted. "I believe much as you do in many ways. The sun is going down now. We better start back. It will be dark soon."

Darkness enveloped Tientsin by the time they reached Paul's home. The moment they entered, Kimiko greeted them, and Sonya had the feeling Kimiko must have been looking and

116

waiting for their arrival. Paul said something to her in Japanese, and she left their presence immediately after bowing and addressing Sonya as "Miss Sonya," in broken Russian. Paul obviously had given her some instructions as to where Sonya fit in the scheme of things. Though Kimiko seemed to care for Sonya and was always overly gracious, Sonya never saw her, but she thought of Paul's relationship with the lovely little Japanese girl. Now, since Sonya also shared his ardent affection, it bothered her even more. She salved the wound by remembering she held with him an entirely different position. And yet, she made up her mind the Japanese custom of having mistresses and accepting free love most assuredly did not suit her tastes.

Sonya wondered how Kimiko felt about her presence in the Japanese girl's heretofore private domain. Surely Kimiko resented the intrusion of another woman. Still, she never showed her feelings, and, quite to the contrary, she made every effort to welcome Sonya. Nevertheless, there were times when Sonya thought she detected a touch of bitterness in Kimiko's manner. Kimiko undoubtedly held a different status in the house when Sonya was not there. When she was present, Kimiko was rarely seen, appearing only when called, and never intruding when Paul and Sonya were together.

The dusty ride on a warm day was evident in their appearance, so Paul and Sonya parted to freshen up. Sonya went to her bedroom and took her time to tidy up, fix her makeup, and comb her hair, tangled by the cap she had worn. She returned downstairs to find Paul waiting in the living room with a tall cool drink for her. He had changed his clothes and was now attired in sport slacks and a shirt open at the collar. Sonya was still in the slacks Paul had handed her earlier in the day, because her skirt was still in the scooter basket.

"Sorry I am not dressed better. It's your fault," she laughed. "You stole my skirt."

Knowing what she meant, Paul responded, "I'll run out and get it."

"Don't bother. I'll change later."

They savored their drinks while talking about what they had seen that afternoon. Paul seemed content sipping his drink, and Sonya was in no hurry, but she was getting hungry and said so. With a snap of his hand, Chang appeared and they were off to the dining room for the usual palatable meal that always seemed ready when Paul beckoned. Back in the living room, Sonya declined an after-dinner liquor and stretched out on the divan. Paul finished his drink, sat down beside Sonya, and lifted her head to his lap. They listened to the radio and talked little, for they were content to be with each other. Conversation added nothing for the man in love and the woman not yet sure she felt the same way.

Sonya looked up and saw the hunger in his eyes. Responding to his expression, her arms circled his neck and she clung to him. She wanted him now. His ardent kisses indicated the feeling was mutual, and he led her to the stairway.

As she started up the stairs he said, "I'll get your skirt and bring it to you."

Paul retrieved the skirt on the scooter. He had turned off the radio and the house was silent. As he ascended the stairs with skirt in hand, he was glad Kimiko had retired earlier to her rooms in the far reaches of the house. When he knocked on the door of the bedroom reserved for Sonya, she called, "Come in. I thought you would just walk in."

When he opened the door, Sonya was standing there as he had seen her earlier that day, in panties, garter belt, stockings, and now she had removed her blouse to reveal a matching brassiere. She gave him a warm impish smile and stretched out her arms to him. Her pliable body held close in his arms stirred his senses. Reluctantly, he relaxed his arms and stepped back only to enfold her again in a mutually close embrace, their lips giving and taking without reservation. Stubbornly, Paul fought the emotions he had promised to control and were peeling through him. With a supreme surge of determination, he withdrew her arms from around his neck and left her standing there, walking out the door and closing it behind him. His determination carried him halfway down the hallway before he stopped short, astonished at his own honorable performance! Trying desperately to still his impulses, he convinced himself he was doing right, and yet the inherent male lust clawed its way back into his thoughts. He fumbled in his pocket, nervously withdrew cigarettes and a lighter. He touched the flame to the cigarette which

118

hung limply from his mouth. Then, in a flash of frustration he tore the cigarette from his lips, smashed it to the floor, and strode to his room.

The walk down the stairs and to his rooms in the far wing of the building cleared his befuddled mind. He forced himself to leave the privacy of his room, because he knew Sonya would be waiting to be taken home. All the time, Sonya's comely face and beguiling body danced before him. The way she had looked at him, that sultry passion twinkling in her limpid eyes! Her fiery love was devouring him, torturing him! Paul faltered as he walked back to the living room, but he need not have been hesitant. Sonya was not waiting for him as he expected, she was still in the bedroom.

When Paul had closed the bedroom door, Sonya wanted to cry out and stop him. She wanted more of his embraces, all of him in her arms and body. Sitting on the dressing stool, she viewed herself in the mirror with eyes that could not stop crying. *What had she done wrong?*

She could not still her desires to see Paul, to talk to him, to have him close. If only he had not left her at that crucial moment, when she needed him so desperately! That irretrievable moment had passed and left her wanting. Still only in her undergarments, she looked around aimlessly for her clothes. Her mind was not on her actions, for it drifted on seared emotions no longer suppressible within her throbbing soul. Helpless tears continued to drench her soft cheeks as she threw herself on the bed.

"I'm sorry, darling," Paul's voice sounded far away. "I heard you crying from outside the door."

Lying face down, Sonya turned uncertainly and raised her head to see if she were imagining his voice. Paul stood in the doorway, waiting, not sure of his ground.

"Oh, Paul!" she cried. Her voice trembled, and she stretched her arms out to him.

In one bound Paul was beside her, enfolding her in his arms. Holding her undulating body close to him, he tried to quiet her as he whispered, "What's wrong? Please tell me."

"I don't know—I don't know," she choked. "When you left me

119

a little while ago, it was like you took something away from me. I'm being silly, I guess. Now you are here and it's all right."

Gently, Paul turned her over and began drying her eyes with his handkerchief. She looked down at her almost nude body and said, "I suppose you think I should not be like this. I have not been very decent."

Paul's eyes took in every detail of her exquisitely rounded figure and inhaled her delectable fairness, her velvety skin softly pink in the pale light, her sleek legs, her firm mature breasts, and her tantalizing thighs screened by shadowy silk. They told of her ravishing beauty! Her allure intoxicated his senses and set his heart beating wildly all over again.

"I love you like this," he mutter hoarsely. "You are so beautiful. I love you, I love you. Oh, Sonya, I want you so!" He bent over her, brutally crushing her lips to his.

Allowing her passion to rage uncurbed under his fervid embrace, Sonya returned his kisses. They stormed her soul, and she gave herself into his keeping, ardently and shamelessly. His hand tugged at the silk, removing the last vestige of modesty from her yielding body. She did not care, for she wanted Paul more than anything else in the world, and she wanted him close to her, part of her! She did not remember his undressing, for she was aware only of his return to her responsive embrace.

Locked in harmony, they were not two but as though one. Not experimenters, nor two people sipping uncertainly of love— they were a mature couple, giving and taking their consummatory ecstasy without reservation. They floated away, higher and higher, on billowy waves of fire. The stinging pain increased incessantly, and then when reaching an unbearable pitch, it multiplied a million times and flooded way, leaving them peacefully content in each other's arms. For a long time they rested in their selfish little world, set apart from all earthly existence.

Finally, Sonya stirred and, cuddling next to Paul, whispered, "Oh, darling. I love you—love you so terribly much!" For awhile she lay there musing, and then added reflectively, "And I discovered it in the space of a few hours. Funny how life works, isn't it?"

"Yes, peculiar it is that I should know you love me, that I have realized full gratification of that flaming love—after all these awful months of waiting, praying some day you might be mine. Are you happy?" Paul spoke slowly, feeling his way in the midst of contentment.

"Terribly happy!" Sonya wormed her way closer to Paul, fondly entangling their legs. "And I'm not sorry, or ashamed. I wanted our love this way."

"I'm glad, Sonya," Paul answered simply. His fingers idly twisted her hair and rubbed her delicate ear. "I'm convinced our miserable feelings of a little while ago were mutual. God must have willed it this way, drawing our hearts together—here, in this room."

"Yes, darling," Sonya's voice drifted away dreamily. Every tiny part of her body was completely relaxed, gratefully tired, and she craved endless sleep in the security of Paul's arms.

She woke to the touch of Paul's lips on her cheek. "Sonya, wake up. We must get you home."

She lay in his arms. As her sleep-deadened senses cleared, she remembered where she was. Slowly, the events of the night ran through her mind, creating a warm satisfying glow throughout her entire body. She was unashamed, and the realization of this fact brought a soft blush to her cheeks, which she concealed by burying her face on Paul's shoulder.

"What time is it?" she murmured lazily.

"About noon," Paul smiled as he answered.

"Noon!" Sonya exclaimed, sitting upright in the bed. "I must get home—to work. Mr. Hecht will be mad, and he is doing so much for me."

Paul corrected her. "No work today, it's Sunday." Then he added, curiously, "What is he doing for you?"

Sonya was caught. She had not wanted to tell Paul about her moving until she had done so, and now she had to explain the words which slipped out. So, still dressing, she explained Mr. Hecht was helping her and she would be moving to her own flat sometime that week.

"Great, it's about time. I'll help you."

Paul's enthusiastic response was a relief, but Sonya had decided long before she did not want him involved. "Thanks for wanting to help, but Mr. Hecht is doing everything, including raising my salary a little bit, and I don't want to let anything

121

interfere. He might be offended."

"I understand," was all Paul needed to say as they left the bedroom and started on their way.

But that was not all Sonya needed to say. She had to tell her parents and decided to do so when she got home. As it turned out, her mother greeted her at the gate and asked why she had been missing for half a day on Sunday when she normally slept late. Sonya found it convenient to avoid the truth.

"I just couldn't sleep. I've been out walking around and wondering how I could tell you."

"What?"

"I've found a small place of my own, and I'm moving there some time this week. Mr. Hecht is helping me." The silence that followed was only a few seconds long, but it seemed like an eternity before her mother spoke.

"You are an adult, a mature woman. I only hope it is not because we are bad parents or have done something wrong. We'll do all we can."

Sonya took her mother in her arms and hugged her tightly. "Never that. I love you and always will. And I promise to take you to the beach as planned. Please look forward to our being together then."

It was done! Sonya was glad she did not have to tell her father. Her mother would do that.

15

Mr. Hecht greeted Sonya with good news when she arrived for work Monday morning. He had already taken care of the necessary paperwork, and the flat was hers. Also, some of his employees had helped him find the basic furniture and put it in her new home. His pleasure was evident as he continued to explain. "You may need a few items from your room, and of course your personal things. I can have a couple of my people help you do that. You seem so eager, I suppose you should get the day off to do it."

Sonya bubbled over with her thank you's. Yes, she wanted to do it today. "Could we go now? Can someone go with me now?"

Mr. Hecht showed her a fatherly laugh. "I sort of thought that would be your reaction. Two of my men are standing by to go with you." As an afterthought, he added, "There is going to be a big party this weekend, the opening of the new Del Conte restaurant. Suppose you have heard of it. My wife and I are taking a few friends. You are welcome to join us."

"No, I couldn't do that. You've done too much for me now. Thanks again," Sonya replied as she started for the door and her new home.

Yes, Sonya had heard of the gala opening of the ultra-new Del Conte restaurant/night club. Considering the war was still raging and the Japanese controlled Tientsin, it was surprising anything was new. It would be an affair where the gentry of the city could see and be seen. Sonya had refused invitations from some of her normal suitors who she had stopped dating. Explanations of her refusals were not given, because Paul was the cause and she dared not speak of him. Besides, the party was Saturday, and she had a date with Paul. He had again asked her to meet him early, at five o'clock. To be with him was all that mattered.

However, as Sonya rode their rickshaw to meet Paul, she thought about the Del Conte party and the formal attire of tuxedos and long dresses that would be evident. Maybe there would be some early activity that she could see, but such was not the case because arrivals would not start for hours. Paul opened the car door and beckoned for her to get in quickly. It was still light, and he had to be careful about being recognized.

Paul's hurried action prompted Sonya to say, "Why do we have to meet in a public place? I now know where your home is, and I'm sure the rickshaw boy who picks me up also knows I've moved. You must take me there tonight so you know and can tell him." As an afterthought, she added, "I'm not sure I want him to know where I'll be living alone."

"I'm delighted you've moved. It will be much easier for us to get together. Don't be concerned about the rickshaw boy. I pay him well, and he is trustworthy. Yes, he has known for a long time where I live. That's where we are going now," Paul answered. He added with a mischievous grin, "You're not properly dressed for our date."

"Why, was I supposed to wear a formal?"

"I understand that's what they are wearing."

Comprehension of what he meant by this statement hit Sonya immediately. "You're not planning on going to the Del Conte thing are you?"

"If not, I'm stuck for the price of an expensive reservation."

"We can't go there. Everyone is going. We'll be recognized," Sonya said in a horrified tone.

"Don't worry, darling. I've taken care of everything," he said calmly. "I won't explain now. I'll let you see for yourself when we get home."

"Oh, Paul, you're impossible," Sonya exclaimed, excited at the prospect of attending the Del Conte opening. Also, going with Paul added distinctiveness—and a dark current of intrigue.

Sonya expected the procedure she met upon arrival at his home—up to a certain extent. The moment they entered the door, Paul called for Kimiko. Kimiko must have been expecting his summons, for she appeared instantly and bowed before them. Paul glanced at his watch and turned to Sonya. "Honey, we must get on with it. We don't have a lot of time. Kimiko knows exactly what she's supposed to do and how to do it. There's a great deal to our preparation, so cooperate with her. All right?"

"Yes, darling," Sonya laughed as she curtsied in gay obedience. "I expect you realize you've got me so mixed up I don't know what to do."

"Yes, dear," he grinned, leaving her standing alone as he walked down the hall.

Sonya promised herself to do just as he said, and once in the bedroom, she placed herself in Kimiko's control, questioning none of the Japanese girl's wishes. Having undressed, Sonya was ushered into the adjoining bathroom. The tub was filled with what looked like a mass of soap bubbles, and Sonya caught the scent of the fragrant bath. The fact that the bath was drawn and waiting indicated Kimiko had anticipated Sonya's arrival at a designated time. That was like Paul—everything planned.

Though Sonya would have liked to soak in the warm foamy water, Kimiko rushed her through the bath. Toweling off, she found Kimiko waiting with powder and perfume. The powder she used freely—the perfume she used tactfully. From then on Sonya's destiny of the moment lay with Kimiko, who seated her and began making her over—swiftly and efficiently. When Kimiko produced a large makeup kit filled with paints, powders, and tiny brushes, Sonya's curiosity was aroused, and she found she had many questions. But she suppressed her curiosity and dutifully endured Kimiko's treatment.

To Sonya, it seemed like hours before Kimiko nodded completion of the makeup and produced the tantalizing new evening gown she was to wear. Sonya slipped into it and consented to more fussing from Kimiko. Jewelry was added. Impatiently, she received Kimiko's final scrutiny and then moved to the full-length mirror to see the result of Kimiko's expert work.

The person Sonya saw in the mirror shocked her. She found herself looking at an exotic, oriental half-caste! Under the skillful makeup, Sonya Petrovna could be seen only vaguely. Somehow her own natural beauty had been accentuated by Kimiko's deft handicraft, and Sonya expelled gasps of amazement as she moved to convince herself the lady in the mirror was really her. Paul's plan was now evident.

Her skin had been tinted the color of light mahogany. Her eyes, which laughed impishly, were cleverly shaded near the edges to give the impression of being slanted, and her naturally long eye lashes had been carefully blackened to appear even longer. Actually, Sonya's lips were heavy, but now they seemed thin. In typical oriental fashion, her golden hair had been given a dark tint and drawn into a severe upsweep to form a round bun on the top of her head. She wondered about the color of her hair, which should be darker for an oriental but decided the tint and hairdo would show properly.

Sonya's seductive body was tucked into a strapless, gold lamé gown which hugged her full bosom and fell to the floor in a distinctive full-side drape. The earrings, necklace, and wide bracelet of exquisite aquamarine accentuated the shimmering dress. Her sandals matched the dress, and brilliant red toenails peeked out from under the straps to match her manicured fingernails. Kimiko brought a matching cape and threw it over Sonya's shoulders. Gleefully, Sonya made one last turn before the mirror and then, anxious to see if Paul was also masked in makeup, she hurried to meet him.

She was not disappointed. He waited in the reception hall, and although she knew him, he looked completely different. He was adept at all kinds of disguises, and it showed here. Dressed in a glistening white dinner jacket, he could have been mistaken for any truly occidental man in Tientsin. He had toned down his Japanese features and stressed his white characteristics. The results amazed her, for he had remade himself so thoroughly she could have passed him on the street without recognizing him.

"My eurasian lass, you are positively radiant," Paul greeted her in exacting Russian.

"And you will pass for a Russian anywhere," Sonya flipped back gaily. "Oh, Paul, are you sure we won't be recognized?"

"Quite. You see, darling, I'm well-versed in the principles of deception. Kimiko and I pride ourselves on being the finest makeup artists in all of China. The idea is simply to make you what you aren't. That's what we've done, right?"

"I suppose so. I look so oriental I feel that way."

"Good," he emphasized, "because you must act that way also. Remember to speak only Chinese. Are you ready?"

"Yes," Sonya answered dutifully in Chinese, "but I'm scared half to death."

"Why should you be? We won't be recognized. Even if we

were, what difference would it make to you?"

"None, I guess," Sonya admitted. Nevertheless, she could not dispel her uneasy feeling, and she knew it could be costly for him.

"Chinese, Sonya. Remember to use Chinese," he cautioned. Sonya had unconsciously answered in Russian.

She smiled and took his arm. When he had helped her into the car and arranged himself behind the wheel, Paul remarked, "We'll have to leave the car some distance from the Club. It might create suspicion."

Sonya understood and made no comment. Instead, she smoothed her dress, thus drawing attention to it. "Your taste is women's clothes makes me believe you were a clothes designer somewhere. There isn't another gown in China like this."

He laughed at her assumption. "I must elaborate on my education some day."

"Undoubtedly. Why not now while we're riding?"

"I said some day," he repeated good naturedly. "Some day soon."

As far as she was concerned, his determined statement closed the subject. She turned her thoughts to the evening, an evening already marked to be one of the most thrilling in her life. If only she could remember to act her part and not greet people she knew, all would go well—she hoped!

They parked the car about two blocks from Del Conte's and began their short walk to the club. As they strolled along with Sonya clutching his arm, he leaned close and whispered, "One last thing. No names. Not ours or anyone else's. We don't know anyone, and they don't know us, no matter what happens."

As they neared the entrance, they heard the soft strains of music from within. Outside, they saw formally dressed couples dismounting from rickshaws and cars, and they threaded their way through the accumulated crowd of curious Chinese. Some were children begging for anything one might give. Paul passed out some coins and politely waved them aside.

The uniformed doorman greeted them with the wave of a gloved hand, and they stepped into the Club. Sonya was nervous and having trouble controlling her emotions. Though the evening was warm, she was shaking and declined when the cloak room attendant offered to take her cape. And then the inevitable happened. There in front of her, standing a few tables away, was Mr. Hecht. He glanced her way while seating his wife, and Sonya could feel his eyes devouring her. She had the uncontrollable urge to walk over and greet them. Paul immediately noticed and put his hand on her arm, steadying her, giving her confidence. Sonya breathed a sigh of relief. The worst was over. She had passed the test.

Paul presented a card to the maitre d', who promptly called a waiter. He took the card and beckoned them to follow. Pressing Sonya ahead of him, Paul urged her along as they threaded their way through the maze of tables. Once through the tables, the waiter led them up the short flight of steps to the mezzanine floor and designated a table set apart from the others and next to the railing. It obviously was a select table, because the position permitted a view of the entire Club.

Unfortunately, this table also gave those seated on the floor below a clear view of that table's occupants. Sonya had the feeling every set of eyes in the place were boring into her. This sensation had been with her from the moment they entered the Club, and it was well founded. The entry of the finely dressed strangers had created an undercurrent of interest. Tongues wagged as heads leaned together for whispered comments. The women detested the way their men ogled the gorgeous Eurasian girl and secretly envied her. The men speculated on the position and background of the handsome gentleman who escorted this dazzling woman.

After the initial stir, an occasional furtive glance was the only noticeable attention paid to the unknown couple who, apparently oblivious to it all, conversed quietly at their table. They discussed the splendor of Del Conte. It was even finer than rumors had described. Modernistic planning, combined with oriental luxury, had produced the design of this neatly decorated restaurant. Heavy oriental carpeting covered the dining salon, and long Chinese-designed drapes hung at the masked windows. Brightly colored tapestries hung on the walls. Amid this Far East de'cot were chrome-framed tables, red leather covered chairs, and mirrored pillars. A few steps above and set apart from the dining area was the ebony bar and small dance floor.

Lounge chairs and small tables around the dance floor were filled by the drinking crowd.

The Del Conte staff performed their duties with perfection. The waiters were so attentive they anticipated every desire, and the excellent orchestra, playing from a raised dais between the barroom and dining room, produced soft music appropriate for the evening diners. Throughout the Club could be seen formal dinner clothes and colorful evening dresses, ranging from the novel strapless one Sonya wore to the silk, sack-like affairs worn by the Chinese ladies. All of Tientsin seemed to be represented, but with the exception of Mr. Hecht, Sonya could not see a person she knew well. This discovery relieved her mind and helped her relax.

Basking in the light of her distinctive status, Sonya thoroughly enjoyed every second of the party. In keeping with Paul's customary attention to detail, his arrangements were carefully made—from the rare champagne to the last morsel of tasty food. They dined, wined, and danced while the hours slipped by unheeded. Throughout, he managed the evening with finesse, and it was a tremendous success.

All too soon it was over. In the car, Sonya dreamily rested her head on Paul's shoulder, expressing her complete satisfaction of the glorious time. The champagne tickled her brain, reminding her of its bubbling freshness and sharp flavor. She liked champagne. She had tasted it before, but this night she had drunk all that she wanted, and her head felt light, giving her a carefree attitude.

"Paul, darling, it's been the grandest evening of my life. You are so sweet," she murmured.

"Grand for me, too," he said warmly. He squeezed her hand. "You made it grand for me."

"You always flatter me," Sonya scolded. She held his hand, looking at it and idly spreading his fingers. "I don't deserve such flattery." She looked up to see his face.

Paul kept watching the road, but his lips turned up in a smile. "You deserve the compliments. They *are* compliments—not flattery."

"You're prejudiced."

"Naturally," he agreed simply.

129

"I'm still throbbing from the excitement. I was paralyzed when Mr. Hecht looked at me, but I don't think a soul recognized us. Do you?"

"I don't think so. They stared only because of you."

"Honest?"

"Honest," he said matter-of-factly. "You were by far the most glamorous woman there. I was proud of you."

"I wanted to be," she whispered in his ear. She clutched his arm impulsively in both of hers. "You're responsible for it. I can hardly wait for us to get to your house and make love."

"I'm glad you said that. I've something to tell you," he said as he stopped the car and turned to her. They were parked along a secluded road on the outskirts of Tientsin. He grasped her shoulders in his hands, holding her before him. "Sonya, we should get married. We can't do it right away, but I want to marry you. Will you?"

Sonya's face went blank. She was too dumfounded to speak and stared at him in utter bewilderment.

"I'm asking you to marry me. Do you hear? I mean it. I love you—love you with all my heart."

Sonya fought to collect her wits, to calm the champagne hum in her head. She wanted to wake up from this dream and think seriously about his amazing words. She tried to comprehend his meaning and consider it logically, but her brain seemed numb.

"Paul, I, I—" she stammered.

"Don't answer now," he said softly. "Think it over. Tell me tomorrow, or whenever you like."

"I'll try to—" Sonya trailed off amidst swirling indecision. Churning thoughts filled her mind. Paul seemed to possess all the attributes she had dreamed of in a man. But he was eurasian—even worse, Japanese. She could not picture herself married to a Japanese. He had relaxed his grip, and she instinctively pulled away in a cool gesture.

Meditating, Paul sat looking out across the shadowy countryside. For a long time neither spoke. Then, evidently satisfied with his decision, he turned to Sonya. Determination filled his expressive features. "I know what you're thinking. My Japanese position makes it an unfair question. I hope to change that.

130

Please give me time."

"You're vague. Asking for my hand is not unfair. I expect I've known all along you would ask me, but I didn't expect it tonight. That's all."

"I must explain something," Paul began slowly. "I know you think I'm just another Japanese officer. Everyone does."

"You *are* being vague," Sonya was instantly intrigued by his unusual words. "What else could one think? You obviously govern the Japanese forces here, or at least carry a great deal of authority with them."

He turned serious. In the dim moonlight, his eyes sought out Sonya and probed through the night, as though examining her soul. "Darling, I love you more than anything else in the world. I know in some ways you love me. I also know you dislike Japanese. You have given yourself away too many times."

"But, Paul," she cried, "I don't dislike you!"

A tiny smile worked at his lips. "I know that. But our relationship is unorthodox. On that you have to agree."

"Please, what are you driving at?" pleaded Sonya. "I'm all mixed up."

"Simply this." His tone was even and steady. "Yes, I am eurasian, or Japanese, or whatever you want to call it. And I work with the Japanese. *But I do it for the United States of America.*"

16

Paul, *Paul who?* An American acting as a Japanese officer for many years! Sonya could not believe what she had just heard. Her hand covered her mouth to stifle the gasp of bewilderment. Paul sat quietly, watching her reaction and waiting for a response. Getting none, he decided to make it perfectly plain. "To use a common distasteful term, I am a spy. I am an American spy."

Completely shocked, Sonya bit her hand to keep from sobbing. She hardly realized his last words had been spoken in English. It was the first time she had ever heard him speak in English. Tears began to fall as she struggled to say, "Oh, Paul! You're not lying!"

As he took his handkerchief and began drying her eyes, he continued to speak in English. "No, I'm not lying, and I probably should never have told you. But I guess it was going to happen eventually. Our love made your knowing inevitable. Now, if you'll clear those beautiful eyes and listen, I'll explain everything truthfully."

Sonya could not speak. She did not know what to say. It was easier to simply nestle in the comforting arms which reached out for her. She squirmed until her head rested on his shoulder, together in mutual understanding. Both gazed out in the direction of Tientsin, content in the light of the moon and stars.

"Sonya, I emphasize again. I probably should not have told you. You have to promise to keep this secret, *absolutely*. *My life, even your life*, and the lives of many others, depend on it."

She gave him a serious, straightforward answer. "I promise, with all our love, I promise."

"Relax. Now you should know what there is to know about me." He began, "My life started in Japan over thirty-five years ago." He momentarily closed his eyes as if to live in the memories he desired to tell. He talked on, slowly and modestly, in perfect

English. "I had the most loving, tender mother in the world. She was American. I always idolized her. Though I was never able to find out much about her before she met my father, I suspect she wasn't the kind people would think of as a good mother. She was born in the United States and somehow ended up in Japan while still quite young. She met my father and eventually I was born. I've never known for sure if they were married."

Paul hesitated, as though planning the best way to express his thoughts. "She named me Paul York. I believe it was her maiden name, but I've never known for sure." He stopped and smiled at Sonya. "Yes, my real name is Paul York. You must have surmised Paul was actually my name. There is no reason to give you my Japanese name. In fact, you are better off not knowing it, and as I've said before, I'll answer to Paul when you call. So, to repeat, my mother was American and loved America. I guess she *must have* married my father, because she had dual citizenship. And I guess he loved her as much as was possible for him."

Reflecting on his father, Paul stumbled over his words. "He is a wealthy, influential man in Japan. Still living. He was very demanding and made sure I was given all the typical Japanese training, including all the important languages, even English. But there was always conflict with my mother, who had to be obedient and yet she insisted I be allowed to go to the United States for a college education. Somehow she prevailed, and I was sent off to the United States. I've always believed she had influence from some source in the U.S. that put pressure on my father. And my automatic acceptance at a top U.S. university evidenced that. There's a lot I have never known about my father—or my mother. As a Japanese son steeped in tradition, I dared not question their actions. I did understand one thing. My father told me pointedly that I was to return and live in Japan when called. He was convinced he had won, but a lot has happened since then."

Paul laughed outright at his last statement, and it drew an amused look from Sonya. She remained silent, completely spellbound. She did not want to distract him from his story or train of thought. For months she had waited for this moment when Paul would finally enlighten her on his life, and now he had started, she was not going to change his mind by even a single word.

"I get carried away thinking about my crazy life, and I'm boring you. Maybe we should get out of the car, stretch, and talk about it," Paul offered.

"I'm not bored. I want to hear everything," Sonya insisted. "But a stretch sounds good."

Back in the car, they sat comfortably, and Paul continued. "My father's wealth gave us every material thing we wanted. Unusual for a Japanese husband, he made money available to my mother. But the one thing she wanted most of all was to take me to America, which he would never allow. I'm sure my going to school in America partially satisfied her strong desire to go back."

There could be no doubt Paul loved his mother very deeply, purposely neglecting to say how he felt about his father. He faltered for a moment to gain control of his emotions and then continued, "I am not sure when she died and don't know any of the details. It seemed strange she kept sending me money and writing to emphasize I should stay in the United States. I'm sure my father was not aware of this, because he also sent me ample money. I had graduated and was working at a brokerage firm when he notified me she had passed away."

Sonya noticed Paul was beginning to speak in a halting way and decided it was time to pick up the jovial atmosphere they had shared on leaving the Del Conte. "You're tired. Let's get on home and rest together. You can tell me whatever else you want to another day. Mostly, I would like to know how you ended up here. But that can wait."

"No, now that I've started, let's be done with it. I'll try to speak faster or say less. At least get to the answers to the questions you have. For once I realize you have wondered how I spend money so freely. I have a lot, usually available. Dollars in the United States and yen in Japan. It came from saving what my parents sent and investing well as a broker at the proper time. So much for that."

"How did I get here? I did well at the university and afterward, by hard work. The stigma of being eurasian made me want to excel at everything, at being accepted, at making friends. Many lifelong friends still are influential in the United States government and military. But, back to the point. My father continued insisting I return to Japan. Eventually, he became adamant. He wrote, he phoned, even had a member of the Japanese embassy call on me. What the embassy officer said, or didn't say, made me curious. It was 1939, and the Germans were taking over Europe."

"I contacted those friends in Washington and learned U.S. relations with Japan were very tense. That made me realize my father's strong demands to return to Japan involved more than his desire to see me." Paul stopped, looking for the right words to explain the relationship with his father. Finally, he said simply, "We were never that close."

The pause gave Sonya a moment to ask, "What do you mean, Washington? Who were these people?"

"Government officials in Washington, D.C., the seat of the U.S. government. Some day you may meet some of them, maybe sooner than you think."

"Meet them? Here, or in the United States?" Sonya asked, hoping he would answer the latter.

"Could be here. We'll get to that later. One in particular who I trusted completely asked me to come to Washington for a meeting. I was pleased and accepted immediately. It was not far to go. I lived in New York."

"The meeting with a select group of officials behind guarded doors actually did not last very long." Paul looked seriously at Sonya and continued. "Father has never known that I had pledged to support America years before when I became a United States citizen. Now I had an opportunity to prove that pledge. Of course, I still held Japanese citizenship, so it gave me dual citizenship. It sounded easy to be an American informer, becoming a spy in a country where I grew up. It didn't take long to get my private life in order and leave for Japan. Figured I would only be there a short time. *That was over four years ago.*"

Paul hunted in his pocket and brought forth cigarettes. Sonya detached herself from his arms and took one. For a moment, their faces glowed in the night as Paul snapped his lighter. Then Sonya pulled her feet under her long dress, curled up in the corner of the seat, and, facing Paul, slowly drew on her cigarette. Patiently, she watched him. As he puffed heavily on the cigarette, the burning tobacco threw a red glow over his fine

135

features, outlining his face with soft shadows. The white coat glistened in the night, marking his broad shoulders. In that instant, she could see nothing in him that resembled a Japanese. She controlled the urge to tell him she wanted to go now so he could take her to bed, fulfilling the desires throbbing through her.

He went on in the same even tone. "Where have those years gone? They've been exciting, and I can't complain. They have also been difficult, hiding the truth and wondering about my home in New York. Our secret channels have kept me informed, but not in every respect. I have missed the good times—and the bad times—in the States. There were parties and travel between New York and Florida. Everything that goes with a lot of money."

"So, back to the important stuff. I landed in Japan. Father greeted me warmly, and I greeted him with forced enthusiasm. As I suspected, he had my future planned. It took time. I was allowed my freedom, but knew I was being watched. After a few months, my father and other influential authorities were convinced of my loyalty to Japan, and I was placed in the Army Intelligence Department as a ranking officer. They thought my U.S. experience would be beneficial."

Paul stopped and laughed as he said, "It was—for the United States." Then he continued more somberly, "My secret channels to U.S. authorities had been planned before I left the U.S." He looked to see if Sonya was paying attention. Satisfied, he squirmed around, hunting for words to address the serious question. "Could I have stopped the attack on the United States—Pearl Harbor? Yes, had I known. I was very aware of the deteriorating Japanese-U.S. relations, but I had no indication of an attack. It was a closely held secret. I doubt I would have believed it was going to happen had I been told. So be it. Then everything changed for me."

"Soon thereafter, U.S. instructions told me to get to Northern China immediately. The U.S. now needed regular information on Japanese actions there. I was also told my new secret channel from them would be contacts located in the capitol, Chungking." Paul paused again and gave Sonya a soulful look. "That was a long time ago—early 1942. At that time you may have heard of U.S. pilots working for the Chinese. They flew fighters from a base in Kunming to help protect the southern china Area around Chungking from Japanese bombers and raids."

Leaning his head back on the seat and looking out into the faint light in the sky far away, Paul said, jokingly, "Maybe I can get the whole story out before sun-up. The urgency of my getting to this area was emphasized when, a few months after the United States declared war on Japan, the Americans bombed Tokyo and their planes had to crash in China. I thought maybe I could help some of those pilots. Well, anyway, I talked my Japanese commanders into sending me here, and here I am."

"To make sure the Japanese authorities here did not wonder about my parentage and question my dedication to Japan, I made it a point to prove my hatred of the United States. For instance, I ordered and personally directed the destruction of all American and English literature in the area."

"I remember that," Sonya exclaimed, but Paul continued to talk, as if he had not heard.

"When I got here, my U.S. contact was now Chungking, and Rangoon, India when necessary. You can guess the rest. We have worked out a secret underground system that sends regular information to America. That's about it, darling. I've covered a lot of living in a few minutes." He hesitated, and then added with deep emphasis, "I haven't been home in a long time. It was mighty lonely until I found you."

The manner in which Paul said those last words and the way he turned to Sonya prompted her to say, "I'm glad you found me. And I'm glad you told me who you are. It makes a great difference."

"Since the day I landed in Japan—all these years, I've not touched a white woman. The other night with you was wonderful."

"I know," Sonya blushed and tugged nervously at her cape. "Let's go."

"You do understand? You see now why I have had to tell you, even though it's dangerous for both of us?" whispered Paul, leaning toward her.

"Yes," Sonya's voice was barely discernible.

Paul was close to her, and his eyes said it all. "Will you marry me, Sonya? Will you marry me when it's possible?"

Sonya gave her answer. She slipped into his arms and raised her lips for his kiss. Tears filled her eyes. "I love you, Paul," she murmured.

For a long time they warmed their love in each other's arms. Words were superfluous following their passionate kisses. Paul stirred and said, "It is really late. We should get on home and out of these fancy clothes."

They drove to Paul's residence slowly, in order that he could steer and still cradle her in the crook of his arm. She was living in a dreamland, far away, and she wanted never to awaken. When the car stopped and Paul disengaged his arm, she disliked the interruption of her moody thoughts. Roused from her reverie, she slipped from the car into his arms. She wanted more of his kisses. She wanted all of his love, all that could be crowded into their short hours together. Her arms encircled his neck as she clung to him. He swept her off the ground and carried her gently through the doorway and up the stairs, letting her slip out of his grasp at the bedroom door. Holding her head between his hands and looking deep into her eyes, he said, "I'll give you some time to erase the Chinese and look like my Sonya again. I'll be back. No hurry. We are going to have a long wonderful night together. You don't have to run home anymore."

When he closed the door, she hoped he would be back soon to provide the security of his embrace. *She was in love—yes, in love. Engaged—engaged to be married, and her great dream of living in America would be fulfilled.* Having pledged herself to Paul York gave her pause to wonder if she could assimilate the full meaning of that pledge, but the excitement of the day and her love for him overwhelmed all else. As she sat on the dressing stool, Sonya viewed herself in the mirror. Seeing the tears of joy ready to spill form her eyes, she wiped them dry and proceeded with her undressing. At the moment, dresses did not interest her, and she threw the gorgeous party clothes on the floor where they remained disregarded. She moved aimlessly into the bathroom to bathe her face. The makeup clung stubbornly, but she did not care. She did not want to hurry, because the water soothed her feverish skin.

Paul stood at the bathroom door admiring Sonya's nude body and waiting for her to look around. Absorbed in her

138

thoughts, she had not heard him enter. He reached out and she gasped with ecstasy as he picked her up and carried her to the bed. She lay waiting while he undressed. Then they were together, body to body, tongues exploring through full mouth kisses. As their passion rose beyond control, his lips warmed her breasts as his hand stroked the intimate folds of her body. Finally, deep inside her, she moaned with rapture as he carried her closer and closer to the peak of human emotion. Having found unabated love again, and enjoyment beyond expression—they would experience it often in the future.

Both slept soundly, completely relaxed, until early morning when Paul got up and dressed. He shook Sonya gently. "Come on, loved one, it is time you got dressed and to your own place."

"Why?" murmured the drowsy Sonya.

"I know it is Sunday and not much of a problem, but we have to be a little careful not to invite suspicion." They dressed swiftly. A quick peek in the mirror and a few rapid strokes with the comb completed Sonya's preparations. As she acknowledged her readiness and moved to the door, Paul opened it for her. Both stopped short, for there in the doorway stood Kimiko!

Sonya gasped. The color rose in Paul's cheeks. Her hands clasped within the loose sleeves of her kimono, Kimiko remained before them and made no effort to leave, though the expression on her face gave every indication she wanted to flee. Humbly, she lowered her head and took one step backward as Paul's voice knifed the sickening silence. He spoke in Japanese so Sonya did not understand, but his words must have been cruel, for Kimiko prostrated herself before him. Then she jumped to her feet and ran down the hall.

"Paul, was she—was she spying on us?" Sonya demanded in a horrified tone.

"I don't know. Come, Sonya, we must move along," Paul said, trying to conceal his perplexity.

Even when they had entered the car and driven out of the courtyard, the memory of Kimiko standing at the bedroom door bothered Sonya. The same thoughts persisted, and though she knew Paul did not want to discuss the matter, she again broached the subject. "Darling, Kimiko *must* have been spying on us."

"And even if she were, does it really make any difference?" Paul asked.

Sonya raised her chin and spoke defiantly, "I don't like it. That's the difference it makes. Having someone watching—well, witnessing, you know what I mean."

"You're being absurd. The door was closed. How could she have seen anything?"

"Through the keyhole."

"I know Kimiko. She would never do a thing like that," Paul said dryly. He was becoming irritated.

Sonya was insistent. "What did you say to her?"

"I simply asked her why she stood there," answered Paul, now out of patience. He got control of his rising temper and added hastily, "Look, it's been a glorious night. Let's not mar it by pursuing a ridiculous little incident which means nothing. We must enjoy every minute together, because I have to leave Tientsin soon."

"Leave Tientsin! What are you saying? We just start to really live in what little happiness we have, and you talk of leaving!" Paul's words had thoroughly upset Sonya. She moved close to him and clutched his arm.

"I'm sorry, darling. I was brutal saying it in such a way."

"But what are you talking about?"

Paul's hand slipped to her leg and pulled her closer to him. His hand remained there, pressing her leg affectionately. "Please, darling, don't worry about it. We still have time together."

Hurt and sad and in the love she had just discovered, Sonya dropped her head on his shoulder. She wanted to be reasonable, but she found it difficult to subdue her grief at the idea of his leaving. When she finally spoke, her voice was lifeless. "Where are you going?"

"Here, this won't do. Cheer up." Paul pressed humor into his tone. "I won't be gone forever."

"I don't care," Sonya pouted.

"Sometimes we have no control over our destiny," he started to explain. "You see, my work here is nearly finished, and I must report to the U.S. offices in Chungking. I'm not sure when, but soon. The plans are still not definite."

"Doesn't that mean once you leave you won't be able to return until after the war?" Sonya dreaded the answer she knew he would give her.

"I'm afraid so, but the war will end soon. It's just about over." He spoke confidently.

"How can you be sure?"

He laughed wryly. "That question demands an involved answer on international intelligence. Take my word for it. I know Japan is about to collapse under the punishment she's taking."

"Why should you have to go back till after the war? Why can't you carry on here as you have been?" Sonya demanded, grasping for any reason to keep him near her. "Then we could go to the United States together."

"Orders—it's that simple. I'm being ordered back. I can't give you the reason, but you may as well know, our lives together may depend on it. Rather, I should say, mine does," Paul explained matter-of-factly.

"I understand," said Sonya, but the thought of his leaving deadened her spirit.

"Let's make a bargain. Let's promise not to talk about it anymore," Paul urged. He stopped the car near Sonya's new apartment, and as she got out he said, "I'll phone."

She closed the door, hesitated a moment, and then leaned through the window. Love sparkled in her eyes as she wrinkled her nose in a slight gesture of impish delight. "I love you, Paul."

When Sonya said, "I love you, Paul," she meant it, because life began to assume a different meaning for her. At last she could visualize the end of her drab existence in Tientsin, and she planned her future in the United States. It would be a cherished dream come true, but it still seemed far away. The exact meaning of her new position in life floated on the outer circle of reality and at times was lost in the obscure fringe of fantasy.

Sonya found herself living apart from her every day existence. This resulted from the fact she was compelled to live within herself, and she dared tell no one of her love for Paul and their glorious times together. For that matter, she dared not tell anyone anything about Paul. Thus, she failed to derive wholesome satisfaction from her secret life, because she could not realize the basic requisite of uninhibited happiness—that of sharing

141

it in the eyes of others. Still, she treasured the hours spent with Paul, and when apart from him, she reveled in the memories of their time together.

Paul's intended departure created the one smear on the beautiful picture they designed together. Sonya dreaded it. Why? That involved more reasons than she cared to admit, even to herself. To pacify her own apprehensions, she resolved it must be her deep love for Paul, combined with the fear he would not return—or that something would happen to prevent his return, or that he would forget her. Had Sonya logically and truthfully analyzed her situation, she would have realized she did not fear only Paul's infidelity, but also her own!

17

Sonya delayed making definite plans concerning her vacation at Peitaiho Beach, even though Paul encouraged her to go on with her original arrangements. He insisted strongly, and she prepared for her departure the middle of July. Netti wrote she had obtained a cottage for Sonya and Katilka. She said it was some distance from the one she occupied, but it was comfortable. She added she looked forward to Sonya's arrival and was having trouble curbing her impatience to see her and hear all about Mr. X. When Sonya answered, she made it a point not to enlighten Netti on her romance, but she did tell her to hold the cottage if she could without too much cost. And yet she still refused to set a definite date of departure because she knew it meant separation from Paul, and that cast an ominous shadow over her once happily contemplated vacation.

With all the details completed, Sonya awaited the final decision from Paul. Although he had not informed her that his departure for Chungking would coincide with her leaving for Peitaiho Beach, he had intimated such was his intention. Evidently he was delaying telling her until sure she had completed her plans. The middle of July was creeping near, and Sonya knew she would be compelled to set a date with her mother within the next few days. Therefore, she made up her mind to settle the question with Paul, for they had a date in the evening and could discuss the subject.

Much to her chagrin, Paul phoned to say an unexpected matter had arisen and their date must be called off. He said his rickshaw boy would pick her up, and he would see her the next night. He did not say more, for he seemed agitated and in a great hurry. His unusual manner roused Sonya's anxiety and prompted her imagination to manufacture a variety of causes for his change in plans. She spent an uneasy evening reading and trying to sleep as agonizing thoughts plagued her. Relief finally came when Paul phoned her at the office the next morning.

"Hello, darling. I'm sorry about yesterday. Now I have great news for you," he began enthusiastically.

As a result of his phone call the day before, Sonya was reticent. "What is it?"

"I can't tell you. You'll see tonight."

Sonya spoke harshly. "Look, Paul. I'm tired of your unusual plans and jokes. I want to know now."

Her insolent tone took Paul by surprise, and when he answered his words were sharp. "I don't make jokes."

Realizing her nasty comment, Sonya was ashamed. "I'm sorry. Guess I'm just in a foul mood. I was a little annoyed last night."

"Of course, I understand," Paul answered. "To make you feel better, I'll tell you a little. Two friends are here, and I want you to meet them."

His statement dumbfounded her, and she stammered, "But we can't go out with anyone."

"This will be strictly a private affair in the house."

"But even that. You know we can't be—"

"Don't worry. You will understand tonight," he interrupted. "Bye, darling." And he hung up.

As Sonya rode along in the rickshaw sent for her, she wondered who Paul meant by friends. Her curiosity had been aroused. Although she abhorred the idea, she assumed they must be Japanese, maybe family friends from Japan. The question was foremost in her mind when she entered his home.

"Where are the friends you told me about?" she asked, looking around and seeing no one.

"Patience, my dear. You shall meet them," Paul chuckled. "I wondered why you didn't ask me about them on the phone."

"Because I did not want to appear eager. But now I give up. I am eager, and I do want to meet them."

"I'll tell you what," he hedged. "You run upstairs and get dressed. Kimiko is waiting. When you come down, I assure you they'll be here."

Paul's eyes twinkled. Sonya had noticed his unburdened nature when she greeted him. He was fresh and jovial, to the extent where it seemed he had not a care in the world. Wanting

144

not to disturb his mood, Sonya obediently went upstairs to her room.

Paul watched as she moved up the stairs, following every graceful step she made. He was proud of Sonya, and he experienced a great deal of self-satisfaction in knowing she belonged to him. Tonight, for the first time, he would present her to friends, and his ego rose as he visualized their enthusiasm over the captivating beauty of this Russian girl. He turned and headed in the direction of his rooms. David and Burl would be waiting, and they would be impatient. Also, they would be drunk if he left them alone much longer, for they were in rare form when he pried himself loose from them earlier in the evening.

Paul opened the door to his lounge to be greeted by a cloud of smoke and the smell of liquor. "My god, it smells like a pool room in here," he exclaimed, walking to the wall and turning on the vent fan.

Burl had his plump torso stretched out in an enormous chair, and his stocking feet were crossed on a coffee table. He was dressed in the suit Paul had told him to wear, but he had the collar open and the tie hung loosely on the stiffly starched shirt which pooched out in front to receive the ashes from a big cigar. Removing the cigar to take a long drink from the glass balanced in his hand, he squinted at Paul through the haze and began to chuckle.

"Well, I'll be damned. I was just telling Dave I couldn't see him, and I was blaming it on this foul vodka you left us to drink. Now you tell me it's nothing but smoke. By god, Paul my boy, you've saved my life—thought the stuff was making me blind."

Paul laughed. Burl Manning was always the same—happy-go-lucky, humorous, and good-natured—he was a typical American playboy. He did somehow have the knack of being serious at the right times, but even his serious moments were usually smeared with dry wit. Everyone liked the rotund little fellow from the moment they met him, and Paul could not remember ever seeing him mad—or anyone mad at him. That was good, because what looked like fat was really muscle and he could handle himself with anyone.

Both of Paul's friends were Americans and had slipped into Japanese-infested Tienstin only the day before. Burl insisted

145

they came to see Tienstin and take in the night spots, but David Rousch, in his serious way, gave Paul the real reason. They were there to pick up some key Japanese documents, which Paul was to obtain, and take them back to Chungking. The officials had not wanted to trust the regular underground channels in the transmission of these particular papers.

It may or may not have been coincidence that Burl Manning and David Rousch were selected to run this grave errand. Both were Paul's friends of long standing. The three of them had attended college together and in recent years worked together as employees of the Office of Strategic Services, the secret unit of the United States Government. Stationed in Chungking, Burl and David had been in and out of Tienstin a number of times in the past few months, and there was no doubt in Paul's mind they had asked for the dangerous job of slipping into Tienstin once again.

Burl's words prompted Paul to look around the room for David. His eyes found him stretched full length on the divan, his long form turned up on either end, his feet resting on one arm of the divan and his head resting on the other. A drink dangled from his hand, and he puffed reflectively on a cigarette as he stared at the ceiling. In contrast to Burl, David was dressed meticulously. In fact, there was a great deal of contrast between Burl Manning and David Rousch.

Burl was short and stocky, possessing a dark complexion with straight black hair and big expressive brown eyes. His round face, which laughed continually, was set off by a bump he insisted was a nose, and he reserved the right to call it anything else. He derived his heritage from a long line of millionaires. He had never worked and insisted he never would. His motto was: "The world is full of ambitious people, and I intend to be different." Only when thoroughly aroused and deeply interested did he ever deviate from his indifferent attitude. The war did arouse him, and his work with the OSS had been superb, but he liked to make people think he retained his lackadaisical style. In any event, Burl readily acknowledged it was a fortunate quirk of fate which brought him into a family of wealth and provided him with more money than he could spend in a lifetime.

Burl's close friend, David Rousch, discovered at an early age that life was not quite so kind. Born to impoverished parents who separated when he was a small child, David found nothing came easy. He worked hard all his life and struggled through college with barely enough money to exist. Many times in those days, Burl had offered to help him over the rough spots but his pride rebelled. He graduated with honors and did well in business until the war demanded his capable ability. That ability was unlimited, and his genius ranged from being an excellent pilot to being a mental gymnast in mathematics. Few men could match his natural skill, and both Burl and Paul found it a master job to keep abreast of him.

Physically, David was handsome. Six-feet-two in his stocking feet, David was every inch a man's man, and his lanky figure rippled with sinewy muscle. His blonde curly hair matched his straight nose and steel blue eyes, which were capable of warm humor or cold decision as his mood demanded. Mostly, David found it easier to be serious than nonchalant, but he possessed a broad sense of humor rarely detected save by his closest associates. Consequently, he and Burl fit well together and presented a formidable pair in either business or pleasure. In the final analysis, Paul York made up the third of this closely knit trio, and it was he who invariably led the others. Now they were together again, and though fate brought them together under weighty circumstances, they were determined to celebrate.

"Well, she's here," Paul announced proudly. "Sonya's upstairs now. When she's dressed, I'm going to treat you two imbeciles to a sight for sore eyes."

"What's a-matter?" yawned Burl. "Did she come naked?"

"Sure, women run around that way in Tienstin," Paul joked in an off-hand manner. "Why so pensive, Dave?"

Burl continued to talk aimlessly. "I read a book once where it said Russians were barbarians or something—that all the pretty girls bathed nude in the public square and..."

Burl's chatter was cut short by David, who began talking as if Burl were not present. "Pensive, am I? Yes, maybe. I was thinking, and somehow I can't get excited about your romances, Paul. She must be a wonderful girl—beautiful and all that—but I can't put much faith in your being serious about her. Then, too, there's..."

"I prefer not to discuss that," Paul interrupted sharply.

Dave shrugged his shoulders and took another drink. "Okay—okay, I just wondered how far your thoughts had taken you. Of course, I know you love this woman. I knew that a good many months ago. But maybe it isn't that easy."

"It's just that easy," flipped Paul. "And remember, no talking out of school. I want this to be a good party."

"I'm with you," David said nonchalantly, still gazing at the ceiling.

Paul emptied the remaining vodka into a glass and took a long drink.

"My god, do you drink that stuff, too?" cried Burl. "I was under the impression you saved it solely for your enemies. Look, chum, I'm no damned Russian. How long do you intend to keep me on this vodka diet? I know you've got a lot of good stuff somewhere."

"Sure I have, but it's limited stock and in a couple of days you two will be back where you can get all the good liquor you want. But if you really want something else, go in the bar and get it."

"Do you mean I'm supposed to walk that far? You know I'd drink bathtub gin rather than do that," joked Burl. "Tell me seriously, old pal, do you think your fair damsel will fall in love with me at first sight, or won't she want to hurt your feelings?"

"Not a chance, unless you straighten up that tie and brush your teeth," answered Paul. "Even I damn near choke on the stink of that cigar. Where in the name of hell did you ever get it?"

"I warn you, you're hurting my feelings and abusing my best girl," Burl said dryly. "I'll have you know my little chicken sent me a whole box from the States. Dollar cigars they are, too, and darn hard to get there these days. I guarded a pocketful with my life—all the way from Chungking, and every time I crawled on my belly I remembered those cigars and put them in my hat."

"Ah, cut it. You make me sicker than the cigars," inserted David, arising from the divan. "Paul, are we ready?"

"All ready," answered Paul. "Sonya will be down soon, and we'll have dinner. What say we have one drink before she gets here?" Paul produced another bottle of vodka from the liquor closet and began pouring three drinks. "Burl, I presume you can't get any drunker, so this won't hurt you."

Burl straightened up from tying his shoes to give Paul a soulful look. "Please, I drink only for the lack of something else to do. 'Course I'm kinda lazy and never have much else to do."

"Well put," agreed David, laughing at his friend who was wrestling with his bow tie.

In some miraculous way, Paul had been able to get dress clothes for his friends. He wanted this to be a special party for Sonya. All three would be attired in dark jacket, white shirt, and bow tie.

As David looked over the tie problem, Burl growled, "I entered the OSS to get away from the goddamned uniforms and ties, and here I am cornered for Paul's benefit."

David took his drink from Paul and spoke seriously. "Aren't you taking a chance telling this woman everything?"

"It's my neck," Paul responded.

"Not altogether," David soberly reminded him.

Paul hesitated. "I know what you mean. But she's loyal and I'm sure of it. Here, how about a toast?"

Standing close together, the three men raised their glasses and a warm smile crossed the lips of each. Indeed, any one of them would not hesitate to give his life for the other if necessary.

"Good to be together again," croaked Burl. "And to a memorable occasion. We're meeting Paul's dream."

After the drink, David was the first to speak, and his words were spoken slowly again, with deliberation. "I heard what you said, Paul, so don't be offended and fly off, but are you really sure of this girl? You've taken a big chance telling her about the true nature of your duties here."

Paul accepted reproaches and criticism from Burl and David which would unleash his fury if they came from anyone else. David's last statement fell into this category. Although it irritated him, he controlled his anger. "I told you, I'm sure of her," Paul said coldly. "I thought about it a long time before telling her. Anyway, it makes little difference now. You told me the chief said I can secure this detail and skip anytime now. And I plan on doing it soon."

"Make it soon, Paul. You're just sticking your neck out to stay longer. In fact, why not go back with us?"

"Impossible. I'll be coming along in a few days," hedged Paul.

"Oh, I see," David grinned wryly. "Unfinished business of a personal nature?"

"You might interpret it that way."

"It's your life, Paul," inserted Burl. "But be damned sure she's worth it. Russians, Americans, Japanese, Chinese, what have you, a female is a female, and my conviction is they're all alike. Kissing you and with their legs around your ass and one hand in the pocket of the pants you left hanging on the bedpost."

"If I didn't know you were kidding, I'd kick your teeth in for that," snapped Paul.

"It's still my philosophy," laughed Burl, gulping long on his drink. "Maybe it's the vodka that's got you Russian happy. This slop gets better with every drink. I must remember to introduce the true blend to my friends in the States. How about a new slogan—I can see it now. 'Get the vodka habit. So clear, so strong, so easy on the heart—one drink and it stops'."

Burl's imitation of a radio commercial was accomplished with antics, and it wrested chuckles from Paul and David. However, David quickly revived the subject at hand. "You really love the girl, don't you, Paul?"

"Yes," Paul admitted deliberately. He remained unabashed, and the manner in which he said that one word convinced David it came from his heart.

"I'm forced to say I'm surprised. Yes, I actually am surprised. After all the women you've played around with—this one comes along and makes a slave of you," observed David. "But damn it, I'm with you if that's the way you want it, even though you know I'm bothered by something else."

"I have to keep on the good side of Dave, so I agree," added Burl.

Though given in Burl's usual joking mode, Paul knew those words spoken in jest were just as deep and sincere as David's. Paul felt good, but David's "something else" hit home, and for a moment a dark feeling surged through him. He erased it immediately, because what he wanted now was for two friends to meet

150

the woman they had accepted without seeing.

"Come along, you characters. We must meet her when she comes down."

18

As Paul indicated, Sonya found Kimiko waiting to dress her. Eager to start the evening, which promised to be a momentous one, Sonya signified her impatience, and they proceeded rapidly with the toilet.

Since the time Kimiko was discovered waiting outside the bedroom door, Sonya's contact with her had been limited. While in the house, Sonya made an effort to stay away from Kimiko, and she told Paul she preferred it that way. However, there were occasions when Kimiko and Sonya were thrown together, and in those instances a cool aloofness existed on the part of both. Though Kimiko remained servile and appeared more attentive than ever, Sonya believed the doll-like Japanese girl harbored a burning hate for the white rival she was required to attend. Still, Sonya did not dislike Kimiko. Instead, her feelings toward her were more that of pity, accented by self-reproach in knowing she was the sole cause of the girl's misery. Under the circumstances, Sonya tried to be unassuming, but this was a hard task, and her mistrust of Kimiko continued to grow.

By women's standards of dressing, it took a relatively short time before Sonya was ready to make her debut with Paul's friends. She was dressed in a long white evening dress which accentuated her dark beauty, and she felt as dazzling as she looked. Her heart fluttered as she hurried along the hallway, to stop suddenly at the top of the stairs. There, waiting at the foot of the stairs were three men, and she knew instantly that Paul's friends must be Americans.

The men watched as Sonya descended the stairs, moving slowly to try and conceal the wild beating in her heart. Soft music filled the house, and she knew Paul had put on the records just for that moment. The realization that Paul was showing her off to his friends filled her with pride and created a warm glow deep inside. As she reached the men, Paul smiled and reached out to take her hand.

"Sonya, this is Burl Manning and David Rousch," he said, motioning to them in turn.

Sonya nodded graciously and extended her hand to Burl. "It's so nice to meet you."

"You're gorgeous!" exclaimed Burl. "Just what I've been waiting for. May I have this dance?"

Paul and David laughed spontaneously at Burl's comment and Sonya's reaction to it, because it was evident she did not understand Burl's dry wit. Taken aback, Sonya tried to laugh with them, but she did not understand their laughter and ended up blushing amid her confusion. Paul put his arm around her and hurried to explain.

"You'll get used to Burl. He was kidding you, darling," he smiled. "You'll find David more mannerly."

Still blushing, she extended her hand to David and laughed, "I guess I'll get used to both of you."

Burl remonstrated dryly, "But you are gorgeous. What a sensation you'd create in that sewing circle of painted wenches back home. When I saw you coming down the stairs, I wanted to whistle and stomp my feet."

"And I agree with him," chimed in David, giving Burl a withering glance and smiling warmly at Sonya. "Burl and I have been looking forward to this pleasant experience for some time, and I must admit, we aren't disappointed."

Burl's uninhibited appraisal of Sonya's beauty served to confuse her even more, but she curbed her blushes and answered, "I'm very happy to meet both of you. You're Americans, aren't you?"

"Yes indeed," flipped Burl, "and fine examples of American manhood we are. Am I not, Paul?"

"Heaven forbid," laughed Paul. "I'm proud of America."

"I think I grasp the meaning of your subtle insinuation," Burl snapped defiantly.

Sonya rapidly accustomed herself to the banterous flow of words. The conversation was being carried on in English, and she liked it. Having regained her poise she said, "I knew you were Americans the moment I saw you. And then when you spoke, Mr. Manning, I was positive. Only an American could be so straightforward and still be appreciated."

"Fair enough, fair enough," grinned Burl. "Now I can sit in my corner for the rest of the evening. And if you are an example, I think I'll like all Russians," Burl decided.

"I've noticed a bit of formality in the conversation," inserted Paul. "Suppose we drop the misters and misses."

"An excellent idea, my friend," agreed Burl. "And furthermore, why should we continue to stand here being dull when we could be exercising our harmony over a bottle of spirits?"

"I'm in accordance with that suggestion. My throat is parched after all that vodka," said David. "Sonya, may I?"

"Thank you," said Sonya, smiling as she took the arm David offered her. They led the way to the bar room while Burl and Paul followed. Burl was mumbling something about losing the pitch or being asleep at the switch and cursing David under his breath, but his faint groans were softened by the music. Taking over as aide to the host, David seated Sonya on a barstool and took his place behind the bar. Paul and Burl arranged themselves on either side of her. While Burl beat on the bar and demanded service, David began throwing ingredients together preparatory to producing one of his matchless concoctions. In the midst of these skillful maneuvers, David stopped.

"Knowing those two beside you will drink anything with liquor in it, I completely forgot to ask you, Sonya, if you have a preference. I suppose you want vodka?"

Sonya began to laugh. "Just because I'm Russian doesn't mean I drink only vodka. Truthfully, I much prefer anything else. Why is it Americans think we Russians drink nothing but vodka?"

Burl supplied the answer. "When I think of vodka, I think of Russians. When I think of ham, I think of eggs. See, it's all the same. Ham and eggs, Russians and vodka."

"Well, it's a misconception," insisted Sonya. "And David, I'll take whatever you mix. What is it, anyway?"

"He hasn't a name for it," Burl offered. "There's none strong enough to fit it, unless it might be limburger. You know, like cheese."

"I'll vouch for it, darling. Dave makes a good drink, and I've been drinking with them off and on for years," said Paul. "I do think he puts everything behind the bar in them, but they come out well."

David served his drinks in tall glasses, and they were good. Sonya liked hers so well she soon asked for another, and it was permitted on the basis the men were ahead of her. They sipped their drinks, laughed, talked, and enjoyed each other's company to the fullest. Always, the men toasted Sonya and gave her the place of honor while Burl furnished the wit necessary to a well-rounded party.

The close understanding of these three men saturated the atmosphere and permeated Sonya's soul. She basked in the glow of the flame which sealed these stalwart men together. Burl was irresistible, and she adored David's quiet manner. Sonya caught on to the feeling that by falling in love with Paul she had also drawn Burl and David into her heart to anchor them there with more than just strings of friendship. In the space of a few short minutes, she discovered a deep attachment to them and knew they always would hold a distinct place in her life.

Sonya wanted to know more about Burl Manning and David Rousch—their previous friendship with Paul, their jobs, what they were doing in Tientsin—if they were in danger being in Tientsin, and ever so many other details which would allow her to know them better. However, she failed to find the right way to approach such questions and left them unasked. She knew Paul would tell her later, but she hoped Burl and David might talk about themselves before the evening ended. In any event, she was determined to have them answer such questions for her if the chance presented itself.

By the time someone thought of dinner, the group was hilariously happy, but Burl outdistanced all of them. He demanded he be given the honor of escorting Sonya to dinner, and Paul granted his request on the grounds that he needed Sonya for support. Upon entering the dining room, Sonya was surprised to find Paul had ordered the big table removed and replaced it with a small one which nicely seated the four of them.

They seated Sonya at one end of the table, and Paul took his place at the other end, with Burl and David on either side. Before the men sat down, David lifted his wine glass and proposed a toast. "To Sonya." The men drank and seated themselves while

Sonya beamed approvingly. She appreciated David's respect and thoughtfulness.

"We should toast Paul—he found her," suggested Burl. "But having all the luck, I'm of the opinion he doesn't deserve any more. Anyway, I'll take another sip of this wine before food quenches my thirst."

"It's my guess we'd better feed you the food first," calculated David. "The way you've been mixing your drinks, I'll probably have to carry you out of here tomorrow."

"Oh, are you leaving tomorrow?" asked Sonya. "I hoped you might be staying awhile."

"Well, it's rather difficult to say," evaded David, giving a sidelong glance at the two Chinese servants who were serving the first course.

An awkward silence prevailed. Then, when the servants left the room, Paul hastened to put Sonya's mind at rest. "Yes, darling, they're leaving tomorrow."

"Oh, I'm sorry," said Sonya, watching David, who concerned himself with some item of food on his plate. "How are you traveling, David?"

At Sonya's question, David raised his eyes from the plate, looked at Paul and shrugged his shoulders, which indicated he did not know how to answer her.

Paul took the meaning from David. "Darling, I may as well explain to you in a few words what you probably already know," he began slowly. "Dave and Burl are here from Chungking on secret business for the U.S. To get here, they came by plane, walking, donkey cart, whatever. They must go back the same way. They are in danger here and should leave as soon as possible. The Japanese would kill them and ask questions later."

"I'm sorry to have pried. I really didn't mean it that way," Sonya apologized, taking in all three men with an ashamed look.

"That's all right. Forget it," flipped Burl in an off-hand manner. "You were bound to find out, and we should have told you before. Of course, Paul exaggerated a little. The Jap hasn't been made yet who could kill any one of us."

"I do hope so," Sonya answered warmly. "I want to propose a toast. To a safe return for my friends, David and Burl." Sonya held her glass high, and three arms raised to match hers. The

156

look she bestowed upon David and Burl was one of sincerity and respect, for her dark eyes sparkled from the genuine pride flowing through her.

And Paul was proud of Sonya. It was revealed in his eyes when he said, "That was thoughtful, darling." Noticing Sonya had cocked her head to listen to the music, he added, "We'll dance after dinner if you like."

Sonya accepted Paul's warm smile and started to answer. Before she could speak, Chang, Paul's Chinese number one boy, stepped into the room and beckoned to Paul.

"Yes, Chang, what is it?" asked Paul.

"Some gentlemen to see you, sir," Chang said in Chinese. "They wait in the reception hall."

Chang's words seemed to ring a bell of disaster. Simultaneously, Burl and David shot inquiring glances at Paul, and both waited expectantly for his answer. Burl returned the forkful of food to his plate, freed his hands, and dropped them to his lap under the table. Sonya followed his movement and guessed the reason for it. She trembled. Instantaneously, the atmosphere in the room had changed from warm joviality to chilled silence, and a cloak of formidable tension dropped over the group sitting rigidly at the food-laden table.

At Paul's nod, Chang left the room, and the instant he left, David broke the hideous silence. "What do you make of it?" he shot in a strong whisper.

Paul rose to his feet and placed his napkin on the table. When he spoke, his voice was cold and calm. "Sit tight. Could be our goods are being delivered early. Carry on with the meal, and I'll take a look."

Watching Paul, Sonya caught no sign of an explanation which would serve to remove the uncertainty and relieve the suspense in their minds. Yet, by his few words, he evidently conveyed a definite set of instructions to Burl and David, for he had no sooner left the room than they resumed their convivial attitudes. To all appearances they became completely oblivious of any existing danger. Sonya felt like an outsider to this intimate circle of men who knew each other so well that words were not necessary to make themselves understood.

"I've been waiting all evening to get rid of that mug and have

157

you to myself," chirped Burl, turning to Sonya. "I met him in college, and he's been taking my girls away from me ever since. I'd like to get even. How about it? I can make you real happy."

Both David and Sonya burst into laughter, because Burl had spoken with romantic gusto about as fervent as a dead lobster. He met her laughter with a forlorn look, shrugged his shoulders, and returned to his eating. Still eating, he mumbled, "I warn you, Sonya, you're missing the chance of your life. There's an awful lot of lovin' in this man."

"I'm sure there is," Sonya answered coyly. "That's why you scare me so."

"Speaking of being scared. Sonya, are you afraid of Paul?" David asked placidly.

David's sudden injection of a serious note amidst the rivalry shocked Sonya. For a brief instant she was stunned by his forward question. Then she recovered her poise to say gravely, "Why do you ask?"

"Because I know Paul. Because Paul is my close friend, and I like you," David said evenly. He remained composed under her vicious stare.

"I wonder if you're not being rude," snapped Sonya.

"Ah, stop it, you two," interceded Burl. "The trouble with you two is that both of you are too damn serious. It gives you gray hairs and makes you old. Relax, relax."

Sonya and David ignored Burl. They were too busy sizing each other up.

"I'm not being rude," David said firmly. "Rarely has anyone ever said I was rude. Honest, straightforward, but never rude. I think you're the same way."

"Yes, I think I am," agreed Sonya. She admired David's direct manner and found herself approving of his uninhibited approach. "Therefore, I'll give you a straight answer. No, I'm not afraid of Paul. I love him."

"And isn't it possible to love and be afraid at the same time?" pressed David.

"Possibly."

"Sonya, maybe I should enlighten you," began David. "Paul is probably one of the best friends I have in the world. I even take the liberty to say I probably know him better than anyone else.

Furthermore, I know his—well, I know what he's like. With such a feeling goes a great deal of understanding, and I'm compelled to be serious about this love affair. That's the way I am. Now, take Burl there. He probably feels as strongly toward you and Paul as I do, but he won't bother to give it any serious thought. He's been too busy for the past ten or fifteen years trying to spend the million or so dollars his grandparents unwittingly gave him."

Burl took David's statement as a matter-of-fact, exhibiting a soulful expression and then turning it into a grin of approval.

"Of course, he's big-hearted and does a lot of good with his money. I said that simply to emphasize my point of view. I have never found it possible to be nonchalant about problems. But back to the question which prompted this little speech. Sonya, my only interest is that I want you and Paul to be awfully sure, and even if I must be brutal to do it, I'm determined to make both of you think farther than just the moonlight. You may remember a letter you received before you met Paul. It warned you about his state of mind and possible danger to you. I wrote that letter."

"You! You wrote that letter!" stammered Sonya. "I didn't have—that is, I had no way of knowing. I'm sorry, David. I'm the one who has been rude."

"Forget it—no apologizes necessary. I just wanted you to realize I know a little about your romance." David pondered, intent on pushing a bit of food around the plate with his fork. Then he continued talking, and his words were slow and deliberate. "Yes, I wrote you the letter. You see, I saw Paul a number of times during that period, and I realized his almost chaotic sense of proportions. I received information from other of our men here which was quite disturbing. In all, I felt bound to warn you."

Sonya started to speak, but David checked her. "Wait, before you say anything let me add this, I hope you love him—love him as much as he loves you."

"I do. That's what I was going to say. I love him, David. I love him with all my heart."

"I pray you mean that, and I thank god if you do." David's voice was stony, and one could not fail to catch the note of foreboding it carried. "For I say now, deliberately and without reservation, Paul loves you so much he would not hesitate to kill for you. Even kill himself —or you."

The horrifying import of David's words left Sonya cold and sick with apprehension. She twisted the meaning within her mind and came up with a stunning realization. She, herself, was aware of that fact, but it had taken David to drive it home forcefully.

Paul's sudden entrance caught the group at the table in a clumsy situation, but as usual, Burl smoothed the road.

"Boy meets girl, proposed, refused. That's my record," he lamented. "And so help me, I think it's the broken record. Always the same, over and over and over. Hell, it's enough to make me drink myself to death."

As Paul laughed, Sonya slipped Burl a heartfelt look of thanks. David was busy taking a manila folder from Paul.

"That's it, Dave. Delivered on schedule by the well-trained Japanese," Paul smiled. "Honest, I feel guilty—like swiping the baby's rattle."

Impatiently, David thumbed through the papers. "Hot!" he exclaimed. "This stuff's so hot it burns my hands. Paul, you'll be able to name your own ticket with the chief after he sees this. Tell me, will your contemporaries miss these plans?"

Having seated himself, Paul stopped eating to say nonchalantly, "Undoubtedly. But not for a few days—I hope."

"Don't tarry, Paul. It's not worth it."

"Right," Paul said as he looked adoringly at Sonya. "But whether it's worth it or not is for me to decide. I think she is."

Sonya tried to quell the tumultuous emotion rising within her. The significance of Paul's words was very clear. He would be leaving in a few days. He just said so. And he had to go—now that the Japanese would soon be investigating the loss of those vital plans. Sonya wanted to grab the folder from David and return it to the Japanese—do anything to keep Paul from leaving. David's act of carefully placing the folder under him was like sealing her fate. She suppressed the urge to cry out her objections, to scream her hatred for the things which were to take Paul away from her. Yet she knew the dreadful feelings would inevitably have to be faced.

Paul sensed Sonya's distress. "Darling, I know exactly what you're thinking," he soothed. "And you can forget it and enjoy the party. Come on now, how about a smile?"

"You two must have a code of your own, cause I'm completely in the dark," interrupted Burl. "However, I'm definitely sympathetic with one idea. Let's all enjoy the party. After seeing our mission fulfilled so easily, I'm ready to get drunk."

"Drunker," corrected David.

"Have it your own way. I refuse to argue," grinned Burl. "The evening is altogether too gay to argue. Here, another toast, to my first dance with Miss Petrovna—right after dinner."

As they drank, Burl's wink at Sonya produced a tiny smile and erased the disheartened expression she wore.

Burl was destined to have his dance with Sonya, but not for some time. The dinner rambled on amidst fine wines to savor, excellent food, and jovial conversations, reaching a befitting climax over dessert. Paul gave a prearranged signal, and Chang entered the room, balancing an enormous cake on a silver platter. Sonya sat spellbound as Chang gingerly placed the heavy tray before her, bowed, grinned broadly, and left the room. Sonya looked at the frosty white marvel in front of her, and her eyes fixed on the little man standing in the middle of the cake. He was standing facing her with his arm outstretched, and dangling from his tiny hand was a plain golden ring, appearing gigantic in relation to the little man who held it.

As she reached for the ring, Sonya looked around the table through misty eyes. David watched her with a genial smile. Obviously embarrassed by the sentimental setting, Burl was blushing and mumbling something about he didn't think the toy looked a bit like Paul. Paul was watching her closely, and his whole expression radiated the love throbbing in his heart.

"Yes, it's for you, darling," Paul said serenely. "Read the inscription on the inside."

Sonya turned the thin, golden band in her hand. The dainty engraving was done in English and read, "SP, My Love Forever, PY." Sonya could not stifle the tears which spilled from her eyes. "Oh, Paul," she choked.

Paul stood beside her, lifting her to her feet. "It's for your right hand," he whispered. "For your right hand until we can transfer it to the left."

Burl and David remained seated at the table, watching, and

feeling self-conscious. For the first time all evening, Burl had nothing to say, and would not have said it had he thought of something appropriate.

Paul took the ring from Sonya and slipped it on the third finger of her right hand. As he did so, he said hopefully, "Promise me, Sonya, promise you'll leave it there until I can put it on the other hand."

"I will, I will," murmured Sonya. She raised her tear-stained cheeks, and her lips caught his in a long, sweet kiss which attested her voluntary pledge.

Still holding her close to him, Paul whispered in her ear, "It's really not much, darling, but I wanted it simple so you could wear it without fear of unpleasant questioning."

"I know that," she answered, and her words were barely audible. "And the ring—it's wonderful. I love you so."

"Hey, you two. You're repeating the first act. Do I have to sit here drooling over this luscious cake and wait for you lovebirds to stop cooing long enough to cut it?" Burl inquired in his usual jesting manner.

Paul and Sonya turned to their guests, and Sonya blushed just a little. "Honest, Burl," she said as she wiped her eyes with the back of her hand, "I forgot you and David were here."

"Obviously," chirped Burl. "But we forgive you—that is, if you'll now cut the cake."

Sonya cut the cake and served the portions. The cake was delicious, but the diners were much too full to eat it. Nevertheless, each one forced down a small piece in respect to the reason for its conception. Then at Paul's suggestion, the group moved into the living room for a smoke and a sip of brandy.

For Sonya, the evening seemed destined to carry an extreme range of emotions—both joyous and painful. Her next wound, though inflected unintentionally, resulted from words uttered by David. Sonya had asked to be excused for a few minutes, and while she was gone from the room, the conversation among the men changed to a discussion of her qualities. Unfortunately, she entered the room to hear David finishing a sentence, and she caught the phrase, "...beautiful, but you should remember another lady." David's words knifed Sonya in a vulnerable spot and brought her to an embarrassing halt in the doorway. She hesitated, and as she walked toward the men lounging in the soft chairs, they arose to acknowledge her presence.

Burl had seen her entrance and, knowing she heard David, acted quickly to conceal it from David and Paul. "No, don't sit down, Sonya, it's finally time for my dance, and we're going to find out where that good music comes from."

With that, Burl took Sonya by the hand and headed toward the ballroom where the overhead speakers provided the music from Paul's record collection. With a mighty gesture, he waved at the two men left standing and amused at his antics. He pulled Sonya toward him and they were soon dancing. Despite his large round form, Burl was agile and an excellent dancer. Amazed, Sonya told him so, only to receive a whispered lecture saying all young men in America have to pass dancing tests before being let out of grade school. She liked his jest and comfort provided as they continued to dance easily, as if they had known each other forever.

Burl told her, "We also learn self-preservation in America, and I'm going to be shot about now if I don't get you back to the others." Whereupon Burl escorted her to David, who rose and took his turn dancing. Sonya danced on and on with David and Burl, but Burl demanded most of the attention. He barred Paul, insisting this was the only time he would be able to dance with her while Paul could do so any evening. Paul graciously conceded and contented himself by watching the enjoyment derived by his friends.

It was Burl who proposed they all take a ride and see the city. Paul vehemently vetoed that absurd idea, reminding Burl his hide was at stake and instead forwarded the bad news that the party must draw to a close. Touched by his drinks, Burl bitterly fought the termination of the party, but he finally had to concede. He pretended to brood while the three men waited for Sonya to change her clothes and come downstairs. Only when Sonya impetuously kissed him and David good-bye did his face light up.

"That was worth my entire trip to Tientsin," he beamed. "Honestly, Sonya, I'm sorry to see you go, but I know we'll meet again—many, many times."

"Yes, I'm sure we shall," she answered, and she honestly believed her words. She had established a warm feeling for the happy, rotund Burl in the short time of one evening.

19

Sonya brooded over her packing. She did not want to leave Paul, but the die was cast. It just so happened she and Paul were both leaving Tientsin. On Wednesday morning, Sonya and Katilka Petrovna would be going to Peitaiho Beach, and although this was only Monday, Sonya decided to accomplish some of her packing before the last minute.

On the way home from the party, Sonya and Paul agreed she should go to Peitaiho Beach and he to Chungking as soon as possible. She faced it bravely, and they discussed their plans with determination. There had been a number of things to consider. For instance, Paul wanted to be sure of the exact day and time Sonya would take the train for Peitaiho Beach, explaining that his departure could be varied to coincide with hers. Further, they were compelled to make some provision for the handling of gifts Paul had given Sonya over the course of their relationship. Their arrangement of storing them in Paul's home worked well, but he would abandon the home when he left for Chungking. Paul finally agreed to have them packed and stored in a warehouse where Sonya could get them if and when she chose.

A knock on her door interrupted Sonya's thoughts. "Yes?"

She recognized the voice of the Chinese houseboy who worked in the apartment building. "Man outside to see you."

"I'll go with you." She turned and closed the door. Outside she found a well-dressed and clean-appearing Chinese man of middle age. She did not recognize him and immediately questioned his reason for wanting to see her.

"Mr. Paul is waiting to see you. Please come with me," he explained in Chinese.

"Yes, of course," agreed Sonya, her pulse rising. *What was wrong? Why did Paul want to see her at such an hour in the afternoon?* As she secured the door and followed her Chinese guide, Sonya developed a weak sensation which was a direct result of the apprehension consistent with her feeling of impending disaster. Paul awaited her in a secluded doorway of a deserted and shadowy alley. They greeted each other with a warm kiss, then Paul turned Sonya to face her guide.

"First, I want you to meet Huang Chu," he began, speaking rapidly in a low tone. "You and Chu shall be seeing a lot of each other in the future. He will be our contact from now on. He is good and trustworthy. He likes to use his English but leaves parts out, so you better converse in Chinese."

"I'm glad to know you, Mr. Huang," Sonya said pleasantly as Huang Chu bowed to her. Turning to Paul, she asked, "This means you're leaving now, doesn't it?"

"Yes. I know it isn't the parting you wanted, but conditions will not permit any other way. I must leave today—this afternoon."

"How are you going?"

"Don't worry about it. I have worked out a plan where I'll have a good start before the Japanese discover I'm missing. They, of course, will be looking for me. I want to be absolutely sure you are on the way to Peitaiho Wednesday morning as planned. I'm concerned the Japs may put us together and come to you. However, they aren't likely to cause you any harm as long as Russia stays out of the war. Anyway, you'll be better off in Peitaiho Beach, and I'll keep you posted on what happens. Okinawa is falling to the Americans. Next will be Japan, and the war could spread to here."

Sonya was having trouble holding back her tears. She reached out, clutched Paul, and said, "I'll try to understand."

Paul pushed her back, looked deep into her eyes, and said, "You are my prized possession. Take care of yourself for me." Taking her hands in his, he turned the small golden band on her finger. "Always wear this ring and believe the words it carries. I mean them. And always remember, I will not give up."

Those last words—the words that had brought them together—said a lot, and Sonya knew he had purposely used them. *No, she would never forget,* she kept saying to herself.

Impulsively, Paul took Sonya in his arms and smothered her with fervent kisses. He kissed her lips, her eyes, her throat. Wanting him to go on showering her with kisses and to never stop crushing her closer, her body melted into his, and she clung to him in pathetic desperation.

"Oh, Paul, I love you so!" Sonya cried hoarsely, uncaring of the tears streaming down her cheeks.

Paul pushed her away from him and held her at arm's length for a last look at her. Then he turned to Huang Chu, who stood nearby. "Chu, see that she gets home all right."

Before Sonya was aware of his action, Paul quickly left the alley and disappeared, leaving her with an empty feeling deep in her heart. They had parted quickly, as Paul had wanted. He hated drawn out good-byes.

Early Wednesday morning, Sonya and her mother arrived at the station to board the train for Peitaiho Beach. Katilka was perturbed concerning her daughter. Sonya's attitude the past few days was not in keeping with a prospective enjoyable time in Peitaiho Beach. Moody and despondent, Sonya merely shrugged off her mother's inquisitive anxiety. In addition to the pain created by Paul's departure, another disquietude was evident. Paul's insistence she leave for the beach earlier than planned, and his formidable reference to her safety, warned her. It was just a matter of time until the Japanese gendarme would discover he had abandoned their services. That might lead to their eventual discovery of his true work, and if that happened, Sonya knew only too well the consequences. No stone would be left unturned in their desperate efforts to corral him and his collaborators—and Sonya would appear in the picture.

As Paul pointed out, such developments were unlikely, and yet, the sight of Japanese policemen, soldiers, and other questionable characters took on a fateful importance for Sonya. She viewed them with annoyed interest, fearful under the apprehension that she was now a marked woman. When the Japanese military police inspected her bags, she trembled under the certainty they concentrated on her, when actually they made a simple routine examination.

Her alarm was again aroused when a seemingly harmless old Chinaman with scraggly white beard and bent cane appeared to drift with her wherever she moved about the station. If she walked down the platform to see if the train was coming, he changed his position to oversee her action. If she entered the station waiting room, he soon was seen in the doorway or among the milling crowd there. Once or twice she turned suddenly and was positive the old fellow had been scrutinizing her. Still, there was no way she might be sure, and thinking her imagination was working overtime she passed it off.

In due time the train arrived, and after a more than normal amount of confusion, it puffed out of Tientsin with Sonya and Katilka Petrovna aboard. Fortunately, the two women had managed to squeeze themselves into a small seat among the packed mass of humanity. When they had stowed their bags under the seat and arranged themselves as comfortably as possible, Sonya began to read. In anticipation of the long dull ride, Sonya brought along a book, and she became so absorbed in it she did not notice when the same old Chinaman with the cane limped into their car, pushed a couple of people aside to make room for himself, and sat down across from her.

Many miles had passed under the pounding wheels of the blowing and wheezing train when Sonya finally closed the book and stretched herself to untangle the knots in her limbs. She glanced idly around the car and saw the same old Chinaman who sat across from her—asleep, nodding with the motion of the train. *Was he really asleep?* she wondered. She believed he was watching her. Further, his constant presence near her was foreboding. She decided to find out if he was following her.

Explaining to her mother that she intended to walk around the train a little and loosen the kinks in her legs, Sonya rose and moved nonchalantly along the aisle in the direction of the nearest door. She found the vestibule vacant, thus suiting her purposes, so she stood at the window apparently intent on the passing landscape. From the corner of her eye she watched the doorway and waited. Only a few minutes elapsed before her expectation was fulfilled. The door opened and the old Chinaman hobbled into the vestibule. Sonya acted indifferent and seemed oblivious to his presence while she concentrated her gaze on the passing countryside. An instant later, she was painfully conscious of the old man's presence close beside her. Terror-stricken, she moved quickly to one side but continued to look out the window, hoping it was only her imagination.

"Stay as you are, Sonya, and don't turn around," whispered

the old man from the corner of his mouth. "This train is crawling with Japanese secret service men."

It was Paul! The mixture of relief and incredulity which surged through Sonya left her faint. For just an instant she turned to see him standing beside her, also looking out the window. Then she collected her wits and played his game. Pretending interest in the passing landscape, she gasped, "Paul! What are you doing here?"

"Sshhh, keep your voice low and listen."

A man walked into the vestibule and Paul stopped talking. When he had passed through, Paul again took up his low-toned conversation with Sonya. "When I left Monday, I waited outside Tientsin for my underground contacts. Before I could leave, Chu came with the word the house had been ransacked. All hell has broken loose. Somebody squealed on me—squealed the moment I left. I had to see about you."

"Kimiko!" hissed Sonya. "It must have been Kimiko. Where did you leave her?"

"Maybe, but I doubt it. I arranged passage and saw her off to Peking. She has relatives there. No, I don't think so, she had money enough for the rest of her life. No matter, it's not important who talked, but rather that someone did."

Again Paul stopped talking while a man passed through the vestibule. When he had disappeared, he continued in the same whisper. "There is the possibility you are in danger. That's why I'm here. I wanted to make sure you get to Peitaiho all right."

Sonya forgot their caution and turned fearfully to Paul, but he sensed her feeling and hastened to calm her. "Careful, darling, don't get excited. I doubt very seriously if they know anything about you. It's just that I'll feel better knowing you arrived in Peitaiho without mishap."

"But what about you? You'll never get out of this country alive! You know they will torture your friends—do anything to find you."

"Don't worry about me. I'll get to Chungking. It's you we're interested in. Even if they're wise to us, they won't have proof—and to touch a Russian national at this stage of the war without proof would be unthinkable. No, I'm sure the worst they can do at this time is watch you. Be careful what you do and don't give

169

them any reason to suspect you."

"I'll be careful, but how can you be so sure they won't touch me?"

"You are a Russian and under the wing of the Russian Consulate. Last February, Russia denounced her non-aggression pact with Japan, and that means she may start firing on Japan any day. Japan's handling Russia with kid gloves. They won't do a thing which might give Russia an excuse for declaring war. They know harming a Russian national would start an investigation."

"Will Russia declare war?" Sonya whispered nervously.

"Undoubtedly. It will soon be July—a long time since Russia broke ties with Japan, and Japan is backed up to the wall. Russia will want to be on the side of the Americans. The Japanese are well aware of their situation—I know."

"That's what I mean. What will happen when Russia declares war? I'm frightened."

"Shush," clipped Paul, as two Japanese policemen entered the vestibule.

Paul waited while the soldiers stopped to light cigarettes and loitered in the vestibule. They casually sized up the old Chinaman and pretty white girl standing idly near the window. Aware of their glances, the aged Chinaman coughed and hobbled into the next car. A minute or two later, the white girl moved back to her coach.

Sonya reseated herself and waited impatiently. She pretended to read, but she saw not a line in the book. For over an hour she endured the suspense, fighting nervously and praying Paul would return. The train had stopped twice since she saw him, and she was beginning to wonder if he had departed. There were a great many things they had left unsaid, and she felt sure he would come back. Sonya was pondering the advisability of scouring the train for him when the old Chinaman came shuffling down the aisle. For the first time she realized the perfection of his flawless disguise. Even as she watched the old fellow, knowing it was Paul, she still doubted her own eyes. His makeup was incredible, exact to the most minute detail.

Ignoring Sonya, Paul took his seat across the car and proceeded to engage himself by eating from a sack he withdrew from

170

a battered carpetbag. Sonya kept one eye on him and continued to wait for some sign of instruction, but none came. He evidently was not taking any chances. They still had a long way to ride, and he bided his time. Sonya played the game, but after a time it began to tell on her nerves. Almost to the breaking point, she took the initiative and attempted to attract his attention by subtly swinging her arm in his direction. He ignored her.

Then, when Sonya could endure it no longer, he made the move she had been waiting for. The sack slipped off his lap and onto the floor. As he stooped to retrieve it, he moved close to Sonya and whispered, "In the vestibule. After I've left."

A short time later, the old Chinaman rose and left the car, but Sonya waited. She wanted to be positive their departures from the car did not attract attention. Leisurely, she rose and started down the aisle. Then she stopped, reversed her steps, and left the coach by the same door the old Chinaman had taken.

Sonya found Paul standing near the window and took up a position beside him. Since the vestibule was devoid of any other person, she reasoned it safe and said in a muffled voice, "You had me scared stiff—I'm a nervous wreck. I thought you left me."

"Don't get jumpy, darling," Paul answered under his breath.

"Well, remember, I'm not used to this cat and mouse game."

Paul could not suppress a little laugh when he saw her cute expression smothered by honest dismay. "Of course," he sympathized.

"I want to ask you, before we're interrupted again, what should I do if Russia declares war?"

"Nothing. You can stake my life on that."

"You haven't answered me."

"You'll be well off in Peitaiho. Colonel Yosuki is the one to fear, and his headquarters are in Tientsin, which means he can't act on the spur of the moment. I'll keep you informed through our underground agents, so don't be surprised how you get my messages. I'll take action to help you, if necessary. In the meantime, don't worry."

"I'll try."

Paul hurried on, eager to give her all his instructions as fast as possible. "Another thing, do as I say. *Do as I say, do you understand?*" he asked seriously, repeating for emphasis. "If I send you instructions, follow them, and don't question my word or my reasons. It may sound like blind faith, but you absolutely must follow them."

"I promise."

"Now, for the present. We are passing through Tangshan, and I'm due to meet Chu here tonight. I'll be leaving at the next stop. I'm satisfied you'll make Peitaiho safely. I recognize many of the Japanese secret service men aboard this train, and you aren't being watched."

"How will you get to Chungking?"

"I've booked passage on a mule cart."

"Stop joking," Sonya snapped irritably.

"It amounts to that."

"Oh, darling," she cried impulsively. "I don't want to see you leave again. One good-bye is enough."

Paul reached out and clasped Sonya's hand. Significantly, he turned the gold ring on her finger. "This isn't good-bye. We'll be together sooner than you think."

"I love you," choked Sonya, suppressing her tears.

"And I love you very much," Paul whispered. "Now scoot back to your seat." He dropped her hand and turned away. There was no more to say—there was no more that needed to be said.

Sonya hesitated reluctantly. Then she marched determinedly into the coach, took her seat, and fought to bury her grief in the pages of her book. The sad-appearing old Chinaman took his seat across the aisle, and his presence comforted her. A short time later, she looked up to see his seat vacant.

20

If Paul could have known how right Sonya was to suspect Kimiko of lighting the fuse to his explosive dilemma, his temper would have soared into a rage heretofore unequaled. But he did not know, and it was just as well, since the explosion already had taken place.

Paul did not believe Kimiko the culprit. He knew she loved him and consequently reasoned she would do nothing to harm him or his friends. The factor he did not contemplate was that the dividing line between hate and love is so thin people step from one to the other instinctively. And, too, the hate on the heels of love is a hate deadly and vehement, like no other. Such was the hate which surged in Kimiko's soul. This hate for her "master" did not spring spontaneously, pushing love aside. It began slowly, starting the first night Paul brought his white girl to "their" home, and it ate into her vitals until the love she treasured was completely devoured.

When she was very young, Kimiko's poverty-stricken father bargained her into the House of Matsunaga, one of the influential families in Japan. She worked dutifully and learned a great deal about the family. She did not, however, learn that the master of the family had a son in the United States. Neither did she learn the mother of that son was a white woman residing in Japan. Eventually, she met Paul's aunt. The old lady immediately adored the attentive and comely Japanese girl. She asked that Kimiko live with her, and it was permitted. In the employ of Paul's aunt, she led a good life but an uneventful one, and she became resigned to her servient life of waiting and praying.

Everything changed for her when Paul returned to Japan and was introduced to her as Mr. Matsunaga. She referred to him as "Master" and never knew him by any other name until he took her to Tientsin and became "Colonel." She had loved him from the moment she bowed in front of him. She wanted him and

173

pledged herself to be his servant. Kimiko worked toward that end, and, though he ignored her at first, she waited on him every opportunity. Finally he had acknowledged her attention.

It all happened one evening after arriving in Tientsin and Kimiko was serving Colonel Matsunaga dinner in his room. She executed the meal faultlessly, and afterward as he started to unlace his shoes, she hurried to bring his slippers and help him. As she crouched in front of him she felt his hand on her shoulder. Then his hand grasped her by the neck and the back of the head, tangling in her black hair. He raised her to his lap and kissed her fully on the mouth. She had never been kissed before. It was new to her, and it sent tremors of passion racing through her body. Instinctively she pulled away, but he held her tightly, kissing her again and again. Under his kisses, she went limp and gave herself into his hands—not knowing or caring what he did.

In Kimiko's young mind, and rightfully so, chastity and love went hand in hand, and she gave both to Colonel Matsunaga. She gave them honestly and gracefully, on her own volition and without inhibition. She loved him, and that meant complete submission to his every desire.

From that day forward, Kimiko made herself part of Colonel Matsunaga. She cared for his home, attended his every want, and wrapped herself in his arms when he so desired. She carried on as his servant and never questioned his actions or his orders. Due to her heritage, Kimiko knew her place and was content and happy in her own little realm of influence. Literally, and in her opinion, life was being unduly kind to her. There were times when she wondered why she did not have children. She secretly hoped she might conceive, thus tying her more firmly to the unpredictable Colonel Matsunaga, but no such event took place. She finally conceded it never would.

In the eyes of the public, Kimiko was the colonel's attendant. She also was nothing more than an attendant in his eyes, though through the years he did develop an affection for her. Cognizant of her place in his world, she never overstepped her boundaries. After all, he did treat her considerately. He provided her with more than the necessities and always made sure she had a comfortable set of rooms in his homes. In his last Tientsin home, the gorgeous mansion, he arranged her rooms to suite her tastes.

Those rooms were her private domain, and rarely did he intrude.

Kimiko approved her existence in Tientsin, for it seemed to strengthen her hold on Colonel Matsunaga, who began living more to himself. All went well until that fateful night when he knifed her sensitivity by bringing home a white girl. Then he seared the wound by ordering her to serve this white girl, whom she later learned to call Miss Sonya. Still, Kimiko suppressed her uncertainty, rationalizing that this was a temporary love affair. But the seed of hate had been sown. As the days lengthened into weeks, more seldom did Colonel Matsunaga require her services and less often did he demand her love. The seed of hate sprouted and grew, and Kimiko's antipathy increased. The last remaining tie of affection snapped within her the night she listened outside Sonya's bedroom door. A few minutes later, when Colonel Matsunaga towered over her, Kimiko knew she hated him.

Fear of his power held Kimiko in check, but meticulously and cunningly, she began to lay the groundwork for his eventual destruction. Outwardly, she carried on without the slightest indication of the treachery which pulsed within her, and never was Colonel Matsunaga given reason to doubt her fidelity. In direct contrast to her feelings, Kimiko showed more understanding for Colonel Matsunaga and his relations with Miss Sonya, thus discounting any suspicions he might have had and leaving him more vulnerable than ever. Under no condition did he sense the villainy which lurked under her agreeable nature.

For a long time, Kimiko had doubted Colonel Matsunaga's loyalty to the Japanese government. Because of her personal contact in his home, she had occasion to see many discrepancies which did not fit harmoniously with his position in the Japanese gendarme. Around this fact she laid her strategy, and secretly she prowled the house—searching his rooms, investigating his secret hiding places, thumbing through masses of confidential letters and documents. Many of his papers were written in English, and she was unable to decipher them, but they multiplied her suspicions. She often watched him and learned hiding places she did not know existed, but they failed to reveal much due to her limited ability. Sometimes she crept to the living room door late at night and listened while he worked over his hidden radio, sending and receiving messages. The conversations were in English, and she was at a loss to know what was being said. Actually, had she understood English it would have done her little good, since all the messages were in code. Nevertheless, the fact that he secretly kept a powerful, two-way radio and used it in English confirmed her doubts. There remained some question, and she was determined to have positive proof before becoming an informer. She knew only too well if she brought the Japanese gendarme down upon one of its most powerful members without unquestionable evidence, her fate would be sealed as well before accomplishing her objective.

Thus, Kimiko waited. Then, on the night of Paul's party with Sonya, Burl, and David, she was provided with the conclusive information she needed. Eavesdropping on the revelers, she learned beyond a question of a doubt the two strangers were American spies affiliated with Colonel Matsunaga.

From that moment on, Kimiko confidently bided her time, awaiting the precise time to bring the Japanese gendarme swarming in upon the man she once loved. By her vehement way of thinking, that precise time would be when Miss Sonya was in the house with the colonel. She wanted to unleash her vengeance upon both of them, and in that way it could be accomplished by one stroke. Well aware of their habits, Kimiko reasoned she would not have long to wait—but by this reasoning, she inadvertently allowed Paul York and Sonya Petrovna to slip away before she could act—saving them from a horrible death. Miss Sonya did not come to the house again, and Colonel Matsunaga did not give Kimiko sufficient warning he planned to leave Tientsin.

Colonel Matsunaga withheld the decision of his departure from Kimiko simply because he desired to avert any more grievous scenes than necessary. If he told her too soon, he knew there would be days of arguments and unhappiness. Knowing of her relatives in Peking, he arranged for her passage there and told her only a few hours before her scheduled departure that she must leave.

Stupefied by his decisive statement, Kimiko did not believe his order. Whereupon, he emphasized it firmly, suggested she start packing the items she needed most, and began to help her. Colonel Matsunaga whisked her through the packing routine so rapidly Kimiko was unable to cope with her plight. While thousands of thoughts raced through her mind, she pled to go along with him or at least to stay in Tientsin, but he remained adamant. Kimiko visualized the collapse of her traitorous scheme, and she cursed herself for having been a fool to wait. Now, she found herself caught in his constant company and unable to slip away to the Japanese officials. Only one chance remained to fulfill at least a part of her lethal plan. She must board the train under Colonel Matsunaga's guidance and then scamper off before it left Tientsin. If this plan worked, she might warn the Japanese police in time to thwart his escape. Also, she might be able to implicate her other victim—Miss Sonya. Settled on this line of action, Kimiko stilled her protests and sullenly completed her packing.

At the train, Colonel Matsunaga squeezed her hand in a fond good-bye and saw her into the coach. Momentarily, he wondered at her composed attitude, but he did not tarry over the thought for his mind was filled with more important matters. Even then, an underground agent waited to take him to his contact point outside Tientsin.

From the car window, Kimiko watched Colonel Matsunaga thread his way through the station crowd until he disappeared from view. Then, she gathered up her bags and scurried through the coach, reaching the station platform just as the train began to move. Standing hesitantly on the platform, her first impulse was to scream for a Japanese policeman, but she thought better of it and hurried off to find a rickshaw which would take her directly to the headquarters of the Japanese gendarme.

The sentry at the doorway of the gendarme headquarters scrutinized Kimiko disdainfully when she blurted in Japanese that she must immediately see the officer in charge. After some questioning, she finally managed to impress him with the graveness of her mission and he called an officer.

"What do you want?" asked the officer.

"I don't know," blurted Kimiko. "All I know is that Colonel Matsunaga is escaping and you must catch him."

At the mention of Colonel Matsunaga's name, the officer focused his attention on the girl and said dubiously, "You're mixed up. What do you mean—escape?"

"He's an American spy," Kimiko said in a low voice. "I know because I've been living with him for years. He's leaving Tientsin. Don't you believe me?"

Her words left the officer aghast. He caught his breath. "No, I don't believe you, but you better be telling the truth," he threatened.

Only a few minutes elapsed before Kimiko sat across the desk from Colonel Yosuki. A few more minutes after that Colonel Yosuki had gleaned from her the information he wanted. For months he had waited to get something on this man he hated—this man who, by political influence, had stepped into his private domain and beaten him down so often. Never, however, did he expect such a turn as this, and he knew well that he dared not take a girl's word for such calamitous accusations. It would be suicide for him to take Colonel Matsunaga into custody and then find out the girl lied. He must prove her statements first, and rapidly.

Under Kimiko's guidance, screaming automobiles carried Colonel Yosuki and his select group of investigators to Colonel Matsunaga's residence. Systematically they searched the house from end to end. Paul had done a fine job of disposing of all information, and Colonel Yosuki began to fear his mistake. He was on the verge of unleashing his violence on Kimiko when his men hauled a battered and twisted radio into his presence. One glance proved its previous use and the statement Kimiko had made concerning such a hidden radio. The men explained they found it buried in the backyard.

"That's it," said Colonel Yosuki, coldly vicious. "This radio proves the girl's statements beyond a doubt." He jumped to his feet and began to pace the floor. Absorbed in thought, he ignored the three officers who stood rigid in his presence, awaiting his orders. Kimiko cowered in one corner of the room, completely terrified, and spoke only when asked to do so.

As though thinking aloud, Colonel Yosuki muttered, "That rat, that stinking rat. Colonel Matsunaga an American agent— and for years he's been duping us all. I've suspected all along he wasn't right. Now I know, after he's made his escape. But he *will* be caught. *I swear it as a servant of the Emperor.*"

Colonel Yosuki stopped mumbling to himself and vehemently turned to the Captain standing near. Hate danced in his eyes. "Captain, Colonel Matsunaga was supposed to take a plane for Peking over two hours ago, which means he should have arrived by now. Contact Peking. Find out if the plane arrived and if so, give orders to arrest Colonel Matsunaga. Report back to me in my office."

The Captain saluted and hurried from the room. Colonel Yosuki focused his attention on another of the officers still in the room. "Return to headquarters. Compile a complete description of Colonel Matsunaga. Send out a general alarm to all headquarters in China to arrest him as an *American spy!* Remember, he may be traveling under disguise. Be sure all border outposts are notified. Don't worry too much about the Tientsin area, you can be sure he isn't around here."

When the officer had departed to carry out Colonel Yosuki's curt and efficient orders, the colonel again started mumbling to himself. Suddenly, he stopped his pacing and laughed outright— a cold laugh that would freeze the soul of anyone within hearing. "It's ironical, positively ironical! The influential Colonel Matsunaga in the employ of the United States—deceiving not only me but everyone." To the one officer remaining in the room he said, "But he will pay, and his accomplices will pay. He must have had accomplices. Check his actions for the past year—what he did, where he went, everything. Arrest for questioning everyone even remotely connected with him. Do you understand? Everyone even remotely concerned with him."

The officer acknowledged his orders and departed, leaving Colonel Yosuki alone in the room with the frightened Kimiko. The colonel concentrated his gaze on her. "Now, what about the Russian girl who visited Colonel Matsunaga? You called her Sonya. I think I know who she is. What proof can you give of her affiliation with him?"

Kimiko cringed, trying to think of some evidence she might produce to bear out her statements concerning Sonya. Then she remembered the clothes and jewelry which Paul had given her. He could not have taken them with him, and they must be somewhere in the house.

"He gave her clothes and jewelry, and they always left them here in the house," answered Kimiko, trembling from the onslaught of the demon before her. "They must still be here, probably in the room she used."

On the way to the bedroom, Colonel Yosuki picked up two of his assistants who were waiting outside the door. He wanted witnesses to their discovery, because he did not trust higher authority to take his personal word in such a grave matter. To his disappointment, they found the room had already been thoroughly searched and revealed nothing. Colonel Yosuki considered his defeat and made himself believe Kimiko's testimony would be enough.

He turned on Kimiko and said tersely, "I'll have to keep you in custody until we find him and the girl."

Kimiko did not care where they took her or what they did, for her life had ended in the death of her love for her master. She submitted listlessly to Colonel Yosuki's declaration she must remain in his custody. But she could not contain herself completely, and the brutal attitude of Colonel Yosuki disturbed the sense of guilt beginning to simmer in her soul.

Kimiko was following Colonel Yosuki into his office when the captain stopped the colonel to inform him of his progress. From the rapid conversation which followed, Kimiko overheard enough to convince her Colonel Matsunaga was still a free man. He had not taken the plane. They did not know where he was.

Hearing this information, Colonel Yosuki turned livid with rage and began cursing everyone within shouting distance. When he finished giving orders, the headquarters was in a turmoil, and every effort was concentrated on one objective—to find Colonel Matsunaga! Kimiko stood cringing under his angry cursing and realized a great deal of relief when he ordered her left in a small anteroom.

Pacing around his office, Colonel Yosuki centered his efforts on tracing and compiling information on Sonya. Memory stood him well, because he clearly remembered the Russian girl named Sonya Petrovna who had been brought to his office by the solicitor, Feng Hu. As a result of that humiliating encounter with Colonel Matsunaga, Colonel Yosuki had his investigators make a file on her, complete with picture and pertinent data. He was aware of the ties of love—and if this was the same woman the Japanese girl claimed visited Colonel Matsunaga—to find and

180

torture the woman would be the way to find Colonel Matsunaga. He had already ordered Sonya Petrovna arrested and brought to him immediately. However, before he had finished inspecting his file, an assistant informed him that Sonya Petrovna had obtained a visa and was now in Peitaiho Beach.

"What do I care where she is," he screamed. "I said arrest her. Bring her here. If this Kimiko identifies her, I'll have her arms stretched till she tells where that traitor is."

The assistant jumped to obey the Colonel's wrathful order but stayed his exit at Colonel Yosuki's command. "Wait, we'll have Kimiko identify her right now."

His eyes had alighted on a picture of Sonya Petrovna which was laying among the papers on his desk. Scooping it up, he beckoned the assistant to follow and then entered the anteroom. Colonel Yosuki was not prepared for the sorrowful scene he found there! In a pool of blood, Kimiko lay on the floor—a gilt-handled dagger through her heart! She had taken her own life in true Japanese fashion. Cursing, Colonel Yosuki jerked a crumpled piece of paper from her limp hand and found it was a picture of Colonel Matsunaga.

"Hold that order of arrest for Sonya Petrovna," Colonel Yosuki muttered coldly to the assistant who was looking sorrowfully at the pitiful sight before him.

"You mean let her go, sir?" asked the assistant, somewhat confused.

"That's what I mean. Our evidence lies dead in front of you," snapped Colonel Yosuki, letting his temper fly unchecked. "Get this mess cleaned up."

When the wretched Kimiko plunged the dagger through her heart, she did not know that by taking her own life she had saved the life of the woman who originally created her misery. In one blundering stroke, she preserved the very cause of her own death—and as is often the case in the ways of life and love, a quirk of fate ironically cheated her. However, she died realizing one mission of her twisted mind. The bloodhounds were loose on the trail of the man she once loved, and the extent of that vital hunt raged beyond her wildest dreams. The fire ignited by the match of Colonel Yosuki spread spontaneously, leaping unchecked through all ranks of the Japanese military, until even the lowest private and the highest general were aware of the China-wide hunt for Paul York. Priority dispatches from the Supreme Command in Japan carried curt orders to all commands: *"Apprehend Colonel Matsunaga, alias Paul York."*

21

Good luck favored Paul when he left the train and went back a few kilometers to Tangshan without incident. Although he possessed a valid visa which allowed him to travel this area as a Chinaman, he realized it might take more than credentials to convince the Japanese in their present state of turmoil, so he was relieved not to meet any Japanese sentries.

It was nearly midnight when he reached the pre-designated corner in Tangshan. A good-sized city, Tanshan was a logical place from which the Chinese-American underground could operate. Paul had been instrumental in organizing and manipulating the secret channels there, but ironically enough, he did not know the exact location of the underground headquarters. Furthermore, he was not aware of the procedure for making contacts, because he had always made it a point to stay away from such areas. He was now compelled to wait for his contact with Huang Chu.

He began to feel a little uneasy after waiting patiently for the first hour. He did not doubt Chu's efficiency, nor did he once consider the possibility of confused arrangements, but he did linger on the hazard of Chu's abduction by the Japanese. Roving Japanese policemen passed him numerous times but paid little heed to the old Chinaman who sat cross-legged in the shadow of a building.

Paul's anxiety was approaching a feverish pitch when he finally discerned a Chinaman stumbling aimlessly in his direction. Closer scrutiny proved him to be Chu, but Paul sat still, waiting for directions. Chu bowed before him and acted as if he were apologizing for stepping on him in the dark. "Follow me. Enter the house where I stop," whispered Chu.

Since Chu had moved on, Paul got to his feet and hurried to keep him in sight in the dim light. Their destination turned out to be a mud hut on the outskirts of town. Placed among many others of like appearance, Paul could never have found it without Chu's directions, but Chu made his stop evident, and there was no possibility of error. Yet, when Paul pushed open the door and found himself in the tiny room, he was sure Chu had blundered. A single candle burned dully on a rough table, and beside the table sat an aged Chinese woman. She glared at him with sunken eyes and made no effort to speak or move as he pulled the door shut. Then, without so much as the flicker of an eyelid, she jerked her head in the direction of the door across the room. Paul skirted the wrinkled woman in the chair and opened the door. To his utter amazement, he found nothing but a closet with filthy clothes hanging from a bent ridge pole.

Dumbfounded, he turned on the old lady who watched him from her chair. His vicious countenance should have frightened the devil himself, but the expressionless woman only raised her arm and waved it toward the clothes. Understanding the possibility of her meaning, Paul parted the ragged clothes, stooped, and stepped between them. There, in the darkness, he discovered a wooden stairway leading down to places unknown. As he felt his way along the stairs, he heard the closet door close. The old lady had moved from her chair.

At the bottom of the stairway, Paul practically fell through another door and found himself in a large cellar illuminated by a mass of candles. There, sitting at a table and grinning broadly, was Chu, and beside him lounged Tian Wei, another of Paul's trusted Chinese aides.

As Wei jumped to his feet to welcome Paul, Chu laughed, "Did the old woman scare you?"

"Good to see you again, Wei," said Paul, shaking his hand and then taking a seat at the table. "Yes, the old vulture rather bothered me. Where did you ever pick her up?"

"A trusted soul with a venomous hate for Japanese. She's our eyes and ears in Tangshan," offered Wei.

"Does she haunt houses in her spare time?" quipped Paul.

"For a man who has a noose around his neck, you joke a lot," Chu answered dryly.

"Keeps up my moral," laughed Paul. "By the way, how did you get here, Chu?"

"By the escape hole," answered Chu, nodding in the direction of a blanket hung over the entrance to a tunnel. "It leads to the railroad back a little ways from here."

"So this is your headquarters?"

"Hardly," explained Wei. "We have places like this scattered all over the area. You know the old saying about never putting all your eggs in one basket."

"Not to change the subject," Chu interrupted seriously, "but Mister Paul, you are hot like a firecracker. This place is boiling for your skin. I suggest we get started."

Paul had taken off the long, ragged Chinese coat, exposing two revolvers nestled in holsters under his armpits. He moved to a washbasin and began scrubbing the greasepaint from his face. "Yes, Chu, I expect you're right. Think I'd better assume a bit younger manner for the rest of this trip, so I'll get this makeup off. Don't want to be encumbered by old age and a long coat if I have to run."

Chu and Wei could not resist a chuckle at the pun dropped as easily by this man who joked about danger and thought about death as a fate for others. They watched and admired, and they were only two of the many Chinese who praised Paul York—an American with nerves of steel and a heart of gold. He understood the Chinese and they understood him.

Soon the three were clustered around a rough map which Chu had unfolded on the table. Both Chu and Wei knew the country and, taking the initiative, Wei began to explain the plan of action by directing attention to the map with a sharp stick.

"Paul, Chu will have to make this escape with you because he knows the way. Your destination is here." Wei placed the stick on the map. "A small flat area, here among the mountains where planes can land. It's sort of a strip, and we have used it a number of times for pickups and contacts with American planes. It's about two hundred fifty to three hundred kilometers as the crow flies."

"My god, can't we arrange a pickup closer than that?"

"Hardly," answered Wei. "We cannot depend on an adequate explanation by radio in picking some unknown place. Our people in Chungking know the exact location of this place, and it will be simple to request a plane for there. All we have to do is radio the time. They have always been right on."

185

"But the area is also under Japanese occupation," Paul pointed out.

"True," agreed Wei. "But there is a minimum of danger in those mountains."

"It's settled, then," stated Paul. "Now, how do we get there?"

Wei smiled. "By foot mostly, unless you are fortunate enough to slip aboard a train running from Peking to Chengting. The railroad runs from Peking to Paoting to Chengting, along the edge of the mountain ranges. On this side of that railroad, the country is flat with little or no vegetation. On the other side, it is all mountains. Going overland from here to the railroad won't be bad, and by striking a line direct, you should hit the railroad between Peking and Paoting. Then, if you're lucky, and I do mean lucky, because we cannot be sure trains are even running that stretch, you can catch a train and ride to Paoting. You should leave the train before it enters Paoting, because Japs are pretty thick in that area. When you reach Paoting, you are only about fifty to sixty kilometers to the pickup point. That is, if you take a direct line through the group of foothills."

"I see," said Paul. "We have a hell of a long way to walk, even if we catch a train in between."

"Right," emphasized Wei. "I don't see any other way. You have to go for it."

Paul nodded agreement. "If that's it, we'd better get started before sunup. But first, let's get a message off to Chungking requesting the plane. Is your set here?"

"We have it tucked away out in the valley," said Wei. "I'll take care of the message. When do you want the plane?"

"Think that is pretty much up to you and Chu," said Paul.

"It must be figured closely. Food will be a problem, and you can't wait too long for fear of discovery," calculated Wei. He remained silent as he thought about it. "I figure if you work hard and keep going, you can make it in a week—even if no train. So I'll give you eight days and have the plane there at dawn, nine days from tomorrow."

Wei looked at Paul and Chu as if waiting for their okay on the decision, whereupon Paul smiled and said, "Whatever you say, Chu. I'm just along for the ride."

"We will make it," grinned Chu.

"Right, I'll send the message tomorrow night," decided Wei.

"Fine," acknowledged Paul. He opened the old bag he had been carrying and produced a number of papers which he sorted carefully. Then he handed some to Chu. "Here are your credentials. On this trip you are going to be a Chinese furrier. I'll be a Russian."

The next morning found a Russian fur buyer and his Chinese associate trudging along an isolated cart trail. They looked to the northwest and the broad expanse of nothingness lying there and paid little heed to the sleepy town of Tangshan which dwindled from sight to their rear. They were dressed unobtrusively as professional travelers and carried small bags attached to their shoulders. The bags held water and food, which would last if they were careful, and their pockets held money they hoped would buy more.

Paul and Chu plodded onward. Ever vigilant and cautious, they catnapped at intervals, usually at night, and one watched while the other slept. Food and water had not been a problem, because they carried food enough to last and found some water to boil for replenishment. The journey, however, was giving them a physical beating, and the constant threat of capture preyed heavily on their endurance. Also, there were many times when Paul insisted they were hopelessly lost, but after checking his compass and visible landmarks, Chu would say he knew they were right. Their only contact with civilization was an occasional farmer or a group of dwellings where the Chinese inhabitants cared not who the travelers were or where they were going. However, Chu warned that once they hit the railroad, Japanese would be found in abundance.

On the fourth night out from Tangshan, Chu suggested they get a good night's sleep in order that they may face the obstacles they were sure to encounter, but Paul objected on the grounds they had to make the plane contact on time without question. If he missed the plane, Paul was doomed to weeks and possibly months of hide and seek with the Japanese while new arrangements were made to pick him up—or he could make his way to Chungking through Japanese-infested areas. The alternative was death. Consequently, they pushed on—cursing their tired muscles which ached from hours of walking without rest.

Their first reward came the next day when Chu was able to recognize mountains far in the distance. When he said the railroad would be along the side of those mountains, Paul was jubilant, but his enthusiasm was squelched when Chu said, "Don't get excited. We good many kilometers from those mountains. Better be train when we get there."

Chu's piecemeal English prompted Paul to say, "Stop the English, Chinese only."

The sun was dropping on the horizon when the two men sat down on the hot rails of the track. They turned tired eyes to the windswept areas of the northeast, where the track dwindled from sight, and prayed for the train they knew had to come. Paul insisted the Japanese were supposed to be keeping this track open, and the rails appeared bright from constant use, but this was little consolation. It might be a week before a train passed, and it might be going the wrong direction. Also, they still had the problem of getting aboard the train if it did come. A train had to be their salvation. They knew it had to come, and they must find a spot to board it, some place where it slowed down or, preferably, where it might stop. To climb abroad while the train moved slowly might be possible, but it would invite attention. Plodding along the track in the direction of Paoting, their prayers were answered when they spied a cluster of mud huts near the track. Aware of the train system in China, Paul and Chu hugged each other, because they knew trains stopped at such places which were isolated from the main terminals.

Their next objective was to remain undetected and still get close enough to the settlement to mount the train when it stopped. With this aim in mind, they worked their way by crawling and crouching to within throwing distance of the mud huts. They picked a clump of weeds near the track and lay down to wait and pray for the sight of a train. Peering across the tracks from his concealed position, Paul could see naked children romping near the houses and guessed correctly the farmers living there were slaves to the soil they tilled for survival. Turning to comment about the children, he discovered Chu's eyes closed in exhausted slumber. Paul did not begrudge Chu the sleep, for he needed it to finish their journey. Paul also found himself dozing, in spite of his desperate effort to carry on the vigil for both of them.

The night passed, and as the next day wore on, Paul's hopes dwindled. He dozed more and more and finally resorted to scratching designs in the earth to keep awake. Then, his benumbed brain heard the pronounced sound of a train! Though he had been looking down the track, his eyes had not registered what he was seeing. Startled, and thinking he was surely dreaming, he saw the unmistakable trail of smoke hovering in the air over a puffing engine. A train was approaching, and it was headed toward Paoting!

Insanely stimulated by their stroke of luck, Paul vigorously shook Chu, but he lay as if a man dead. Paul slapped and beat him until he opened bleary eyes. As Chu looked groggily about and collected his senses, Paul began giving him their plans. They had no time to waste, for it was possible the train would only slow down and not stop at all.

"The train, Chu, the train—it's coming," Paul breathed hard. "Now listen carefully. We'll lie right here and stay out of sight. If it stops, we are close enough to slip aboard. If it keeps moving, stake everything on grabbing the last car. Once aboard, we can't keep together for awhile, so meet me at the rearmost part of the train after a few kilometers. If we lose each other, it's each man for himself and at least one of us *has to meet that plane!* I think maybe I can find the location of the airfield if I lose you. Got it?" Chu nodded agreement.

His eyes glued to the approaching train, Paul said grimly, "With this week's growth of beard and as dirty as we are, we should be well-camouflaged and fit perfectly with the local passengers."

The train churned past, leaving a cloud of smoke and soot in its wake, and then ground to a stop before the huts. Instantly eager to stretch their cramped muscles, occupants of the train jumped to the ground and began milling around while the naked children ran among them like wild animals. Multiplying this anxiety, Paul noticed some of the passengers were Japanese soldiers but reasoned they were no more dangerous than any of the other travelers.

"We go now," Chu whispered nervously, starting to rise.

"Wait," snapped Paul, reaching out and pressing him back to the ground. "Wait till they start boarding the train. No one will

189

pay any attention to us then—they'll be too busy stuffing themselves into the cars." Even as Paul spoke, the train whistle sounded and the passengers began mounting the coaches.

"All right, Chu. Saunter naturally into the group and climb aboard. Take the far car. I'll wait a few seconds and grab the near one," instructed Paul. He watched Chu disappear into the crowd and hastened to make his own entry. For all the attention he drew, Paul could have been riding the train all the way from Peking, and he breathed a sigh of relief when he had settled himself into an inconspicuous corner of the coach. If Chu had managed as well, the big stumbling block of their treacherous journey had passed.

After days of walking, the steady beat of rolling wheels eating away the kilometers pleased Paul, resting his mind and body. Presently he was sound asleep, nodding with the roll of the train. What awakened him he never knew, but he came to with a start. Terrified that he might have overslept, he looked at his watch. Although it was starting to grow dark, his watch told him he had been sleeping less than an hour. He must hurry—Chu would be waiting.

Paul found Chu alone and slumped over the platform railing on the rear of the train. "Afraid you no make it," Chu greeted Paul with obvious relief.

"I fell asleep," explained Paul. "Chu, this train won't travel far after dark—they never do."

"Yes," agreed Chu. "Getting close to Paoting. Thirty, maybe forty, kilometers."

"Passengers will be checked at Paoting."

"Yes," Chu agreed emphatically. "We jump before Paoting."

Cursing silently, Paul muttered, "At this speed! I can think of a simpler way to commit suicide."

"It will slow down when we enter Paoting," Chu said. He definitely was not in the mood for joking.

Chu's irritable response closed the conversation. The two men sat down on the platform to await their hectic departure from the train and said nothing as time slipped by. Darkness moved in and shrouded the train in gloom. Its presence prompted Paul to reason that at least one factor was in their favor—no one would see them leap into the night.

190

That leap took place when the train broke speed to enter Paoting. Paul watched Chu's form spin into the dark and disappear. He followed by placing his hand on the railing and vaulting to the roadbed. The train was traveling faster than he calculated. He landed on his feet but was slapped to the ground, rolling over and over down the roadbed and hitting something hard. Excruciating pain shot through his ankle, leaving it numb. Cursing vehemently, he staggered to his feet. The thought of injury goaded him not nearly as much as the fact he would fail to make his goal—to meet that plane which dared not wait for him. He slumped to the ground and gingerly began removing his shoe.

Paul's curses brought Chu running to his side. "Are you hurt?" he inquired breathlessly.

"Hit my ankle on a rock or something," gritted Paul. "Don't think it's broken, but it's badly bruised or sprained, cause it's swelling like hell. Here, give me a hand. We'll bind it up."

Chu kneeled to remove Paul's shoe and stocking while Paul pulled off his shirt and undershirt. He ripped his undershirt into strips. "Here, Chu, wrap these around my ankle tight as you can."

"If you can't walk, we never make plane."

"We'll make it, we have to," Paul said between clenched teeth. "Pull it tighter, damn it. Pull it tight as you can."

Their temporary operation completed, Chu helped Paul to his feet. Paul was forced to let Chu help him walk, and he put his arm around Chu's shoulder. In this manner, they struggled to skirt the town as fast as possible. They wanted to be a good distance from Japanese-filled Paoting when sun-up caught them. From this point on, Chu knew the trails well and led Paul directly toward the nearby mountains. Required by Paul's injury to stop more than they should have, they were only to the mountains when daybreak overtook them. Progress on the steep trails of the foothills presented a forbidding obstacle to a crippled man, but other obstacles were also piling up against them. They were out of food, and the mountains would offer them nothing more than water. For the exhausted men, water would help, but only iron-willed stubbornness could carry them through the remaining forty-eight hours of walking uphill without nourishment.

Paul's ankle had swollen until the flesh bulged over the

edges of the bandage, and the sickening blue color of the flesh told them the circulation of blood was being seriously impeded. Still, Paul refused to let Chu remove the bandage. In its present condition, his entire leg was numb, and he could maneuver it like a wooden limb. He hobbled on with determination generated by his long-standing desire to win.

Grimly intent on the steep trail ahead of them, they were not aware of the close proximity of another person until they were hailed by a shrill shout given in Chinese. They turned to see a Chinese boy prodding a small donkey up the trial. The donkey was pulling a two-wheeled cart filled with straw. The boy evidently noticed their labored progress and called to them to wait. When the boy reached them, the normal greetings were made, and Chu asked if his crippled friend might ride. He explained they were fur buyers headed for the interior and that Paul had just fallen and sprained his ankle. In turn, Chu learned the boy lived in a small settlement further up the mountain and was returning from Paoting after peddling his vegetables there the day before. They were headed in the same direction, and the boy agreed after Chu settled the matter with a couple of coins while Paul managed to crawl upon the cart.

Constant prodding and haranguing by the boy failed to impress the nonchalant donkey, which moved at its own slow pace. However, Paul and Chu did not complain, for their progress was fast by comparison to their previously arduous walking. As the donkey plodded along, Chu took up a low conversation with Paul. By now, he was quite sure of the boy's exact destination, and he informed Paul that, even though it took them slightly off course, they would make time by riding nearly the entire distance. Further, he estimated the boy had timed his journey to reach home shortly after dark. They could leave him at dark and take up the proper direction to their own destination. Chu estimated they would have twenty or thirty kilometers.

Settled on their plan of action, silence fell over the group, and the only sounds were the wheezing donkey and the boy's shouts echoing through the valley. Throughout the day, all went well, but as darkness began to settle over the valley floor and Chu began looking for a likely spot to make their departure, an unexpected event occurred.

From the confines of a darkened thicket, two Japanese sentries stepped into the middle of the trail and halted the travelers. Both held their rifles in a position of readiness, and as one of them stepped forward to better scrutinize the party in the dim light, the other kept his rifle pointed menacingly at the group. Paul and Chu remained silent, awaiting developments.

Evidently recognizing the boy, the sentry focused his attention on Chu, who stood beside the cart, and demanded in poor Chinese, "Who are you? Where do you go?"

Not sure of his ground, Chu hesitated. At this hesitation, the boy spoke up. "They're fur buyers. The man in the cart hurt his leg, and I gave him a ride. They paid me well, too, and—"

"Shut up," barked the sentry. Then, shaking his rifle at Chu, he ordered curtly, "Your papers?"

Chu rummaged through his pocket and handed his credentials to the sentry. As he did so, the other sentry stepped forward with his rife cocked and ready, waiting while his associate inspected the papers. Producing a flashlight, the sentry studied the credentials. Then he snapped out the light and handed them back to Chu.

"Seems to be in order," he growled dubiously. "But what are fur buyers doing here at this time of the year?"

Paul took the initiative. "Merely setting up our contacts," he explained calmly in Chinese.

"That—you'll have to explain to the Commanding Officer of our garrison," the sentry snapped. "Where are your credentials?"

"Right here," answered Paul. He reached inside his shirt to obtain his papers, and the sentry stepped closer to receive them.

A series of blinding flashes followed the sentry's sudden expression of bewilderment, for Paul fired his pistol point blank at the two Japanese. Both sentries crumbled to the ground from the burst of fire. Panic-stricken, the Chinese boy screamed and bounded into the darkness, leaving the donkey standing in the middle of the trail.

Paul clammered to the ground. "Knew I was going to have to shoot those bastards. We can't stand a delay of any kind, and we wouldn't have a chance under a lot of questioning. Let's get out of here. Don't know how many soldiers are in this garrison, but all

193

of them will be beating the brush in this area looking for us. If they heard the shots at the garrison, it's minutes."

"You're right," agreed Chu, jumping to help Paul, who teetered on his bad leg.

Contrary to Paul's expectation, the day's ride had not helped his ankle for the now-needed purpose of walking. By not using it, his ankle had lost its numbness and become tender. Now, his every step resulted in agonizing pain, but the graveness of their situation pushed him on. Paul and Chu doggedly fought their way through the scrub brush, finally emerging into a long narrow valley bounded by high, jagged cliffs. The black of night was smothering all landmarks, and the first concern was to establish their location.

"Chu, do you know where we are?"

"Not sure. Valleys look alike at night. This may be one I know later."

"And if it isn't?"

Chu shrugged his shoulders wearily. "Make no difference now. No time to look. Tomorrow is last day."

"I know tomorrow is our last day. Suppose this is the valley. Where are we? How far are we from our contact point?" Paul asked in a tired voice.

"Don't know—quite a ways. Through this valley and over the hill," Chu answered without conviction.

"All right—this is it," Paul said resolutely. "We have to gamble everything on that fact. Let's go."

"Wait," Chu whispered. "Hear that?"

In the distance they heard the unmistakable sound of running feet and cursing voices. The hunt was on! Prolonged movement by Paul and Chu would surely attract attention. They must find a place to hide until the search subsided.

"We hide in the bush in the valley."

"No. That's where they're going to look," calculated Paul. His eyes were piercing the darkness, searching the rocky cliffs. "There, up there on that overhang. It's big enough for the two of us, and we can lay flat on top of it. It's too obvious—they'll never look there." He stopped, and then as an afterthought, added, "By tomorrow they'll have questioned the boy. They will know what they are looking for—us. Now they don't."

194

Paul's predictions proved accurate. From their lofty position, Paul and Chu followed the sounds of the search until the
soldiers assembled and marched off. The rest of the night they
forced their beaten bodies forward, and by morning commanded
a view of the valley from the rim of the high divide at the extreme
end. From there they watched the actions of the refreshed pur-
suers. There could be no mistaking the seriousness of the search.
They were combing every foot of the valley floor, but paying little
attention to the high rim of the valley. This gave Paul and Chu
the opportunity they needed. Completely exhausted, they
needed rest and agreed now was the time to take it. They drank
freely from a little spring, found a crevice in the rocks, and
relaxed. Throughout the morning, they took turns watching and
sleeping. Finally, it became obvious the Japanese searchers had
given up and left the area.

Paul could think of only one thing, as if by perpetual concen-
tration he might make it come true. This was the right valley—
this had to be the right valley! Toward dark, when they stopped
on the rim of a shallow valley, Chu screamed. They had made it!
Paul stood transfixed. Reverently, he turned his face to the heav-
ens, and an expression of gratitude crossed his countenance,
lighting his drawn features and leaving a film over his eyes. His
eyes closed, and Paul York's powerful body crumpled to the
ground, unconscious.

Chu dragged Paul's limp form under a tree, placed his
blouse under Paul's head, and went in search of water. Paul's
stupor did not particularly perturb Chu, for he knew it resulted
from exhaustion multiplied by the unrelenting pain he had been
forced to endure as a result of his bad leg. Paul needed sleep
more than any other tonic, and since they had reached their goal,
it could be allowed without neglect of their mission. For hours,
Chu kept watch. Finally Paul stirred, opened his eyes, and
raised his head from the ground. It was dark, and he kept rub-
bing his eyes in an effort to bring Chu into focus.

"How you feeling?"

"Guess I collapsed," muttered Paul. "We better move on."

"We are only a little ways," emphasized Chu. "I'll wake you
in time. Go to sleep."

Paul needed no urging. He promptly dropped his head to the

ground and fell into a deep slumber. For Paul, it seemed that his eyes had just closed when Chu awakened him.

"Night coming up. Now to the contact point."

"I guess so," Paul answered groggily.

He tried to rise, but his whole body felt stiff and heavy. Chu had to help him to his feet and practically carry him for the first hundred yards. Eventually, Paul managed to help himself and hobbled along with Chu's assistance.

When they broke into the clearing, the sun had begun its fight to remove the darkness. A deep haze hung over the grassy area Chu pointed out as the spot where the plane would land. Trees bordered both sides of the narrow strip of open country which began at the foot of a small mountain and ended abruptly in a mass of heavy trees.

"Is this the place?" Paul asked. "How they can land a plane here is beyond me."

"They do. Few people come here. It makes a good place."

"Obviously. The grass is knee deep in places," observed Paul. "Listen!"

They heard the spasmodic roar of powerful engines. Paul was wondering why the roar of the plane would vary in volume when he caught sight of it weaving among the peaks, at times turning to evade the towering crests. Since the plane was flying extremely low, the mountains and valleys were deflecting the sound to produce a weird effect.

"It's a transport," moaned Paul. "How will they ever land a hearse like that in this cabbage patch? There's a brisk wind blowing down the landing area toward the mountain end—it might help if they can bring it in past the mountains. Chu! Run out in the middle and wave your arms to show them how to land! They have to come in past the mountains to take advantage of the wind, and they might not be able to tell it up there."

Chu ran into the open area and began waiving his hat in long sweeps from the mountain end of the strip to the tree-blocked end. The big plane came rolling past the side of the mountain, dipped down into the valley only a few feet above the ground, and zipped past Chu with a deafening roar. As it did so, the wings wobbled back and forth. They had understood! The pilot pulled the plane up in a steep climb and winged over to make his approach. The landing gear came down as the plane slipped out of sight behind the peak. Paul next saw the plane settling in past the mountain. Under full flaps, the enormous ship looked like a gigantic bird as it careened crazily to miss the mountainside. The next instant it hit the end of the open area with a resounding smack and came skidding through the tall grass with the brakes on. Chu scurried for cover. Paul unconsciously crossed his fingers as the plane raced past him. He knew the plane could never stop before ripping into the trees. What Paul did not know was the pilot had been there before. With propellers reversed, he suddenly released the brake on one wheel. The plane spun around at the edge of the trees and came to a stop. Chu ran to help Paul hobble out to meet the plane now taxiing back along its path. As the plane rolled to a stop, the door opened, and a man in a flying suit jumped out. He came running to give Chu a hand with his crippled burden.

The man halted in front of them. "Jesus Christ! Can this be *the* handsome and dapper Paul York?"

"Burl!" exclaimed Paul. "Might have known you'd come."

Burl grabbed Paul's free arm and helped propel him toward the plane. "Sure, who did you think would come? Nobody else would bother to pick you up. Wait till you see who's herding this crate."

"Dave?"

"Right," nodded Burl. "What happened? Did they wing you?"

Paul forced a smile. "Try jumping from a speeding train sometime. I want to be around to pick up your remains."

"Never in too bad a shape to be nasty," countered Burl. "God, you're a mess."

Paul grimaced and cursed as they lifted him into the plane. For the first time, Burl turned his attention to Chu, who stepped back from the ship. "Chu! So help me, I didn't recognize you. Come on, get aboard."

Before Chu could answer, Paul called from his position in the doorway. "Chu, take a message to Sonya in Peitaiho Beach. Tell her I made it."

"Oh, that's it," perceived Burl. "Hell, he isn't going to walk, is he? Chu, have you ever used a parachute?"

"*No.*"

Burl laughed at Chu's very definite answer, for it implied far more than the one word he used. "Well, my friend, you'll have your first chance, cause we're giving you a lift and throwing you out where you can get to the beach. Know just the place—Dave and I have tried it out a couple of times. Get abroad."

Chu hesitated, whereupon Burl settled the question by grabbing Chu's hand and pushing him to the doorway where the flight sergeant reached down and pulled him in. Burl was the last one on. He secured the door and waved his readiness to David, who was shouting greetings to Paul from his seat at the controls. David straightened in his seat, eased the throttles forward, and the ship bumped along the rough grassland, taxiing to the end of the open strip.

Burl turned his attention to his passengers. "Soon as we hit the air, the sergeant and I will get some hot coffee and sandwiches down you two, and fit Chu with a pack of silk and a bag of food." The pathetic look on Chu's face indicated his reaction to Burl's words.

The plane swung around. David shouted, "Tie everything down back there, including yourselves. This is going to be a close pitch."

The engines took up a screaming roar and the plane vibrated like a fluttering leaf. The locked wheels skipped along in little jumps under the powerful thrust of the speeding propellers. David released the brakes and the plane jumped forward, throwing the passengers sideways against the safety belts of their hard metal bucket seats. The tail came up immediately as the ship tore through the grassy field. There was a breathless minute and then a sigh of relief as the tail dropped and the ship rolled easily. They were airborne. David cut the throttles to cruising speed and the roar of the engines subsided to a steady drone.

"Didn't take her off that time," David called back. "Just retracted the landing gear and pulled the wheels off the ground."

"He's telling me!" grumbled Burl as he unfastened his safety belt. "I was looking out the window. The damn fool didn't fly over those trees, he flew between 'um. He's a flyer—the best."

The sergeant began breaking out food and coffee for Paul and Chu, while Burl went forward to inform David of their necessary sweep through north China to dump Chu. The army lieutenant flying co-pilot for David was handling the navigation, so he proceeded to plot the new course under Burl's management. Burl wanted to be sure they dropped Chu at the right point, because he and David always used a certain spot on some of their trips into Tientsin. He knew a low jump at that point would be neither dangerous or picked up by curious eyes.

Returning to the rear, Burl confronted Paul. "We've got a mattress right here on the deck which you're going to use as soon as you suck in some more of that coffee. And I want to get that bandage off your ankle before gangrene sets in. Those sadistic bastards we have for doctors may want to saw your whole damn leg off."

Burl spread some blankets on the mattress and rolled one up for a pillow. Next, he helped Paul onto the mattress, cut away Paul's pant leg, and removed the makeshift bandage.

"Boy! What a beaut!" exclaimed Burl. "How you ever walked on that is a mystery to me! If it isn't broken, it should be."

Burl's probing brought a burst of profanity from Paul. "Damn you, Burl. You must be sadistic. You wouldn't know the difference between a broken leg and a broken neck!"

Burl ignored Paul's blasphemy. "You may as well get some sleep. We're going off course to drop Chu, so we'll be in the air quite awhile. Sergeant, wash off this stinking leg. Then get that bottle of alcohol and rub it down."

As the sergeant carried out his instructions, Burl turned to Chu. He hauled out a parachute and fitted it on the terrified Chu, giving instructions in the "simple" manipulation of the ripcord. Then he strapped a bag of food to Chu's stomach and slapped him on the back.

"My friend, you are now ready to float through the air with the greatest of ease. Just like a bird," said Burl solemnly. "Don't you agree, Paul?"

Chu failed to see the humor in Burl's words, and Paul did not answer, because he was sound asleep. It was too bad Paul slept, because he might have witnessed the comedy which transpired when Chu jumped.

"Ten minutes and Chu gets off," called David. "We're giving him about two thousand feet."

Burl opened the side door and led Chu to the open exit. Chu's heavy breathing could be heard above the blast of the slipstream, and his face assumed an ashen hue as he looked through the door into nothingness. Poor Chu. His feet worked adversely, moving him father away from the door instead of closer.

Faced with a pitiful plight, Chu began to plead with Burl. "Mebby it no good. Take back—I walk."

Intent on his watch, Burl pretended to ignore him. Then Burl looked up, pointed calmly to the exit and said, "Look, Chu, isn't that a pretty color out there?"

Chu's eyes followed the direction of Burl's fingers and, with the aid of Burl's foot, his body followed his eyes. Burl stepped to the door, leaned out into the slipstream, and shouted in his best form of dry wit, "Oh, yes, Chu, don't forget to pull the ripcord."

A white umbrella blossomed over Chu's hurtling form, swinging him gently toward the earth.

22

Arriving in Peitaiho Beach without mishap, Sonya was gleefully greeted by Netti and Zota. After their fond embrace, the girls escorted Sonya and Katilka to the cottage they had rented from them. It was only a few blocks away from the one occupied by the Seivbergs and Ruriks and built the same—a structure facing the beach.

Netti was eager to hear from Sonya all the many things she knew Sonya had to tell and she had trouble subduing her impatience. She and Zota finally got Sonya and Katilka settled in their cottage and lured Sonya away. As they trekked to the beach, Netti was asking questions which Sonya purposely ignored. By now Zota had been extended the privilege of knowing about Mr. X, and she shared Netti's anxiety.

At the beach, Netti brought her questioning to a head by saying determinedly, "Now, tell us all about it—Mr. X, I mean. And that ring. What does that mean?"

"Paul, Mr. X, gave it to me," Sonya answered in an evasive manner.

"But what does it mean?" Netti persisted. Seeing the impish twinkle in Sonya's eyes, she said knowingly, "You're engaged. Is that it?"

"Maybe," Sonya smiled. The way she said it told Netti and Zota the answer was yes.

Sonya finally conceded to tell them more, provided they promised not to interrupt. Zota and Netti agreed eagerly. Whereupon, Sonya began with the departure of the girls from Tientsin and carefully told all her experiences until her arrival in Peitaiho Beach. Sonya went into ecstasy over the most minute details, meticulously describing her dresses and her wonderful times with Paul. Naturally, she left out the chapter on her intimacies with Paul and skirted them gracefully, thus creating only the impression of a passionate romance culminated by restraint.

Throughout the story, Zota and Netti spaced Sonya's descriptions by rapturous sighs and gasps of amazement.

Properly impressed, Zota said, "Gosh, Sonya, it's so thrilling! Honest, it's like a fairy tale. I envy you. Are you going to get married?"

"I'm afraid that will be awhile yet," Sonya replied.

"I'm so happy for you, Sonya," said Netti. "I'm honest in saying I have some misgivings about it, but if it's the way you want it, I'm with you and happy for you."

"Thanks, Netti," Sonya answered warmly and inferred by her tone that she wanted to change the subject. "Now what about you two? I've told you everything that's happened to me since you left, and it's fair you should tell me what you've been doing up here on the sunny beach. I hear there are scads of men."

"Yes, plenty of men," exclaimed Zota. "We've been having a great time swimming, dancing, hiking. Haven't you noticed our suntans? And Netti has been dating a new fellow."

Sonya turned to Netti. "You never mentioned anyone in your letters. Do I know him?"

"No, but he is eager to meet you," Netti explained. "We date a little, but it doesn't amount to much. His name is Arturro Ramon. He goes by Arty."

"You'll meet him tonight," offered Zota. "The group is getting together."

As Netti and Zota departed, Sonya said pointedly, "Remember, no date for me."

The group, as Zota called them, showed up in the evening on Sonya's porch. She knew all of them except the one man Netti quickly introduced as Arty. Sonya was seductively tucked into a white silk dress, and it was obvious Arty was immediately taken in by this sensuous creature he had wanted to meet.

Netti followed the progress of the introduction and watched Arty's reaction. She saw the spark in his eyes which evidenced his spontaneous desire for Sonya. She was thankful Sonya was pledged to Paul and would not pick up the clue, but she could not erase the knowledge of men's reactions to Sonya. She wondered what Sonya would do now when Arty pursued his advances. It was inevitable he would, sooner or later.

The group arrived at the little club on the beach where there was dance music provided free by some locals who just liked to play their instruments. As usual, the group mixed up the dances with different partners, but Arty kept going back to Sonya. She cautioned him concerning the lack of manners involved in his actions. When he guided her into a darkened corner and dropped his hand lower than good manners decreed, she jarred him back to being a gentleman by her well-stocked knowledge of curt phrases for such circumstances. The party ended with Arty noticeably quiet.

It was not until the party was over that Netti had the opportunity to talk frankly to Sonya. Sonya and Katilka were staying with the Ruriks the first night, and Sonya had gone home with Netti. They were preparing for bed.

"Sonya, do you have a conscience?" Netti asked as she stood at the mirror brushing her hair.

"Of course. What makes you ask?"

"No, you don't have. If you did, it would be tormenting you to death right now," Netti went on coldly. "Honestly, I wonder after the way you carried on tonight if you really love Paul York."

Netti's reference to her love for Paul knifed Sonya in a vulnerable spot. She took offense immediately and snapped sarcastically, "What's the matter? Are you jealous of Mr. Ramon? Surely that isn't possible the first day—and after you told me you weren't serious and didn't care."

Netti took Sonya to task, gently and firmly, for her deliberate speech carried wisdom, as well as affection. "If you'll think a moment, you know I'm not the type to care about men—at least not yet. Sure, maybe some day I shall find the one I don't want you to play with, and I'll scratch your eyes out if you do, but Arty isn't the one, so let's just skip that aspect. Right now, I'm interested in you and Paul. I'm sure he is the finest thing that ever happened to you."

Sonya was pensive. "I didn't mean to be sarcastic and say nasty things to you. It kind of hurt when you intimated I don't love Paul. Believe me, I do. I've never been serious with anyone else and Arty is no exception. But I'm not going to sit and mope. I'm not the type, and I won't let being here without Paul ruin my time here."

"Just remember, you know Paul can be vicious, and he

would never understand your going out with another man. I'm guessing before you leave here you'll be having dates. You better be careful."

Netti was right. In the days that followed, Sonya and Arty would free themselves from the group and walk along the beach. Sonya never evidenced too much enthusiasm for Arturro and carried him as passive entertainment. Despite this fact, she was forced to acknowledge his genial nature and the pleasant times he provided for her, so she submitted to his primary advances much as one paid a check for services rendered. She was well capable of handling herself, and early in the game she gave Arty a thorough understanding of her position. Nevertheless, she discovered soon enough that she had not emphasized her point sufficiently.

On their usual stroll, Arty suggested they leave the beach and view the town and ocean from the hillside. Sonya consented, and a while later, they were relaxed comfortably on a grassy knoll, breathing in the beauty of the picturesque scene spread out before them. The town of Peitaiho Beach was tucked neatly in its little valley, and the glassy bay dotted by idle sampans and fishing barges lent a dreamy atmosphere to the spectacle. Amidst the vicious war raging nearby, the tranquillity of this spot set it apart in a tiny world of its own. Sonya really was closer to the fury of the world, but she was not aware of it and felt only the restful mood of the picture.

"It's gorgeous, isn't it, Arty?" she mused, stretching the full length of her lithe figure on the grass. "From here, one doesn't see all the filth of China."

"Yes, it is," agreed Arty, more intent on Sonya's enticing body than the view before them.

"You're not even looking," reprimanded Sonya.

"I'm looking at something *much* more gorgeous," Arty answered throatily.

"Thank you for the compliment, but the way you look at me makes me feel naked."

"I wish you were."

"Arturro!"

"I mean it, so why not say it?"

Sonya laughed. "Brutally frank, to say the least, but no

thank you. I prefer clothes in the presence of men."

"All men?"

"You're being insolent," snapped Sonya.

"Now, Sonya, you mistook my meaning," apologized Arty. "I meant that as a compliment. Such a gorgeous creature should not conceal her charms."

"This conversation is going too far," Sonya observed.

"Then I'll change it." Arty leaned over and kissed her. "Is that better?"

"I haven't made up my mind."

"Make it up, you're driving me crazy," croaked Arty. He stretched himself beside her and propped his head in one hand in order to look down into her face. "I love you, Sonya."

"You *are* crazy!"

Arty ignored her words. He kissed her again and let his body pin her to the ground. After the kiss, he did not release her but kept pressing his body upon her. Sonya struggled and started to cry out, but his lips crushed hers and stifled the scream. His passion raging beyond control, heat surged in Arty's inflamed body and sped to Sonya, whipping her amorous emotions. Too vitally alive, too full of loving, Sonya could not fight her own inherent desires and also the savage advances. She stilled her struggles and her arms encircled his neck, straining him to her and burying his face in the downy hollow of her neck and bosom. His hand groped for the hem of her dress, and she felt it burning her leg.

Then, inches before her eyes, Sonya saw Paul's ring. "You beast!" she screamed wildly. "*Stop it! Stop it!* I told you I don't like such things."

Somewhat bewildered, Arty got up, offered Sonya a hand, and said, "I apologize. We have both learned something. It won't happen again." And it didn't. They stopped being alone altogether.

Peitaiho Beach was wearing thin for both Netti and Sonya, and they had not had a serious talk for some time. Something was bothering Netti, so she decided it was time for that serious talk when they found themselves alone at an inexpensive little café. Being more observant than Sonya, Netti had become aware of the invariable presence of Japanese policemen in their wake. Wherever Sonya went, some Japanese, usually uniformed but sometimes civilian dressed, could always be found loitering nearby. Well aware of the graveness of Sonya's position with the Japanese, Netti reasoned this was not merely coincidental, so she made Sonya cognizant of her fears.

"For instance, there are two Japanese policemen sitting at the third table from us. No, don't look now. Those men came in right after we did, and I'll bet they leave when we do."

"Ah, Netti, your imagination is taking advantage of you again," discounted Sonya.

"No," persisted Netti, "I know I'm right. Just wait and see when we leave. You'll see I'm right."

Netti's words created some concern and prompted Sonya to remember seeing Japanese quite frequently. Maybe Netti was right. Paul had warned her she may be watched and to be careful. Paul also said he would contact her. It had been days, and not a word—that was not like Paul.

True to Netti's prophecy, the two Japanese followed them when they left the café. The nudge Netti gave Sonya was not necessary, for Sonya noticed and automatically agreed with Netti's previous observation. Now thoroughly convinced she was being watched, Sonya decided to conceal every possible affiliation with the infamous Paul York; and the one tie she instantly remembered was the ring she wore. It carried Paul York's initials! She decided she should stow it somewhere for safekeeping, but soon abandoned that idea because she had made a solemn promise to Paul to never take it off.

"I'm frightened," confessed Sonya in a low whisper. "You're right. I am being watched, and no telling when they may decide to investigate further."

As they parted in front of Sonya's cottage, the two Japanese policemen sauntered by, presumably making the rounds on their regular tour of duty. However, Sonya knew their mission, and that night she retired with a troubled mind.

Due to her night of restlessness, Sonya thought she was dreaming when she heard loud words and strong arguing outside her window. The commotion increased until the pitch of excitement awakened her, and she discovered the disturbance to be a reality. Though the argument was being carried in Chinese, Sonya recognized her mother's voice mingled with that of some

206

man, and they were engaged in a heated controversy.

Going to the window, Sonya looked down to see a ragged Chinese peddler standing in front of the house. His baskets of vegetables were dropped on the ground, and he waved his hands, evidently arguing with Katilka, who stood on the porch and was shielded from Sonya's view by the roof. The peddler kept screaming that the day before a woman of the house had underpaid him on an agreed price for his vegetables, and Katlika was vehemently denying it. She insisted she had never seen the man before.

Having taken stock of the situation, Sonya shouted at the peddler. "Get out of here and leave us alone before I call the police."

At the sound of her voice, the peddler looked up, and Sonya saw his face under the cone-shaped mass of straw he used as a hat. The face startled her, for she instantly recognized the peddler as none other than Huang Chu. A slight smile crossed his face as he looked at Sonya, and she detected a tiny wink which carried an unmistakable message for her.

Competently sizing up the situation, Sonya shouted to Katilka. "Mom, I recognize the peddler. I remember I did buy some things from him and there may have been a mistake. I'll hurry down and straighten it out."

Sonya's explanation satisfied Katilka, and the peddler bowed acknowledgment. Thus pacified, the peddler again bowed respectfully and retired to the street to await Sonya's arrival. Impatient to learn Chu's message, Sonya allowed her anxiety loose rein as she rapidly fumbled through her dressing and raced into the street.

"Act natural," Chu cautioned in a subdued tone the instant she reached him. "Pretend you are straightening out our mistake, and you might be looking over my vegetables."

"Yes," Sonya breathed hard. She withdrew money from her purse, and they passed it back and forth. Then she knelt beside his basket and began looking over the tomatoes, lifting each one and inspecting it at length, thus going through the characteristic motions of a good buyer.

"What is it, Chu?" she whispered impatiently. "Where is Paul?"

"He's on his way to Chungking," answered Chu, bending close to her and rolling the tomatoes back and forth for her examination. "Be cautious, Miss Sonya, this country is boiling because of his escape."

"But is he all right?"

"Patience, Miss Sonya. He is on the plane to Chungking with Mr. Burl and Mr. David," Chu said, keeping an alert eye on the street and the people sauntering past.

A few minutes later, Sonya returned to the house with a small purchase of tomatoes and explained to Katilka the peddler was happy. She had received her first message from Paul York.

23

Much to Burl's assumed chagrin, Paul suffered nothing more than a sprained ankle, and under the watchful care of David and Burl, he was walking painlessly in a few days. His few waking hours were spent relaxing in the comfortable apartment David and Burl occupied in Chungking, talking over old times and drinking with his hosts. The evening was typical, as the three intimate friends inhaled the amiable atmosphere. Liquor, mixer, and glasses littered the coffee table, and mutual conversation filled the smoke-laden room as they reclined in various positions of leisure.

"What a life," mused Paul. "You characters work hard here in Chungking."

"Our duties consist solely of waiting," said David. "We're specialists, work only when asked to do so. Right now we're waiting for the chief to return from being called by the top brass. He's probably on a ship somewhere. That's why he didn't meet you. He told us to give you his regrets and take care of you till he returned."

"It'll be good to see Mac again," said Paul. "You say he's a Brigadier General. It'll be strange to see Joe McLawhorn wearing a uniform and packing a star."

"Oh, we're all in the army," offered Burl, "including yourself."

"Afraid I fail to grasp your meaning," said Paul. "You guys mentioned something of the sort the last time you visited me in Tientsin, but I'm still a little vague on the subject. Remember, I've been part of the Japanese Army for a number of years, and the two organizations don't carry on much of a correspondence."

"I've sort of noticed that," quipped Burl. "Now if I were running this war, I'd arrange transportation and communication from one side to the other—send women envoys back and forth. International fornication would produce friendliness faster than

any other thing. Why, hell, you know as well as I do the invei-
gling arms of a woman'll take the fight out of you. Can't you just
see whole harems moving from..."

"Remind me to make you president some day," David cut in.
"Here's the setup, Paul. The war created a necessary organization for the United States known as the OSS—Office of Strategic
Services. It's the international gestapo of America and is a hush-
hush outfit. Very few people are even aware of its existence. They
built it with care and drafted the people who could do the job. It
includes army, navy men, marines, and civilians like ourselves.
Naturally, we all work under a common head for a common purpose. Though you didn't know it, you were part of it since the day
you came to Washington and agreed to go to Japan."

"I wondered how you fitted in with the army—flying their
planes and whatnot. Just hope they don't plan on regimenting
me—I'm not the type."

"Don't worry, my friend," said Burl. "You can ask and receive
anything you want. Bet you pack more weight than most of our
generals."

"You flatter me, I didn't know that."

"Seems there are a lot of things you don't know," suggested
Burl. "Did you know you're due for a rapid trip to the States?"

"Goddamn it, Burl, you weren't suppose to tell him. We were
going to let it come as a surprise," reprimanded David.

"Ah, he'd have found out soon enough anyway. Simmer
down."

Paul said nothing. He drank long from his glass and
remained absorbed in thought.

"Hell!" exclaimed Burl. "Aren't you happy about it? What did
you expect?"

"You can't *want* to stay out here!" exclaimed David, obviously perplexed.

"I'm not sure—hadn't thought about it," reflected Paul.
"Odd, isn't it. After so many years away from the country you
love, and you don't have the enthusiasm expected when finally
you hear you *are* going back—that it isn't a cherished dream
anymore and that you're really going."

"I think you need a psychiatrist. You're mentally unbal-
anced—in other words, nuts!" expounded Burl.

210

"After all these years, I have no urge to go," Paul continued, as though thinking aloud. "Maybe it's ridiculous, but maybe I'm afraid of what I might find."

"You'll find everything just as you left it," David offered.

"I think that's what I'm afraid of—that everything will be the same. Maybe I don't want it that way. I'm not sure. I am sure of what I have here."

David settled back in his chair and peered knowingly at his friend. "Sonya," submitted David. "Sonya, that's it."

Paul straightened up and fire danced in his eyes. "Yes, damn it, that's it! That's what I want more than anything else on earth, Sonya. They don't build barriers high enough—they don't breed arms strong enough to keep me away from her."

An awkward silence settled over the group. David wanted to say more, to remind him of a few matters, but he had tried before and failed. To bring up the subject again would only bring Paul's wrath around his head and terminate in a nasty quarrel. He felt too strongly for Paul to argue or fight with him in any way. It was not that David disliked Sonya. Quite to the contrary, he thought she was wonderful and probably good for Paul. Still, Paul did not face realities. A loud banging on the door interrupted David's moody reflections.

The door swung open, silhouetting a man of medium height and strong build. His dark complexion, hawk nose, and black eyes were barely discernible against the light of the hall. When he stepped into the room and doffed his cap, they saw he wore the uniform of a major in the United States Marine Corps.

"Was told I might find a man by the name of Paul York at this address," the major said briskly.

"Jack!" exclaimed Paul, bounding forward to crush the major's hand. "Jack Shull—my god, I haven't seen you for years. And a marine yet. Give me your jacket and get comfortable. These two characters with me are David Rousch and Burl Manning. They keep me out of trouble."

Having finished the greetings, Paul added, "Do I see a paratroop emblem on that jacket?"

"Yes, I'm a paratrooper. Had to find excitement the hard way. You guys must also know I'm affiliated with the OSS. Believe I was ordered here because of that."

Quick to get a word in, Burl said, "You must have jumped from the wrong plane. What the hell are you doing here in Chungking? Can't believe anyone would come here just to see Paul."

Laughing at Burl's wit, Jack turned to Paul and said, "I was on the right plane. Just luck and a pleasant surprise to learn you were here. And to answer your friend, I was ordered here to head up a small group of paratroop specialists if needed in the China area. Doubt I'll be needed now. Just left Okinawa. We now own that place, and the mass of ships around there must mean the next stop is Japan."

Burl gave Jack a glass and pointed out they should get on with some serious drinking before the war ended. At least Burl had decided that was a good excuse for boozing it up.

Paul returned to questioning Jack. "How did you know I was here?"

"No problem. As I said, I've been involved with the OSS for some time. The information I got on you was stamped 'Top Secret.' You're well-known and respected in the organization."

Burl spoke up. "Enough of that great stuff about Paul—let's talk about me and be serious. When do the fireworks start in Japan? I want to be in the States when that happens."

"We'll know more when the general gets back here tonight or tomorrow," David interjected. "Let the war be. Let's drink a toast to good luck and off to bed." And they did.

Early the next morning, Paul was awakened with a splash of cold water over his face. Burl stood over him with the evidence and joked, "Thought I was the only one that got drunk last night."

Wiping his face, Paul controlled his anger. "At least I don't have to wash now—what's up?"

"General Mac's in and wants to see you," Burl answered, as he groped around on the bureau for his watch. Finding it, he exclaimed, "It's only ten o'clock! What kind of war is this, getting a man up at such a ridiculous hour in the morning?"

Escorted by Burl and David, Paul reached the general's office shortly before eleven o'clock. When he gave his name, the desk sergeant ushered Paul and his friends into the general's office without the slightest hesitation. Grey-haired Joe

McLawhorn was not old, as one might think at first glance, for one look at his ruddy face and sparkling eyes proved him to be in his late forties. Upon seeing Paul, he smiled warmly, arose from his desk, and stepped forward to shake hands.

"Paul, it's good to see you. For years, I've been looking forward to the day I might welcome you back home."

"Mac, it goes without saying I'm glad to be here, and I'm glad to see you. You haven't changed a bit—other than the uniform and the weighty star which goes with it."

General McLawhorn greeted Burl and David, seated his visitors, and after arranging his wiry one hundred and fifty pounds behind his desk, took up Paul's conversation. "So the star surprised you. Well, I guess they decided if I was to govern military men as well as my department men I should have the badge of authority. Paul, it's been a long time since our little council of war back there in Washington. There have been many changes."

"I'm aware of a few of them."

"Yes, I expect you are," said the General, looking directly at Paul with his straight honest gaze. "Before I go a step farther, I want to personally congratulate you on the fine work you've done. The United States picked up a good one when you agreed to leave your U.S. home and go to Japan. Few people know of your incredulous performance, but someday it will be told after this war ends. That's the disconcerting feature in our work. Our heroes can't be presented to the public they fight for—at least, not until after the war, and then few care to listen."

"Your speech makes me sound like some sort of martyr."

"I mean it. America can be truly proud of you," General McLawhorn emphasized. "You've done so much for us I hesitate to ask for another favor. Paul, I had planned on having a special plane stand by to fly you directly to the States, and it is still ready if you choose to us it. "However," the general stopped and with a slow sweeping glance took in all three men who sat across the desk from him. "We now hold Okinawa and the invasion of Japan has been settled and will take place soon—exact date not set yet. It will be very costly in lives for both America and Japan. There are rumors Japan wants to negotiate for peace, or will draw the war to north China and Manchuria for a last stand to save destruction of their homes and land. Even now our bombers

213

are tearing up Japan."

The three men listened intently to the general's simple, deliberate words. He was giving them "Eyes Only" information, more sensitive than "Top Secret." He paused, allowing the full meaning of his words to penetrate their astonished minds. Then he continued. "We believe our contacts in North China and Manchuria have the information which will give us a clue to Japanese plans, but are not sure enough of the information to transmit it. They obviously are afraid it would prompt military action which would be wrong. Time is of the essence. Many lives may depend on that information. Someone must analyze that information and give us a quick, accurate answer. Only one man is capable of that analysis—a man who has worked with the Japanese command throughout the war years. His name is Paul York."

Paul's acknowledgment was simple and direct. "When do I leave?"

"Not so fast," the General cautioned. "There are a few matters to be considered. The best place for quick information is probably Tangshan, and for you to go there is like walking into a lion's den. They must be after your hide. Remember, I said a plane is ready to take you to the States, and that still goes. You can take it and not be ashamed."

"Don't believe an answer to that is necessary," Paul said without hesitation.

"All right, you go, but something must be understood. That plane will still be waiting when you return, and I'm putting you aboard it whether you like it or not. Believe me—I mean it." The General's firm voice was evidence enough that he meant it. "Now, I want to get you out of here as soon as possible—tomorrow. It's a rush job, so we'll have to fly you in. You can pick your pilot and anyone else."

David spoke up. "That's settled."

"Not quite," interjected Burl. "There's going to be at least three people on that plane."

General McLawhorn and Paul both laughed. David and Burl had made it clear immediately who would be Paul's choice to go with him. Eager to facilitate Paul's rapid departure, the general pressed the subject. "Paul, is it possible to land a plane near

Tangshan and cover it?"

"Maybe," Paul answered thoughtfully. "There are a couple of places where it might be done, depending on the type of plane and some close maneuvering. About concealment, I don't know. Jap patrols pretty well cover the areas I'm thinking about."

The General frowned as he said, "It's a chance you'll have to take. We haven't got time to let you work your way in. The plane must wait to haul you out in case of trouble and get you back."

"And, if something does go wrong?" Paul asked.

"Get the information to us as best you can. If you find the rumor groundless, a negative reply on the coded channel will suffice. Now, what about the plane? Dave, your thoughts?"

David did not answer immediately. He was looking out the window. "We've had good luck flying over that area, but the Japs have some AAs and fighters. We need something fast and light as possible. That A-20 sitting out there is probably best. It would have to be stripped of every bit of weight—guns, ammo, everything. And we will need a drop fuel tank to make a round trip." David smiled as he added, "Even though it will accommodate three people, weight is a problem, and we can get rid of a lot by leaving Mr. Manning here."

David's comment eased the solemn mood evident in the office. It prompted Burl to point a finger at Dave and say, "Be careful. I know how to fly, and we may not need you."

The General returned to the serious situation. "I'll have it ready by tonight. We'll put in a week's rations, just in case. When do you want to take off?"

David gave a pensive response. "I'll need some light for a guide-in landing, and Paul has to be able to spot the place. Guess we should plan to get there at sun-up tomorrow. What do you think, Paul?"

"With good luck, and if I can get to the right people in a hurry, we should be able to get out of there in a couple of days."

"Hopefully you can do it in a few hours, but I know that is optimistic," the General said as he stood up. One by one he shook the hands of the three men. "Any questions?"

"No, Mac," Paul answered.

"Then get together with your plans. May god be with you and speed your return. *And be careful.*"

When Paul, David, and Burl left the General's office, Joe McLawhorn stood in the doorway with a fond and admiring expression on his usually stern face. The success of his orders was fixed. He had placed a grave mission in competent hands.

24

The takeoff was routine and they were air borne on a dangerous mission. It bothered David sitting at the controls, wondering if they could find that landing spot Paul described. Paul would be giving directions on the intercom from his better view of the ground from the bombardier seat in the nose.

"Want me to keep the original course you gave me?" David asked.

"Right. It's getting light enough so I can make out a few ground features. I'll keep an eye on the landmarks and orient you rapidly when we come in."

The seriousness of the situation was eased when Burl could be heard singing merrily in his whiskey baritone, as he idly watched the stars disappearing high over his head. "—and when I die, you kin burrie mee, just a mite ways in frum the Chinee Sea."

Listening to Burl ad lib to the tune of "The Lone Prairie," Paul grimly watched the ground speed beneath him and wondered why the world did not produce more such men as Burl Manning. It would be a much, much better world. Paul waited with one eye on his watch and the other on the dim horizon. Then he was rapidly giving David concise instructions in a calm voice. They worked well together, and a few minutes later the plane bounced to a stop in the shadow of an abrupt hill.

The location proved superb for their purposes. The sun was sending a little light over the horizon when three figures jumped from the plane and began covering it with brush and weeds, from a nearby patch of undergrowth. The process took about half an hour even though they worked feverishly. The camouflage was not good but would have to serve. Then the figures huddled for a hasty conversation.

"It's a good thing I came along," Burl croaked. "I'm the same as old Lady Luck herself. We drifted in here without so much as waking a baby. Course, Dave, I must give you your due—you dropped that baby in like a gliding angel."

"Well, Miss Luck, let's don't ride you too far," cracked David. "Suppose we organize this thing and get moving."

Paul took over. "Somebody has to stay with the plane. Dave, obviously you're elected. You're the pilot and can get out of here if something goes wrong. Burl, you and I are going to town. I know one of the contact spots and don't think we'll have any trouble. Dave, if you haven't heard from us by tomorrow morning, you'll know the jig is up and get your ass back to Chungking. Also, don't shoot us when we return. We'll give you three sharp whistles. You return ours. Keep in mind we are only about twenty kilometers from Tangshan."

"Okay, get going," David responded.

Paul and Burl dirtied their faces and hands with makeup and pulled on the ragged mandarin coats brought along for the purpose. Without too much scrutiny, they could pass for old Chinese. Next came a check of their pistols, and they were ready for their hike into Tangshan. For an instant, the three men stood silently intent on each other. Theirs was a friendship which needed no words for emphasis, and in that moment of silence, each had a prayer for his two companions. Then three hands locked in strong farewell, and Paul and Burl started off, walking briskly.

There could be no doubting Burl's lucky influence. They arrived at the mud hut without one moment of suspense, despite having passed Chinese and even a few Japanese soldiers. Rapidly, Paul checked his bearings to make sure he stood at the door of the right shack. Having been there only the one other time when he left Tangshan a few days before, he experienced some difficulty in ascertaining the right hut. Finally settled on his decision, he pushed open the door to find a familiar scene. There sat the withered old woman, giving Paul the impression she had been sitting in the same spot since that night he entered the room for the first time. This time, however, she shot a wicked glance at her intruders, and it prompted Paul to make his identity and business known immediately.

"I'm Paul York looking for Tian Wei or Huang Chu."

Although she had recognized Paul, the old woman's expression did not change. She remained silent and alert. Paul experienced a sensation of misgiving before she relieved the tension by waving her hand to the familiar closet door. Paul grinned at Burl and nodded for him to follow. To their surprise, they found the cellar hideout deserted.

"What do we do now—wait for that witch to ride in on a broomstick and spirit us away?" Burl commented dryly.

"At least we wait, we have gone as far as we dare. I think that old vulture has sense and knows a lot—like the owl that watches and listens. It has to be her move."

"Move! I still bet she uses a broomstick," grimaced Burl. "At any rate, I hope she herds Chu or Wei in here without delay. She gives me the creeps."

Paul's confidence in the old lady quieted Burl's anxiety, but nearly an hour elapsed before the woman in question proved her worth. The stairs creaked under the rapid descent of some person, and Chu greeted his callers.

"Mr. Paul," he exclaimed, astonished to find it was really Paul. "Why you back?"

"Business, Chu. Speak Chinese so we can understand you. How did you find Sonya?"

"She was fine. Happy to hear you escaped."

Chu deliberated as though hesitant to go on. Then he added brightly, "It is funny. After all that bad trip you are back where we started. Makes no sense. Why?"

Paul detected Chu's obvious effort to escape the subject. "About Sonya," he insisted sternly. "Is everything all right?"

"Yes, of course," Chu blurted. "She seems to have enjoyment where she is, and the Japanese only watch her." Chu stopped again, but knowing he was pinned down he went on, "She walks with a Spanish man by the name of Arturro Ramon."

"And?" Paul snapped.

"And that is all," Chu hurried to answer. "I said they only walk together."

Paul said nothing, but Burl noticed he paled visibly from Chu's seemingly harmless information. Cleverly, Burl snatched Paul away from certain fury by flipping gaily, "So she dances with another man. Hell, there's nothing wrong with that—most wives do. Tell me, Chu, how did you like your descent from an airplane?"

"Me want no more," Chu gasped in English, fearing Burl planned another parachute jump for him.

Burl laughed, and they chatted while Paul brooded. Finally Paul shook off his morbid attitude, issued a strained laugh, and took up his reason for being there. Within a few minutes Chu departed with instructions to round up all the agents and all information on the subject at hand. Some time later, Paul and Burl received their first caller. The hours melted away as Paul questioned man after man, examined documents and bits of miscellaneous information, and tied his reasoning together. At last, he shooed the last informer from the cellar and turned to Chu and Burl with his decision.

"Sure, they're thinking about giving up, but such ideas are only off-hand comments. I knew that much before I left Tientsin. There's no firm basis for such rumors, no foundation for actual belief. The competent Japanese authorities are mum. In fact, my guess is they're giving the impression of an all-out fight to the finish. Mind you, they act on orders direct from the top and think little for themselves. Of course, I believe the word will break any day. Now there's no positive proof to substantiate our lead."

"Then that does it," Burl said with finality. "I'm ready to warm up our winged buggy and have a good meal in Chungking."

Paul ignored Burl's words. He was busy writing a coded message on a small slip of paper. He handed the paper to Chu and said, "Radio this to Chunking. It's a negative reply to General McLawhorn and is all the information he needs. Do you have to go far?"

"No," answered Chu. "There is a trusted man standing by for such purposes. He can see it's sent."

"Good," said Paul. "Give it to him and get back here. I want you to go to the plane with us."

Burl put Chu's astonishment into words as Chu left the room. "May I ask why you desire Chu's company?"

"He knows where to find Sonya," Paul stated simply. "But he doesn't know where the plane is and I want him to bring her there."

"He what? Damn it, Paul, you're crazy. You'll see her again in the future. Why take such a chance at this stage in the game?"

"Because I'll be going back to the States as soon as I reach

Chunking. You heard Mac say so," Paul answered coolly. "Sure I'll see her again, but there's an if or two attached. Only God knows how long it may be."

This might have been one of Paul's reasons, but Burl thought of at least one more. He tried to approach it subtly. "She's being true to you, and she's waiting for you. After all, it's been just a few days since you saw her and they don't write you off that quick."

"You're wandering in the wilderness," snapped Paul. "You may as well save your breath because I'm going to see her even if I have to go to Peitaiho Beach and get killed trying."

"And that is just what might happen," declared Burl. "It's asinine to risk everything because of a woman."

"Have you ever been in love?" gritted Paul. "So in love with a woman that her shadow falls over your every action, so in love her face smiles at you each time your eyes close, so in love you find her beside you in your every dream, so in love the mere thought of being with her warms your blood, and the thought of being without her leaves you numb with fear. If you've never felt that way, Burl, you can't possibly understand me."

Paul's cold acid tone meant just one thing to Burl. *Paul was going to see Sonya.* That tone clearly conveyed to Burl the futility of any argument. The words which rose in his throat to denounce this absurd idea were choked back and he shrugged his shoulders, thus signifying his helplessness. Maybe David would be able to pound a little sense into Paul's love warped brain. Burl knew the tremendous will power of Paul York and he acknowledged defeat.

Chu returned, beckoning eagerly. "Must get out of this area. Lots of Japanese patrols when it starts to get dark. And it's getting dark."

When they were finally able to sneak out of the mud hut, the sun had turned its duties over to the moon, but the moon was blotted out by haze leaving the night jet black. They did not object, for it suited their purpose as they followed the path that would lead them back to the plane. Progressing cautiously, all was going well and the three men were constantly on the alert with readied automatics. They stayed close together and moved in single file, Paul leading, followed by Burl and then Chu.

221

They were making good time, and Paul estimated they were getting close to the plane. Despite their dangerous mission, he was in a happy frame of mind. Soon he would see Sonya again. Soon he could take her in his arms and feel her warm pliable body close to his, her soft lips, her caressing hands on his face and neck. Challenging words from a Japanese voice rudely snatched his mind from its rapturous musing! A pistol barked unexpectedly. It belonged to Chu. Somehow he had fired automatically under the tension of the moment. Instantaneously the darkness exploded with the sound of coughing guns. Blinding flashes seared the night, leaping back and forth, while burning lead sought to knife human flesh and bone.

As suddenly as it started, the firing stopped and deathly silence reigned. Paul stood with feet wide apart, alive but fighting desperately to master the numbness, which crept through his body and left him teetering drunkenly. The bone shattered above his elbow, his left arm hung like a limp rag. His right hand still clutched a smoking automatic. Not everyone faired as well, for death had walked boldly through the night.

"Burl!" Paul cried hoarsely. "Are you okay?"

Chu's voice came back through the night to grip Paul's soul and twist his senses into a pounding turmoil. "He's here, *dead*."

Paul stumbled in the direction of the voice and found Chu kneeling beside Burl's still form. Brutally insane, Paul grabbed Chu by the collar and flung him away from the silent figure. Then he dropped beside Burl and reached out to check his pulse. Paul stopped his movement. Such action was unnecessary because a bullet had left a gaping and ghastly hole in the side of Burl Manning's head. Burl had died as he wanted to—instantly, and fighting. His hands still clutched two revolvers not yet cold from their rapid firing.

Spontaneous and unrestrained tears gushed over Paul's cheeks as he dropped over Burl's lifeless body and began mumbling and sobbing like a heartbroken child. Chu picked himself up from the ground, wiped away a tear with a soiled shirtsleeve, and moved out into the night. He was not a part of this last embrace.

A few minutes later, Chu returned and stood over Paul. "Three Japs, all dead."

Chu's voice aroused Paul and he straightened up. Still kneeling, he looked up and Chu saw his face—a bloodless face lined with cold determination. His unseeing eyes were dull and glassy like those of a man mentally dead. Fear crept over Chu, for he could only guess at the thought behind that almost ghastly face staring up at him.

"Mr. Paul, you hurt?"

"Yes, my arm, also a slug in my belly, low down on the left," he answered dully. As though trying to figure out what happened, he added, "Must have hit a Jap patrol. No sentries up this way."

Chu acted efficiently. He cut away Paul's shirt and bound the smashed arm. Then he inspected Paul's abdominal wounds. "One hole is bleeding badly. Bullet must be inside." Chu wadded up strips of cloth and padded over the wound.

"Guess it musta lodged at my hip bone," muttered Paul. "Burl, we can't leave him here. We have to get him back to the plane."

"You, too," added Chu.

A fever was starting to rise in Paul, but his mind remained keen. "Those Japs, hide them before we leave. They may not be found for some time."

"Have already rolled them off the trail and covered them with weeds," Chu said.

Paul nodded his approval and staggered to his feet. Chu stopped and worked Burl's body across his shoulders to a carrying position. The dark night was fading away as they staggered along the path, which would lead them to the plane. They rested frequently for Chu's burden was heavy, and since Paul continued to lose blood, his strength diminished with each step.

David saw them coming and rushed forward to lift Burl from Chu's shoulders. For a long time, he stood with Burl's lifeless body cradled in his arms, and then reverently, he lowered Burl gently to the ground. He spoke not aloud, but a prayer crossed his lips as he brushed away a stray tear. He turned to Paul who had slumped to the ground in a semi-conscious coma. One look at Paul had him running to the plane for first-aid equipment.

As David worked over Paul, cleaning and bandaging his wounds, Paul murmured, "Burl—gone—I—I can't believe it. Oh

223

god, Dave, why couldn't it have been me instead of Burl? There were three of 'em and we got all of 'um but, but Burl's worth a million Japs and more."

"Forget it, there's nothing we can do now," David said. "It's done, and you'll be done, too, if we don't get you to a doc and have this arm fixed. Also, that slug needs to be cut out. The bleeding has checked some but even a little loss of blood is too much now."

Paul raised himself to a sitting position. "Not yet, I'm not going back yet. I have to see Sonya."

"In the name of God, you're out of your mind. You must be," spat David. "Christ man, you're dying. *Do you understand? You're dying.*"

"I know it." Paul's voice was cold and unemotional. "That's why I want to see Sonya—have to see her before that happens. After I see her, I don't care."

Confounded beyond expression, David scrutinized the wounded man sitting before him. A fever flushed Paul's cheeks, and his eyes carried the glint of a madman, defiantly refusing to give way though cornered like a wild beast.

"Damn it, Paul, I won't hear of it. This is one time you do it my way," gritted David. "If necessary, I'll put you aboard that plane by force and tie you in." He dropped his eyes and turned away. "Expect we'd better give Burl his burial. No point in trying to get him back to Chungking—would require an explanation and create more problems. He deserves a burial with all the trimmings, but I guess our services'll have to do. Chu, see if you can find anything in the plane to dig with while I collect his personal items."

Hoping it might stop the flow of blood, David made Paul lie still while he and Chu dug the grave a few yards away from the plane. After a few feet they were forced to quit, for they could not break the ground further with the bucket and steel rod they had for tools. They carried Burl to his final resting place and lowered him gently into the shallow grave. Just showing itself over the far horizon, the sun peeked in upon a touching scene as three bareheaded men bowed respectfully over the humble grave of their fallen comrade.

David paid homage to the man they all loved by a few well-chosen words which would provide the feeling in the heart of everyone who ever knew Burl Manning. "Burl, we've laughed, loved, played, and fought together. Your parting leaves a vacancy in all our lives. We thank God that your short life was well-lived—full and plentiful—and no man ever deserved more than you. May the Lord keep you always, and be kind and considerate as you have always been here on earth. I, I..." Tears filled his eyes, and the lump in his throat checked his voice. Finally, he blurted pitifully, "Please, oh Lord, please take good care of him, he needs a lot of taking care of."

Paul was submissive. Loss of blood had taken its toll and he could not get off his knees. David lifted him up. "We better get you to Chunking in a hurry. Chu, help me get him in this plane."

When Chu put his arms around him, Paul, in pain, mumbled in Chu's ear, "Get to Sonya. Tell her I'll come back and I love her. Chu, promise me."

"I promise," was all Chu could say. He was caught in the agony of the moment as he watched David place a cross of twigs at the head of a mound of fresh earth and turn away. He heard David almost whispering.

"Burl, you named it right again."

With Paul strapped in the bombardier seat, David jumped out of the plane and gave Chu a hug. "Thanks again, Chu. I hope to see you again and I'll make sure your name is known where it counts. When I start the engines, you get the hell out of here as fast as you can. Good luck."

Chu answered with the nod of his head and a big smile as David climbed aboard.

The thundering engines spun the plane around on one braked wheel and took up a screaming crescendo. Leaning her sleek nose into the darkness, the ship hurtled through the tall grass, and jumped into the sky. As the pilot brought the plane on course, it was not strange to hear him humming the strains of "The Lone Prairie." He knew Burl Manning would be listening.

225

25

When Sonya awoke unusually early and found the morning sun throwing torrid rays through her bedroom window, she decided it was an appropriate time to wash her hair. Since it was not yet seven, she tiptoed quietly about the cottage to keep from awakening her mother. Then, having gathered up the necessary items for her purpose, she took up her toilet on the back veranda where a large water basin sat on a washstand.

Contrary to her normal procedure, she had retired early and after a healthy night's sleep, felt spirited. As she worked up suds and dropped her long, golden hair into the frothy water, she hummed merrily to herself. She stopped, cocked her head tone side, rubbed the soapy knot on her head, and attempted to place the tune she hummed. "Sweethearts," that was it. Paul had played it for her many times and she loved it. She had not heard it since the last night in Paul's home. Satisfied with her memory, she dunked her hair and went on humming the same romantic song. Now her mind was not on the swim she had previously contemplated. She was thinking of Paul and remembering that last night together—remembering with girlish enthusiasm the intimate moments in his arms, remembering with pride the strong influential man who was to be her husband. Her thoughts skipped to America and built a dream life there, wild and frivolous yet full of prestige as the wife of Paul York.

She toweled vigorously, picked up her hairbrush, and moved out where the sun could dry her hair. To aid the sun she sat down on the veranda step, dropped her head and began brushing the dangling mass of silken locks. She brushed in rhythm to the melody floating in her heart, for she reveled in the knowledge that Paul was safe in Chunking and only a few months must pass before he would return to make her Mrs. York.

"Be quiet, do not move," a voice whispered near her back.

Sonya's brush caught in mid-air. Momentarily terrified, she

turned and saw a person crouched at the end of the veranda. It was Chu in dirty Chinese clothing. His hand brushed across his mouth indicating silence, which she understood.

"Keep doing what you do. We could be watched. I tell you everything. I hurry," Chu spoke in Chinese.

Sonya started brushing again. "Something wrong?"

"Yes, I tell you. Mr. Paul near here on American job. Now on plane to Chunking."

Fighting to suppress her excitement and keep her voice low, Sonya asked, "Is he alright?"

"Yes, but he's wounded. Shooting with Japanese. Arm and belly, maybe hip shot up. He told me to let you know his love. He will have to go to America and will be back for you."

Her sigh of relief was shattered with Chu's next words. "Three Japanese soldiers killed, Mr. Burl killed."

"Burl Manning dead!" Sonya choked on the words, tears filled her eyes and flowed over her cheeks. The man she liked and loved immediately, that jovial person who showed her how to laugh and have fun without a care. And Paul wounded. "Chu, *you must be wrong, you must be.*"

"No, I there in the shooting. You must believe and wait for more word. I go now. Be careful, you're being watched." With that, Chu jumped up and disappeared in seconds.

Sonya needed consolation and advice. As always, she turned to Netti. Half walking, half running, she made her way to Netti's beach house. Netti was still in bed and surprised to feel Sonya shaking her at such an early hour, but her surprise vanished when she realized Sonya was crying. Sonya did not give Netti time to question her, and even before Netti had completed wiping the sleep from her eyes, Sonya blurted out what Chu had said.

Netti put her arms around Sonya. "At least Paul is alive and we can't help Burl. We'll take a walk and relax. No more crying."

Netti took Sonya to the beach. They were together throughout the day, and it was the most miserable day Sonya had ever spent. Only Netti's constant reassurance and understanding kept her from breaking down completely. When evening came and darkness began, they sat on the veranda with Catherine. It was difficult to make conversation and act natural in front of

Netti's mother. Finally Catherine excused herself and went off to bed.

The girls now had the opportunity to walk freely out to the beach again. They wandered aimlessly along the beach and back along the streets of the small town. It was nearing midnight and they headed for Sonya's cottage.

"We're being followed," whispered Netti.

Even as Netti spoke, Sonya became aware of two men sauntering along behind them. She knew instantly they were Japanese police.

"I'm always being followed," whispered Sonya. "They follow me home and I think they even watch the house all night. I often see a couple of policemen around here first thing in the morning."

"We better get on to your place. We can sit on the veranda without disturbing your mother. Maybe they'll leave."

When the girls turned in to Sonya's cottage, the two men walked on past and out of sight. Sonya breathed a sigh of relief as Netti got up to leave and said, "It is you they watch so I won't have any trouble walking to my cottage. See you tomorrow. Get some sleep and don't worry about Paul."

Loud laughter aroused Sonya from her lethargic reflections. She had spent a restless night and been awake for some time but remained in bed, idly piecing together the events which had fired her once-dull life. She wondered if maybe she had asked for a lot and received too much. She tried not to think of Paul and did not want to remember happy-go-lucky, lovable Burl gone. Now Paul's life, in effect her own life, hung by a thread stretched taut and held together only by the will of his indomitable spirit. She wanted the noise outside to black out the ugly thoughts and let her wake up to find them nothing but an awful dream. Reluctantly, she dressed and went out to greet the laughter she knew belonged to Arturro Ramon and friends. She dreaded facing anyone.

Set for a swim, Arty had been urging Netti to call for Sonya to join them, but Netti was ignoring all their pleas. When Sonya appeared, Arty took one look and exclaimed, "What happened to you?"

"I told you she doesn't feel well," snapped Netti. "Go swim and leave us alone."

Dismayed at Netti's curt attitude, the men left and Netti turned to Sonya. "Come on and sit down. Sometimes I recognize those fellows for what they are."

Sonya continued to worry and brood. She spent the days idly wasting her time. She did not want company, refusing to go out with any of the usual crowd. One afternoon, when Arturro pressed the point after having called on her, she set him straight in no uncertain terms and he perceived immediately the door was closed permanently as far as his entrance was concerned.

Only Netti managed to stay close to Sonya, because Sonya appreciated Netti's presence and Netti knew Sonya's problems. Rarely did they talk of Paul, but his presence lingered with them, whether they swam or walked in the surrounding hills. Occasionally, Sonya liberated the thoughts foremost in her mind. They always revolved around Paul and the hope that soon she might hear from him.

Then the eventful day came! It was August 8, 1945. Sonya would never forget the date, for it carried a momentous message, which affected her life and millions of others. She was on her way to pick up Netti for a late afternoon swim when approached by a Chinese peddler who insisted on selling her some green beans. She waived him away but he persisted in following her. Even though she pretended to ignore him, she felt ill at ease, and the suspense hung heavily as she turned from the main street.

"Miss Petrovna, I have a message for you."

Sonya's heart skipped a beat and left her weak. She spun to see the Chinese peddler practically at her side. He bowed quickly and began showing her the vegetables in his basket. Having played the game before, Sonya did not hesitate to focus her attention on the vegetables he pretended to offer her.

"Who are you?" she said, wondering immediately how he knew her name.

"Tien Wei, a friend of Paul York. He sent an important message," he answered in Chinese.

Excitement flushed her cheeks and Sonya gritted her teeth to control her emotions. "Yes, what is it? Is he all right?"

"He is much better. David Rousch is flying him to the United

States for further treatment." The peddler held out a large head of cabbage for her inspection.

"Go on," Sonya urged.

"Russia declared war on Japan today. It means you may have problems." Wei spoke calmly and in such a matter-of-fact tone, Sonya momentarily doubted his statement.

"What?" Sonya's voice rose above a whisper. "Ssssshhh," cautioned Wei, glancing furtively up and down the street to see if she had attracted attention. "Yes, tomorrow Russia will be at war with Japan. Paul says you are to stay in Peitaiho Beach as long as you can. If you return to Tientsin now you could face trouble. Even here you are in danger. Remain calm if approached by Japanese and answer only routine questions. Those are his exact words for you."

"Oh!" Sonya gasped.

"Another bit of news," Wei continued soberly. "A couple of days ago the Americans dropped a devastating bomb on Hiroshima, Japan. It demolished the entire city. Paul says it may end the war soon. *Remember*, stay in Peitaiho."

The peddler slung his vegetable baskets over his shoulder and paddled down the street, leaving Sonya rooted to the ground. The message she had received spun in her head, froze her rigid, and left her sick with apprehension. The news of Russia's entry into the war should not have been a surprise, but now that it took real form she shivered from the shock. Also, the news of the terrible bomb seemed fantastic, and yet Paul was in a position to obtain reliable information. He would not mislead her. However, the bomb was a minor point considering the solemn fact of her own danger and Russian friends. Instinctively, she ran for Netti's cottage.

The shock of Sonya's appalling news rocked Netti's customary equilibrium. Safely on his way to the United States, Paul York was forgotten in lieu of the grave condition at hand. The entry of Russia into the war made every Russian in north China and Manchuria an enemy of the Japanese who had stood on the doorstep for the past decade. Remembering the Japanese action against the British and Americans after the Pearl Harbor attack, Sonya and Netti had cause for anxiety. There was no barrier to hold the brutal Japanese in check. Japanese soldiers might now feel free to ravage, rape, and torture the Russian nationals on one hand—and pillage their homes and property on the other. The scope of their drastic actions could run unbounded.

Guessing the news would soon be made public, the girls told Netti's mother that Russia had declared war on Japan. Her reaction was immediate. "Where did you get that kind of serious information? If true, it would be announced by the Japanese."

Sonya groped for an explanation. "Some men, some men on the street were talking. They waved their arms at me. It must be true."

Catherine was not convinced and shooed the girls toward the door. "I'll wait and see. In the meantime, you two better go to the beach, take a swim and cool off."

Catherine Rurik did not have long to wait for her proof. The next morning, official word came from the Japanese police unit in Peitaiho Beach stating Russia and Japan were at war. Catherine remembered Sonya's words but had no time to wonder about Sonya's amazing source of information. Like every other Russian in the area, she was too busy deciding what to do. Peitaiho Beach was full of vacationing Russians who were many kilometers from their homes and families. She knew there would be a scramble for train tickets and travel permits. What else? She decided to start packing and advised Netti to get busy and help her.

Despite all the concern by the Russians, the Japanese police of Peitaiho Beach went about their duties in a routine manner. It mattered little to them whether the Russians stayed or returned to cities such as Tientsin. The cities remained in the iron-clad grip of the Japanese.

A massive problem faced Sonya and Netti. Paul's message emphasized in no uncertain terms that Sonya should stay in Peitaiho Beach, and though they could only guess at his reasons, they did not question his word. Even as they discussed the matter, Katilka Petrovna was busy packing. How might they convince her that she should stay in Peitaiho when everyone else scurried homeward? Proof for such an argument must materialize from nothing and be invented without a basis. Netti argued the point for Sonya. Netti pointed out everyone was panicky, that they acted in haste without sufficient cause, and the Japanese were not likely to pounce on them in the space of a few days. Furthermore, what could be gained by fighting the mobs in order to return to Tientsin when Mr. Petrovna was there and capable of handling their home and belongings. After all, Sonya and Katilka had been vacationing only a short time, so why break it off abruptly when it was well possible Mr. Petrovna would want them to stay longer. In a few days, the mass hysteria would die, making traveling easier, and the homeward journey would be more comfortable at a later date if conditions actually warranted their return to Tientsin.

Netti ended her plea by saying she would contact Mr. Petrovna immediately upon her arrival in Tientsin and explain it to him. Then, if he wanted Sonya and Katilka home, he could wire them that word. When Netti finished, Katilka remained dubious, but Netti's persistent reasoning coupled with Sonya's ardent pleas finally convinced her, and she stopped her packing. Had Katilka been observant, she would have noticed the obvious expression of relief which flowed through the girls. Later, Netti explained to Sonya, the telegram from Mr. Petrovna would be sent by her, and it would say, "Everything fine. Stay as long as you please."

26

Netti found a touching scene when her train pulled into Tientsin. Waiting were many nervous Russians, apprehensive and worried about members of their family who were out of the city. They met every train and excitedly inquired of everyone as to the whereabouts of their daughter, or son, or wife, or husband. Some found the person they sought, and midst thankful tears, hurried them away to unobtrusive seclusion. Others looked in vain as they ran from traveler to traveler, begging a word of assurance about their loved ones. Mr. Petrovna was one of the latter, and when he spied Netti running toward him, his face lit up happily for he knew Sonya and Katilka also must be present.

When Netti informed him that his wife and daughter had stayed in Peitaiho Beach, he gave vent to his consternation by a series of explosive cuss words demanding an explanation for such a foolhardy trick. Hastily, Netti soothed his tense disposition by saying Sonya and Katilka were perfectly all right and had waited a few days because of crowded traveling. She managed to help Mr. Petrovna regain his composure by her confident tone, and leaving him to simmer, made off to send the phony telegram. Where the girls' actions would end up after the telegram they did not know, but at least they would gain a few days respite by the maneuver. Such was Netti's calculation as she entered the telegraph office. When the Japanese operator rudely informed her telegraph communication had been discontinued for civilians, she knew not whether to be sad or happy. At least fate made it impossible for her to lie, but now on the action was strictly up to Sonya—and Sonya alone.

Sonya wondered why they did not receive the telegram while Katilka expressed grave concern. After two days of fruitless waiting, Katilka insisted they make arrangements for the trip back to Tientsin before it was too late. Sonya held her ground, arguing they should stay a while longer. Though Katilka questioned her daughter's attitude, she temporarily conceded, hoping for early word from Mr. Petrovna.

Fast on the heels of the original alarm, prompted by Russia's entry into the war, came numerous rumors of Japan's plea for peace. The rumors varied in text. Some said Japan had surrendered under an interpretation of the Potsdam Ultimatum which would leave Emperor Hirohito on the throne, while others stated Japan had thrown up her hands and surrendered unconditionally. These rumors sifted into occupied China and were completely unofficial, but they seemed to have a stabilizing effect on the actions of the Japanese. The Japanese appeared to be taking stock of the situation before exercising force against the helpless Russian nationals. Even though the grave situation actually remained unchanged, the panic subsided.

Having counted the days since Netti's departure, Sonya knew only four had slipped by. Nevertheless, it seemed like months, because the departure of the tourists had left Peitaiho Beach tensely still. The lull of impending calamity hung so heavily around Sonya that she felt like a person being strangled by an unseen hand. Further, the tedious waiting for an obscure result only served to prick her already dangerously taut nerves. Each day she paced the streets in search of some intangible outlet for her fraught impulses. By constant walking she at least expended the nervous energy which gnawed at her vitals and pushed her closer to the brink of collapse.

She was homeward bound from a vigorous walk along the beach when a Japanese policeman, accompanied by a Japanese civilian, stopped her. The civilian lent an authoritative appearance and being one capable of using the Russian language, took the initiative.

"You are Sonya Petrovna, right?" He clipped in a guttural tone.

"Yes, yes, I am Sonya Petrovna," she quavered.

"We have orders to pick you up, question you on certain matters, and search your property."

"But—but why?" inquired Sonya, immediately terrified. "I have done nothing."

"We will see," snapped the man. "How long have you been in Peitaiho Beach?"

"A month—six weeks. I'm not sure."

"And you're from Tientsin. Your father's there, and your mother is here with you. Your friend, Netti Rurik, returned to Tientsin a few days ago. Right?" the soldier rattled on matter-of-factly.

"Yes, that's right," admitted Sonya, stupefied that this man should be so minutely informed concerning her personal affairs.

"Why didn't you and your mother return to Tientsin with your friends?"

"Because—because we haven't been here very long. We wanted to rest awhile longer before going back. The Ruriks had been here for a number of months," stammered Sonya, amazed that he should ask such a question.

"I see," mused the man. "And isn't it barely possible you wait here for someone?"

"Why no, of course not. We plan on leaving in a few days. Who might I be waiting for in this deserted hole?" His question gave Sonya warning, and she steadied herself for the crucial question she was sure would come.

"Does the name Matsunaga sound familiar?" croaked Sonya's examiner, leaning forward and pushing his face close to hers as though inspecting her eyes.

Her reactions obviously disappointed the man because his question fell flat. Sonya had never heard the name and her cool answer demanded no acting.

"No, the name is not familiar."

"How about Paul York?" The man's words cracked like the snap of a whip.

Sonya braced herself. "No, neither is that name familiar."

Waiting for a break in Sonya's calm front, he paused and stared insultingly at her, but she held her emotions in check. Obviously irritated by the results of his interrogation, he nodded in the direction of the town. "Now, we'll take a look at your home. You lead the way."

On the way to her cottage, Sonya tried to remember if there was any incriminating evidence in her belongings. To the best of her ability, she remembered none—except the ring on her finger! Impulsively she started to slip the ring from her finger and then thought better of it. To remove it now might encourage suspicion

235

and where else would it be less likely to draw attention than right there on her finger. After all they were not likely to question the simple ring she wore. She prayed that would be the case.

When Katilka saw Sonya in the custody of the Japanese, she was panic-stricken and visions of violent action danced before her eyes. Seeing her mother's terrified expression, Sonya hastened to explain that nothing was wrong, and the Japanese were simply running a routine investigation. While Sonya comforted her mother, the two men searched the house. They ransacked the building from one end to the other, leaving wholesale disorder in their wake. They seemed to take special delight in throwing Sonya's intimate clothing in all directions. After their fruitless search and vulgar antics, they confronted Sonya and Katilka.

The civilian-dressed Japanese fired a volley of questions at Katilka along the same vein of thought as those previously pointed at Sonya. Katilka's answers confirmed Sonya's words and they gained nothing. Visibly provoked, the man glared nastily and gave a parting word. "Miss Petrovna, you may consider yourself under arrest although I am not taking you into custody. You are to return to Tientsin tomorrow and report to Colonel Yosuki of the Japanese gendarme. He expects you and will be waiting, so don't entertain any ideas about slipping away or going elsewhere. You will be watched constantly. The train leaves in the morning. You and your mother may pick up your travel permits and tickets at the police station this afternoon." Having spoken, he beckoned for his assistant to follow and stomped through the door.

There was nothing left for Sonya and Katilka to do but start packing, and they went about it in morose silence. To Katilka, the Japanese orders seemed simply irrational, but to Sonya they carried a deadly meaning. She could not discount the feeling something terrible would happen upon arrival in Tientsin. Escape from Colonel Yosuki was impossible, and she dared only guess at the vehemence in his heart. She would suffer the brunt of Paul's escape. *What else could wait in store for her?* Surely he knew of her contact with Paul, and now he was free to torture her at will. If only there were someone to turn to, something she might say, anything—anything to save herself. That night she

236

prayed. She prayed for guidance from above, and she prayed for Paul's aid, but she knew Paul was thousands of miles away and unable to help. No one could help her now. Her life lay in the hand of fate, and there was not the remotest indication fate would be other than cruel!

Unable to close her eyes, Sonya spent the entire night in restless anticipation of the next day, which would be the most terrible day of her life. She would be taken into custody by the Japanese gendarme, and could only guess at what would happen next.

Morning found her hopelessly rushing head-on to a total nervous collapse. Katilka failed to understand and tried in vain to stimulate Sonya's crushed attitude. However, Sonya refused to talk and continued to stare blankly, as though a person in a dream. Once aboard the train, Sonya fidgeted, twisted, and prayed—prayed for a miracle which had already transpired. This miracle did not just answer the pathetic prayers of one Russian girl, it answered the prayers of millions of people all over the world!

The day was August 14, 1945, a momentous day in history. Japan had surrendered unconditionally to the United States of America. *World War II was over!*

27

Sonya soon learned she would not have to report to Colonel Yosuki. Like many other devout Japanese, he lay dead in his office, having performed the honorable ritual and dropped his military body on the fine point of his ceremonial saber.

World War II would soon be a memory to last forever in the minds of all who lived and would live for centuries to come in the changed world. In step with the rest of the world, Tientsin, China rejoiced. Since they were the only armed body in the city, the Japanese remained in power, but they restricted their actions and dropped their belligerent attitude. They stood by passively as the once-subjected people held hilarious demonstrations and proclaimed their freedom. However, the Japanese restrained an otherwise uninhibited people, and it was well they provoked a semblance of order since curious Chinese presented a fertile field for mass hysteria.

The Russians, true to their blood, shouted praises for the homeland that had entered the war, but the majority of the people voiced their thanks to the United States as their liberator. Rumors flew as to if and when American troops would march into north China and assume control, but there were no indications such an action might happen. Some hoped for the Americans' arrival, for they contemplated the prosperity which would result from the U.S. occupation, while others hated the thought of having Americans in their front yard. Still, it was logical that American troops would be the first to enter Tientsin. The Chinese Nationalist troops were scattered thin over the broad battlefront of China and Manchuria and did not posses the transportation facilities for large-scale movements. Tientsin waited while the Japanese solemnly allowed unarmed Chinese to take over certain civic functions, such as police duties. At the same time, Japanese merchants and officials began a feverish scramble to put their houses in order for the eventual arrival of occupation troops, whomever they might be.

The most ardent exponents of American occupation were the hundreds of eligible girls, of many nationalities, who foresaw a gala time with the American troops. Some girls even carried their dreams further by thinking of marriage and legal entry to the bountiful country of America. In effect, their nets were stretched for the pleasure-loving Americans who may—or may not—come soon to expectant Tientsin.

These were good times, and a jovial atmosphere seemed to exist everywhere, with many parties prompted by the end of the war. It was one of these gatherings which changed the way Netti and Sonya perceived each other. Zola Seivberg had invited them, explaining the hostess was a girlfriend who occupied a suite of rooms in the hotel which housed the swank Del Conte restaurant. It was a get-together affair where friends invited friends and the hostess merely provided the location for the festivities. Thus, a broad cross-section of Tientsin's population found their way into the crowded apartment and rubbed elbows with strangers amid frequent introductions. Caught up in the lively swirl of men and women, Netti and Sonya were soon separated, but Netti caught glimpses of Sonya and noted she was drinking a lot. In recent weeks, it had been the same at all parties. Netti tried to overlook Sonya's heavy drinking, knowing it evidenced the distress over Paul, and only after drinks did she seem to loosen up and show interest in anything. Becoming disturbed, she began looking for Sonya.

Her search led her through the French doors to the balcony overlooking the street. Though the dimly lit balcony seemed vacant, she instantly perceived two people close together in one of the corners nearest the building. Though their faces were not readily discernible, instinct told her one of those people was Sonya. She sat on the railing with her back to the wall while some unidentified man, standing with his back to Netti, strained toward Sonya in either intimate embrace or close conversation. Horror-struck, Netti noticed immediately that Sonya's dress was pushed back nearly to her thighs, revealing her long silk-stockinged legs. The man's hand lingered familiarly amidst the soft curves of those legs, which glowed white where the silk stockings left off and the velvety skin began. Obviously, the couple were so wrapped up in each other, they failed to realize Netti's presence.

"Sonya!" Netti's shocked reprimand knifed the air.

"Netti—I, we didn't notice you," stammered Sonya, hastily pushing the man away and slipping off the railing to the floor.

"Obviously," snapped Netti.

Under the influence of her numerous drinks, Sonya wobbled toward Netti. "You're making shush a ridiculous scene. Pleash leave." Her thick tongue fouled her pronunciation.

"Not until you go with me." Netti's eyes glittered defiantly.

She stepped forward to lead Sonya away, but she stopped in the act of grabbing Sonya's arm. The man had turned toward the light and she recognized him. It was Rick Simon! Withholding the automatic greeting which rose in her throat, Netti turned away from his ironical smile, laid hold of Sonya, and hustled through the French doors. She wasted no time in propelling her inebriated friend through the crowd, down the stairs, and into the street.

Sonya sulked as she was whisked along the street in the direction of her apartment. Netti remained silent. She was too busy thinking of Rick Simon to indulge in conversation with the liquor-deadened Sonya. Rick Simon! Of all people for Sonya to become involved with, he was the most illogical. Netti knew him, or rather knew of him, as did practically everyone in Tientsin. Rick was a colorful, if not infamous character. A small, athletic type with light brown hair and a thin face accentuated by an aquiline nose, he lived by his wits and his wits alone. His dark murky eyes bespoke of the shrewd cunning person he was, and even the most dubious soon learned to respect his intelligence. Suave and well-mannered, he possessed the uncanny ability to converse fluently on any subject, from international relations to women's lingerie. People both liked and disliked him. He was so subtle he made most people like him. Yet he disturbed them because they wondered what lay under his glossy finish.

Very little was known about Rick's heritage and early life. One might guess his age at anywhere from thirty to thirty-five. Undoubtedly, Rick had found it advisable to grow up rapidly, and he looked thirty, ten years before his time. Rick's real name was Richard, but he had discarded it so long ago practically everyone knew him as just "Rick." Even those who knew him well were not sure of his nationality. He professed to be Russian and carried a Russian passport but his family name and mannerisms indicated he was of Jewish descent.

It was common talk that Rick had been an ardent collaborator with the Japanese and amassed a sizable fortune peddling narcotics for his Asian colleagues. True to his ingenuity, condemning evidence was never produced, but there was little doubt such was the case since he lived luxuriously without working and always basked in the friendly security of the Japanese. As a result of his close association with the Japanese, the Russian group of Tientsin shunned him. Rick was married and the father of a cute redheaded boy about five or six years old. His wife, a streamlined beauty whose activities bordered on promiscuity, had decided a number of years before that all she needed was his money. She lived apart from him, entertaining whom she pleased and squandering the cash he readily gave her. He permitted their marriage to remain legally intact because it provided privileges he could not otherwise enjoy.

The brisk walk sobered Sonya's spinning mind, and seeing her in an intelligible state, Netti pounced on the subject foremost in her mind. "Why, Sonya? Why did you allow yourself to be degraded by such a distasteful person?"

"I don't know. Guess I just felt happy and irresponsible," muttered Sonya.

"And such vulgar antics, is that life for you?" admonished Netti.

"No, of course not, I didn't mean it just that way. It's just that I have giddy desires to—well, oh, what's the use, I don't know how to explain to you. You wouldn't understand 'cause we've always thought differently. Maybe your set of standards are different than mine. Anyway, I'm sorry it happened as it did, and I expect I'm ashamed of it. I don't know! Please, my head feels like a pumpkin, let's not argue about it anymore."

Netti was persistent. "And Rick Simon, that's what dumbfounded me."

"I like him," Sonya snapped irritably. "He's different. I like him, even if you don't."

"I didn't say I don't like him. How could I? I've never met

241

him. Also, I didn't know you'd ever met him."

"I hadn't before tonight. He just walked up, offered me a drink, and that was that."

Netti shrugged her shoulders despairingly. She gained nothing by arguing with Sonya in her present state of mind. In Sonya's own words, Netti conceded to herself there were many subjects upon which they thought differently, and for the first time, she realized they traveled different roads. It had become more and more evident since Sonya returned from Peitaiho Beach and lived in her own apartment. Wanting complete independence, Sonya rarely saw her parents and Netti did not realize her friend had changed. Her associations with Paul and the calamitous events of their tempestuous love affair had made Sonya a woman, now mentally as well as physically. When they parted that night, both knew without speaking that their close companionship had eroded. In its place there would be mutual respect and lasting friendship bred out of many years together.

Something came hurtling through Sonya's open window and hit the far wall of the room with a resounding thud. The strange noise jerked Sonya out of her deep slumber and left her trembling as she sat upright in bed. Instinctively, she bounded to the window, and saw the retreating form of a man as he ran down the alley. Sonya's mind was none too clear, aching from her drinks of the night before, and it took a few seconds of stabilizing before she decided the object thrown through the window might offer some clue. Finding a rock, she discovered it carried an envelope tightly rolled and tied securely to it. She removed the envelope, ripped it open, and withdrew the typewritten letter. When she tried to read it, the words blurred before her eyes. Her agitation in realizing the letter was from Paul, combined with her frightful hangover, was too much. The letter still in her hand, she dropped on the bed to quiet the little devils viciously dancing inside her head. Finally the spinning top slowed down and she was able to read:

August 1, 1945
My Own Precious Sonya,
  You shall have received my radio message many days before

242

this letter arrives because this must go by underground routes, but I wanted to write before leaving for the States. Dave and I are leaving today. It is against my wishes, but the doctors here insist. I tell them I'm all right, but they won't believe me. Dave is typing this for me as I talk. I will read it over when we are done. Want to be sure this letter tells you what needs to be said.

There is great news today because the Japanese have asked for surrender terms, and I'm sure it means the war is over. Darling, it means more to you and me than just the end of a war. It means that soon we can be together for the rest of our lives. I pray for that day when I will see you again and be able to tell you in person how much I love you.

I will be coming back soon. Believe me, darling, I mean that with every ounce of strength in my body. They can't keep me in the States. The world isn't large enough to keep me away from you, and remember no matter how many thousands of miles separate us, we shall always be together because you remain constantly before me. Thank God for that, because just the thought of you gives me something to live for!

I have been thinking a lot while lying here in bed, and I know I must now confess to you. I hesitate to put this in a letter for fear you may not understand. Please, please try to understand what I am about to say. Sonya, I am married. Yes, I have been married to an American woman for nearly ten years. No, Jessica and I do not have children though at one time we wanted them. That has been a long time ago, and you must realize I haven't seen my wife or been with her in well over half of that time. Now I know I am going back and she will be waiting because Jessica is the type who would wait faithfully. It scares me. I need and beg for your support. Strangely enough I don't want to hurt her, and remembering Jessica vaguely as I do, I know she will be hurt. Please, darling, believe me when I say I do not love Jessica now, and sometimes I wonder if I ever did. You are the woman I love, and will love forever.

You of course are wondering why I never told you this before. It is because I was selfish and afraid if I told you I might lose you. I dared not take the chance because you mean too much to me. Also in those days when I should have told you, you would not have understood. Now I pray there is no doubt in your mind as to my love for you. If that is so, this should make no difference. Please forgive me, please forgive me for not telling you, for loving you so desperately I was afraid to tell you.

When I see Jessica, I will explain everything, and I'm confident

243

she will understand. Then I'll be free, free to return and make you my very own. That is my future, my whole life. You are my every-thing. Good-bye for just a little while. Remember, I do love you, love you more than words can ever express.

> *Your own,*
> *Paul*

There was a postscript written long-hand which said: "He has finally told you what I wanted him to tell you from the begin-ning. *My best to you. Always, Dave.*"

28

Please believe me! Please believe me! Over and over, the words raged in Sonya's brain. She laughed, but it was a painful laugh. It was funny, positively funny. She never dreamed Paul might be married, and it appeared so very logical now. She laughed again. Then her mockery turned to grief, and her proud indignation collapsed in the flood of wretched tears. She did not believe Paul because she did not want to believe him, and yet neither did she hate him. Their all-consuming love had burned too deeply into her heart. She stored the anguish within herself, where it grew and tormented her. In a bold attempt to comfort her ego, she turned to Rick Simon, but her thoughts of Paul never left. Despite trying to smother her love for Paul with Rick's attentions, there were many nights when she awoke crying from hurt and loneliness for the man who showed her the way to true love.

Rick Simon also needed companionship, particularly the companionship of a gorgeous and enticing woman, and he handed Sonya all the excitement of Tientsin on a silver platter. In turn, Sonya deliberately cultivated his affection and saw more of him than was good for either of them. He proved to be the acme of perfection in the art of squiring the fairer sex. His suave ability to handle all situations with finesse created in her a feeling of respect which she made herself believe was love. She found herself looking forward to the hours she spent with him and to the mature satisfaction he created. Though she hated herself for it, she began wanting more time with him. Her better sense cautioned her, but she was on a self-induced merry-go-round and could not stop the ride. Rick was adaptable to every situation and possessed the ability to provide an enjoyable time for any woman he dated. There was always a select table for him at the best restaurants and clubs, with choice foods and fine wines that were still a rarity in Tientsin.

Having received approval from Mr. Hecht to work only

part-time, Sonya's freedom actually created more distress thinking about Paul, and ultimately a greater desire for Rick who never seemed to work. Although he had a fully equipped office in his apartment located in an expensive tenement building, he was rarely there. This surprised Sonya, who enjoyed the comfort of the luxurious apartment with two bedrooms and reception room opening out on the second floor veranda. In particular, she liked the bathroom with large tub and lots of hot water often missing in her small apartment, where she had to fire up the stove to get hot water for a shower or sponge bath. Rick had given her a key and full access, permitting use of the place as she pleased.

When there was nothing better to do, Sonya took advantage of this privilege. There was a well-stocked bar of expensive liquors, a record player with a broad selection of records, and comfortable lounge chairs. Rick had managed to bathe his apartment with a lazy amiable atmosphere which was always relaxing. Sometimes in the evening they would sit quietly and listen to the music. Rick played the part of a gentleman friend and did not press Sonya, limiting their physical contact to an occasional hug and kiss on the cheek. She appreciated that because Paul was always there in the back of her mind.

Having spent the day working, the thought of a warm bath on the chilly fall day prompted Sonya to go to Rick's apartment. She found a towel, returned to the bedroom, and undressed. Holding the towel around her nude body, she slipped through the hall into the bathroom and settled in the big tub. She leaned back in the warm sudsy water, wanting to forget the cruel turn of events that had led her to an apartment owned by Rick Simon.

Her long hair fell into the water so she decided to wash it properly. She hated getting her hair wet, but the invigorating result of having the water splash over her face was too pleasant to resist. After her lengthy bath, she reluctantly got out, emptied the tub, and toweled herself hurriedly. Wanting to dress and make herself presentable before Rick came, she realized forlornly that her hair would be hours drying and thus look terrible. It hung in long, water-soaked waves and dripped water on the floor, as she spread the towel in front of her and stepped into the hall.

Shining from head to foot after her extended scrubbing, Sonya thought herself far from glamorous, but to Rick Simon, she presented a seductive picture. He stood in the hallway between her and the bedroom, grinning broadly at her instantaneous confusion. Drops of water still clung to her body as she stood rooted to the floor, frantically clutching the small towel which did a poor job of concealing her nude form. Delightfully aroused, Rick regarded her easily.

"Rick! I didn't expect you. I took, oh, I look awful," Sonya stammered amid her confusion. "Please, my clothes are in the bedroom."

"Good, that's a fine place for them, and to the contrary, I think you're gorgeous just as you are."

When he stepped toward her, it did not dawn on her to retreat to the bathroom. Her only thought was to gain the security of her clothes, which at the moment seemed far from her reach. She started toward the bedroom, but he stepped almost casually into the doorway and blocked her path. The thought of the inevitable conclusion to this spontaneous game fired Sonya's senses and sent the blood racing through her shivering body.

"You're dripping all over my hallway," he smiled, but his eyes held hers and did not take in the wet area, which formed around her bare feet.

"Yes," she murmured throatily. "I guess—I guess I am." Then she was in his arms, and his clothes were absorbing the moisture of her damp body. As their lips crushed together, her arms slipped around his neck, and the small towel dropped to the floor to lay neglected in the little pool of water.

Rick's lovemaking was all consuming and beyond Sonya's wildest dreams. It carried her away to soaring heights never before scaled by her most impetuous emotions and dropped her into rapturous depths. Finally, it left her weak and completely exhausted, incapable of even the slightest movement. Yet, she was content, gloriously content and happy to lie in the arms of the masterfully competent and pompous man beside her. As she dropped off into flawless slumber, Sonya did not realize she had stumbled onto an endless road where the direction signs were painted by the will of Rick Simon. There were no regrets because it was an easy road to follow, and the excitement produced the food for her insatiable hunger.

The little pool of water had vanished when Rick Simon stopped to pick up the towel which lay in his hallway.

29

It was August and WWII had just ended when planes appeared over Tientsin. Impressively grouped in perfect formation, the drone of their powerful motors attracted widespread attention among the curious masses and incited hilarious enthusiasm as the planes circled the city. Dark objects dropped from the planes and burst into white umbrellas, which dotted the pale blue sky. As the planes flew out of sight leaving their human cargo drifting silently to the ground, the exhilarated people below jostled one another in their efforts to reach the edge of the city where the parachutes seemed destined to contact the earth.

U.S. Marine Corps Major Jack Shull gave rapid orders to his paratroopers, and they had disposed of their chutes and zippered flight suits by the time the shouting people reached them. This was the first time Major Shull had parachuted into occupied territory wearing a regular uniform with campaign ribbons and insignia, and he was more than a little dubious concerning the welcome he might receive. Though Japan had surrendered, he had been cautioned his small command would be the first Allied troops to enter northern China and upon his shoulders rested a vital mission.

Following the surrender, American plans to occupy Japan and Japan-held territories were implemented and the Manchuria, north China area, was one priority. The decision was made to parachute in a small military contingent to ready the civilian population for the arrival of American troops as well as ease the sensitivity of the initial contact with the Japanese military. Uniforms rather than fighting dungarees would present the best impression.

Not trained as a diplomat, the major had been thoroughly briefed and knew diplomacy would be required. It would be a drastic mistake if American troops were belligerent when entering Japanese-held territories. Their work had to evidence a good relationship, combining finesse with authority. In the words of General McLawhorn, Major Shull's mission was "to contact the Japanese and Chinese authorities, establish a temporary headquarters for direct communication with the U.S. Command, ready the authorities and people for immediate occupation by United States forces, investigate occupational difficulties, and submit prompt reports." He had collected a small group of carefully chosen men and with such qualified aid, reasoned the job would be simplified.

When the Major made their identity known to one of the English-speaking Chinese, the word spread like wild fire and the jabbering masses lined the road to the city. Although Major Shull, nor any of his troops, had ever been to Tientsin prior to this day, they knew well what to expect. Their briefing had covered every point from building locations to politics. Further, they were well-supplied with the materials necessary to tackle the problems which faced them. Even before reaching the city and the real beginning of his task, Major Shull was thankful for the schooling given him in Chunking, and he was more thankful for the excellent interpreter who was assigned to his group. However, he could not help thinking how simple his task would be if his good friend, Paul York, were there.

When the Americans neared the International Bridge leading into the British concession, they were surprised to see a Japanese delegation approaching them. The crowd parted and the tense silence, which fell abruptly over the heaving masses, lent a calamitous touch to the scene about to transpire. Moving slowly across the bridge, the Japanese delegation produced an impressive picture of a nation not quite sure of its status. Comprised of authoritative civilians and military men who were once arrogant rulers, the Japanese were now unsmiling as they moved to meet the Americans who grimly watched their approach. Led by a straight-backed officer wearing heavy glasses, the body of Japanese moved closer and closer. Jack Shull found himself counting the even, deliberate steps of the Japanese officer. Not a sound was heard from the mass of people who watched breathlessly. There was a moment of indecision as the Japanese officer came face to face with the American Major and stood before him, proudly erect even in

250

defeat. Then the officer removed his cap and bowed low, thus signifying his humble subjection to the victorious country whose representative stood before him. When he straightened up, he removed the glittering saber which hung at his side and handed it to the American major. Throughout the solemn spectacle not a word was said, but as soon as Major Shull accepted the saber, a conversation ensued which ultimately explained the American position. Eager to please, the Japanese then escorted the Americans to the Astor House, which was reputedly the finest hotel in Tientsin.

Contrary to the expectations of the Japanese, Major Shull did not assume a ruling attitude and, in fact, was careful not to disrupt anything. His duties were strictly a matter of liaison between the Japanese in Tientsin and the United Stated headquarters in the Pacific area. He was collecting information and preparing for the eventual arrival of United States forces. To this end, he and his men worked industriously and efficiently, and still found time to investigate the intriguing city which surrounded them. Since they were the first of the victorious Americans to arrive in a city subjected for years, they discovered the populous of Tientsin toasted them wherever they went.

This was the beginning of a new era and a different way of life for the people of northern China and Manchuria. In the weeks that followed, American planes began using the airports at Tientsin and Peking to drop off personnel and equipment. Ships docked at Taku, the sea entrance to Tientsin, and began to unload U.S. Marine Corps personnel. The marines boarded trucks and entered Tientsin to occupy billets made available by the Japanese. They also had permission to confiscate what was necessary to provide adequate living, but had strict orders from the American Command to do so only with property owned by the Japanese, Italians, and Germans. They were to leave alone anything belonging to Chinese or Allied Nation people.

Japanese and Chinese officials greeted the marine leaders, and the citizens of Tientsin turned out to give a hilarious welcome to the American troops they viewed as their liberators. So exhilarated were the boisterous crowds which jammed the streets, the Chinese policemen struggled constantly to provide a path for the moving trucks.

The Chinese had made gigantic preparations for the triumphant arrival of the United States Marines. Enormous signs welcoming them to Tientsin and proclaiming them partners in China's victory were stretched high above the streets and plastered on building walls. Gigantic archways, meticulously constructed and wrapped with bright red paper trimmed in gold, were placed at strategic points along the route, and Chinese schoolchildren lined the streets waving flags.

In return, the marines were a jovial group, shouting from the trucks and bestowing their carefree nature upon the swarming masses. It was difficult for the curious Chinese to realize the laughing boys, who looked down at them from the passing trucks, were veterans of many bloody battles. Neither did these American troops present the colorful picture the Chinese had expected. Wearing battled-scarred helmets, well-worn dungarees, and carrying high-powered rifles, the American troops moved into Tientsin without the slightest show of flashing grandeur. However, their fighting garb was impressively business-like and demanded respect.

Initially, contact between the two races was restricted to quick glimpses as screaming jeeps and powerful trucks began moving through the cluttered streets. The Chinese watched awe-struck at the display of American equipment, and scurried to evade the vehicles which raced through the streets with blaring horns to move them out of the way. Nevertheless, they clapped and shouted gleefully to the marine occupants of these passing vehicles. Tientsin gave Americans the right-of-way as exemplified by the Chinese policemen who held up traffic and changed the streetlights to agree with the requirements of the American drivers. Eventual abuse of that right-of-way, coupled with the Americans indifferent attitudes, created some Chinese dissatisfaction, which would show in the months which followed. The Chinese learned much when they began meeting the American troops on the sidewalks and in their houses of business.

Having spent a few days putting their new homes in order for an extended stay, the marine commanders finally granted liberty to their troops. After months of exile and fighting on desolate Pacific Islands, the marines pounced upon Tientsin like hungry wolves. For nearly all of them this was their first contact with a world which heretofore had existed only in history books. In the minds of most, China was an antiquated country devoid of modern culture and conveniences. To find Tientsin a city comparable in appearance to many United States cities both amazed and delighted them. In addition to the prestige they carried, the marines liked their newfound property in a country where a viciously fluctuating rate of exchange made the American dollar worth thousands of Chinese dollars. They liked the thousands of tiny shops where for a pittance they could buy all types of expensive merchandise including cameras, furs, exquisite jewelry, silver pieces, pearls, silks, and priceless curios. They liked the wines, the liquors, the sumptuous twelve-course meals of steak, eggs, roast duck, seafoods, and rich French pastries. They liked the rickshaws, the cafés, the nightclubs, the music, and, most of all, they liked the women.

The Americans were plagued with invitations of all sorts from the Tientsin populous. These invitations were often amusing because they were motivated by the personal hopes of those wishing to ride the wave with the victors. Some had businesses long ago confiscated by the Japanese and they wanted them back—some wanted to initiate their prewar communications with the United States, some merely waned the friendship of the Americans and more importantly the security which went with it—and some wanted the companionship of the gregarious American male. In the latter category were women of many different nationalities who craved new faces. Under ordinary circumstances, only those lewd and bodacious females, of which Tientsin had its share, would pursue the attention of the foreign men. However, pride was often trod under amidst the scramble to capture the attractive American male, and even many women of better class disregarded their usual propriety.

To the marines who, for years, had foregone the pleasantry of an occidental woman's consuming embrace, it was like stepping into a land of make-believe. Both single and married women pressed their company on them, offered their services, and sometimes themselves in disgraceful antics. Gorging the fruit of endless delight, the Americans loved them all in their

253

typical light-hearted manner. With the married women, strained situations sometimes arose, but, oddly enough, the husbands wisely did not make an issue of it.

30

Netti was not without her share of invitations from the American marines. The display of beautiful silks, brocades, scarves, kimonos, and other ideal gift items for women in the boutique window was supposed to draw men into the shop, but the presence of the good-looking sales girl contributed to the greatest extent. She was amused when a marine would buy a kimono and ask for a date at the same time. Netti was probably right when she assumed that kimono, or the scarf, or the silk blouse was for a woman back home—probably a girlfriend. Despite this, some of the young men insisted on a date and being a good salesperson, Netti would carry on the jovial banter. The stopper for most of the invitations was when the eager marine learned he had to meet and pass scrutiny of Netti's mother.

Occasionally a determined marine was willing to accept the Rurik conditions and would end up with Netti on his arm. The drinks, dinners, and evenings made for enjoyable companionship. Netti liked all of them, but it ended there. She believed the day would come when she would meet the right man, maybe a marine who would take her to the United States.

A surprise announcement came from Catherine Rurik. "Netti, I've made a date for you."

Netti's mother repeated she had made a date and Netti was compelled to go. As it developed, the date was not with any specific person but a blanket invitation to a number of Tientsin girls. A respected Russian lady of Catherine's age, and one of her best customers, had contacted Catherine. She explained a group of American marine officers had acquired the luxurious Tientsin residence of Henry Pu Yi, last emperor of China, and they planned a gigantic housewarming party to show off their new quarters. Catherine's lady friend was asked by one of these officers, who had become rather well-acquainted with her, to provide dates for the party and she explained to Catherine this

255

officer had been careful to point out they planned a fine party for nice people. He wanted only respectable girls, and, in fact, requested the lady act as chaperon. She had accepted and proceeded to arrange the dates. Catherine Rurik was her first stop.

Netti consented, under duress, and prepared herself for a dull evening. At the appointed hour, a young marine officer presented himself at the door of the Rurik residence and was greeted by Catherine.

"Good evening," he said pleasantly. "I am Lieutenant Wilson. I believe arrangements have been made for me to pick up a Miss Netti Rurik at this residence. She was to attend a party we are giving this evening." He smiled good-naturedly and added, "Do I have the right place?"

"Yes, I'm her mother," Catherine answered. "Please come in. Netti will be ready soon."

"Thank you." The lieutenant doffed his cap and stepped into the lighted hall.

Catherine immediately liked the lieutenant dressed in the tailored green marine uniform. She liked the candid twinkle in his clear blue eyes, the engaging smile, and the firm confidence displayed by his gentlemanly demeanor.

Standing in the hall, the Lieutenant started to speak to Mrs. Rurik but Netti's appearance made further conversation with Catherine unnecessary. He nodded politely to Netti and waited for an introduction.

"Hello," Netti said shyly, thus acknowledging the lieutenant's presence.

"Lieutenant Wilson, this is my daughter Netti," offered Catherine.

"A pleasure, Miss Rurik." The Lieutenant stepped forward to help Netti on with her coat.

Netti kissed her mother fondly on the cheek. "Bye, Mums. I'll be home early."

As they stepped through the door, Lieutenant Wilson turned and offered a word of assurance to Mrs. Rurik. "We'll take good care of your daughter. We're having dinner and plan on dancing afterward, but it won't be a late party. Goodnight."

Catherine waved an approval. "Have a good time. Goodnight."

256

Aided by Lieutenant Wilson's firm hand, Netti climbed awkwardly into the waiting jeep and received a pleasant surprise. Two other girls were cramped into the tiny rear seat, and both were her friends. One was Zota Seivberg whom Netti had not seen in some time. "Zota! I didn't know you were going to this party."

"Oh yes, you'll find lots of the girls are going. I directed Lieutenant Wilson to your house." She flipped a gay laugh in the direction of the Lieutenant who was mounting the jeep. "He's a pretty good driver. At least we haven't killed any Chinamen."

Intent on evading the swarming Chinese who smothered the streets, the lieutenant said little during their ride. However, he did offer his apologies to the girls for being the only man to come for them. He explained since the jeeps were so small and there were so many people to transport, the officers had deemed it best to have one man pick up as many people as possible. He went on to say it was going to be necessary for him to make another trip upon depositing them at the house.

It was a cold damp night, and the ride in the open jeep chilled the girls. Thus, they were more than eager to abandon the machine when they reached the Japanese concession and the gigantic home which in previous years had been used as a refuge by Emperor Pu Yi. As they were the first guests to arrive, the girls were met enthusiastically by the officers who awaited them. After Lieutenant Wilson introduced them around and made sure they were in good hands, he excused himself to make another trip.

When Lieutenant Wilson left, he took along Netti's self-confidence, and with all the new names spinning in her brain, she felt ill at ease. Subconsciously, she placed trust in Lieutenant Wilson despite the fact she had known him less than an hour. She smiled and chatted with the officers who took turns waiting on her. She even accepted a tiny drink but she made up her mind the evening would not be satisfactory until Lieutenant Wilson returned. During his absence, more jeeploads of guests arrived, and they included both men and women from the age of sixteen to sixty. There was a grandmother who had been courteously asked because her daughter and son-in-law were coming. One young girl had been forced to bring her

257

brother as a personal chaperon. Netti knew practically all of them and noted that her mother's friend had been careful to select respectable people.

Restricted to the group conversations, the party moved slowly as the officers and guests roamed the pompous living room and neat barroom. When Lieutenant Wilson returned, Netti watched him as he hurried here and there, and she realized he carried the responsibility of the party's success. He laughed and joked with the various guests, subtly steered backward officers in the direction of deserted women and, in general, kept the group alive to produce an amiable atmosphere. Since Netti was well entertained by a host of admirers, Lieutenant Wilson's duties did not include her. However, when he announced dinner and directed the assemblage to the dining room, Netti found him escorting her. Having seated her in one of the two chairs at the end of the long banquet table, Lieutenant Wilson stood behind the other and suitably directed each person to their place at the table. Upon completion of his task, she noted his skill had appropriately seated the large gathering in a manner so the hosts were well-proportioned and no two women sat together.

A Major sat on Netti's right, and during the excellent multi-course meal efficiently served by a host of Chinese servants, she divided her conversation between him and Lieutenant Wilson. She enjoyed herself until the Major placed her in a rather embarrassing position by insisting on being granted the privilege of escorting her home after the party. Unable to picture herself dating the older man, she tried desperately to evade the subject. The Major was feeling the before-dinner drinks and continued trying to extract an affirmative answer from her. Caught without a logical reason for a polite refusal, Netti was hedging awkwardly when Lieutenant Wilson came to her rescue.

Leaning over the table to catch the Major's attention, he said humorously, "You're wasting your time, Major. She has already accepted my invitation to see her home."

The Major laughed good-naturedly, and Netti slipped Lieutenant Wilson an appreciative wink. However, she did not think Lieutenant Wilson meant his statement until later in the evening when they were dancing. He had spread his dancing around to most of the women present, but managed to dance with Netti by far the majority of the time. She did not object because she liked his company. But when he asked for verification of his date, she refused.

"But why?" asked the Lieutenant, leading her to a divan where they seated themselves. "Aren't you grateful to me for getting you out of that scrape? I have to take you home now to make it appear authentic to the Major."

"I don't even know your first name," said Netti, indicating they were not well enough acquainted.

"That's easily fixed. It's Gerald, but I prefer Gerry. Okay?"

"All right, you may take me home, Gerry," she said placing humorous emphasis on his nickname. "But it's home. Straight home. No stops, no detours."

Lieutenant Wilson did not appreciate Netti's assumption he was not to be trusted and responded in a cold tone. "Wait a minute. You have some wrong ideas. I'm engaged to a girl in the States. I love her very much and am going to marry her the instant I get back. Being unfaithful to her will never happen. You need not worry about advances from me."

His straightforward honesty pleased Netti. She said simply, "I believe you and I like you. Maybe we can have some good times together since we understand each other now."

"Sure, why shouldn't we go out together? I'm new here, you can show me Tientsin, and it will help me with the lonely days."

Lieutenant Wilson took Netti home that night and saw her the next day. Having explicit confidence in Lieutenant Wilson, Catherine Rurik condoned Netti's dates that followed. Gerry's pledge of fidelity to his fiancé had discounted any possibility of eventual complications, and Netti trod on solid ground. Going with him was fun and she asked nothing more—nor did he.

Netti became acquainted with Gerry's fellow officers, whom she learned to like immensely. In fact, she liked it all—the dancing at The Forum, meals at the Del Conte, drinks at Gerry's house, movies in the Tientsin theatres which were now receiving American productions, rides in the jeep, and evenings at her home. Mostly, she enjoyed the times they spent at the famous

Tientsin Country Club which had been taken over by the Americans for the use of their officers. There, they could eat, drink, dance, and meet the class of people Netti desired as associates.

31

The American marines were attracted to the beautiful Russian girls who sometimes presented an aloof attitude and ignored their pleas for a date. It was not difficult for Sonya Petrovna to say thank you—and no thank you. She was wrapped up in memories of Paul York, and wondering about his physical condition persisted. There were many restless days where she fought her mixed emotions, and she found relief for her mental anguish by spending more time with Rick Simon, despite the fact he was married and likely to remain so. After all, she salved her conscience by remembering Paul also was married. Her frustration reached peaks, which Rick noted and addressed by his suave methods. But he never allowed Sonya the satisfaction of saying "I love you."

When Sonya started believing she had learned to live without Paul and could put up with Rick, she was awakened by the fact her love for Paul would always be there and needed only a spark to revive it. That spark was supplied suddenly one day when Huang Chu confronted her as she strolled along Taku Road. She followed Chu into a dim doorway, remembering the last time she saw him. It was at Peitaiho Beach when he gave her the information there had been a shoot out with the Japanese, that Paul was wounded, and Burl Manning was killed. Now, here in front of her was the same kindly Chu. *Why did he want to see her?* It had to be news about Paul, and a feeling of foreboding caused her to tremble, even though she tried to remain calm.

"Chu, it's good to see you."

"Makes me happy to see you, too," Chu said in his normal warm manner.

Sonya was scrutinizing Chu and what she saw was shocking. "Chu, you've really aged. You look like an old man. In heaven's name, what has happened to you?"

Chu smiled wistfully. "Yes, Miss Sonya, grow old fast when

261

Japs know I have information they want."

"What?" Sonya blurted.

The far away look, which showed in Chu's dark eyes, told far more than the words. "After fooling them for many years, they caught me."

Chu pulled back the wide sleeve of his Chinese coat. His right hand was horribly deformed. It was obvious the bones on his hand and fingers had been broken and healed without medical attention. "They crush hand in vise. They want information. No talk. Beat me. Guess left to die."

Sonya turned her head away. Her heart cried for the faithful little Chinaman who had suffered such untold agony. Nausea gripped her, and she fought off the faintness which emerged. "Oh, Chu!" she gasped.

"Please, Miss Sonya, don't cry. Will not bring hand back."

"Does Mr. York know?"

It warmed Chu to see the genuine affection this white girl showed for him, and a smile of gratitude spread over his face. He started again to answer in his poor English, but emotionally upset, he became confused and switched to Chinese. "No, Mr. Paul does not know. Our contact is poor these days. Our grapevine used to function officially—now it is mostly personal. I believe it's just as well he doesn't know. He has enough agony of his own. That is why I come to you, to bring you news. Bad news I'm afraid."

Chu's words froze Sonya, leaving her tense and unable to speak. She wanted to cry out and ask him not to tell her, but she could do nothing more than stare vacantly awaiting the message she knew would tear at her very soul.

Chu began slowly in a barely audible voice. "You will probably be getting better information. I know little and was asked to give you this message. He has lost an arm and a leg. They had to take them to save his life."

Taking a deep breath, Sonya was able to get out just three words. "Are you sure?"

"No, it is all I know."

Sonya was not prepared for news such as this. She knew for a man like Paul, loss of an arm and a leg could be a more cruel fate than death. Her mind whirled crazily as she slumped against the wall and would have fallen to the sidewalk had Chu not steadied her. At first, there were no tears because the shock simply deadened her feelings like a powerful anesthetic, leaving a dull expression on her pale face. Then she started to whimper like a frightened child and tears gushed forth to drench her cheeks.

"Oh, Chu, it's horrible. I can't imagine—I simply can't think of Paul like that. Oh, my god!"

Chu continued to hold Sonya upright, and he tried to ease the pain as best he knew how. "Maybe it isn't as bad as we think. You are supposed to get a letter. It may tell you more."

"What letter. Who brings it? When?"

"I do not know. I was simply told a letter was being sent."

For a long time, the white girl and the little Chinaman stood together in the doorway while the passing crowds wandered by without so much as an interested glance in their direction. When Sonya finally gained control of her emotions, Chu stepped into the street and disappeared in the throng of humanity which surged along the road.

Sonya walked aimlessly among the people who swarmed along the busy trading street, her right thumb nervously flicking the plain gold ring she wore on that hand. Eventually, her steps led to the seclusion of her little apartment, and she closed out the rest of the world. Her mental anguish was all consuming as she dropped to the bed and covered her face with the pillow.

Rick Simon missed Sonya for she failed to make her customary appearance in his apartment. This irritated him because he looked forward to the evenings with her. However, he was not the type to express concern and refused to investigate her absence. The second day he received a note saying she did not feel well and would see him soon. Sonya's note appeased Rick, but it did not give him the actual reason for her absence.

Sonya confined herself to her apartment. She was mentally ill, confused and despondent. Realizing she must get control of her feelings, she tried to avoid active consideration of Paul York, but he was there in the conscience, which had never been more evident. His horrible mutilation produced an unanticipated sequence to the sensitive love he had instilled in her many times. No one could advise her. It was something she had to endure

263

alone. True to her pattern she rationalized it was her due and a few days later she went to see Rick with his easy way of life. But the plight of Paul York did not go away and Sonya looked forward to the letter Chu said would be coming.

32

When word spread through Tientsin that more Americans had arrived by plane, intuition told Sonya the letter Chu referred to was being carried by one of them. She was impatient and thought of contacting some one of them to ask about a letter. She realized how ridiculous this would be and fought down the impulse.

Sonya did not have long to wait. Her intuition was right. Only a few days elapsed before she received the contact she expected. It was in the form of Tian Wei, who stopped her as she emerged from her apartment. She was astonished at Wei's dress. He was wearing a U.S. Marine officer's uniform with the rank of Second Lieutenant. Her amazed expression disappeared when he started to speak. His perfect English matched the uniform he wore.

Sonya could not resist. "Wei—I can't believe this is you."

"Yes, just the same. Just a different outfit. You can now call me Edwin Tian if you like. I'm acting as interpreter for the Americans. So much for that. Miss Petrovna, a Lieutenant Lee wants to meet you at the Astor House."

"And who is Lieutenant Lee?" Sonya asked dubiously.

"An American officer who just arrived. He's waiting and has a letter for you. Can you go now?"

When they entered the lobby of the Astor House, Sonya was surprised by the activity in the usually sedate hotel. The lobby was crowded with men chatting in little groups while Chinese attendants scurried around performing various duties. As Wei propelled her in the direction of a small lounge next to the lobby, she asked, "Why all this confusion?"

"Simple. These people are here to see the Americans for business or personal reasons. There's Lieutenant Lee coming to meet us."

Sonya looked in the direction of Wei's nod to see a tall gangling boy detach himself from a uniformed group of Americans and walk toward them. He wore the uniform of a United States Army officer and this youth with a mop of curly blond hair seemed out of place in this uniform of authority. Only when he stood before her did he look much older. The result of hard experience showed in his steel gray eyes.

He did not wait for Wei's introduction. "So you're Sonya Petrovna. I've heard so much about you I feel as if I already know you."

Sonya met his warm gaze with an equally pleasant one. "Yes, I'm Sonya Petrovna."

Wei broke in determined to accomplish his introduction. "Miss Petrovna, Lieutenant Lee."

All three laughed spontaneously, and Wei departed graciously as Lieutenant Lee steered Sonya into a corner of the room where they could talk in reasonable privacy. Even before he spoke again, Sonya decided she liked Lieutenant Lee.

"Miss Petrovna, I apologize for being able to spend only a few minutes with you. I'm the pilot stuck to ferry a group of rank around. Right now I'm standing by to fly some colonels to Rangoon."

"I understand," acceded Sonya. "I'm just impatient to get the letter Wei said you have for me?"

"Of course, Paul gave me specific instructions to give it to you personally, so I appreciate your coming here right away. He also asked me to do something else."

"Yes, what?"

The lieutenant grinned at Sonya's pointed question. "It wasn't to kiss you, but I admit I wish it was. He asked me to see if you were wearing his ring. I assume it must be the one you have on."

"Yes, it is," Sonya blushed. She did not understand these Americans.

Lieutenant Lee noticed her embarrassment and went on hurriedly. "He said it may be a sentimental gesture and yet asked me to read the inscription to you. May I?"

Sonya hesitated. She was uncertain of such an odd request, but knew it would be like Paul to do something of this nature. Dubiously, she slipped the ring from her finger and handed it to

Lieutenant Lee. He took the ring and held it to the light.

He spoke softly. "SP, My Love Forever, PY."

The way Lieutenant Lee read those words created a disturbance within Sonya, which she could not quiet. She wanted to leave—to be free of the involved thoughts brought to mind. If only he would give her the letter so she could take it away and suffer in silence. She trembled visibly as he returned the ring to her finger.

The Lieutenant sensed her discomfort and hastened on. "I saw Paul only a few days ago, and could tell you many things you might like to know. From what he said, his letter will tell you everything, and I had better leave it that way." He reached inside his blouse, withdrew a long white envelope, and handed it to Sonya. "Here's the letter. Now I must excuse myself. It's been nice to meet you and I do hope we may meet again. You can be sure I'll look you up if ever I get back this way."

"Thank you—thank you very much," quivered Sonya, clutching the letter in her hand. "I, too, hope we meet again."

The Lieutenant escorted Sonya through the milling crowd and waved good-bye as she sped down the street. He had been very kind, and Sonya truthfully did hope to see him again. Right now she could think only of the letter which seemed to sear the nerves of the hand which held it. It took all her will power to keep from stopping in the middle of the street to read it. When safely within the confines of her apartment she ripped open the envelope. It was written in longhand without a heading.

My Darling Sonya,

It has not been long since I wrote you from Chungking, and it seems like years. I have thought of you constantly and wondered if I should bother you. Since being restricted to this hospital I've relived every moment we spent together, the sadness, the joy. I can close my eyes and see you, clearly as if you were here.

Even as I write this I know it is wrong to pass my unhappiness on to you. My left arm is gone, and I'm writing this on a clipboard held by my knees. Hope you can read it. My recovery has taken time because they had to take some slugs out of my hip area.

Thinking of you helps. I have come to understand losing an arm does not mean the end of everything but it does mean changes.

I want you darling, I want you now as always—but no one

*knows better than I it would be unfair to deaden your zest for liv-
ing by attaching you to a man crippled for life. You are vivacious
and carefree. That is the way I always want you to be. I know you
date Richard Simon, a man of questionable character. Who am I to
object? If he brings you happiness that is all I can ask.*

*I have Jessica, and she has shown her love for me from the
moment I returned to the States. She will always be true to me and
it's depressing to know I do not love her anymore. I have told her
about you. She makes no issue of it. Just said she understood and
is willing to put up with me—for life I guess.*

*What I have written here has been difficult to say. Always
know I love you. Please write. Chu or Wei will know how and where
to send it wherever I'm settled.*

*Forever yours,
Paul*

The letter confused Sonya. She read it a second time. It still
said the same thing. Paul was bowing out in spite of the love he
still held for her. She could not believe that Paul had accepted a
defeatist attitude even though he had lost an arm. It was not
both an arm and a leg as Chu had said—just an arm, but maybe
that was too much. Paul's love still vibrated deep within her and
his attitude encouraged a surge of impulsive fury, which dis-
torted her reasoning. Had Sonya honestly tried to understand
Paul's letter, she could not have failed to see it was a weak
attempt to be noble. His real plea lay between the lines, where he
asked her to assure him their love overshadowed all else, and his
impairment did not matter. The tragedy once again was Sonya
not understanding the meaning—or did not want to.

Paul asked for a letter. She would send him one—now while
the subject burned in her mind. She began scribbling the note
destined to be the answer to his admirable letter. Her note was
not rude—it was not unkind. It was impersonal. She told him
she agreed with his letter and since he asked for the termination
of their love, she conceded. She added little else, for what could
be added to such a note. They were through. Her act of sealing
the envelope and stuffing it in her purse was like hanging a
mourning wreath on their love for each other.

She was determined to get it on the way and started for the
Astor House hoping to catch the now-Lieutenant Edwin Tian so

she could sent the note to Paul immediately. She was fortunate! Wei was just leaving the Astor House and was surprised to see her.

"Miss Sonya, I was on my way to find you."

"Why?"

"An American officer wants to see you."

"Lieutenant Lee again?"

Wei did not elaborate. "No, another one. Follow me and I'll introduce you."

Sonya's impatience showed with her curt reply. "I'm tired of this. Why do all these officers want to see me? I'm not that popular."

"Frankly speaking, I don't know. I only work for him. He is my superior and I was hardly in a position to ask. You shouldn't be concerned. He is a fine person."

Wei's explanation did not satisfy Sonya but her curiosity was aroused. Meeting an American who took pains to solicit her presence might be interesting. Her day had already been packed with surprises—some joyful, some painful. As she took Wei's arm and let him lead her to the second floor of the hotel, she hoped this surprise would be a happy one.

Wei ushered Sonya into an office and introduced her to a man in military uniform who arose from a broad desk and stepped over to greet her. She was wondering about his age and rank when Wei introduced them, and she failed to catch his name. Wei had left the office.

The officer extended a friendly hand and motioned to a chair near the desk. "Please be seated, Miss Petrovna."

"I'm sorry, I did not get your name," Sonya said with some hesitation.

"Colonel Gordon, Bruce Gordon to be exact," he said in a joking way. "Now you know my first name. I'm called Colonel so often, I've just about forgotten it."

Sonya laughed and said, "Think I better use Colonel."

"I appreciate your taking time to see me so soon. Lieutenant Tian is really efficient. It was only a few minutes ago I asked him to find you."

While the man arranged himself behind the desk, Sonya took time to look at him. She liked what she saw. His square, leathery face and graying hair made him seem older than the forty-five to fifty she guessed him to be. His warm brown eyes and his kindly expression gave him a fatherly appearance which inspired her trust. The tan shirt he wore was thrown open at the collar in harmony with his easy manner. She was not aware of his rimless glasses until he removed them and placed them carefully on the desk.

"You know, Miss Petrovna," he began slowly in a congenial voice, "you and I have a lot in common. We both love Paul York." His words startled Sonya. "You seem surprised that I should know about you and Paul. Well, maybe you should be, but it's quite simple. I've known Paul for a good many years and he's— well, he's sort of like a member of the family. Not many days ago I talked with him and told him I was going to be stopping by Tientsin. I told him that because the week before when I called on him he talked of nothing else but you. I thought he might want to send you some word. He told me he didn't want me to. Said he had written a letter which would suffice. I suppose you have received it by now?"

"Yes, only today," Sonya answered. She was trying to conceive this man's ultimate reason for talking to her.

"I suspected as much. I guessed Paul was sending the letter by some member of our party and didn't want me to bring it. I believe he hoped I would not talk to you." The Colonel spoke low and deliberately. As he talked his hand fumbled for a pencil, but his eyes held Sonya. "He didn't want me to talk to you because he was afraid I would tell you the truth. Did his letter tell you about his arm?"

"Yes."

"I can guess at the rest of the letter," the Colonel continued knowingly. "Despite what he told you, Sonya I want you to know Paul loves you more than even his own life. He talks of nothing else. Somehow I feel his life depends on you." He stopped talking and watched Sonya closely, as though making sure she grasped the meaning of his words. "If you cast him aside now I think he may die mentally, even physically. His spirit is already dead." The colonel paused again to gauge Sonya's reaction. "Do you *understand* what I am saying? I am asking you to help him. I'm convinced you can do more than anyone else."

Fumbling for a sensible answer, she muttered, "I—I expect I

understand but—but he said he didn't want me anymore. He was nice and said it was all over."

"He warped the truth as I knew he would."

Sonya was remembering the letter and realized the true text of its meaning. And her note to Paul? A feeling of guilt restrained her from telling the colonel about it. Paul also wrote it was all right for her to keep seeing Rich Simon. Self-hatred flamed within her and left a distaste for all her miserable entanglements. Hunting for excuses, she remembered Jessica and her thoughts flared into words.

"He has a wife. What am I to be—a mistress of some sort? I have no obligation. He wasn't fair with me. I'm not even sure I love him anymore. I did once—I did love him with all my heart. If that love is gone, he killed it—not me." Sonya raved uncontrollably, and her words became sarcastic. "A wife, Jessica—trusting, loving, devoted Jessica. The words make me sick. Why should he want me? I'm not trusting, or devoted, or even loving. And then he writes a letter telling me we are through. What am I to do in the face of all that—beg at his feet?" Her voice was vicious, taunting, nearly screaming, and she bit her lip to keep from crying.

The Colonel moved slowly around the desk and stood in front of Sonya. "Please, Miss Petrovna, such anger will not help us—or Paul," he said in a fatherly tone. "I admit Paul has a wife, and Jessica is a wonderful woman. The sad part is Paul does not love her."

Sonya jumped to her feet and faced the man defiantly. "I don't care what she is. Jessica! I hate the word, I hate her!" she cried maliciously. "She must be a fool, an idiot!"

The man standing before Sonya reddened, and his eyes grew icy. "Miss Petrovna," he snapped, fighting to withhold his temper. "I realize you are wrought up and saying things you don't mean, but when you degrade Jessica York you carry it too far. She happens to be my sister."

Sonya stood stupefied, then turned and fled from the room. Fate had entered the scene. She had forgotten to give Wei her note to Paul and it was still in her purse.

33

The meeting with Colonel Bruce Gordon changed Sonya's inner-most feelings about Paul York. It brought Jessica York plainly into view, and her position with Paul could not be dismissed. Also, Paul's knowledge of Rick Simon hung over Sonya like a shroud. She now knew she had to address her relationship with Rick.

Rick was good to her and gave her everything she wanted, mostly in a material way. He paid the rent on her apartment, provided food, and purchased the clothes she wanted. Her part-time job permitted too much loafing around and too much time with Rick. *What did she want? Did she want to go on being a kept woman—a mistress?* Longtime friends tried to ignore her dating Rick, but cool attitudes evidenced their true feelings.

Colonel Gordon had sparked Sonya's realization she was living a repugnant life. It left her ashamed and sorry. This was a period of self-blame and bitter distaste with herself before finding the right path. With strong determination, she severely limited her association with Rick and set out to find a full-time job. Someone surely would have faith in her.

Returning from a fruitless morning of job hunting, Sonya was surprised to find Lieutenant Edwin Tian lounging in front of her apartment. She still had trouble picturing him in a uniform and said so. "Lieutenant, you are going to continue being Wei to me. You may as well go back to Chinese clothes."

Wei started to take off his jacket and joked, "Find me some Chinese clothes. I'll do it right here."

That lightened the load Sonya was carrying. She wrapped her arms around him saying, "No need, at least not here. Why are you here?"

"That hug is the best thing that's happened to me all day, let's do it again."

"No way. Again, why are you here?"

272

Wei responded, "Waiting for you. I have another invitation."

Sonya's wrinkled brows evidenced her immediate concern. "It isn't the same officer, is it?"

"The same one, Colonel Gordon. He said to carry you if necessary. Well, not really, he was emphatic and in a good mood."

"No, I can't face him—not after that awful scene. Please, tell him I'm sorry."

"You will be glad to see him," Wei said as he waived a rickshaw to a stop beside them.

Any further protests from Sonya were overruled by Wei's quiet determination as he took her arm and guided her into the rickshaw. He paid the rickshaw boy and gave him rapid instructions. Turning to Sonya, he said, "I'll follow." By the time he mounted his human-propelled vehicle, Sonya's rickshaw boy was loping along Victoria Road in the direction of the hotel. Upon arrival at the Astor House, she waited for Wei, who escorted her to the same second-floor room from which she had fled. The door opened promptly at Lieutenant Tian's knock and Sonya found herself facing Colonel Gordon.

Sonya blushed amid her confusion and smiled awkwardly. She did not know what to say and felt ill at ease. Colonel Gordon took the initiative in his kindly way by saying cordially, "Thank you for coming, Sonya. I was afraid you might refuse."

Words failed Sonya as the Colonel ushered her into the room and closed the door. Only when seated did she find the courage to say what was in her heart. "Sir, I'm sorry about the other day. Please accept my apologies for being so rude."

"By all means," Colonel Gordon said. "I am of the opinion we both owe apologies. I extend mine."

Colonel Gordon pulled a chair close to Sonya's and sat down. "First, I have discovered a job for you. That is, if you think you might like it—being a hostess at the American Recreation Center. A number of local girls work there. Many are part-time volunteers but some are paid for regular work to maintain consistency. You would be perfect and it can be enjoyable. It means entertaining our lonely boys—serving food, drinks, dancing, making conversation, playing games, and so on. No dating required, and in fact, it is prohibited. It won't pay much but pretty good by local standards. So, what do you think?"

"How did you know it was I looking for a job?" Sonya asked. "It was Wei, that's it, Lieutenant Tian."

"Yes, Lieutenant Tian told me. I gather he sort of looks out for you. But you haven't given me an answer. How about it?"

"Oh, I know I would love it. Thank you."

"It's settled then. Here, take this to the officer in charge there. His name and the address of the place is on the envelope," the Colonel said as he handed her the envelope. "And now I want to show you an official document we just received."

He picked up a yellow sheet from his desk and handled it to Sonya. "The message wouldn't interest you, even if you could decipher it. It's military stuff from the States. The line at the bottom is for you."

Sonya scrutinized the official looking document. The word CONFIDENTIAL stood out in bold-faced type at the top of the page, followed by a maze of numbers and words she did not understand. Eager to find the line to which the colonel referred, she skipped to the bottom and spied the word "Paul," which began a line at the very bottom of the page. It said, "Paul sends love to Sonya."

She read the line a second time, choked back the lump in her throat, and handed the paper back to the colonel. Paul sending her a note in this fashion caught her off balance. Noting her distress, the Colonel hastened to say, "Making personal messages with an official one is forbidden. I was surprised to see this and doubt Paul really did this. Yet, his ability to get sensitive things done has always amazed me."

"So, who would do this?"

"I don't know and don't plan to try and find out. Let it be. The important message I want you to get is from Jessica. I phoned her yesterday when this showed up. I decided it was necessary to talk to you before I leave Tientsin in the next day or so."

"Please, I don't want to know anymore about Jessica." Sonya pleaded. "She is your sister and you understand. I don't—I don't know where I fit in."

The Colonel leaned toward Sonya and his expression was soft and serious as he said pointedly, "Sonya, I'm going to tell you where you fit in. You hold the key to Paul York's well-being—maybe his entire future."

Sonya again wanted to flee from the presence of Colonel Gordon but knew it would only create more pain. The colonel ignored the dismay showing clearly on Sonya's face. "Paul is morbid, depressed beyond control. Jessica thinks it is because he has not heard from you. He talks only of you even when Jessica is with him. You have to send him some word. I'll help you."

"How? I can write a letter but I don't know how to send it," Sonya said sadly.

The Colonel reached over and laid a comforting hand on her shoulder. "I can send it for you."

Sonya grasped his hand. "You would, really? Would it help?"

"I'm sure it would. Here, use my desk." He stood up and pushed paper and pencil to the middle of the desk. "I'll be back in a few minutes. Remember, it can't be too long."

Sonya was picking up the pencil when the Colonel closed the door. After some futile starts, she finally finished a short note and waited for Colonel Gordon's return. When he entered the office she handed him the slip of paper saying, "I wasn't sure what to say."

"May I?" he asked.

"Of course." Sonya wanted him to see what she had said but the color rose in her cheeks when she thought of him reading her intimate words to Paul.

Colonel Gordon picked up his glasses from the desk, carefully put them on and held up the note. It read:

Paul my darling,
Please forgive me for not contacting you somehow. I love you. I love you with all my heart and I shall always want you no matter what.
Forever your own,
Sonya

Colonel Gordon nodded approvingly and laid the paper on his desk. Then he walked over, put an arm gently around Sonya's shoulder, and led her to the door. He held her for a moment, locked his eyes with hers and said, "It will go out today. Paul should have it soon. Sonya, you are a good woman, I want you to know it. Be proud. I am sure you will always do what is right, and you have my blessing."

As Sonya walked slowly towards her apartment her prayers were with Paul and it filled her with sorrow. Despite it all, there was certain lightness in heart, a feeling she had not experienced in a long time and Colonel Gordon was now calling her Sonya.

34

Netti had accepted a pleasant companionship with Lieutenant Wilson, but one thought continued to plague her. It did not deal with him. It was her continued concern about Sonya. Sonya had not been invited to the now talked about housewarming party given by the marine officers, and the reason was obvious. The senior women doing the inviting for the marines were well aware of Sonya's romancing with Rick Simon.

The Tientsin tongues wagged. The malicious gossipers viewed Sonya's actions with disdain, others lifted a knowing eyebrow, but most of them talked and forgot. However, no one condoned her actions and she discovered a cold aloofness among even her most intimate friends. Even a long friendship could not override the distaste for Rick Simon, the man who allowed his greed for money to drive him into the receptive arms of the hated Japanese. Though the Japanese regime had collapsed and it was logical to assume the termination of Rick's business with them, the stain remained, and many associates refused to forget easily. Of all the people who stood on the sidelines watching Sonya's impertinent actions, one was deeply grieved. That person was Netti Rurik. It was impossible for her to accept a passive attitude toward her lifelong friend. Continuing to keep track of her, Netti now noticed Sonya was making a real effort to pull away from Rick Simon.

Freezing weather and occasional flurries of snow meant it would soon be December and thoughts naturally turned to Christmas. Tientsin expected a buoyant season for the first time in years even though the lack of coal left many homes uncomfortably cold. The skyrocketing prices were due largely to the American's needless spending which the natives could not match, and many were limited to just life's necessities.

Although Christmas was weeks, away it promised to be a lively season because the U.S. Marines who swarmed through

Tientsin were already bubbling with the holiday spirit. For most of them it would be their first Christmas in years spent in true civilization, and they planned to make the most of it.

As Gerry and Netti absorbed the gaiety of The Forum, they could see and feel the Christmas spirit generated by the revelers around them. The Americans made themselves at home in their adopted city, acquaintances blossomed rapidly, and mixed parties could be seen laughing and drinking throughout the club.

Netti touched Gerry's arm and nodded to a couple leaving the dance floor. "There's a very good friend of mine. I want you to meet her."

Gerry took in the voluptuous woman and her civilian partner and said, "Sure, I'd like to. Why don't you call them over to our table."

"Let's go over to their table," suggested Netti, starting to rise.

When they approached the table, the gentleman stood up and greeted Netti with a warm smile. The woman added a happy greeting, and Netti hastened to make the introductions.

"Lieutenant Wilson, Sonya Petrovna and Rick Simon."

"How do you do." Gerry nodded politely to Sonya and took Rick's extended hand.

"Won't you join us?" offered Rick. "We need some company."

Netti and Gerry took the seats Rick offered, and a lively conversation was soon underway. Rick's instant comprehension of military lingo somewhat amazed Gerry, and his subtle questions on military matters aroused dubious thoughts in Gerry's mind. Ever cautious, Gerry gave vague answers and wondered what it was about the suave gentleman which did not fit the frank character Rick attempted to portray. Possibly it was Rick's almost too clever manner—it intimated subversive cunning. Despite Gerry's curiosity, Rick's brilliant talk incurred appreciation, if not trust, and Gerry found himself enjoying his company.

As the afternoon wore on, Gerry suggested they adjourn to his quarters for a few drinks in privacy. Rick readily agreed and Sonya seized the chance to visit the mansion all of her friends had seen. She spoke emphatically, "Let's go. I'm eager to see the place everyone talks about where the Chinese Emperor lived."

Netti emphasized, "It's really gorgeous and worth seeing."

278

A ten-minute ride in the jeep took them to Gerry's quarters, where they settled themselves in the barroom to sip drinks and listen to the American records. The American occupation of this swank home prompted Rick's subject of conversation. "Tell me, Gerry, how do you manage to rate a mansion like this—here in the Japanese concession?"

Gerry gulped his drink and laughed. "Well, that's a long story. The officers in my company decided we needed a place to live. Our men live in the former Japanese girl's school down the street, which was occupied by Japanese soldiers until we moved them out. It was soon decided we needed separate quarters for the officers so I took an interpreter with me and started out. We began with Chinese cop on the corner and ended up at this Japanese Housing Administration—or whatever they call it. I latched onto the head man down there and told him we wanted a western style home close to where our men were billeted. He assigned a man to help us, and we began the run through the Japanese concession. We drove all over the Japanese concession. When I saw a house that looked good from the outside, and the Japanese authority with us said it was owned by Japanese, we took a look at it."

"But aren't all these places occupied?" Rick asked.

"Yes, of course," Gerry said. "If I saw something I liked, I was going to take it."

"You were taking a lot on yourself, weren't you?" Rick offered. The tone of his voice indicated his sympathy with the Japanese.

Gerry did not appreciate Rick's inference, and quipped, "Not a bit. If we need it, we're authorized to take over anything owned by the Japs, Italians and Germans. I don't think we've abused the Japanese—they've gotten off pretty lucky."

To control his rising temper, Gerry sat silent. He was remembering lying in the mud on Okinawa, flying shrapnel, whizzing bullets, dead comrades. He could not help it—he vehemently disliked the Japanese who started the war with the United States. To get hold of his emotions, he turned to the girls who had been ignored.

"You ladies must be bored. You can't be interested in this stuff. What are you planning for Christmas?"

Gerry's subject change did not work because Sonya hastened to say, "But I am interested, I want to see everything here."

"Me too," Netti added. "I haven't seen all of it and always wondered how you took it over."

"Okay, I'll get on with it."

He offered his guests more drinks, poured one for himself and continued. "Guess we drove around the Japanese concession for about a week looking at Japanese homes. Some looked good from the outside but the lifestyle we found inside wasn't suitable for westerners. You all know what I mean. Interesting part of all this. We drove by the walls and gate to this place every day when I went back to our offices down the street. I kept wondering what was behind the walls, the big gate was always closed. Wondered what I would see if it were ever open. Even drove around the block these walls encompass. Finally, I asked the Japanese authority with us what it was. He said it was Chinese property and he had no authority. We told him we wanted to see it anyway, and under a degree of pressure, he rang the bell at the pedestrian entrance. Don't know what he said to the gatekeeper who appeared but the gate swung open and we went in. A few minutes walking around the property told us it could be fine for our officers' quarters. It was vacant and we needed a key to have a look inside. Then the problem. What could we do about it? More pressure and he told us it belonged to Chinese Emperor Pu Yi."

Netti interrupted to observe, "There are no emperors in China anymore."

Gerry agreed, "And it's been that way for some time. Netti, I thought I had told you Pu Yi was installed by the Japanese as the puppet emperor of Manchuria. Guess you wouldn't consider it China."

"Where is he now?" Netti persisted.

Gerry explained. "The Russian military picked him up at the end of the war. I learned he is under house arrest there."

Now the Russian girl was interested and Sonya spoke up. "If he's in Russia and owns this place, and it's not Japanese, how could you take it over?"

"That's a good question. I don't know if Pu Yi owned or rented it. We turned our Japanese escort loose and the next few days did some investigating on our own. Needless to say, we found the person with the keys. He lives near here, and is a relative of Pu Yi. We were told he is a brother. Talking to him through my interpreter I learned he had legal control and did not want to rent this place. After a bit of a hassle I told him we would rent it or simply take it. That brought out the keys and he took us through. Completely furnished as you see it now and with Western-style baths, it couldn't be better for our company officers."

This statement prompted another question from Sonya. "Where are the officers? We're sitting here presumably in their home and I don't see any."

Gerry laughed, "Another good question. It's early—guess they're out on the town or looked in to see women and decided to stay out. Probably some staying upstairs to give us privacy. Best I get on with it before one shows up and ruins my story."

"The final rental negotiations were simple. Pu Yi's brother required we move some crated items and two safes to a warehouse near his place. We agreed to pay twenty-five dollars per month, all utilities, and the phone. There were rooms upstairs filled with boxes. Our troops brought in a truck and hauled away the boxes. The two safes are still in a corner of the ballroom behind folding Chinese screens. Too heavy to move. I got a local lawyer to draw up a legal rental paper which he and I signed. That did it. All our trouble was worth it for this elegant sixty room place to live in while we're here."

Gerry took a deep breath. "Can't believe you all wanted to listen to my chatter. Oh yes, we added a staff of ten servants. Still, it's been cheap living for each of us."

"Everything in Tientsin is cheap for the Americans," Rick commented. "At one time I understood the Japanese Consulate General to Tientsin lived here. Was that right?"

Rick's affinity to the Japanese irritated Gerry and seeded a feeling of distrust, which he subdued in order to carry on as a genial host. However, his answer revealed his concern. "There was a Japanese family living in the garden bungalow. I don't know who he was. The day Pu Yi's brother signed the rental agreement I told him to take his family and get out."

Rick caught the significant twang in Gerry's voice and elected to keep silent. The awkward silence that followed told

Gerry the jovial atmosphere had vanished. He said, "It's time we find a restaurant, get dinner, and take our lovely ladies home."

"Think we'll pass," Rick said. He stood up and motioned to Sonya. "We'll grab a rickshaw and be on our way. Thanks for the entertainment."

Sonya put her arms around Gerry in a friendly hug. "It's been a pleasure meeting you. Netti is my best friend. Anyone she dates has to be a fine person."

Lieutenant Gerry Wilson also knew he had met a fine person—Sonya Petrovna.

35

"Paul's in Shanghai."

Netti had just opened the shop when Sonya bounded through the doorway. "What did you say?"

"Paul's in Shanghai. He wants me to come there." Sonya repeated. "Tian Wei told me yesterday at the Rec Center. Can you believe Wei is a lieutenant in the U.S. Marines Crops? He was born in the United States. His real name is Edwin Tian."

"I'm not really interested in Tian Wei. All I know about him is what you've told me. Chinaman or American officer. Makes no difference. Guess he has fooled a lot of people as a Chinese citizen, so I am surprised."

Netti was also surprised to see Sonya in the shop. She had not come there in a long time due to Catherine Rurik's cool attitude regarding Sonya's association with Rick Simon. This sensitivity was forgotten by Sonya's enthusiasm and Netti was eager to get more details. "What about Shanghai?"

"All arrangements have been made for me to go, but I don't know. What should I do?"

"Go," snapped Netti without thinking. As an afterthought, she added, "But how are you going to Chungking? I don't think any trains are running. Forget it."

"By plane."

"By plane!" Netti's mouth flew open in amazement. Having never flown, the mere fact her friend was presented that privilege excited her.

"Yes, by an American military plane."

"But that's impossible." Netti gasped. "Civilians like us wouldn't be allowed on an American military plane."

"I expect you're right, but Wei said it had been arranged. I guess it isn't exactly legal. He said it is unusual."

"Explain it to me."

Sonya hunted around for a chair and sat down. "I don't know

too much about it. Wei was in a hurry. He stopped me in the street. He said a plane will arrive here this afternoon. I'm supposed to meet him at two o'clock, and he is going to take me to the airport. He said he would have a flying jacket or something, and a cap. He said I won't be recognized. Anyway, the plane is to take me to Shanghai tonight so I can see Paul. It's to bring me back tomorrow afternoon." Sonya stopped talking and then added, "I packed a purse with my cosmetics, but I don't know. I'm afraid."

"Afraid!" Netti was astonished at such a statement. "I would give most anything to fly in an airplane."

"I'm not afraid of the plane. I'm afraid of seeing Paul. I'm not sure I should go."

"But you will go." Netti spoke with determination. Then suddenly her voice took on a soft sentimental tone. "And something tells me you may not come back."

"What makes you say that?"

Momentarily Netti grinned at Sonya's shallow question. Then she turned deadly serious. "You know why as well as I do. Paul didn't come to China simply to say hello. He has come back for you."

Sonya dropped her eyes to the handkerchief she folded and refolded on her lap. Netti's heart went out to this dejected girl whose gay life had been enmeshed in a web of conflicting and sometimes strange circumstances.

"I remember when the mere mention of Paul's name brought a happy light to your face. Now it seems to bring remorse. Why?" She paused and fumbled for words. "I shouldn't ask why—I know why. But Paul is so good for you. I *know* he is the kind of person you need. You thought so too. You still do."

"Yes, I do and I'm still afraid," Sonya spoke as if she did not understand.

"You've got to find out. Seeing him is the only way you'll ever know."

"I'm going, expect I knew from the moment Wei gave me the plans. You're the only one who will know where I've gone."

"And if you are not back by tomorrow night?" suggested Netti.

Sonya did not answer. She was thinking about the obvious meaning of Netti's observation. Confused and uncertain, she conceded Netti spoke within the realm of possibility. Therefore, why not face the truth.

"If I'm not back by tomorrow, you'll know I've gone with Paul." An expression of resolution crossed Sonya's face and kindled a light in her eyes. "I pray it's the same—that nothing has changed. I must tell him all, and he has to forgive me."

"It will be the same and he'll forgive you," Netti assured her in a confident tone.

Sonya needed the courage Netti gave her, and both knew this might be their last meeting for years—maybe forever. They clung to these last minutes, for such minutes of parting are cherished and never forgotten by true friends. When Sonya left the shop there were no tears, for tears were not appropriate to such a parting. Sonya would soon be standing at a crossroad and the road she decided to take would define her future. Netti truly believed Sonya would make the right decision and have a happy life.

Sonya met Lieutenant Tian at the appointed hour. He drew her into an alley and unwrapped a bundle, which he carried under his arm. It contained a cap, a leather flying jacket and a pair of nylon coveralls used by American pilots. With his help, it did not take long for Sonya to get outfitted. Wei was careful to pile her long hair on top of her head and pull the cap tight over the mass of tresses. He helped Sonya into a waiting jeep, and they headed for the airport.

The paved road to the airport led through the flat grasslands which surrounded Tientsin, and the winter wind sweeping across the unrestricted area made the ride in an open jeep uncomfortable. Sonya huddled on the hard seat and was glad she wore the warm flying gear. At the entrance to the airport, a marine sentry stood at the edge of the road, but he made no effort to stop the speeding jeep, and his only action was to flip a snappy salute to Lieutenant Tian. Wei swung the jeep out onto the gravel taxiway in the direction of a plane, which was parked near the edge of the paved runway. Sonya saw a cloud of dust billowing up from the belly of the plane and realized the two propellers of the glistening ship were already spinning. Wei stopped the jeep and turned to Sonya.

"Our timing is perfect." Intent on the idling plane, he gave Sonya rapid instructions. "The instant we reach the plane, jump out and head for the door there in the side. Keep your collar turned up, and don't hesitate. I'll drive as close to the door as I can."

Sonya nodded that she understood. Lieutenant Tian stopped the jeep before the opening in the belly of the plane, and she bounded for the little steel steps. Hands reached down and lifted her into the plane.

"Thank you." She turned to her helper. "*David—David Rousch!*" She flung herself into David's outstretched arms.

"I see you made it," he said warmly. "It's good to see you again."

"Gosh! Am I happy to see you," blurted Sonya. "I never dreamed you were anywhere in China."

"Yes, I'm still running errands for Paul."

"David, there are so many things I want to know," she began impulsively. "Tell me all about everything."

"Later. Right now I have to get this crate in the air." He pushed her into a seat and began fastening a safety belt around her waist. "In a few minutes, I'll be back and get you out of this harness."

Sonya trembled just a little as the plane crept forward, picked up speed, and began bouncing roughly. Suddenly it stopped and teetered up and down against the locked brakes. It dawned on her they had simply been taxiing onto the runway. The powerful engines took up such a deafening road it terrified her, but she found the courage to look through the little round window. She wanted to see the takeoff. The plane jumped forward, throwing her back against the seat, and the ground flew by the window. She caught a quick glimpse of Wei sitting in the jeep and waving as the plane sped past. Then the bouncing stopped and her seat seemed to float softly on nothingness. As the engines gave up their roar for a pulsing drone, she saw the ground moving farther away from her. The sensation of flying was much different than she imagined. Her tense muscles relaxed and she began a survey of her surroundings.

David stooped through the little door at the front of the plane and greeted Sonya. "Well, how do you like it?"

"Oh, it's grand!" she exclaimed. "You here? Isn't anyone steering this thing?"

David laughed. "Yes, there's a co-pilot sitting up front. He does the work and it gives me time to cavort with beautiful women in the rear."

"Now I wonder just how you mean that," Sonya frowned impishly.

"Guess you can trust me, or would you prefer I locked myself up front?"

Sonya quit joking. "David, I would trust you anywhere. I'm sure you know that."

"We'll be in the air a few hours. Lots of time to talk and bring each other up to date." David said as he settled himself in a seat next to Sonya.

That started the conversation, which drifted into every subject. David spoke freely of his time in the States and answered Sonya's questions. However, when she brought up the subject of Paul York, he declined to discuss it, answering that she would soon be able to talk with Paul in person. David had never before been reticent on the subject of Paul and Sonya. His dodging attitude incurred an uneasy feeling of doubt, and she tried again and again to extract information from him only to be congenially refused.

It had grown dark and David's reference to the lights ahead drew Sonya's attention. She looked through the window to see a sprinkling of lights, which seemed to bob up and down past the black wing of the plane. Shanghai! Realization that she would soon be seeing Paul brought a feeling of anticipation akin to fear, tightening her muscles and leaving an empty feeling in the pit of her stomach. Her nervousness grew by the minute and her mind was a jumbled mass of fleeting thoughts prompted by conflicting emotions. When David went forward to land the plane, Sonya hardly realized he had left her alone.

The plane skimmed in over the mass of twinkling lights. Sonya wondered how David could find the runway in the night, and then she realized he had done just that. The heavy plane hit with a thud, and the screech of tires on the pavement told her they were on the ground. The vicious tossing stopped as the plane settled firmly on the earth, raced past the thin line of lights, and swing sharply around. A few minutes later, David appeared and began tugging at the latch of the heavy door.

"We're here, Sonya, and the car's waiting," he said, swinging open the door and locking the ladder in place. He straightened up and confronted her. "I'll go with you. You better get that cap back on and pull up the collar of your jacket. Hard to tell who may be around here."

The sedan was empty except for a Chinese chauffeur who said nothing. Sonya and David barely had time to settle themselves in the rear seat before he clashed the gears and spun the big limousine out onto the road. Sonya had hoped to see Shanghai, but the buildings with their brightly lighted fronts sped by so fast she managed only a glimpse of them.

"Where are we going?" She tried to be casual, but the excitement caused her voice to quaver.

"To see Paul York," answered David.

"Yes, I know," she retorted impatiently. "But where is he?"

"He's staying at some friend's home—somewhere on the outskirts of the city. Couldn't find it myself without the driver," explained David. "Quite a luxurious joint."

Sonya caught his hint at silence, so she decided to be quiet. David was preoccupied in thought, and she gathered the impression he was disturbed about something. His constrained manner did nothing to improve her anxiety. She even found herself wishing she had never come, but she could not dispel the fact she wanted to see Paul York.

After half an hour of wild driving, the car stopped before a high iron gate, which opened promptly at the touch of unseen hands. The car pulled through the gate and along the drive to the house. Before Sonya realized it, David ushered her into the enormous house. David had said "luxurious joint," and his words perfectly described the two-story structure. However, once inside, Sonya was not interested in the lavish home with its gorgeous furnishings. She looked around expectantly but saw only a Chinese servant who stepped forward to care for them.

"The boy will show you to your room," said David. Sonya still wore the flying gear, and noticing it, David added, "Maybe you better give me those flying togs. I'll keep them so you can have them when we leave tomorrow."

She began removing the jacket. "You're not deserting me, are you?" she asked in alarm.

"Sort of —you may call it that," he conceded. "My duties are over for the time being. Paul takes over from here."

"But I haven't seen Paul. You must take me to him," she said nervously.

"You will see him soon enough," David assured her. "You want to get tidied up a little first, don't you?"

Sonya wasn't exactly sure she wanted to wait, but David's tone made it evident plans had been made which she must follow. That would be like Paul—everything planned to minute perfection, like the car waiting for the arrival of the plane at the airport. Silently, she followed the Chinese boy up the stairs and along the corridor of the second floor. He opened a door and bowed for her entry. When Sonya thanked him in Chinese, he grinned and pattered off down the hallway.

Sonya might have guessed at what she found upon entering the room. Neatly laid out on the bed were her clothes for the evening, complete from undergarments to the short dinner dress of bronze wool jersey. She scooped up the dress, held it to her body for a quick fitting as women will, and inspected her reflection in the mirror. Cut as it was, such a dress must be molded to the wearer, and she wondered momentarily if it would fit. She dispelled this doubt instantly, because she remembered Paul had purchased it and the clothes he gave her always fit perfectly. Sonya glanced over the rest of the ensemble arranged on the bed—brown leather pumps, broad gold-link bracelet, dainty garter belt, and silk stockings. The hose seemed different. She picked them up and inspected them. They were nylon and it dawned on her all these items had been brought from the United States! Thoroughly delighted, she found the bathroom and impatiently began her toilet. However, interest in her new outfit was secondary to seeing Paul. Nervous anticipation began to consume her.

Sonya stood admiring her reflection in the mirror and meditating her next action when she heard a sharp rap on the door, followed by David's voice. "Sonya, are you ready?"

Sonya's heart turned over and created a giddy feeling in the pit of her stomach. A nervous lump swelled in her throat. In minutes she would be facing Paul! "Yes, Dave, I'm ready," she answered. "Come in."

The door swung open, and David followed his entry with a low whistle. "Sonya, you're gorgeous. There just isn't any arguing the point—you're positively gorgeous. I don't know how he does it."

She blushed. "How he does what?"

"How Paul picks those clothes and the woman for them. I told him they wouldn't fit. He knew they would."

"Thank you, David. But where's Paul?"

"Well, come along." He spoke in an off-hand manner and held out his hand. She detected a certain uneasiness in his manner but pushed the thought aside, and took hold of his extended arm. She welcomed that arm because it not only gave her support but also confidence. She needed plenty of assurance.

As they walked down the stairs, Sonya forced out the question, which had been tormenting her since the moment she knew Paul was in China. "Is he—is he sick? Bad, I mean?"

"He's not a well man. Don't be surprised at what you see," David answered.

They stood in front of the broad sliding doors, which Sonya guessed led to the library. David turned to Sonya. "From here on, you're on your own." He pried the heavy doors apart and beckoned her to enter.

36

Sonya stepped into the high-ceilinged room. The words of greeting, which she had practiced over and over, died on her lips. She saw not Paul, but a white woman pacing back and forth in front of the fireplace. The woman turned at the sound of her entry, deliberately inspected Sonya from head to toe, and then stepped forward. Sonya wanted to bolt, but she heard David closing the doors behind her and knew she was trapped.

As the woman walked toward Sonya, her erect carriage bespoke a person of intelligence and culture. She wore a smart, well-tailored suit of gray tweed, and a double string of pearls set off the neck of her dark sweater. Her straight, brown hair was parted in the middle and swept back to a knot on her neck, revealing pearl earrings and making her striking fine-featured face with high cheekbones fit her perfectly. She was tall and thin with small well-formed breasts. Everything about her evidenced refinement and good breeding. Even before she spoke, Sonya knew the name of this woman standing before her, extending her hand in greeting.

"Miss Petrovna, I am Jessica York." Her voice sounded flat and unexpressive, as if she had just given the time of day, but her thin lips turned up in a kind smile.

Sonya was so utterly confused she could not find her voice, and her embarrassment brought a flaming blush to her cheeks. She felt as though she should curtsy or kiss the outstretched hand, but mostly she wanted to run. Instead she gulped helplessly, took the hand, and nodded a greeting.

"You *are* beautiful. I knew you would be," Jessica said as though it were a common assumption and needed no further explanation.

"I thought—I thought..." stammered Sonya.

"You thought you were going to see Paul," supplied Jessica. She was not being rude or bitter. Quite the contrary, Sonya could not fail to catch her warm, understanding attitude. "You shall see him—that I promise you. He agreed to let me talk to you first. I hope you don't mind."

"No, I'm very glad to meet you," blurted Sonya, not knowing what else to say.

"Won't you sit down," Jessica suggested politely, beckoning to a chair. She picked up the cigarettes laying on the coffee table and offered one to Sonya. When Sonya refused, Jessica lit one for herself. She sat down and fixed an honest unflinching gaze on Sonya. "My object in seeing you is simple. I want to beg you to give back my husband."

"But, but..." Sonya began feebly.

"You needn't explain, Miss Petrovna. You needn't even talk if you don't care to." Jessica spoke considerately and congenially. "I don't blame you. I don't blame him. It's quite natural for two people to fall in love, and when they do—well, there just isn't much anyone can do about it. I blame only the war for keeping Paul away from me all those years. When men get lonely they forget—forget even their wives."

"I didn't know he was married," Sonya managed to say.

"Yes, he told me that," conceded Jessica, intimating she knew all the facts. She nervously ground the butt of her cigarette into the silver ashtray and thoughtfully contemplated its remains. Then she looked up at Sonya who sat tensely on the edge of the big chair, and gave a short, hurt laugh. "Yes, Paul is quite noble—maybe that is why I love him so much. Oh, there are thousands of reasons—reasons I can't even explain. I loved him from the first time I saw him as young and giddy as I was. I've loved him every minute since. I shall love him forever. I just don't know— don't know." Jessica's voice caught painfully on the lump rising in her throat. It was her first sign of emotion, and the sincere expression she showed tore at Sonya's heart. Then instantly, Jessica subdued the sting she had evidenced and added in a determined voice, "I don't know what I would do without him."

"But does he love you? Do you want him even if he doesn't love you?" Sonya was not asking for Paul. She realized she was only trying to comfort the magnificent lady sitting before her.

"I don't care. All I know is that I must have him," Jessica

292

answered. "I have thought of nothing else—tried to find some way to make Paul see my plea. I even prayed I would find you a—a common creature, a harlot. I wanted to use that to convince him. I might have known Paul would be attracted only to beauty. I—I have prayed you wouldn't want Paul—Paul as he is now." Her eyes filled with tears, and her voice quavered. "Please, Miss Petrovna, I implore you. Don't take him away from me. He's not well and knows not what he wants. A young woman like you needs a young, healthy man who can play and enjoy life with her. Paul shall never play again because he's beaten and worn out. He needs only someone to comfort him and wait on him. I want to be that someone. I want —I want my husband. Please, oh please!" Her voice trailed off midst her wretched sobbing, as she dropped her tear-covered face onto her hands. She sat before Sonya—a sad, desolate woman devoid of her last vestige of pride. In harmony with her strong, true-hearted character, Jessica York was humbling herself before a strange woman to beg fervently for the only thing she wanted from life.

Instinctively, Sonya stepped to the divan and sat down beside her. She placed her hand on Jessica's shoulder, timidly, as though she was not sure of herself. "I'm sorry, Mrs. York, truly sorry. I hardly know what to say."

Jessica raised tear-filled eyes to Sonya. "Go now, please go," she quavered. "I have said all I wanted to—and more. Go before I make even a bigger fool of myself."

Sonya hesitated. It seemed as if there was something else she should say but she knew not what. Words of comfort, any words, might be drastically unsuited to such a distressing situation. Sonya arose reluctantly and started slowly toward the door.

"Thank you, Miss Petrovna, thank you for seeing me." Jessica's simple words of gratitude stopped Sonya. She turned and looked despairingly at the sorrowful woman who sat watching her departure.

"Mrs. York, you've been so—so kind." Sonya's voice broke painfully as she spoke. Then she turned and fled through the door.

In the hallway, Sonya leaned weakly against the wall and raised the back of her hand to her forehead as though to fight off the faintness which assailed her. She was not aware of David's presence until she heard his soft voice.

"She's nice, isn't she?"

"Yes, wonderful." She looked up to see David lounging near, thoughtfully contemplating the smoking end of his cigarette. "Oh, David, she makes me feel—feel like a beast!"

'That's the wrong attitude, Sonya," he reflected dryly.

"But why? Am I not to blame for all this—this misery!" blurted Sonya. She wanted guidance from the one man who had stood on the sidelines and watched the game from the moment it began.

"I don't know. Maybe no one is," mused David. "They have a word for such things. I think they call it fate. Suppose we blame fate."

"But what does he want? What does Paul want?"

"You raise a question I've wondered about for months. I can't answer it," David answered flatly. "You haven't seen him. Suppose I take you to him and you can ask him."

She acknowledged his suggestion with a feeble nod. The gay spirit she had possessed in the expectation of seeing Paul had been whisked away in the minutes she spent in the company of Jessica York. Now as David led her down the hall, Sonya truthfully dreaded facing Paul York.

David pointed to the door, and his manner gave a formidable accent to his simple gesture. "He's there, in the sitting room. Go on in, he's expecting you."

Without a single encouraging word, David left Sonya staring helplessly at the closed door. She took a second to take firm hold of her tumultuous emotions. Then, forcing a gay smile to her lips, she stepped through the door.

"Sonya, my darling, it's really you." Paul's happy voice was vibrant and enthusiastic. He got up from the straight-back chair and started toward Sonya. He seemed to stumble, hesitated to steady himself, and put his arm around her when she rushed to his side. As she pushed him back into the chair, he offered a pointed excuse for his shaky action. "I sit too much. Have to get more exercise."

Sonya dropped to her knees beside his chair and put her head on his lap. For a long time the only sound was her muffled sobbing as his hand tenderly stroked her hair and cheek. Finally that hand lifted her chin, and Paul leaned to kiss her quivering lips.

Slowly her sobs died away, and she raised her hand to wipe away the tears which blurred her sight. "Paul, let me look at you. Don't say anything, just let me look."

What she saw was not the confident, healthy man she remembered. There were shadows around his eyes. His usually tanned face was drawn, looked sallow, and seemed to lack expression. Flicks of gray hair outlined his temples. There was no question, pain and depression had changed his appearance in a short time. She reached up for the hand he extended and she noticed for the first time the empty sleeve of his jacket tucked into the pocket.

He held her hand and sentimentally turned the simple gold ring she wore. No words were necessary because the significance of his deliberate action was mutually understood. Sonya gripped his hand and held his tired eyes with hers. There she found what she wanted because deep in his eyes was the look she sought, a sparkle that evidenced his love. He had not really changed. Grief had taken its toll physically and he was not well, but he was the same—her lover, her Paul.

Finally, Paul shook off his sentimental mood, looked at Sonya as a man revived and determined. "You saw Jessica?"

Sonya dropped her eyes. "Yes."

"Did you like her?"

"Very much."

"All people do," he said and waited for some comment from Sonya. When none came, he answered the question he knew she held in abeyance. "I didn't ask her to come with me. She insisted, so I agreed in order for her to fly on a government plane. It's probably just as well. Now you know each other and maybe it's for the best. She wanted to see you, alone, before I did. She has been good to me and it was little enough to give her that privilege."

"I'm glad I saw her. I've wondered what she was like."

Paul went on as if Sonya had never spoken. "My ears burned while you were together but I know what she said. There could be only one thing Jessica would say."

There was no use delaying the agony or evading the subject

on their minds. Sonya summoned every once of her courage and asked pointedly, "What about us?"

Paul shifted restlessly and his eyes searched Sonya's wan face. When he spoke, it was not as a lover mumbling endearing phrases, it was as a man talking business in cold hard truths. "I love you. I doubt if a man has ever lived who loved as I do. Never shall I find peace without you." His eyes watered ever so slightly, and he looked down at the empty sleeve dangling at his left side. "Yet, I am a cripple and may never be much more than a burden."

"You talk like a fatalist," said Sonya in a near-reprimanding tone.

"Yes, maybe." Paul remained thoughtful for a few moments and then once again confronted Sonya with a serious look. "I have little to offer, but I want you. I once told you I would always want you and it has never changed. Till the day I die I will want you. Still, it is not for me to decide. Darling, the decision is yours, not mine."

"What decision? Do we have a decision to make?" Sonya asked as she fought to suppress the agony in her heart. "You're married! It was emphasized to me only a few minutes ago."

Her reference to the obvious fact seemed to catch Paul off balance. He groped for an answer and come up with a question he was afraid to ask. "You used to say you loved me. Do you still love me?"

"It's a silly question. Does a love like ours ever die? Yes, Paul, I love you. I will always love you."

"Then my marriage is secondary."

"Are you asking that I should simply be your mistress—be there only when you want me to..." Her words died with an obvious meaning and left a distasteful insinuation.

"Never," Paul said quickly. "I want you as my wife."

Sonya's mouth turned up in a wry little laugh. "You can't mean it. It's crazy. You're wife is even in this house with us."

"Jessica will understand. She would never contest a divorce."

Sonya did not share Paul's confidence that Jessica, the sad lady she had just left, would agree easily to a divorce. Jessica had made it plain she wanted her husband and would fight to keep

296

him. Also, Sonya was remembering Jessica's humble plea and the prayer that went with it.

Paul kept on hurriedly. "I know Jessica's presence changes what we do here, maybe what you expected, certainly what I had looked forward to. There isn't much we can do about it now. There can be more times, more places. Time can remove our obstacles and we'll be together forever."

He took Sonya's hand and led her to the sofa where they sat down and embraced fervently. Somehow they both knew with Jessica in the same house with them, the ardent kisses had to stop there.

As Paul arose and pulled up a chair, Sonya picked up where he left off. Her voice was soft and filled with love. "Yes, my admirer, in fairness neither of us can say any more than maybe. Time will let us find a way." Her intentional use of the word "admirer" struck a chord which brought back fond memories for both of them.

With these words they cleared temporarily the subject of their possible life together. During the hours which followed, both shied away from the slightest reference to the unpredictable future. Also, noticeably evaded was the mention of Rick Simon, and it astonished Sonya that Paul did not so much as remark on her relations with Rick. She had no desire to discuss Rick and was pleased that Paul did not press her with such a discussion.

They received a sumptuous dinner served to them in the sitting room and they chatted freely and gaily. It was a delightful evening and the hours wore on deep into the night. Sleep finally came to Sonya as she lay stretched on the large divan, and Paul was content to sit in his chair and carry on a lonely vigilance over her slumbering form. He loved her deeply and derived unbounded pleasure and contentment from simply being close to her. When Sonya stirred and opened her eyes it was nearly noon and Paul York still sat there, watching her with a mild satisfied smile on his haggard face.

Netti Rurik sat wondering if she was going to be able to spread the news of Sonya's elopement when Sonya walked into the shop. Under her arm she carried a bundle of new clothes

297

wrapped in newspaper to conceal the contents. Sonya did not realize the newspapers, as well as the clothes, were from the United States.

37

Christmas raced into Tientsin with all the normal gaiety and left the customary aftermath of joy, sorrow, memories, gifts received, and gifts forgotten. Sonya wondered why she had not received a gift from Paul York, or at least some word. She had not received a single word since she saw him in Shanghai. Perturbing as this was, she still had to acknowledge she might never see or hear from him again.

Though neither Paul nor Sonya had said so, both knew there were obstacles to a future of being together. They had parted without decision, and without decision there was no direction. Jessica had enveloped them and each was afraid pursuing the subject would result in giving up what they wanted most—each other.

During the weeks that passed without word, Sonya inevitably came to the conclusion Paul had realized the impossibility of their marriage and decided to stay with Jessica. This undermined the determination Colonel Gordon had inspired months before by getting her a job and telling her he knew she would do the right thing. She had reduced her contact with Rick Simon to one infrequent date, giving him back the key to his apartment and tenaciously guarding herself against the weakest moments when she was taken with the impulse to go to his apartment. For unexplainable reasons she clung to the threads of dignity and maintained her independence despite the lonely hours in her small apartment. Her sanity was sustained by her job at the Rec Center and she worked hard at it. She enjoyed her work and had been so conscientious she was given added responsibility.

Under strict Rec Club rules, the girls were not allowed to leave the club with any of the guests, but requests for dates were frequent and Sonya received more then her share. To break the everyday routine, Sonya occasionally accepted a dinner date with some marine who appealed to her, but one date was it. She knew more than one date could evidence something that might lead to an unwanted situation. Her refusal for subsequent dates often annoyed her escort but she kept her self-made rule despite the fact she had plenty of free time. She worked only four days a week, from ten to six.

The free time fed Sonya's desire to have the mature companionship of Rick Simon, and the affection, which was absent. The weeks slipped by. Eventually Sonya gave in when Rick phoned her. Well aware it was unusual for Rick to bend his pride, she took the key from his hand when he held it out. She had learned he never pushed or demanded anything and was always a gentleman. Sonya liked that, she liked Rick, but she did not love him. They both understood and their congenial relations flourished again.

It was nearly six and quitting time, and Sonya was looking forward to a late dinner with Rick when she was called to the phone. As she made her way to the little office, she wondered which one of her new daily acquaintances it would be this time. There usually were phone calls just before quitting time from men she had met that day. He would be asking for a date.

"Miss Sonya Petrovna, is this Miss Sonya Petrovna?" a woman's voice repeated. "Chicago is calling Miss Sonya Petrovna in Tientsin, China."

Her legs turned to rubber. She groped for a chair, and gasped weakly, "Yes, yes, this is she."

"Will you go ahead please. Your party is on the line."

"Hello, darling." It was Paul's voice, so clear he could have been standing next to her.

"Paul, where are you?" quavered Sonya. "You're not really in the United States? Your voice is so plain!"

"I'm in the United States all right," he assured her. "But I wish I were there with you."

"Gosh, I can't—I can't believe it."

"Well, it's true. I'm sorry about your Christmas, darling. Thought I'd have a big surprise for you and could make it your present, but circumstances delayed it. I kept waiting and putting off calling you till I knew for sure. Now I know, so I phoned to wish you a late Merry Christmas and tell you your Christmas present will be coming along soon."

Still trembling, Sonya asked, "What is it?"

"You'll have to wait and see. I know you will like it."

"Oh, Paul, you're impossible."

"I try not to be," Paul responded. "Right now there's another matter we have to talk about. You're seeing Rick Simon again?"

"Yes." Sonya could think of nothing else to say.

"I wish you wouldn't. He's not good for you." Paul's voice was stern and almost threatening. Quickly the tone changed and he added, "I love you, Sonya, with all my heart."

"I know and I love you—so very much."

"It's good to hear that. It means you can stop seeing him. You have to."

"I don't know." She could not make herself lie to him. "It doesn't make any difference. I love you, not him."

"But it does. You know it does," gritted Paul. "Promise me you will stop."

Even though Sonya recognized his temper was about to flare forth, she knew it would be wrong to promise anything under pressure. "I can't promise. Our talk in Shanghai left big questions. It's been a long time since then. Will I ever see you again? Will this game ever stop? Where's Jessica? I can't go on like this. Tell me." A short pause and she repeated firmly, "*Tell me*—tell me when all this will be over."

"Wait for your present," insisted Paul.

"But that won't answer my questions. Please tell me," Sonya said changing her tone to agonized plea.

"I will—just trust me."

"What is the present?"

"Be patient, darling. You're making it difficult for me to keep my surprise." Paul waited for a comment from Sonya. None came. She was wiping away tears and wondering about his continual reference to a surprise. His very tone spoke of a gigantic event, not just a Christmas present.

"Our time is up, darling. I have to say good-bye before we hang up. Remember I love you—love you so very much," he said with emphasis. "Your present will be there soon."

"I love you, too." Sonya breathed softly into the receiver.

A sharp click signified the end of the conversation. Sonya

still sat weakly clutching the receiver. *What had Paul meant?* He had left her hanging in mid-air, trying to decipher the real purpose of his call.

Somehow Sonya felt guilty the next time she used the key to Rick's apartment. Rick had watched her moods and recognized she was wrought with inner turmoil. He was aware of her love for a man named Paul York and he permitted her moods without any reference to him.

Rick loved Sonya in his own way and she was his choice among the other women he knew and dated. But the only person he really loved was himself, and perhaps the wife who did not love him. He would never lose himself in the interest of any woman, and he would never rid himself of the attachment to his wife and child. If Sonya wanted to be part of his existence it was fine—and if she did not, that was fine, too.

Long, difficult weeks went by for Sonya, and then another and another, and no word from Paul. He said she would receive a present soon. None came. The feeling of anticipation dwindled. She stopped looking through every mail delivery and answering every phone call expectantly.

It was April and a warm spring flicked at the gates of Tientsin. The balmy weather began urging life into the winter-deadened plants and vitality into the numbed bodies of the people grown dull by cold days. It was the time of the year, which fosters well-being and inspires romance. Light-heartedness was the rule and melancholy the exception, but Sonya did not show the inspiration created by the season. Inevitably, she went back to Rick and soon Paul's phone call was another fond memory of love she now believed might well be over.

Sonya awoke at the knock on the door of Rick's apartment. A look at her wristwatch verified she had slept late and would have to hurry to get to work. She heard a faint conversation carried on in Chinese as Rick talked with someone at the door. Then Rick walked into the bedroom and handed her an envelope.

"For you," he said and left without further explanation.

As she sat cross-legged on the bed, holding the envelope, Sonya could not ignore receiving a letter in Rick's apartment was bothersome. She concluded it was not too strange because Chinese servants possessed an uncanny ability for knowing every move of their employers. The Chinaman who delivered the letter evidently fell into this class of clever underlings.

Though it showed no return address, she recognized the envelope came from the United States. It had to be from Paul. After tearing it open with trembling hands, she discovered it was a long letter with a number of pages and the signature was not Paul's. It shocked her to see it was from David Rousch. There was no heading, no date, and no location. *Why? Was there a purpose in not saying where he was?* She began reading David's large easy handwriting.

My Dear Sonya,

    A long time ago I wrote you a letter warning you so about a man who pursued you so violently I feared for your safety. This is about the same man. I hope you appreciate this letter as much as you did the other one. I rarely see Paul anymore, and I am not sure I know enough to make sense out of a letter to you. So why am I writing? He seems healthy and vibrant, but I think he is mentally unstable and needs help, which he adamantly refuses. I'll try to explain what I have pried out of him, but he is not very open with me although we are and will remain close friends. I believe you should know what goes on and be prepared for whatever, because you and I are more then just friends. We have worked the problem together for a long time.

    This may be old information for you. I don't know what he has written or said to you, or if he has contacted you at all. So please take this for it's worth and never let him know I have told you or written anything.

    He has divorced Jessica, or maybe I should say she divorced him, because it was evident she could not live with him in his present state of mind. He blames Jessica for going to China to see you and himself for permitting it. You know his confidence and determination to do everything perfectly. You also know his temper. I have learned to listen and say little.

    Again, why this to you? You are foremost on his mind and he talks about you to anyone who will listen. It seems to lighten him up. I'm sure he will come back to China again to get you. Why he waits I don't know.

    I do know there are complications. His father has died and left him a large estate in Japan. He should go and take care of it, but

303

he is uneasy about going back to Japan. Also, he says he will never go back to Tientsin. Really why, I don't know. He thinks he will be killed because of his war experience there. He obviously gets information from your area, because he seems up-to-date on Rick Simon. I share his concern about Mr. Simon. You are a good person and can do much better. Maybe some day I can help you.

I have rambled on and this letter is much too long. Hope I have said the right things. I have a deep attachment to you and believe you should know what goes on with Paul. The rest is up to you. You deserve some true happiness. I will give you support and be there if you ever need me. Just let me know.

Love Always,
Dave

Still holding the letter, Sonya's hand dropped limply to the bed and this dejected action portrayed the abandon she felt. *What could she do? What was there left for her to do?* It was not within her to fight or contrive to make it all come out right. Resigned to fate as David had once told her, she wished above all that he was with her now.

38

The letter from David Rousch alerted Sonya to the possibility
Paul York would return to China. She remembered their last
meeting in Shanghai and spent hours picturing the scene of their
next time together. Guessing at what he would say she planned
her words and actions. Somehow, she thought Paul would simply
appear out of nowhere and confront her on the street or knock on
her door.

Sonya's idea was derived by memories of her first contact
with her "admirer" when he pursued her in secret. She relived
those events—his strange notes and requests, his extreme cunning and uncanny abilities, his unbelievable deception of the
Japanese, the pride she felt upon learning of his courageous spying in a confused world, his gifts to her, and the uninhibited love
he showered on her. She also relived with a smile the masquer-
ade at the opening of the Del Conte, and with a warm glow akin
to reverence experienced their first ultimate embrace. Those
long pleasant hours of lying in his arms and plotting their future
would never be erased. And there were difficult times which
found them even closer together—Kimiko's treachery, delightful
Burl Manning killed, the Japanese watching her every move. All
the memories added to Sonya's confusion.

In contrast to the imaginary meeting Sonya planned for her
and Paul, their contact occurred quite normally. While on duty at
the Rec Center, she was called to the phone. It was Paul calling
from Shanghai.

"Darling, this is my surprise. I'm in Shanghai waiting for
you," Paul began enthusiastically. "When can you come?"

"Oh, Paul." Sonya pressed surprise into her voice. She dared
not give him reason for suspecting she already knew of his plans.

"Is that all you can say?"

"Yes, I guess so," she stammered. "This is a surprise."

"When can you come?" He repeated. His tone signified he

expected a simple answer.

"Come? Come where?" hedged Sonya.

"To Shanghai, here to meet me." He added with emphasis, "To become my wife!"

"Uh..." Sonya checked herself. She was not supposed to know of his divorce and had to be careful.

Paul interpreted her confusion to be a result of the surprise and took time to laugh. That was well, for she needed that moment collect her wits.

"We talked about that before."

"But I was married then."

"And?"

"And now I'm not. I'm divorced, free."

"Oh!"

"Oh what?"

"I didn't know that. It took me unaware," Sonya lied.

"Yes, darling, there are no obstacles in our way now. I removed them," he said decisively. "All our plans are made. I've got a new home for you, everything. You'll love it."

"It must be nice." Try as she might, Sonya could not put enthusiasm in her comment.

"You'll see it in a matter of days if we can decide when you are coming to Shanghai."

Sonya knew she was compelled to face his question and she squirmed uneasily. "Darling, why don't you come here—to Tientsin. It'd be much easier that way. I can't just pack up and leave. I have a good job."

"I know that. You won't need a job. You needn't even bother to pack. I'll see you have everything," snapped Paul, showing his irritation at her evasive chatter. "Everything is arranged. All you need to do is go to the American Military Headquarters and tell them who you are."

"Why can't you come here?" Sonya insisted.

"Tientsin is out. The U.S. State Department approved my coming to China but prohibited my going to Tientsin. They are concerned my wartime actions there could create problems. They were even against my coming back to China. *Do you understand?* You have to come here."

"Yes, of course." Sonya answered without knowing what she

said because she was groping for a proper answer to his appeal. Then she blurted, "Darling, I won't come to Shanghai."

"What?" Paul shouted.

Sonya took a firm grasp on the phone as if she needed support from it and answered in an even tone. "I said I won't come there."

Her words ignited Paul's temper and he exploded viciously. "You won't come because of Rick Simon, *isn't it?* I swore I'd never mention his name, but I have, and now you know you've never concealed anything from me."

She trembled under his wrath but answered courageously, "No, Paul, it's not Rick."

"I don't give a damn who it is, or what it is," screeched Paul, letting his temper rage unchecked. "I'm waiting here and I'll be expecting you!"

Sonya heard the violent clang as he slammed down the receiver. Quivering from his onslaught, she dropped the phone in place. Then, as though she did not possess the strength to hold it up, her head fell on the table. Sonya buried her face in her arms and sobbed without control. She was thankful the small office shielded her agony from prying eyes. She wanted to go—she wanted to see him. *Why had she said no?*

Two days passed without another word from Paul. Sonya was confident he would not leave China without seeing her and yet she feared he might do just that. She wanted him—and was afraid of wanting him. His love still vibrated deep in her heart. And then he phoned again.

He was still in Shanghai and was infuriated by her disregard to his previous plea. Waiting had taken a toll on his patience which was reflected in an ultimatum he gave before she was able to respond to his initial greeting. If she did not come to Shanghai within three days, he would come to Tientsin despite the danger and against official United States restrictions. Knowing the possible result of such action might be trouble for both of them made Sonya's response easy. She would have said "yes" the first time he called, but he had not given her an opportunity.

Sonya made hasty arrangements, followed Paul's instructions, and was surprised to learn she could leave the next day. She was told Mr. York would be notified and a car would be waiting for her at the airport. Realizing someone should know what she was doing, she wrote a note to Netti and gave it to a Chinese Rec Center attendant for immediate delivery.

All went well. Due to Paul's usual planning, Sonya was whisked to Shanghai and to the same mansion she remembered visiting months before. She had talked to Paul's wife on that occasion, but now he had no wife!

When the Chinese boy directed Sonya to Paul's room, she was afraid—so afraid she wanted to go back to Tientsin. Her fear was well-founded. She knew his actions were sometimes unpredictable and he had been angry when he phoned. She stood before the door, breathing heavily, and the thud of her palpitating heart seemed to echo through the ghastly silence in the hallway. When her hand reached out and rapped on the door, it was like it belonged to another person. As she debated her ability to go through the next few miserable minutes, the door swung open and Paul York faced her.

Contrary to Sonya's expectations, he stood there beaming happily and his amiable manner instantly dissolved the foreboding she had felt. His first words verified the elation his expression presented. "Darling, my darling—it's so good to see you." His long arm scooped Sonya close to his body and their lips met as he held her close in a tender embrace.

Paul stepped back and held her at arm's length. "You're more beautiful than ever. Yes, you've grown more gorgeous with every day. Though I've always been able to picture you in exacting detail, I had forgotten how exquisite you really are. Funny, isn't it, how even a short time allows one to lose his way."

Paul signified much by his last sentence, but Sonya was not listening carefully and failed to catch his subtle insinuation. Amazed at his good nature, she was thinking of how wrong she had been to worry.

"Oh, Paul, I'm so glad! I was so afraid you'd be mad. Please stay as you are. Promise you'll let us talk tonight without getting mad."

His unflinching gaze held her with a sincere look of both acceptance and satisfaction. "You have my word," he said simply as he took her coat.

Having arranged herself on the spacious divan, Sonya

watched Paul walk across the room and lay her coat on a chair. He had improved immensely since the last time she saw him sitting in this very room. He was alert and moved about with ease. His hair was now definitely gray. Lines showed in his face, and his once-powerful body was thin.

As Paul drew a chair up in front of her and sat down, she said by way of making conversation, "How's David? Have you seen him lately?"

Reaching for cigarettes, Paul hesitated in his action of offering her one and then proceeded to light one for himself before answering. "All right, I guess. Haven't seen him for a long time." He looked up and caught Sonya's pensive gaze. "Sonya, I'm not interested in David. Why are you?"

Sonya changed her mind about not wanting a cigarette and awkwardly groped for one. Having extracted a cigarette from the package, she leaned over for the light he held for her. *Though she did not realize it, she had in that instant made up her mind on the ultimate course of her life in respect to Paul York,* and she wished David was waiting in the hallway as he was the last time she was in this room.

"Just wondering," Sonya finally responded.

"Let's discuss us. I'm asking you now to go back to the United States with me and be my wife." Paul said his eyes begging for an affirmative answer.

"You make it difficult."

"Difficult!" he exclaimed. "There is no difficulty. We love each other—that's all that matters."

"No, darling, that's not all. There must be something else."

"What?" Paul snapped.

"Honestly, I don't know," she answered softly. "But we don't have it. I'm sure of it."

His voice rose in anger. "You don't know what you're saying!"

Sonya sighed, as though she had lost all strength to think or face the gigantic problem at hand. "Maybe you're right, I've given up thinking about it. There doesn't seem to be a solution where either of us can elude suffering." She lifted a tiny Buddha from its place on the coffee table and contemplated its chubby figure. "I'm sure of this much—marriage would only magnify our suffering." Paul started to say something. "No, wait, let me finish. For one thing, you are insanely jealous—not because you want to be, but because you can't help it. Don't say you'd change, you can't, nor can I. A marriage for you and me would be continual hell on earth. We're far better off apart, cherishing a love that can only die by our own hands if we're together."

"You want Rick Simon!" snapped Paul.

"Paul, you promised."

Her plea strangled his rising fury. He fought for control of his rage and subdued it. "I promised not to get mad. We made no stipulation that we were not to discuss Rick Simon," he said in a cold, collected voice.

"I'm willing to discuss him," volunteered Sonya. "I didn't think you'd want to."

"You love him, don't you?"

"I don't think so. I've never thought much about it."

"What can he give you? He's married and plans on staying married. Is that what you want?"

"No, it isn't. He affords me happiness, at least some happiness—and that counts for something," Sonya admitted.

"So help me god! I can't understand it," Paul said in a cold expressionless voice.

"Why try? He's not important to us. Please, let's not discuss him anymore," pleaded Sonya.

Without answering, Paul granted her request. He realized any more said concerning Rick Simon would only serve to broaden the breech between him and this woman he loved.

"Then your mind is definitely made up?" Paul asked, knowing it was. He clung to one last hope that she might change her mind.

"There's no other way."

"I'll never marry again," Paul offered, as if it were an obvious conclusion.

"I guessed as much," Sonya acknowledged sadly. "But I wish you would."

"Never." He clipped the word off. "I'll always be wanting you if you ever change your mind and want me."

Sonya, listening remorsefully, knew he meant every word of it.

It seemed there was no more to say. When Paul rang for

drinks they both knew would be their last together. When the Chinese attendant brought the drinks and departed, Paul stood up with his glass, toasted Sonya with a warm smile, and sat down beside her on the divan. They talked about meaningless things, avoiding marriage and personal feelings. Holding each other gently, the night slipped away.

It may have been the will of fate which lifted two planes into the air at the break of dawn and headed them northward to different destinations. It was not fate—it was determination that made a sad young lady stop her rickshaw on the bridge in Tientsin where she had often met her lover. As she fumbled in her purse, she remembered her last words to Paul York as she left him in Shanghai. He had not acknowledged what she said. "When you see David Rousch, tell him to come to Tientsin and see me."

What had Sonya Petrovna really meant? Maybe some day her dream could come true and she actually would get to see the United States of America—even live there. Having found what she wanted from her purse, she held the key to Rick Simon's apartment. A little smile crossed her lips as she tossed it into the river and watched the little bubble it made.

It was not fate, but more coincidence, that about the time the lady was leaving the bridge, a tall gaunt man got off a plane in Tokyo and into a waiting limousine. He was on his way to the United States, and a deceased father required a stop at a home he had not seen for years. On the little finger of his only hand was a plain gold ring inscribed "SP, My Love Forever, PY." As he worked it around and around on his finger, phrases from a poem he had learned as a student in the United States came again to mind. They held no meaning then, but now he remembered and understood.

> *"And yet my love for thee still sings*
> *Having robbed my soul of all earthly things*
> *Leaving contentment only in the heavens above*
> *My life on earth pledged for thee my love."*